Also by Francesca Segal

FICTION

The Innocents

The Awkward Age

NONFICTION

Mother Ship

WELCOME TO GLORIOUS TUGA

Welcome to Glorious Tuga

A NOVEL

FRANCESCA SEGAL

An Imprint of HarperCollins*Publishers*

HarperCollins books may be purchased for educational, business, or sales promotional use. For information, please email the Special Markets Department at SPsales@harpercollins.com.

Ecco® and HarperCollins® are trademarks of HarperCollins Publishers.

Originally published in Great Britain in 2024 by Chatto & Windus.

Illustrations © Conrad Garner

FIRST U.S. EDITION

Library of Congress Cataloging-in-Publication Data

Names: Segal, Francesca, 1980- author.
Title: Welcome to glorious Tuga : a novel / Francesca Segal.
Description: First edition. | New York : Ecco, 2024.
Identifiers: LCCN 2023053530 (print) | LCCN 2023053531 (ebook) | ISBN 9780063360457 (hardcover) | ISBN 9780063360464 (trade paperback) | ISBN 9780063360471 (ebook)
Subjects: LCGFT: Novels.
Classification: LCC PS3619.E374 W45 2024 (print) | LCC PS3619.E374 (ebook) | DDC 813/.6—dc23/eng/20231120
LC record available at https://lccn.loc.gov/2023053530
LC ebook record available at https://lccn.loc.gov/2023053531

24 25 26 27 28 LBC 5 4 3 2 1

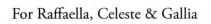

For Raffaella, Celeste & Gallia

Dramatis Personae

Charlotte Walker — London vet and academic herpetologist

Islanders

Dan Zekri — the new doctor, coming home after fifteen years away from the island

Lusi Zekri — Dan's mother; Saul Gabbai's sister

Johannes Zekri — Dan's father; died in a boat accident

Saul Gabbai — community doctor; chief medical officer; Lusi's brother

Moz (Fermoza) Gabbai — the schoolteacher; Saul's wife; Garrick's sister

Garrick Williams — island pastor; Moz's brother

Joan Williams — Garrick's wife

Levi Mendoza — bartender and handyman; Charlotte's landlord

Walter Lindo-Smith — Maia's husband; Levi's brother-in-law and good friend

Rebecca Lindo-Smith — Maia and Walter's six-year-old daughter; Levi's niece

Annie Goss — eleven-year-old islander

Alex dos Santos — eleven-year-old islander

Marianne Goss	Annie's mother, and the island's baker
Ruth dos Santos	Alex and Caleb's mother; former island councillor; Marianne's beloved foster mother
Sylvester	keeps the general store on Harbour Street
Betsey Coffee	runs Betsey's Cafe on Harbour Street
Taxi	cabbie and radio announcer
Elsie Smith	customs officer; mechanic; amateur reptile enthusiast
Grand Mary (Mary Philips)	Island Elder, the oldest (and by far the richest) Tugan
Martha Philips	a tortoise
Katie Salmon	incoming physiotherapist

Miscellaneous, Off Island

Maia Lindo-Smith	Levi's sister, left to work in England
Caleb dos Santos	Alex's much older brother, now living in England
Martin Blackburn	visiting optician from the See the World Foundation
Lucinda Compton-Neville	Charlotte's mother, a QC in London

WELCOME TO GLORIOUS TUGA

I

Islands are places you flee to, or places from which you flee.

For days the ship had been anchored, waiting for the seas to calm. They were a mile off the reef-wrapped coast of Tuga de Oro, a tiny British overseas territory, the world's most remote inhabited island, on which life was variously described as "turning the clock back a hundred years" (*Lonely Planet*), "an English community life from a bygone golden era" (*Time Out*), "a modest British seaside hamlet airlifted to the Tropics" (*Fodor's Travel Guide*) or, less warmly, "stuck in the fifties, just possibly the eighteen-fifties" (*The Wanderer*). Certainly the weeks of this ocean voyage had felt positively Victorian. They were nearing Tuga, but Charlotte Walker had so far seen nothing of her future home except roiling ocean through her cabin's filmy porthole. A few days out of England she had hoped some fresh air might quell the rising nausea and had opened this window, but instead had almost asphyxiated herself with a warm cloud of diesel fumes from the engines, and would not make that mistake again. Now, finally, the lighters would call in the morning and with them salvation, at least from seasickness. Soon she would be in the dense beauty of a pristine jungle, with her tortoises.

Charlotte was twenty-nine, and held a PhD conducted at the Institute of Zoology in Regent's Park, investigating the impact of non-native newts on the UK amphibian populations. She had always loved amphibians and reptiles, particularly tortoises. They were easy metaphors for resilience and independence, and as a sensitive child, a homebody, and the daughter of a commanding and intrusive single mother, she had envied their ability to retreat into a physical space that literally no one else might enter. This affinity was disapproved of by Lucinda Compton-Neville, herself a sociable and highly sought QC, who considered her only child's achievements to be assets of her own, and found no social cachet in slimy things.

Charlotte's early childhood had been overseen by nannies, and populated with small creatures the housekeeper resented; gerbils and hamsters and funfair goldfish, and at one stage a bearded dragon she lovingly named Joan, after Joan Beauchamp Procter, the first female curator of reptiles at London Zoo. Lucinda detested this animal in particular and refused to speak its name, while slug-hunting for the bearded dragon had pushed the nanny to the edge of resignation. Only pity for her preternaturally well-behaved charge had kept her in the job.

When Charlotte was ten, Lucinda had married a fellow barrister, Adrian Walker, and had ruthlessly dispatched the creatures that had till then been Charlotte's solace, reasoning that a spirited trio of much smaller stepbrothers would be menagerie enough. Charlotte's prep school got the hamsters, a terrarium of dart frogs rode grandly back to Palmer's Pet Shop in a black cab, and the stick insects were set loose to try their luck on the box hedges of the Inner Circle. Charlotte Compton-Neville was reborn as Charlotte Walker. At night she sobbed, quietly, unobtrusively, for these lost companions. Still, she had offered up her small heart to Adrian Walker, full of hope that here, finally, had come a father, and a reward for all the years of unspoken longing. But the step-siblings rarely visited, and the underwhelming and unresponsive stepfather was divorced within the year, reappearing in their lives intermittently and only as Lucinda's opposing counsel, periods during which her mother's mood would be dangerous and erratic. Lucinda became Compton-Neville again. Charlotte, by then at secondary school and wise to the semiotics of a double-barrel, would not relinquish Walker. She did not wish to be remarkable, in any direction. From then on the animals in Charlotte's life had been mostly imaginary or theoretical, until college.

As an undergraduate, Charlotte was made anxious by the distance between herself and her fellow veterinary students. The others studied together and drank together and exercised together and slept with one another in various configurations, and Charlotte would join them in the library, and usually slipped away from the pub after the second round. She wanted to fit in, but not enough to do the things they did. She suffered real fear of silliness, of social risk, of emotional exposure. She could not pretend to enjoy rappelling in Wales, nor racing up peaks in the Lake District, nor downing pints on a Bloomsbury pub crawl in animal fancy dress. She had never downed a pint, nor smoked a cigarette, nor had a one-night stand, and had she done any of these things it would only have been to disguise herself as someone whose natural behavior it was, a pretense that would have fooled no one. It did not help, of course, that most of the students at the RVC came from outside London and lived together in halls, bonded by the constraints of student loans, while she still lived in alienating privilege and splendor in a white stucco Nash house in the park, so grand that she was ashamed to ask anyone home.

On graduation, most of these contemporaries joined small-animal practices or took advisory roles in farm-animal husbandry, while Charlotte sank with gratitude and pleasure into a PhD based in a multidisciplinary lab at ZSL, and a life with the newts. Newts were plentiful in England. She felt at home with the team of academics, biologists, and bioinformaticians, recognizing herself in their introversion and rigor. Academic herpetologists in particular were usually an obsessional lot—patient, dogged and retiring; playful, but on their own terms. Not unlike tortoises.

*

"Knock, knock." The door opened a fraction and Charlotte quickly smoothed down her covers and combed through her tangled hair with her fingers. Dan Zekri appeared, bearing a small stainless-steel tray on which stood a mug of soup sealed with cling film, and a brown roll. He had dark skin, very blue eyes, and deep, unexpected dimples, a striking combination that Charlotte did not yet know was characteristically Tugan. Charlotte herself had dimples, and felt both kinship and competition with the rare others whose dimples were exceptional. Dan was not tall but solid, square as a rugby player and courteous as a footman, and was so gleaming and healthy that her squalid state had at first made her want to curl up with shame. Then the seasickness had taken a turn for the worse and she ceased caring if she lived, let alone how handsome was the man who held her hair back as she retched. Dan came each day in an apparently unending supply of clean white shirts, smelling of menthol and sea air, and in her cabin Charlotte sweated and festered and was sick. She longed for a breeze. Dan arrived with a portable fan.

"How's my patient?"

Charlotte sat up in her bunk with trepidation. She waited, but the impulse to vomit did not come. The room rocked, but did not spin.

"Better, maybe?"

"Good news. Last tinned broth, I promise; I happen to know there are carrots and onions in cargo. Once we land you'll have more chicken soup than you know what to do with." Dan handed her the mug and then sat in his traditional place, on the floor of the cabin by her feet. He leaned easily against her bunk and picked up a slim journal.

"Right, where were we. Keep drinking, please. We'd just finished 'Genetic differentiation over a small spatial scale in the smooth newt.' Next is 'Supplementary Materials for "Genetic differentiation over a small spatial scale in the smooth newt."'" He threw his head back to regard her. "I presume you don't want the supplementary materials? Too much of a good thing, maybe."

Charlotte could not answer truthfully, for one did not look in the mouth any gift horse willing to read aloud from the *British Journal of Herpetology*. Dan regarded her steadily.

"I just want to know what's *in* them," she admitted.

"A table of the latitude and longitude of each surveyed pond. The most potent narcotic yet discovered."

"OK, no, you're right. I don't need that. Next article, please."

" 'Effects of aquatic and terrestrial habitats on the skin microbiome and growth rate of juvenile alpine newts?' "

"Yes, please."

"'Alpine newts' sounds like a condition. I'm sorry to tell you, you're suffering from a terrible case of alpine newts."

"Can't be worse than motion sickness," mumbled Charlotte, obediently peeling cling film. Then she sipped tepid bouillon and listened to the now-familiar cadence of Dan's voice, letting the words wash over her. She watched him, safe to study his face while he looked down at the pages. When he had finished the article, Dan set the journal down on the floor, and got to his feet. He regarded her, obviously gratified to see the mug empty in her hands.

"Well done. I'll head back and get organized now, I think. Do you need a hand packing up before tomorrow?"

"No thank you." She handed back the cup. "Will there be a big crowd?"

Dan nodded, and looked, for a moment, uncharacteristically uncertain. He had paused in the doorway and now began to study the mechanism of the lock, jiggling it a little, frowning at it while he spoke.

"Oh, you know. There's always a crowd on Ship Day, but it's mostly for the cargo, really; people have waited so long ship to ship. Baked beans, or a new wheelbarrow, or the next James Patterson, or whatever. A loo seat. Whiskey. Flour. You cannot believe how much cake Tugans consume, for an island that isn't wheat-producing."

He spoke lightly but he was anxious about the landing tomorrow, Charlotte sensed, and she wondered again how it would be to return to such a small community an adult, to step straight into a senior island role, having left as a teen. She watched him quietly from the safety of her narrow lower bunk, this man she had known for only a brief period, but one with such a strange and intimate intensity to it. Her heart went out to him. After weeks of his professional confidence, his sudden nerves were affecting.

"If you're really feeling better, will you try and come up tonight? Watch the Island Day fireworks with me? We'll be able to see them on deck." Dan released the handle, apparently satisfied.

Charlotte's stomach turned over, and she closed her eyes. It was unfortunate that butterflies shared so many symptoms with seasickness. She opened her eyes again.

"I might have to bring my pet bucket. Just in case."

Dan grinned. "No need. There's the whole of the South Atlantic at your disposal. See you in a bit." Then he was gone and Charlotte lay back.

She was young and strong, and until these last weeks had existed in the blithe ignorance of near-perfect health. Intensely private and habitually defended, she could not help but see this motion sickness as a failure of her own self-possession. It seemed a betrayal, for where possible Charlotte avoided vulnerability, and mess. She had experienced a new alienation from the body she had always seen as herself, and was now as unreliable as everything else. It had been a year of shifting sands.

On this purgatorial sea crossing, Dr. Dan Zekri had come to Charlotte as a savior. She guessed him to be about ten years older than she was, in his late thirties, returning to his native Tuga de Oro after many years living in England. A cargo ship with only eleven passengers has no legal requirement to carry a doctor, and so it was merely good luck that a medic happened to be a fellow traveler. Dan had visited her cabin that first terrible night and then every morning and evening since, with cinnarizine tablets and magical injections, with salted crackers, with blackcurrant squash, with sluice bowls, a sense of humor, and apparently unending kindness and patience.

He was also traveling alone, and had time on his hands. Unlike a passenger ship, there was nowhere on board to go, nowhere but the modest cabins to escape the roar of the engines, and the pervasive smell of stale cigarettes and diesel. Dan talked about growing up on Tuga (the first silent bat swooping across the evening sky, he told her, was the island sign that all children had to stop playing and go home for supper, though he was unable to tell her with any satisfaction what subspecies of bat they had been). He took a medic's interest in the fellowship that was bringing her to the island, an invitation to spend a year surveying the dwindling population of Tugan gold coin tortoises in the island's lush, canopied interior. Charlotte, who had long ago learned that most people did not want to hear about herpetology as much as she wanted to talk about it, felt the rare pleasure of encountering someone whose intelligent enquiries made clear a genuine interest in the answers. She could speak with ease about reptiles in a way she never could about herself. Indeed, her own escape into academia had been spurred by the realization, at college, that domestic-animal patients necessitated a great deal of interaction with their human owners. Wildlife was owned by no one.

But Dan was an appealing human. He laughed with self-deprecation when she risked a classic veterinary joke, about doctors. ("What do you call a vet that can only treat one animal?") She was touched by how terrified he confessed to being of cats, one of the advantages of his return home to Tuga, he declared, where there were none permitted, in order to protect the endemic bird population. He read esoteric articles aloud to her and, though he often praised their untapped power as a tranquilizer, could not help but go on to ask about reptile viral expression. He was secretly fascinated, she was sure of it.

Dan was driven, which she admired, and obsessional, which she recognized. He was full of plans for public-health initiatives on the island, additional training for the clinic's two and a half nurses, and incentives to recruit four more. He feared he had been away too long to be accepted, but also that he had been away too long to submit himself to all the idiosyncrasies and limitations of impoverished, isolated medical practice, while acknowledging that attempted change, even for the better, would itself be a barrier to acceptance. He seemed to have the confidence to confess his limitations. Charlotte did not feel she could be her true self with Dan Zekri, for she could not imagine anyone would want to meet that weak and spindly person. Practiced at evading intimacy, she made light of her family when he asked her questions. She would recite her mother's curriculum vitae—a single mother lauded at the Bar, who worked hundred-hour weeks and was devoted, with an equally meticulous focus, to the care of her daughter either directly, or by proxy. On the day she'd made silk, Lucinda had also made Charlotte a vanilla-sponge tortoise birthday cake, the scutes tessellated slices of Marks & Spencer's chocolate Swiss roll, to be presented early the next morning before school, and court.

Over time this anecdote came to represent as much about her family as she wished to communicate, and all the right things. The story had been so often on her tongue that it was worn smooth, and snagged no further questions. To Dan she then added the frank lie that Lucinda was overjoyed about her Tugan fellowship. Charlotte wished it had been so. In fact, Lucinda herself was in Grenada for almost a month for a case, and when she eventually returned home, a note on the kitchen table confessing to this yearlong relocation, five months in the planning, would be the first she heard of it. Time would tell, when her fury broke, whether the world's most isolated island was sufficiently far away.

It had always been hard to explain the unique constellation of circumstances that made Lucinda what she was, the central deity and influence in Charlotte's life, without listeners mistaking this intensity for dysfunction. Charlotte yearned for her mother, sometimes even when she was present. Her only significant ex-boyfriend had misapprehended their dynamic, when no longer in the first flush of Lucinda's concerted charm offensive. But Lucinda had not been wrong about him, in the end. All men were unreliable, Lucinda often counseled her daughter, and he had done Charlotte a favor by revealing his fuckwittery so fast.

It was hard to talk to strangers about her father too, but for different reasons. At its worst, her ache for her mother bloomed into an ache for her father, a more diffuse, pervasive sorrow for the lost, for the never-known. Fathers were anchors and bodyguards and disciplinarians; teachers and comforters; heroes or villains; fathers were embarrassments or cheerleaders or letdowns. With nothing—no name, no history—her own father was a void she could not try to comprehend, a shadow, just outside her vision. Lifelong she had believed he had not wanted her, and this rejection was all of him she had, its legacy a craving for the protective armor of emotional self-sufficiency. Charlotte looked forward to an island famously resistant to outsiders on which, she thought, no one was likely to take much interest in a quiet, self-contained herpetologist. The journey had been a torment, not to mention the confusion of her reasons for making it. Nonetheless, ahead lay Tuga de Oro. And sitting with Dan Zekri beneath a tropical sky alight with fireworks was not a bad way to begin an adventure.

2

The last time Charlotte had been on deck they'd been a day past the Azores and into the open water of the North Atlantic, whipped by frigid winds. Here the air was warm and soft, the seas finally calmed. Above was velvet blackness pricked with unfamiliar constellations. The deck lights were lowered but in the gloom a voice called her name. Dan stood as she approached him, and sat again only when he had seen her into the white plastic chair beside his own.

"You look much better."

"It's pitch-dark."

"Still. It's exciting to catch a glimpse of you upright."

"Like a rare wildlife sighting."

"Exactly, like your first gold coin tortoise. Can I get you a ginger tea? Actually, you're probably sick of it—would you like a soft drink?"

Charlotte nodded, and Dan went to the mess and returned with two plastic bottles of Coke.

"We call this fizzycan, on Tuga."

"Fizzycan? Really, that's what you'd call it? But it's not currently in a can."

"Even so. You can imagine how hip I was in Freshers' Week. 'Hey, man, I'm going to the bar, want some fizzycan?'"

"Oh God. *Some* fizzycan, not even *a* fizzycan."

"Yeah, well. One day I'll tell you how my leather bumbag went down with the ladies." He touched his bottle to hers. "Cheers. Welcome back to the land of the living."

"Thank you." Charlotte took an experimental sip of icy Coke. "You've not told me about moving to England."

"God. It was an exercise in humility. I left feeling like such a big man. I don't know what you know about the island's educational opportunities but English university really doesn't happen often, so I thought I was pretty world-class."

Charlotte smiled. "You were only a teenager."

"I was a cocky little so-and-so. I'd heard people describe big cities so often and I thought, *I've seen a million movies, England's just like Tuga but bigger.* And then you get there and people started to work out I'd never seen an escalator. Or a lift. Or a motorway. Or heard of mugging. Or—it's hard to explain. And *then* you realize that motorways are actually terrifying, and also there are thirty different kinds of toothpaste." Dan put his feet on the railing and lay back, looking upwards. "I didn't know all the things I didn't know. People would laugh and I'd have literally no idea why what I'd said was funny."

"I did work experience in a clinic that sold eight flavors of canine toothpaste."

"Exactly. *Exactly.* And also, until then I thought I was British. Or, Brit-*ish.* Tugan independence is a whole other conversation, but back then I was going—not home, obviously, but I had the same passport as everyone else, so it was honestly a shock to discover that no one else really thought I was British, or felt much reciprocal affection. I arrived in midsummer, because if you're starting an academic year in England you have to leave on the Island Close ship, or you'll not get off Tuga till Christmas. My father had an old friend at Southampton Hospital and she got me a job as a security guard there for a month, and that felt incredible, being in a hospital. Like a movie. But then term started, and daylight savings ended, and honestly I wore all my clothes, all the time, I was so cold. I got every single respiratory virus that first winter. I got flu, I got slapped cheek, I got hand, foot, and mouth, and who knows what else. Like I was an infant. It makes you realize just how limited the exposure to the outside world is, when most Tugans have never had RSV, never had chicken pox. And whatever it is, either none of us has had it, or all. I think I had overlapping colds for a year."

"But you stayed."

"I stayed, and it got better pretty soon. I got an English girl-friend." Dan gave her the grin of a naughty schoolboy and she felt her body respond, an unexpected contraction of the stomach utterly unlike its previous weeks of torment.

"First trip home since I left fifteen years ago, and it's my last one. I can't think about it too much or I get sort of—wild." He gave a long, slow exhale. "Chief medical officer of Tuga, when my Uncle Saul retires."

"Doesn't get much realer than that."

"It's so mad to think that it's why the island sent me in the first place, just a kid, really, to one day come back for this. And, and the thing is—I love my island. I love Tuga, I want to be a community doctor, I love people, and I love these people, but—somehow it's come round so fast."

"I don't think I'm very good with people," Charlotte admitted, surprising herself.

"Oh, I don't know. You seem to be doing all right." Dan turned slightly to look at her and she felt the heat rise to her face. "OK, bad with people. Good with newts. Got it. So why Tuga? In fifteen years in the UK I think I've met about, oh, a dozen people who have even heard of it, let alone people wanting to move there. You could be doing tortoises in, like, the Galapagos. Or the Seychelles. Some-where easy to get to. Somewhere with an airport."

"Not moving, it's just a year. Long story."

"Always is. Folk are drawn to Tuga, it can be a bit like Jerusalem syndrome. People running away, or searching." His accent was not English, though it was not not English, either. Now he assumed a BBC formality. "So tell me, Charlotte Walker . . ." Here he extended an imaginary microphone, like a news anchor. He was so corny, Char-lotte thought with disbelief, corny and old-fashioned and attractive despite or perhaps because of it. "How does a beautiful young veterinary postdoc from London find herself en route to the world's most remote island community? Which are you? A runner or a searcher?"

Both, she thought, unsettled by the precision of the question.

"Neither. I'm just the new Martha Philips Visiting Fellow. There's opportunity there, and I wanted to do work that really matters. I mean, all conservation work is vital but remote island ecosystems are so fragile and you'd be shocked how many critically endangered species get no attention, no funding, no nothing; they go on a list, and that's it. But then a chance like this comes along to really understand one species. Gold coins don't seem to have any close genetic relatives left, so they represent what is possibly a unique evolutionary strand, by this point." As she talked she felt a return to herself, and a safe return to the places within her that mattered. "A paper I wrote ages ago on waif tortoises was published last year and then this fellowship came up unexpectedly, and I was ready to do field research again. It was serendipity, it was like it was tailor-made for me. Twelve months of funding, accommodation, and passage on this ship, which I understand usually takes years to book or whatever."

"And is thousands and thousands of pounds."

"Yes, that too. It's seemingly very well resourced, this grant, it's a new conservation program in honor of an islander. Apparently Martha Philips was an important elder?"

In the darkness she saw Dan was smiling again. There was starlight in his eyes. His dimples were black holes, she thought, and it was very important not to fall into them. When she was off the infernal ship she could work, and equilibrium would return. Equilibrium and boundaries.

"Martha's still an elder of the island. You'll meet her."

"Really? No one mentioned that. I'm excited to talk to the older people, they might know if the gold coin territory has shifted or contracted over time. And I want to know if anyone still remembers hunting them for meat."

"Well. I don't know how an interview with Martha would go, but

I can promise you'll meet her." Dan drained his glass. "I'll tell you something. This delay, rough seas, missing Island Day, has made it all feel very real. It's such a Tugan thing to happen. Islands force you to abandon illusions of control." He stood up suddenly. "Can I get you anything else? I'm having a brandy, before the fireworks start."

"I'm not much of a drinker, really. Alcohol doesn't suit my obsessive need for control, illusory or otherwise."

"Probably for the best. You're not that long after a whacking great dose of promethazine, you'd go to sleep and never wake up again. I'll get you a saloop."

When he came back, Dan handed her something viscous and violet-colored, in a teacup.

"Thank you. This really looks quite terrible, like amantadine syrup. I've noticed something, I think. You know you switch between 'we' and 'they' whenever you tell me about Tuga."

He took a sip of his brandy and exhaled. For a moment he frowned. "I'm coming back to reality on the world's most remote island after fifteen years in outer space. It might take me a while to, to—know where I am, I guess. But I must tell you, knowing that you'll be there has made me feel a whole lot better. A fellow astronaut."

They sat in a silence that was not a silence, as the waves washed the tall flank of the ship, and the lifeboats creaked behind them. Charlotte clinked her teacup against Dan's glass, and turned towards the invisible island thinking—thinking what? Thinking that to the rest of the world it was Tuga that lay in outer space, the extremity of its isolation central to the island's identity. Thinking, as usual, in order to avoid the more treacherous practice of feeling.

If for Dan Zekri reality lay ahead, for Charlotte Walker reality now lay far behind. The reality of being a woman of almost thirty who lived alone in the basement flat of her mother's house. The reality of discovering—in the course of one, till then unremarkable, conversation five months earlier—a first truth about her father.

It had been at last year's Christmas party: champagne; devils on horseback; tartan; poinsettias in gold ribbon; too many floral scented candles in the close, closed air, and the living room filled mostly with guests whose acquaintance Lucinda cultivated for professional advantage. Too much, all of it, with hindsight; cloying, braying, raucous, overheated. At the time, Charlotte had squeezed Lucinda's arm and said, defiant, "Look at everything you've built. It's my father's loss, to walk away from us," and her mother had kissed her cheek and clinked her Veuve Clicquot with Charlotte's sparkling water and said—why then? Why ever?—"Oh, sweet girl, don't be naive. You mustn't go on feeling all rejected and sorry and pathetic. Of course I never told him I was pregnant. We weren't in a relationship, he didn't abandon me when I was knocked up like some sort of soap-opera cad, or whatever you've cooked up in your imagination. You were my baby, I wasn't taking risks with you like that. He left and went back where he came from and I simply never contacted him again. He was from the absolute ends of the earth, darling."

A lifetime's lie, dismantled. Her self had formed around an aching absence, and now that self was collapsing. Not sinner but a father sinned against, denied the chance to try. She had hated him and longed for him for so long. Centerpiece of her sixth birthday party, the sponge tortoise cake had not distracted her from the pain of watching Olivia Perez arrive on her father's shoulders to spare her new shoes from the puddles; Olivia's small fingers twisted in her father's hair; his low voice explaining to Lucinda that Olivia did not like drop-off parties, she preferred him to stay. And he had stayed, and he had helped, and at intervals Olivia would twirl over to him and retreat from the party to the perfect, separate safety of his lap before running back to watch Safari Simon, and all through the chinchilla and the rabbit and the tree frog Charlotte could not take her eyes from Olivia's father, this easy, smiling man who handed round flimsy paper plates of tortoise cake with his huge hands. He would never leave his daughter, not even at a party, not even for an hour. But now, who knew now what sort of man

Charlotte's father had been? Maybe he too would have joined in with musical statues.

As ever, it was work that came to her rescue. Fieldwork was the unimpeachable right and terrain of an animal researcher—no one could accuse Charlotte of anything but professional advancement for snatching at this strange, lonely island adventure when it had come to her, out of the blue, as if summoned from her deepest wishes. Work would make her, whatever the truth of her mounting suspicions; work would save her, whether or not her father was really from Tuga de Oro.

Already the recollection of that awful Christmas party had receded, for here was its opposite. Space and sky and ocean and emptiness. Here she was, then, at the ends of the earth.

They were reclining side by side in plastic garden chairs, legs extended, and Dan briefly touched his foot to Charlotte's. At that moment the sky above them exploded with ruby and emerald.

3

Tuga de Oro lies more than two thousand miles from the nearest landmass and nearly seven thousand miles from England, and even once the intrepid voyager came close, her shallow harbor was only accessible fewer than half the days of the Island Open season. This ship called roughly once a month during Island Open, bringing essential cargo, as well as the lucky few passengers able to secure a berth. Traveling to or from Tuga often necessitated years of advance planning, and a high tolerance for unexpected changes of schedule. An oil tanker called to fill the diesel tanks, and occasional yachts would drop anchor, bringing bucket-list tourists or round-the-globe adventurers whose arrival was always a source of island interest (and welcome income). During these busier months, the seas around Tuga could often shimmer like glass but placidity was hard to predict, and ships were known to drop anchor at the kelp beds for weeks waiting to off-load, before giving up and turning round for home. With typical Tugan understatement, Island Close was the benign name for a hurricane season that locked the island into total isolation from late June to early December. That was another animal altogether.

Charlotte's passport had been taken ashore and declared satisfactory. Stamped and signed, it would be returned to her "at home," and Charlotte felt obliged to explain that she didn't yet know where home would be. In an email the fellowship administrator, Joan Williams, said that she entirely understood Charlotte's reticence to lodge with a family, and that a cottage would be found within walking distance of New Recife. Their subsequent communication had mostly been about tortoises.

The customs officer, Elsie, had come aboard during breakfast, and had joined Dan and Charlotte and the other passengers in the mess. A broad-shouldered young woman, she had on a pair of scuffed, steel-capped work boots and a boiler suit, the lapel of which had been hand-embroidered in orange with the words "Elsie Customs." Elsie had been much younger than Dan at school, and seemed somewhat overawed to be welcoming him back.

"It's an honor, Dr. Zekri," she told him reverentially, drawing herself up. Charlotte wondered if a salute might follow.

Elsie assured Charlotte that she'd be staying at the Mendoza place, a house in which they always put important FFA ("Folk From Away," Dan clarified), and then wished her a speedy recovery from the seasickness that Charlotte had not mentioned she'd been suffering. Elsie recommended Marianne Goss's gingerbread as a remedy, whoever Marianne Goss might be.

"When you're settled, Dr. Walker and Dr. Zekri, I'd love to introduce you to my red tegu lizard," Elsie added.

"She's going to be living at Levi Mendoza's place," Dan had repeated with indeterminate expression, ignoring the tegu invitation, and Elsie had nodded, helping herself to a pear, which she wrapped in a paper napkin and zipped into a leather pouch at her waist. Charlotte felt sure she'd seen a look pass between them.

"I'll tell Marianne to make you some biscuits, shall I?" Elsie said to Charlotte, who said thank you and that of course it would be a pleasure to meet any resident lizard, wild or domestic, before Elsie moved on to the next table.

"First Tugan bumbag," Charlotte observed, once the officer had gone.

"First of many." Dan was finishing his dried-egg omelette. "Be warned my pack'll come out of retirement within the week. God.

Marianne Goss was about twelve when I left. And I'm sure Elsie had no front teeth. I feel very old, suddenly."

Now Charlotte was in a life jacket that smelled strongly of damp, seated shoulder to shoulder with Dan in the stern of a small lighter, moments away from dry land. Here was the place she had so often tried to conjure. It was as wild as seeing Treasure Island shimmering in the ocean before her. On Tuga de Oro lay—what? Research. Refuge. Answers. Adventure. Freedom, on an island the size of an English county. A miniature world, a British Overseas Territory, and yet ferociously proud of the unique cultural history that made it entirely unlike anywhere else in the world; a community founded on the principles of compassionate collectivism by a series of deliberate arrivals, terrible calamities, and happy accidents.

The fifty square miles of dense jungle had been uninhabited until the Lindos, the Mendozas, and the Altarases had escaped from Recife, fleeing the anti-Semitic Portuguese conquerors of Dutch Brazil. On their way to Curaçao, they had stopped for fresh water at this strange small island in its angry sea and had decided, on a whim, to stay. Persecution here would merely be from the sun, the sea, and the isolation, which seemed a fair trade for the chance of true home. Those first settlers found no trace of native human occupants, and so claimed the island from no one but Mother Nature, a landlady they swore to respect. No sign of endemic mammals, even, save the bats. They really were the beginning, then.

But as with buses, so with settlers. An island can wait millennia to be populated and then, barely six months after these first arrivals, came the British, intending to establish a staging post. The idea was abandoned in the absence of a safe and dependable harbor, to what must have been the great relief of the recent arrivals. But a number of British men decided to stay on their own terms, perhaps for the climate (perhaps after catching sight of the Altaras and Mendoza daughters).

The two groups came to a reasonably peaceful accommodation, for able-bodied men were needed, and it would take collaboration to survive. Abraham Mendoza and William Smith together drew up the constitution on what became the first Island Day, and Tuga de Oro was born.

Today's Tugans were thus descended from some or all of the following: seventeenth-century Sephardim; the British sailors who jumped ship, taken with the Sephardi girls; four Dutchmen sick with scurvy and put ashore to die, who then ate pineapple and lived; nine Nigerian Igbo slaves from Aba who survived a catastrophic shipwreck; three Puritan American whalers who passed by, married Igbo women, and stayed; and later a boatload of Eastern European refugees in the final months of the Second World War, refused Tugan landing rights by the governing British and brought ashore by the Tugans nonetheless, in the full knowledge that Island Close would prevent their deportation.

The overwhelming majority of these disparate founders had in common their flight from the storm of murderous European colonialism, and had no interest in replicating its values. Tuga was thus not simply collectivist but predominantly atheist, adhering to a rational humanism that esteemed reason, fact, and empathy in place of religion. And, though the closure of the Suez Canal led to a pragmatic decision to become a British Overseas Territory (ensuring an annual supply ship would replace diminished passing sea trade), it was also now entirely self-governing.

And to this history of unexpected arrivals was added Dr. Charlotte Walker, BVetMed MSc MRCVS PhD. Her maternal line was upper-middle-class English Anglo-Saxon. Her paternal line was anyone's guess.

4

Nothing stood above two stories. The buildings of the seafront were low and candy-colored—pale mint, creamy lemon, marshmallow pink, dusky lilac, mushroomy beige—with thick walls and small windows, built to withstand the heat, the rain, the hurricanes. Their roofs were palm thatch, which looked mostly to have seen better days but was, in fact, meticulously and endlessly maintained against the theatrical weather and salt erosion. The little boat drew closer, and Charlotte could see that the road that ran along the seafront was cobbled, and that at one end these cobbles gave way straight into white sand. Here, a familiar red London phone box stood beneath the palms, a bright primary color among chalky pastels, embodying the contradictions of the place, as Charlotte had understood them. Beyond and behind this phone box was verdant jungle.

At the other end of the road stood the municipal buildings: the Old Kal, the Residence, and Customs House, a mansion whose entire facade had once been painted with the Union Jack for some long-ago celebration, now faded to faint memories of color by the salt and the wind. Everywhere Charlotte looked hung the territory's flag—the Union Jack in the canton, and the crest of Tuga de Oro in the blue of the ensign. It was too far to see the details but she was a diligent researcher and so already knew the coat of arms: a gold coin tortoise, a coconut palm, and a string of the blue conch pearls that had, in the eighteenth century, paid for the island's brief golden age until the unexpected and devastating extinction of the Tugan conch.

The rest of Town was hidden inland, glimpses visible down narrow streets that climbed up a slight hill behind.

Dan was still chatting, explaining some sort of Shrove Tuesday custom of flipping a pancake thickened with sheep's wool down from the roof of Customs House into a crowd of small children who would fight for the biggest piece, to be weighed and exchanged for a prize; whether Charlotte would get away without being called in to help with lambing; but while he spoke his eyes were scanning the shore, and he was fidgeting, his leg beside hers bouncing up and down. He cracked his knuckles.

"Fifteen years is a long time," she said softly, and was surprised when he grabbed her hand and squeezed it. Then, as if her words had fortified him, he scrambled to his feet and was standing in the bow, waving hugely, and almost tipping a startled Charlotte into the sea.

"What, ho!" he called, "What, ho!" and the cry came back from what sounded like a hundred voices, "What, ho! What, ho!"

Her camera and her now-defunct smartphone were packed in a sturdy case in her duffel bag, inaccessible. Nonetheless, she wanted to remember each word, to record everything, to study every person; every countenance. For this was it. She had not allowed herself to feel the immensity until now, leaving behind the beige and gray of the ship's cabin for this panoramic, dazzling color, gold light flashing on deep navy and then turquoise water. Suddenly she was light-headed with it, struck with vertigo at the magnitude of what she had done. Then they were in, and the lighterman threw a loop of rope, leaped out, and pulled them in to dock. Dan jumped out beside him and turned back to Charlotte. She took a breath, grasped his outstretched hand, and, with the rough egg of a walnut shell closed in her other palm, stepped onto Tuga de Oro.

*

A roar went up at their approach. To Charlotte it sounded like a football stadium, though in reality there could only have been forty people or so, calling and clapping and stamping. She was under no illusions that this was for her—the joy was all for Dr. Dan Zekri, Tuga's returning son. An actual chant began. "Zek-*ri*! Zek-*ri*!"

"I've no idea who's meeting me," she shouted, scanning the faces, her heart in her throat, looking, looking.

"Everyone's meeting you!" Dan called back, without turning, and then ran forward into the crowd, which enfolded him. "*Ke haber!*" she heard over and over. "*Ke haber!*" She had lost her anchor and for an uncertain moment stood watching.

Yet it seemed that some of this fanfare was for Charlotte too, because a brass band she had not previously noticed now struck up with Cliff Richard's "Big Ship," and two little girls in party dresses began to scatter pale velvet frangipani flowers at her feet, and a third sprang to attention, holding out a glass platter of what she explained in a soft voice were fig jellies. A tiny boy in a starched shirt and bow tie stepped forward to give Charlotte a bunch of maroon calla lilies, intoning a well-rehearsed, "Welcome to the island, Dr. Walker," and then adding in an entirely different voice, "But she too small to take care of all ours cows an' bulls, ain't she?" before being hauled away by a slightly older child, perhaps a sister. Now Charlotte understood why she and Dan had been sent alone in the first boat, together with the precious post bags. They were the VIPs.

The scrum around Dan loosened, revealing him bent almost double, enfolded in the arms of an older woman she presumed was his mother, and who now stepped back to look up at him, her hands on either side of his shoulders. Lusi Zekri was laughing and crying and shaking her head, and Dan, too, had tears in his eyes. Charlotte presumed that the round and smiling man beside Lusi was Dan's uncle, Dr. Saul Gabbai. It could not be his father, she knew, for he'd been killed in an accident five years ago, and Dan had not been able to return for the funeral. There had been no berths; even if there had been, he could not take off from work the months required for a round trip and, more to the point, as a junior doctor could not afford the many thousand pounds. In any case, his father had died at sea, with no body to bury. All this must be on their minds as they embraced, a grieving mother and son who had not, till now, been able to offer one another comfort. The Tugan internet connection was rarely good enough for video calls, and Dan had seen his mother only in the photographs she would painstakingly upload and email to him, weddings and community events in which she herself was usually one small face in a crowd. Fifteen years had passed since their last embrace.

Charlotte was surrounded by children all watching with covetous interest while she tasted her first fig jelly, and could not help but overhear.

"I can't believe it's you, it's like a dream. I never thought you'd come. Look at you, *mi vida*! And you're really staying?" Lusi held her son's face between her hands.

"I'm taking on the practice. CMO. No going back now."

"I know, I know, oh, I just can't believe it. I think maybe it will sink in, I'll start to believe it, when it's Island Open and your wonderful Katie finally arrives, and I'm dancing at your wedding, maybe then I'll be able to believe it. Saul, isn't it wonderful?" The man beside them nodded, though he seemed moved beyond speech. His life altered, too, by Dan's return.

Charlotte stared. She couldn't pretend not to have heard, especially as Dan's mother and uncle were both beaming at her in welcome, including her in their reunion. Happiness made them generous, frothing over, inviting everyone to share their own good fortune. Before they moved away, Dan glanced at Charlotte, and his expression of embarrassed apology was all the evidence she needed.

5

The children scattered, and Charlotte came back into focus to find that a man about her own height was frowning at her. He wore a pink baseball cap from which thick iron-gray curls escaped, and beneath it his eyes were very green. He too had Tugan dimples, but Charlotte would not learn of these for some time, for his severe expression did not alter. He offered a brief, firm handshake.

"Garrick Williams. Island pastor."

"How do you do."

"Yes. Well. How d'you do, I suppose, though none of this is at all to do with me. My wife, Joan, arranged for me to meet you. She's the fellowship administrator."

"Oh, Joan's been so helpful," said Charlotte, further disoriented by this unfriendliness. She offered a wobbly smile, which was not returned.

"Well. She could have done with giving a bit less help, as it happens, but what's done is done. She is sorry not to meet you this morning but, as I said, she's indisposed. Any bags with you, or all in cargo? Come down this way."

The arriving passengers might have missed Island Day but tatty decorations remained, red, white, and blue bunting strung across the cobbled street, between oddly enormous Victorian lampposts that wore royal crowns like the Kensington originals from which they were cast. On Tuga de Oro these stood taller than many of the buildings they illuminated, ten in a row down candy-colored Harbour Street, donated by the London Electricity Board in the 1890s and now solar-powered, like much else on the eastern side of the island. Charlotte touched each with a fingertip as they passed. Relics of London transposed, strange in their familiarity. She followed the oddly hostile Garrick along Harbour Street, feeling skinless and slightly dizzy. A general store called Sylvester's, a cafe called Betsey's, a gift shop that doubled as "The Tuga de Oro Post Office: Home of the World's Rarest Stamps," a nameless hardware store, some local handicrafts and pottery on display beneath a swinging painted sign that read BOTIKA MOSHAV. She had studied photographs of this seafront so often that she knew these with a recognition that was almost bodily.

Beside the harbor wall a child of about five was clinging to her mother, weeping, though Charlotte could not hear anything, for the sound of her sobs was swept out to sea by a stiff wind. The mother bent to whisper to the child while small, sturdy arms locked around her neck, two blonde heads together, long hair mingled. Behind the pair stood a broad man with a hand over his mouth. He too, it seemed, was crying.

Charlotte's eyes suddenly brimmed with her own stupid, shameful tears. She was not five; it was she who had left her mother to come here, however, many times, in childhood, it might have been her mother who went away. This distance, at least, had been a choice. Still, after the exhaustion of weeks and weeks of motion, the illness, and the sheer emotional overload of being, finally, on Tuga de Oro, she felt an ache of longing for Lucinda's arms around her. It was she who had been silently furious since Christmas, but now she wanted her mother's forgiveness for her own months of anger. She had risked the only parent she actually had.

A frowning Garrick turned to see what was keeping her and followed her gaze across the road. His expression softened.

"Rebecca Lindo-Smith. Mother's leaving on this ship, taking a job in England. Tough stuff, very hard for everyone. Now let's leave them in peace, bit further this way. I'm in a hurry to get back to Joan, as it happens. Oh, do come along." He set off again and

Charlotte glanced back once more to see the mother lift the girl into her arms and bury her face in the child's neck, while small legs wrapped around her waist, and the man step forward to embrace them both. It was a scene alight with love, and pain. Charlotte hid her stinging eyes behind her sunglasses, and looked away.

Where the road ended a dirt track began, winding upwards and disappearing out of sight. Here they found a black London taxi idling, engine on, doors all open. The vibrating diesel of a hackney cab was incongruously familiar above the slap of waves and the shrill, scraping call of some small white birds wheeling overhead. Atlantic fairy terns, pale as cotton. Another first. She listened, and took a breath.

"Taxi," Garrick called, oddly, for he was standing with his hand on the bonnet of the taxi. Before Charlotte could thank him, he turned on his heel and left.

"Don't worry about your things," said a voice from the far side, "jump in and I'll have you up the Mendoza place in a jiffy. I'm Taxi."

When he came into view, Taxi was revealed as a very short man in a white button-down shirt, neatly pressed khakis, and a pair of green plastic clogs. The few teeth he retained were of a deep earth hue. Taxi gestured with some pride and Charlotte looked inside to find—what? What would you call this, exactly? The black-and-gray fabric seats had been lovingly reupholstered in sheepskin, for which upgrade the seat belts had all been removed, and a miniature woven rug lay in the center of the floor, in a pattern Charlotte would come to recognize as a traditional Tuga de Oro design of rudimentary donkeys, tortoises, and conch shells.

Charlotte climbed in. A sudden hot wind carried sand and dust through the open windows, and when she went to roll them up she found they had no glass. The thick Perspex passenger screen behind the fold-down seats had also disappeared.

"I'm Charlotte," she called.

"We know all about that." Taxi leaned back and handed her a very cold Evian bottle filled with a glowing yellow liquid. "Tugan

27

gold," he said, lurching the cab unexpectedly six feet forward into the jungle. "We've just got the one apple orchard but Betsey gets the best of a keg of juice, still. The trees are right elderly now. Like the rest of us." Here he descended briefly into an alarming fit of coughing, brought on by his own joke. When he recovered he began to reverse the cab at speed, scattering the group of people who had been standing in the middle of the road behind him. A man banged a fist against the side of the cab, but when Charlotte spun round she saw the hammering had merely been in greeting. As they began to edge forwards again someone else smacked the bonnet, like a fond slap on the side of a favorite mare, and Taxi sounded his horn several times for good measure. Charlotte had imagined a small island to be a place of quiet, but so far everything from the stiff breeze to the brass band to her own, frantic inner monologue had all been very loud.

They began to wind their way up the track. Leaving behind the creamy pastel palette of the seafront, this was a return to a more traditional tropical island, as the road curved between banana palms and fronded coconut palms and, closer to the ground, huge frilled club-shaped leaves, the size of coffee tables, that Taxi pointed out as a common wild taro. The light seemed full of chlorophyll. Everywhere was lush, heavy, curling, creeping; here and there splashes of carmine and blood-orange and crimson. It was cooler, instantly. Something tiny fed upon the back of her hand, and would soon itch.

Taxi explained that she'd be staying on the land of one of the founding families of the island, a ways up this road, he told her, but still walking distance into Town if she was "a plucky one."

"Now. Usually at this point with Folk From Away I'd give you a tour, but as you've been dreadful seasick I reckon I'm going to take you straight to the Mendoza place and let you get your land legs back. Where was I? Yes. There are a few Mendozas around the island, a few Lindos, some Smiths, a few Lindo-Smiths, the

Altarases, a fair few Davenports. All those are names from those first settler families. Levi's old Tugan stock. The house you'll stay in, Levi built it with his own hands. Not the grandest, mind, not a big fancy mansion like Martha House up the other side, but authentic, you know? There's not many as honors the old ways on the island anymore, but Levi Mendoza's one of them. He's someone as knows what matters, he values what's right here, not chasing around after the latest whatchamacallit. An honest craftsman, like his father. We put all the important FFA in Levi's house, when they don't lodge with a family."

Charlotte had visions of a doddering island patriarch, evicted. Taxi caught her expression in the rearview mirror. "Don't you worry, he done this for years, he does it for the optician and the dentist when they visit."

"But they don't come to stay for a year, do they? Will he be all right?"

"True that they don't, they come boat to boat, a month or so. But don't you fret. No one ever made Levi Mendoza do a thing he didn't want."

"I didn't know there were—" Charlotte was about to say taxis and then realized that sounded odd. "I didn't know there were hackney cabs on the island."

"I'm the only one," said Taxi, with some pride. "I'm also the radio announcer and disc jockey. Of course, that means people who don't know their manners have been known to call in to the show and ask if I can go and get their granny from the orchards, but I don't encourage that unless it's urgent. Best way to know if I'm driving, you turn on the radio and you hear a lady called Oluchi chatting away, she's the other one at the station, or you hear a lot of Cliff Richard playing without a disc jockey, just music on till the next show, then you know I'm out in the cab and someone can always track me down. Now, I'll put on something nice for you and you just relax and look at the scenery."

She fell silent for a moment and then, over the opening bars of "Devil Woman," leaned forward. "Does Cliff Richard have a particular significance on Tuga de Oro?"

Taxi frowned at her in the mirror.

"Cliff Richard has global significance."

6

Charlotte lay back. The sheepskin was warm, an unexpected texture against the bare skin of her legs. The winding dirt track was vertiginous, shaded by banana palms from which hung deep purple flowers, huge and pendulous, as well as startling bunches of actual bananas, twenty at a time, massive green hands of ripening fruit. The other side of the road dropped away down a steep hillside she was still too queasy to survey. It didn't take long, in the end, and they passed no other cars. Taxi's taxi turned left into jungle and began to lurch over a sandy track veined with cashew roots, and juddered to a halt.

Two low buildings faced one another across a clearing, in the middle of which stood a large single tree with a generous canopy. There was jungle on three sides, and a vegetable garden on the fourth. Both houses were painted peppermint green beneath the palm thatch and one had a wooden porch, round which climbed a vine spangled with tiny tangerine-colored blossoms, and was flanked by two young frangipanis. Its neat solidity and quaint prettiness sang to Charlotte. In her mind she was already through the door, looking out of its small, single upstairs window across the garden and jungle beyond. A home of her own, at least for now.

She got out, and looked up into the glossy dark leaves above her and experienced a moment of sheer, childish delight.

"Is this an actual avocado tree?" she called back to Taxi.

"Yes, ma'am," said the tree, and Charlotte screamed. A man swung down from the branches, apparently naked. When he landed lightly she saw he was, in fact, wearing a very small pair of black swimming briefs, but his sudden appearance remained entirely terrifying. Charlotte backed away, while the man reached forward to shake hands with Taxi through the window of the cab. He jerked a thumb over his shoulder in her direction.

"This my vet?"

Taxi nodded. "Any sign of Annie Goss up here? I'm heading back down to Marianne now."

"Nope. Tell her I went all up around the Lakes and beyond, and the folks at the moshav'll keep an eye out. They'll bring her in if she pitches up."

"She won't."

"You know it and I know it, and neither of us going to be the one to tell Marianne."

Taxi laughed and mumbled inaudibly, saluted Charlotte, and sped off.

The semi-naked man turned back to Charlotte. He was much taller than she and had a square jaw, rough with stubble. He looked like a swimmer, not simply because of the Speedo but also the neat waist and broad, rippling, hairless torso. It was all utterly surreal. She held her bag to her chest like a shield and stared.

He said, conversationally, "We lost ourselves a scamp who's meant to be on that ship for her own betterment. Not so easy finding good hideouts on Tuga. I thought I knew all of them but Annie's got me stumped." He shook his straight black hair from his eyes and began to consider her. "Damn, girl, you for sure ain't the vet I was expecting. You can check my puppies any day of the week."

Charlotte drew herself up with dignity.

"Please can you point me towards Levi Mendoza and perhaps then, you know, go away?"

The man laughed, showing very straight, very white teeth. He stepped back, palms raised, and then stretched, long and slow, forcing her to acknowledge a set of gleaming, corrugated abdominal muscles. Charlotte averted her eyes primly. He then extended a hand, which she glared at.

"Levi Mendoza. Your landlord."

It was the final straw. Dan Zekri had evaded her usually formidable defenses under the world's most unpromising circumstances, and Charlotte now felt that his gentleness and good listening and near-comedic chivalry made him no better—and in fact considerably worse—than the rest of them. Her mother had built their lives on a lie, and Lucinda's flight home landed any moment, which meant she would shortly learn of her daughter's own betrayal, in return. And her father. Her father had not met her at the dock. But then, how could he, when he did not know she existed and might not even be from Tuga? It suddenly seemed a conclusion she'd drawn on the flimsiest childish evidence, and only now that it had failed to happen did she realize with what hope she'd scanned that waiting crowd for a face in which she might glimpse an echo of her own. The passenger list for each approaching ship was announced on the radio—if her father was here he should have heard her name, and though he did not know it, its notes ought somehow to resonate within him like remembered music. That was the rightful fairy-tale ending to this pilgrimage, which had already gone so far awry. Instead, Charlotte was alone in the jungle with a creep in a Speedo. She had reached the end of the day's forbearance.

"Wonderful. I've been lodged with the island sex pest." She had never spoken to anyone with such candor before in her life. It felt unexpectedly cathartic so she added, "Absolutely fucking brilliant."

"Cool your jets, girl, it was just a friendly offer from one healthy young person to another. You're safe with me. Though I must say, I enjoy a woman who curses like a sailor, it's as if you know my tastes already. Where's your stuff?"

"Someone's bringing it. Could you put some clothes on?"

A small pair of shorts were hanging on a branch and Levi hooked these down and stepped into them, followed by a pair of purple plastic flip-flops, which had been lying in the dry leaves beneath. "Better? Follow me. That one's my workshop." He gestured to the left hut. He ambled towards the other one, the one she had wanted. "This is my house. Your house, now."

Moving closer, Charlotte saw it had a stable door painted the same tangerine as the nearby flowers, with two halves that opened independently. At the center of the top half was an iron knocker in the shape of a tortoise. Despite the unwelcome presence of Levi Mendoza, despite everything, her heart lifted. It was a door for warm weather and daydreaming, for gazing out at the ripening avocados while eating one, freshly picked. It was a tortoise-lover's fantasy door. Levi remained on the threshold, arms crossed, handsome, mannerless, apparently finding her amusing. The distracting abdominals remained on display.

The perfect door opened straight into a single downstairs room, whitewashed and low-beamed. It was kitchen at the front and living room in the back, where a gray linen sofa sat opposite an open fireplace, tiled in shades of ochre and brick. A small wooden staircase disappeared up the far wall.

"Bathroom's at the back under the stairs, if you're still vomming."

"I don't underst— How does everyone on this entire island know I was ill? This is so beautiful. Why is there a bed taking up the whole kitchen?"

"Some wires were crossed. I heard professor, I thought you might be elderly."

"Can you move it back into the bedroom?"

"That's a big bed, girl. I had to rebuild it down here. On the bright side, now there's a desk upstairs with a nice view. I understand you're the studying sort."

"I can reach the kitchen sink from bed."

"And the fridge. Useful if you get thirsty. It's spring water from the tap, by the way."

"Great. Can you go away, now?"

" 'Thank you, Levi, for lending me your beautiful home.' You're welcome. Oh, also Joan Williams made you the quilt, that's yours to keep." He nodded at the bedcover, donkeys and tortoises again, marching in wide concentric rectangles.

"She's very generous, I will treasure it."

"So you do have some manners. Very good. I'm up here at the workshop most mornings if you need help with anything in the house. Or if you just get lonesome."

"Ugh," she said, pushing the door shut. Only the top half responded, and Levi's bare legs and purple flip-flops were still visible in the remaining aperture. She shoved this lower section closed too, and his laughter grew quieter. The man at least could make a good solid door.

7

Dan had asked to walk with Lusi, so that he might slow the beating of his heart. He did not want Uncle Saul speeding and jouncing him too quickly towards his childhood home. It had been fifteen years, but he needed just a few more minutes.

Harbour Street had been overwhelming, memories layered upon memories, familiar and yet no longer his. For reasons he could not imagine, someone had painted Customs House with a Union Jack, and he had forgotten the Tugan devotion to a flag that was surely known only to Tugans and perhaps the odd Foreign Office civil servant, for it hung everywhere, great swathes of patriotic bunting from lamppost to lamppost, possibly for Island Day, possibly just because. The scent in his nose was the same—salt and kelp, frangipani and vanilla, donkeys, woodsmoke, diesel. The feel of the cobbles beneath his feet, slippery with seaspray near the harbor wall. And his mother, jubilant and generous, whose every word nonetheless betrayed how much she'd missed him, and how much he had missed. In his childhood she had always worn her hair in an afro, but now the slim twists that fell almost to her waist were gray, and her face was lined as he had not remembered it. He had been away a long time.

But once out of Town, Lusi's chatter began to soothe him, familiar as a caress, and then she mentioned that Caleb, back in England, had been instructed to collect Annie Goss when she disembarked, and he had felt a sudden liberty and mirth, and a release of the tension that had been building since he climbed down from the ship into the lighter. This chauffeuring—driving a sulking eleven-year-old from port to boarding school—was exactly the sort of task that might have fallen to Dan himself. Expat islanders were expected to link arms in a robust support network, providing everything from housing to meals, company to transport, and his time away had been punctuated by requests to assist arriving or departing Tugans. One month he would be issued the sudden command to collect an old man coming over for a hip replacement (Island Council hoped that Dan didn't have too many stairs to his flat, for the patient would also need lodging, in the week before his hospital admission); the next to spend his day off driving to Bath to collect a parcel of forty pairs of donated reading glasses, and then to deliver these onwards into the charge of a trio of old ladies awaiting transfer back to the ship in Southampton. Katie accompanied him on many of these adventures, and took seriously the associated responsibilities. Preoperative patients billeted in their tiny spare room had more attentive physiotherapy sessions from Katie than they would later have as inpatients, and were loaded back on to the boat with a full sheaf of printed instructions. Dan had no particularly warm feelings about the saturnine and evasive Caleb dos Santos, who got in touch only to borrow money, and who certainly did not usually make himself available to do the eccentric bidding of the Island Council. But it seemed that Dan's departure had left him in the firing line. At the very moment Dan was trying to face the implications of his own return, this was the perfect reminder that true independence had in any case been a delusion. No man from an island is an island. Not even Caleb dos Santos, openly despising the smallness of the world he'd left behind, concealing his heritage with an adopted accent so peculiar that even Dan (burdened with an unusual accent of his own) could hear veered wildly from Wales to Liverpool. One was Tugan anywhere and always, and some relief would surely come with being again a Tugan on Tuga. This insight gave him hope that by returning home, finally, the battle within was ended.

Ended too was the walk, for here they were, outside the cottage in which he was born, freshly painted the color of buttermilk beneath its palm thatch. The front door had been hibiscus crimson in his childhood and was now white, and standing open. Otherwise the building looked the same, and it was only in the trees that he was struck by the passage of time. Long ago, after his own brief trip to England, his father had planted three kadota fig saplings along one wall. These had thickened and grown, and now spread heavy branches over the east side of their yard, cloying with green sap. Dan put his arm around his mother and they stood together for a moment, looking in silence at the little house and its big trees. His father was dead—that too was a change.

Dan was led into the small kitchen where Lusi and his aunt Moz had laid out a lunch that would have been worthy of Pearl Day. Aunt Moz gave a cry when she saw him, and threw her substantial arms around his neck. Lusi watched them with obvious pleasure, each new reunion reigniting her own joy.

"You saving your uncle," said Moz with feeling, squeezing Dan's cheeks, and when Saul protested that he did not require saving she said, "All right then, you saving me. Oh, the very second you take over, I am disconnecting that phone."

Moz was tall and full-figured, a giantess to the worshipful schoolchildren she taught, to whom Miss Moz was the ultimate authority on all matters. They loved and feared her, retaining this passionate combination long into their own adulthoods, for Miss Moz had by now taught generations, her flaming red hair long faded to a sleek silvery-gray. Despite her insistence that it was high time Saul retire from medical practice, no one would dare suggest that Moz retire from teaching, least of all her husband. The schoolhouse without Miss Moz was inconceivable.

Seated at the table, Dan found himself undone by the unexpectedly familiar scents. A pair of roasted chickens, their crisp skins stuffed with preserved citron and island mintberry; sweet coconut rice; a pyramid of deep-fried taro keftes. A meal for twelve lay between the four of them.

Saul clapped Dan on the shoulder, and took the chair beside him. "You should come home every ship. Look at this feast."

The phone rang and Saul stood again. A look of weariness crossed his face, but he answered brightly and immediately took up a pen, listening, taking notes. Moz was pointing theatrically.

"You see, this is how we live. *Decades* like this, finding him wherever he is. Any minute now he'll say he can't eat his chicken, he's going to an urgent poisonberry sting, or a life-threatening splinter." She dropped a kiss on the top of Dan's head and then sat down at the table. "We made all the things you might have missed, *kerido*. Nancy reminded me you liked keftes."

Saul was gesturing for her to be quiet.

Dan whispered, "Ahh, I've not had keftes since I left. Where is Nancy?"

"She working, you see her later."

"At the clinic?"

"At the Rockhopper," Lusi told him. "She's at the Rockhopper on the days she isn't assisting at the clinic."

"And she teaches science at the school," Moz added, "on Tuesdays."

"Which you can do too, of course," said Lusi, with no little pride.

"I'm going to get that new conservation vet woman teaching biology, I reckon," mused Moz, who had a capacity for sniffing out visiting expertise, and co-opting it for her pupils.

"By all means ask the vet, but Dan's going to be far too busy at the clinic to be teaching anyone anything," said Saul firmly. He had set down the receiver and now returned to his place at the table. Moz heaped food onto his plate in aggressive quantities, as if challenging him to remain seated until he'd finished it all.

"Actually I was thinking about teaching." Dan leaned back as from either side his mother and aunt built a similar mountain on his plate. "Not the kids, the nurses. I thought maybe we could run a training session once a week for clinic staff, I started making a list of topics, I'll show you."

Saul frowned slightly. "Who's seeing patients when we're running a training session?"

"Well, I wondered if we could cancel routine clinic appointments one morning a week, just block it off for training. And emergencies, obviously." When Saul didn't respond, he went on, "You'd said you thought motivation was a bit of an issue with the nurses, and on the way over I was wondering if professional advancement was the answer. An answer," he amended quickly, not wanting to imply that he had already solved a problem Saul could not.

"It's an interesting thought." Saul spooned sauce over his rice and chicken. "Eat up, we've got to get to a rash."

"I told you," said Moz, crossing her arms. "Can't get through a single lunch without urgent impetigo. How was the food on the boat, *mi vida*?"

"Terrible."

"And the food in England?"

For a moment, disloyally, Dan's mind flew to Camden Town, to Brick Lane, to Borough Market. He thought of pad thai with crushed peanuts and lime juice; he thought of sushi and brisket and bao buns and Korean fried chicken. He felt a sudden pang for Camembert. The rest of his life held fresh fish, and ripe fruit, but soft cheeses did not seem likely to appear on the island unless someone learned to make them.

"Nothing on this," he said and smiled at his mother, whose love and pride filled the small room, and who was aglow with the pleasure of feeding him. "Nothing like this. Not like home."

8

"Home is where you are, I'm not leaving you," said Annie, fiercely. She and Alex dos Santos were up a sycamore fig near the old cemetery, looking out over the glittering water. It was the day after their eleventh birthday, and each was fighting tears.

"You won't be allowed to stay. Everyone's looking."

"I'll hide till the island's closed. They can't hold the ship for me, it's late in already."

Alex nodded, though he did not dare to hope. He could not take his eyes from the blue and red lights of the cargo liner, anchored far off at the kelp beds.

Annie Goss and her mother, Marianne, were Alex's twin suns. Marianne had nursed him as a baby, when his own mother had been sick from a hard birth. He had been lifted from Ruth's exhausted body onto the heat and safety of Marianne's chest and it was here that he had first found Annie; on Marianne's sternum that Annie's hand first grasped his fingers. Marianne had looked down to see their two bent arms like the wings of a single delicate bird, vernix-feathered. Annie was color and magic, his milk sister, blood sister, twin flame. Foretold since her babyhood like a fairy-tale curse, the threat of Annie leaving for an English boarding school sat like a stone he had swallowed, leaching poison into everything. He had dreaded this day for the whole of Island Open.

When during the days her ferocious little face was close to his, her breath hot on his cheek, vowing insurrection and triumph, Alex allowed himself to hope. But late at night, when his own mother's troubled wanderings woke him, then he knew the truth. The adults would send her.

Marianne had found him just yesterday morning on the beach, curled at the foot of a palm as if expecting a blow, had picked him up almost without effort and held him on her lap, her big little boy, newly eleven, and in all ways yet a child. And she had stroked his hair and whispered through her own tears that they who most loved Annie must be brave, must palliate their grief with generosity of spirit, that true love lets go. Marianne had nothing of her own to give her daughter, only this, a bequest made long ago. She did not pretend that Annie, once she had gone to England, would ever come back. They might suffer, but their beloved would fly.

Alex scrambled down to the jungle floor and a moment later Annie landed, silent as a cat. Even in the deep shade he could see that her eyes were swollen.

"I'm going up to the waterfall. Go and say you can't find me." Annie pushed him in the chest, not gently.

"They'll never believe me."

She stamped a dusty bare foot. And Alex, sidekick, devoted follower, fellow knight and brother squire, wiped his tears with the back of a dirty hand, and made his vow. He began to run.

"I won't tell," he shouted over his shoulder. For Annie he would disobey them all. For Annie he would smash the island into pieces. And at that moment the ship's low horn sounded its departure, and the island answered with its own peal of bells. The relief was too much for Alex, who fell to his knees at the foot of an ironwood, leaned his forehead to the rough trunk, and sobbed.

Eleven years earlier

It had long been considered good luck to give birth on Island Day, but neither Marianne Goss nor Ruth dos Santos's pregnancies had seemed, till then, especially propitious. Then again, it was also tradition for children born during the festival to be named Tuga, but as it had not happened for a hundred years there were no Tugas remaining, and everyone had all but forgotten. And so, that Island Day, were born Alex dos Santos, a late-in-life second son to the beloved and formidable island councillor Ruth dos Santos and her estranged fisherman husband, and Annie Goss, unplanned and unexpected daughter to poor teenage Marianne Goss and who knew which deadbeat father. If the arrival of these new souls augured good luck, such luck was far from obvious.

Marianne had caused no one any trouble until this pregnancy, though many had worried for her, knowing what they knew of the mother. As a crew member from a cruise ship, her mother had come ashore and stayed illegally, had given birth to Marianne four months later and, with her temper and her drinking, caused trouble with fatiguing regularity. She ran up debts; she picked fights. On Tu B'Av she mooned the pastor. The island had difficult characters of its own, and felt considerably less tolerant of public nuisance when it was made by an FFA.

Marianne had been a pallid, skinny little girl, silent and unsmiling. By evening, island children were often dusty or mud-splattered but they set out for school each morning on a full stomach and, though their clothes were likely handed down through half the island, they were always clean. Miss Moz went out of her way to touch the girl with kindness, to stroke her cheek, to hold her hand, determined to overcome her distaste for a child who so often smelled of unwashed hair, who itched, who bit her nails to bleeding, and who would not meet her eye. Moz took the issue to Ruth dos Santos, the senior island councillor responsible for child welfare, among various other things, but before the two women had agreed on a course of action a cruise liner called at Tuga. The following day, eight-year-old Marianne was sent to school with her meager belongings packed into her satchel, and when the ship left, Marianne's mother was aboard.

There was no one Moz revered more than Ruth, who seemed to run the island with one hand while baking for half the community with the other. She was known for wisdom, fairness, and a brisk efficiency, and her moral courage had more than once set her against the rest of the Island Council. Ruth tied back her own huge mass of black curls, a sign, to those who knew her, that she meant business. Then she sat Marianne in the yard and cut to chin-length her long, splitting blonde hair, suffocated the lice with coconut oil, and combed, while the girl picked her cuticles in silence. Ruth massaged more oil into the tender scalp, and treated the torn nails with ginger honey. The next morning she stood the little girl on a chair by her side and began to bake biscochos.

Woman and girl suited one another. Each was quick, watchful, independent. Ruth was a talker, Marianne a listener. Ruth's son Caleb was almost grown, her husband worked trawlers and was away from the island for months at a time. Ruth had the space and energy to devote to Marianne (Ruth had space and energy for limitless projects, Moz felt, envious. Ruth had more hours in her day than others).

The love Ruth came to feel for quiet, careful Marianne took time but was profound, when it one day surged upon her. Marianne loved Ruth devotedly from the first day, for making the itching stop. In later years, Ruth was the only person she trusted with the whole scabbed and filthy mess of her early childhood and Ruth had held her and said softly how sorry she was, they should have realized sooner, they should have protected her. But that wasn't how Marianne saw it, not at all. She had not told, so how could they know? Now Ruth was her berth, and nothing more could hurt her. Ruth had not let her down; she had come like a rescue mission. Ruth was safety. Ruth was home.

It was a good joke, or a bad joke, when Ruth and Marianne, by then seventeen, fell pregnant at the same time. Everyone suspected Levi Mendoza had fathered Marianne's baby, but it was without evidence, and only because everyone suspected Levi Mendoza of everything. Such a total absence of information was not the usual way. The island was wreathed in confected myth and only partially apocryphal mysteries, but there were no mysterious islanders, and certainly no mysterious conceptions. On the subject of her own pregnancy Ruth felt merely tired, and that by her age she ought to have known better. Her husband David was rarely home, and that suited a couple with little in common—though he was home often enough, the island observed tartly. That momentous visit turned out to be his last, for before he could even have known of the pregnancy, he'd joined up with the crew of a Kiwi boat he met in the Falklands, and left permanently for New Zealand. But if anyone had the energy to start all over again with not one but two newborns in the house, it was Ruth dos Santos.

Ruth's labor went wrong from the beginning. It was Marianne who went for Rachel, the midwife, by then two weeks overdue with her own baby and cycling at speed over the rutted track. When Rachel felt the danger come for Ruth—the whole air of the room changed—it was Marianne who went again for Dr. Gabbai. Perhaps it was all that frenetic cycling, in the end. Marianne lay on the bed beside Ruth, breathing heavily with her, eyes locked, willing her strength into the other woman's body. And then suddenly she had given a laugh that quickly became a moan, and grabbed Ruth's hand and said, "Ahh, streuth, so sorry, sorry," and Saul and Rachel had exchanged raised eyebrows. "Let me look at you, girl," Rachel had said, but Marianne hadn't seemed to hear, had turned onto all fours and buried her face in Ruth's damp neck, and Rachel, leaving her post between Ruth's open knees, pushed Marianne's dress up and took the scissors to the girl's soaked underwear to discover her fully effaced, and more than three inches dilated. Forty minutes later, Annie Goss was born.

That night, Ruth's baby finally came out gray and silent, flaccid as a fish. Rachel saw to the child, Dr. Gabbai to the mother. But after some minutes a faint flush rose on the infant's chest, which heaved, and juddered. A sign of life was enough—it was Ruth who needed their urgent attention. Rachel lifted the frog-body and laid him down in the best place she could think of, on the hot chest of the healthy teenager, only a few hours a mother and already nursing her own baby with apparent ease. Marianne accepted the next infant without comment, and without apparent surprise. In her arms were two new souls, her daughter and also Ruth's boy, who felt as much a part of this moment and of herself and of her strange twinned pregnancy as anything else.

Across the room Ruth was flushed and feverish. "My baby, is he OK?" she managed, and Rachel nodded and soothed and wiped back the damp black curls that had long been threaded with silver. "He's fine, he's here with us," and Ruth gave a faint smile, and her eyes rolled back. The boy would live. And Ruth would go on to live, if you could call it living. Saul added intravenous diamorphine. Rachel held the light and Saul sutured and sutured, and hoped, in the end, for the best.

Outside the Island Day parade had begun down Harbour Street, flags whipped and cracking in a stiff sea breeze. Inside the cottage, on the heat of Marianne's chest, two hands met like the hands of a gimmel ring, above her sternum, just to the northeast of her heart.

9

The ship's low horn sounded its departure and the island answered with its own peal of bells, announcing Island Close. What was meant to be four days anchored by the kelp beds had instead been compressed into the time it took to unload the cargo, load the small quantities of fish frozen for export, and board eleven departing passengers. Someone had presumably found the errant eleven-year-old Annie Goss and hauled her aboard. After all, how far could she really have gone on a teacup island, a child known to everyone? And that other little girl, Rebecca Lindo-Smith, would now not see her mother's face again for a year.

The horn woke her, and when she looked at her watch Charlotte found she had slept for most of the afternoon. She was grateful for it. There were things she was not ready to consider.

The adrenaline of her rushed and covert departure from London had stayed with her all the weeks on the ship, stoked by the bodily emergency of her illness and then by the unexpected spark of hope that meeting Dan had ignited. But now she had arrived at a destination towards which she had been traveling for weeks. Longer, if imagination counted. Now she had stillness and silence, she was no longer seasick, and the emergency became her thoughts. Lying in a bed that was not her bed, looking at a kitchen sink that was not her kitchen sink, it was hard to remember all, or indeed any, of the reasons she had come. The preservation of a threatened species. The pursuit of knowledge. The solving of other mysteries, perhaps.

For a year, Charlotte would live like a Tugan. She would learn to greet passersby with "*Paz*," and a raised hand. If she wanted to travel any distance across the island, she would have to learn to catch a donkey. She would drink violet saloop, ground from the dried, heart-shaped fruits of the endemic korason palm and sweetened with coconut syrup; she would pick ripe mangoes and wild vanilla; in season she would be offered scrambled booby eggs. (Tourist reports were equivocal on the subject of booby eggs.) She would scour the jungle for tortoises, and scour the bookshelves for historical tortoise accounts. She would find her father, or she would not find her father.

Here she was, alone in the middle of a huge ocean, on a remote island to which no more boats would come for months. She was intrepid, or she was unhinged. They were not mutually exclusive.

She had earlier kicked off her shoes but otherwise was still dressed, partly from exhaustion and partly because the kitchen windows had unlined cotton curtains hung from large nails, and afforded a fairly unobstructed view of her bed. It was also for this reason that she had earlier not allowed the rising tears to come. The sea was still rushing in her ears, and there was a note on the doormat, together with a jar of hot chicken soup.

Dear Dr. Walker,

Please forgive my absence on the dock this morning, I have been under the weather. I do hope Garrick conveyed our warmest welcome, & the depth of our pride and gratitude not only that you are here but that you were so accommodating of our somewhat rushed schedule. You were very understanding, and of course we were lucky with the berth. I'm sure en route you learned the eccentricities of travel here, and that even among the most willing, very few visitors find themselves on Tuga so soon after deciding to come!

I trust the Mendoza house is in good order. I have left milk, butter, and yogurt in the fridge, as well as some of my own mangoes & papayas. Levi will walk you through his garden, which is plentiful, & at your disposal. In the tins beside the sink you will find a coconut cake and a loaf of bread. Please keep everything perishable in tins, to defend against ants. It is safe to drink the water. I can only apologize for what must have been some error of my own communication with Levi regarding the bed. However, at my direction he has taken a desk upstairs, which has a beautiful view, & I hope will prove an inspiring place to work. If you need them, Levi will make additional bookshelves.

This evening at six p.m. it is the annual Island Close party at the Rockhopper, & it is my great hope to see you there. You are perfectly safe anywhere that you can reach on foot from your house, but please take the large torch with you whenever you go out near dusk. Night falls very quickly here, & is very dark.

I so look forward to seeing your face at the Rockhopper, and it is to summon the strength to do so that I have spent this morning resting. On behalf of all the administrators of the Martha Philips Veterinary Research Fellowship, welcome to Tuga de Oro. It is my our great wish that during your time here you find a home from home, productive research, & the answers to all your questions.

Yours warmly,
Joan Williams

PS I am sending this note with Alex dos Santos, a somewhat shy & diffident little boy, full of sweetness. If he is still nearby as you read this, perhaps you might find a task for him, fetching or carrying etc., he has a broken heart & is in need of occupation. His twin sister is to be sent to England today—may already have left as you read this, in fact.

49

PPS I fear Garrick was somewhat brusque this morning. He has disapproved of my exertions in preparing this fellowship only because he worries for my health. I implore you to find it in your heart not to judge him, he is truly the best of men.

There was a great deal in this note to consider. But not now. Now, Charlotte thought wearily, standing up from her bed and stubbing her toe on the pedal bin, now she had to go to a party.

10

Island Close at the Rockhopper was a quiet affair. After the exuberance of Island Day, Island Close marked a shift, an end not only to the festival but to the season of tourism and travel. There was no longer anyone for whom the Tugans needed to perform Tuga. Remaining were only islanders and the long-resident FFA (who retained the acronym, even those who'd been on Tuga more years than they'd lived anywhere else). Fishermen still went out when the conditions were right, understanding the idiosyncrasies of the local waters, and in a few months it would be September and booby-egg season, with all the feasting and festivities that entailed. Supplies of everything were plentiful for now, but what there was, there was. No more curry powder would arrive till December; no more baked beans, or Rice Krispies, or shampoo. No more letters. If you had ordered a new sink, or a pair of running shoes, or a roll of polythene, or a special size of rivet, they'd either come on shore, or they hadn't. Either way. It was time to batten down the hatches.

Charlotte had followed the hand-drawn map at the bottom of Joan's letter, minimal but accurate, and before long the noise drew her from the main road, laughter and music drifting out on the warm evening. The Rockhopper was halfway between the Mendoza house and Town, a long, low building of yellow-painted breeze block, windows latticed with fairy lights, and set back from the track in the sandy clearing of a walnut grove. On one side it had a dusty car park, at present filled with motorbikes and 4x4s, two of which seemed to have their lights on and engines running, although no one at the wheel. On the other side were a few picnic tables, on which were set flickering electric storm lanterns. Several donkeys were tethered next to a bucket of water and their open, comical faces gave Charlotte her first uncomplicated pleasure since disembarking. They were friendly beasts, responsive to her approach, and to stand quietly with her palm on the rough warm neck of an animal redeemed the whole miserable, humiliating day. These were her reminder, she told herself. It was for the animals she had come.

When eventually she tore herself from the donkeys, she went up the steps of the Rockhopper to find the threshold barred by Elsie, now in a different boiler suit with "Elsie Mechanic" hand-stitched across her lapel. In this context she loomed like a bouncer, and for a moment Charlotte wondered if she would be refused entry.

"Ah, Dr. Walker, did those donkeys check out all right? You're very thorough working in the dark and all. I'm glad I've run into you again. I wanted to ask about windscreens. In winter, in England. I know you're not meant to pour boiling water on them."

"No, I understand that makes them crack," Charlotte said vaguely, grateful to be pulled so entirely into any conversation, however eccentric. Her anxiety had instantly returned. She scanned the room over Elsie's broad khaki shoulders, looking for Dan. On an island with a population smaller than her London postcode, she was nonetheless fervently hoping never to see him again. Yet catching sight of him would at least locate him in one single spatial point, and relieve the discombobulating sense that he might be everywhere.

She could no longer remember why she had assumed he was single, nor what had made hope flare within her that he had reciprocated the sudden intensity of her own feelings. All in all it had been a humiliating error of judgment, and a salient reminder that no good ever came from letting down her guard.

"Well, technically it doesn't crack them," Elsie went on, stepping back just far enough to admit Charlotte entrance but remaining at her elbow, linking arms with her, in fact, "and I bet you're thinking what does Elsie know, she's never seen snow! Well. Elsie doesn't know snow, it's true, but I do know windscreens. Actually it only cracks if there is a weak point already."

"I see. I didn't know that. But I suppose you can't know if you have a weak point till it's too late."

"Precisely!" Elsie looked pleased. "Do you generally prefer to use chemical antifreeze, or a scraper?"

"Both, usually. One then the other."

"Both," Elsie repeated. "Goodness. What about salt? Would you ever salt the windscreen, do you think?"

"You could, I suppose. Bit messy. Scratchy, even. Might you know if Joan Williams is here?"

"Joan'd be out of date, I should think. Antifreeze technology has moved on a bit since she left England."

"I'm sure. Is that—" but beyond Elsie, Charlotte saw that someone was moving towards her, a slight woman in navy blue, with gray hair cut very short and, inexplicably, tears coursing down her pale, lined cheeks. One hand was extended, the other lightly at her throat. She was simply dressed, in a straight, homemade shift that fell mid-calf, a sturdy pair of plain brown sandals, and was unadorned but for a large cocktail ring on her index finger, incongruous with the modest simplicity of the rest. It caught Charlotte's eye, huge and round as a penny, made of royal-blue enamel patterned with small gold stars and ringed with pavé diamonds that winked in the low yellow light.

Stepping gratefully away from Elsie, Charlotte reached out for Joan with perhaps more longing than she might otherwise have, and the two women embraced in silence, a moment of connection that felt less like a greeting and more like a reunion after many years. Charlotte had liked Joan in all their correspondence, and now felt an emanating warmth that threatened her composure. She wanted to speak to her mother, who by now was home, and presumably hysterical to the point of spontaneous combustion. Charlotte didn't know how nor where she might check her emails, but had no doubt that fire and brimstone burned within them. She missed her mother, and feared her.

Joan drew back and was looking at Charlotte, still clasping her hand. The surprising ring pressed into Charlotte's fingers. Joan dabbed her cheek.

"Forgive me. This has been so long in the planning and I'm moved—I'm just so very glad you're here. I will take you over to Garrick in a minute, but first I wanted you to myself, just for a moment. Will you tell me about your journey, are you feeling any better?"

Charlotte was not in a rush to reunite with Garrick. She told Joan about the weeks at sea, finding herself unable to describe the voyage without at least passing reference to Dan, which led Joan to explain that Dan's Uncle Saul, the current doctor, had married Garrick's sister, Miss Moz, who was the teacher, and to suggest that Charlotte draw spider diagrams of the Tugan families she met, or risk hopeless confusion. Joan revealed that the public library had been catalogued, the final amendments made this week. The catalogue was in a box file on the table of the Rupert Whitten Library, awaiting Charlotte's first visit.

At that moment Charlotte caught sight of Dan Zekri, at a table in one corner between his mother and his uncle again. Their table seemed in conversation with a group at the next, at which she now recognized Elsie and Taxi, both of whom waved. Dan was laughing but when he saw Charlotte the smile fell. He stood as if to come over, and so Charlotte asked hurriedly to be taken to Garrick. As she followed Joan in the opposite direction, she saw Dan in the far corner close his mouth, and sit back down.

II

Alex dos Santos had thought himself safe, in the darkest corner behind the buffet table, but someone had seized him by the ear. He could not turn to see, but knew nonetheless. He dropped a biscuit back onto the platter. Marianne released him.

Marianne extended her hand and Alex yielded up the bundle he clutched. She opened the tea towel to find a stack of crab sandwiches, squashed against a slice of chocolate cake. She closed this back up with deliberation and stared at Alex, who in turn stared resolutely at his own dirty feet. He and Annie had defied Marianne on the grandest possible scale and, against the odds, they had pulled off the impossible. The boat had gone and Annie was not on it, and no one now could send her. He waited for the sentencing he deserved. Anything, anything, would be worth it. But Marianne's voice was soft, when it came.

"I'll let you take this to her. But you tell her she'd better be home and in her own bed by the time I get back tonight, and I expect her clean. She's to wash her hair and scrub her nails before she sets foot in my house."

Alex, who had been expecting lashes, or the stocks, or some other medieval punishment furnished by his fervid imagination, began to cry with relief at this clemency. He threw his arms around Marianne and sobbed incomprehensible words of gratitude against her shoulder.

"There there, my love. Listen. It's all right, shhh. It's OK. Alex, my darling. It's all over now, she didn't go. Don't cry. You take some sandwiches to your mother first, OK? Take her some fig jellies, too. Just put them by her, if she's sleeping."

"You might have been more welcoming. You've chased her off. Were you that stony when you met her at the boat this morning?"

Garrick blew air through his lips. He knew he had been forbidding with the new tortoise researcher, and felt defensive. "I don't see why we should be rolling out any red carpets. Your anonymous donor has had some crackpot ideas in his life, but you can tell him from me, this is the worst of them. You are supposed to be slowing down, focusing on getting better, and precisely what we did not need was a big project. Those creatures have been here longer than we have. Why a population survey now, all of a sudden? I can see what the pressure has done to you these last weeks, you're ill with it, it's set you back months. And that girl with her demands, expecting you to provide a fully functioning London townhouse—"

"She only asked if there was air-conditioning," Joan interjected mildly.

"Asking whether there will be air-conditioning in a Tugan cottage implies an almost total lack of understanding of this island she's so keen to visit. And that business with the library catalogue."

"The air-conditioning was to do with scientific samples, as I understood it. And it's been a pleasure doing the catalogue. She didn't ask me to do it, she just asked if we had one and I realized we didn't."

"Balderdash. Her tortoise mumbo jumbo can go in the kitchen fridge, and most of those books have nothing to do with her research, as you well knew before you began. And it's not been a pleasure for me watching you do it, I can tell you that for nothing. You've been like a headless chicken since that boat left England, and this morning it caught up with you and you couldn't get out of bed. Well. I went to get her today because you were indisposed but it took all my restraint not to load her straight back on to the lighter and send her back to England. What earthly use to Tuga is an academic vet? Will she help with lambing or gelding or vaccinations? Will she look over the insemination plans for the cattle? No. We need her like a fish needs a bicycle. This community needs practical support for livestock, not rummaging around in the jungles chasing the animals that take care of themselves. Saul and I are united in our disapproval."

Saul Gabbai had appeared, putting a jovial arm around his brother-in-law.

"United in all things, *badjanak*. What do you have me disapproving today?"

"That." Garrick nodded towards the jukebox corner, where Charlotte Walker was standing once again with earnest Elsie Smith, whose rhythmic gestures suggested they were discussing shovels or perhaps axes. "The donor's new Fellow, come here tortoise-bothering."

"Everyone's very excited to have a vet here longer than boat to boat," Saul told him. "Everyone I see has been piling up questions for her."

"But she's not going to be seeing patients; supposedly, she's coming to poke about, and shoot things into the poor gold coins who never did a thing to her, and to be a nuisance to my wife. It is ecological imperialism and we can well do without it."

"You are being positively horrid," said Joan, unexpectedly. "And you're forgetting that our donor created this fellowship specifically for tortoise research, it wasn't Charlotte's idea, she's not a, not an ecological imperialist, or goodness knows what. I never thought you'd be so unwelcoming to a young woman we've invited so far from home. She's a reptile expert, and in the long term that research will benefit the island. We want scientists coming, and conservationists, and anyone who can bring us a bit of attention, a bit of energy. The island lost its native conch to extinction and it would be terrible if our tortoises went the same way. And she actually doesn't owe us her expertise, there shouldn't be an automatic tax on visitors who happen to have skills we want, and she's very brilliant and we need her. I need her. And you will need her."

They were both looking at her in astonishment. Joan had never before been known to contradict Garrick, least of all in public, and she certainly did not raise her voice. She did not elaborate on why Tuga de Oro might need a herpetologist with such urgency, and this unexpected outburst seemed to have winded her, for her color was high, and she had run out of words.

"Have a caper with me, Joanie," said Saul, bowing, and Garrick nodded and returned to his whiskey. Joan took Saul's hand.

"I will, sir."

Saul led her to the dance floor, where they joined in a slow galop, played on the accordion by Sylvester, who owned the Harbour Street general store. Taxi had taken up a harmonica, and Joan and Saul revolved away from Garrick, sedately.

At a safe distance, Joan said to Saul, "Island Close, finally."

"Island Close. How do you feel?"

"Relief."

"Truly?"

"Truly, Saulie. No regrets. Remember that." She tightened her grip on his shoulder.

Miss Moz took Marianne's hand between her own, and squeezed it, and together the two women watched Alex dos Santos dart out of the Rockhopper clutching his treasures, disappearing into the blackness beyond. He was a timid little boy, made anxious and acquiescent by his mother's long illness. Yet for Annie Goss he had withstood the outrage of the entire island. It was hard to know if Annie was his kryptonite or his superpower.

"*Kerida*, I know what you're thinking, I do. It's going to be OK."

"Is it?" Marianne looked up at her old teacher, searching her face for reassurance. Miss Moz knew more than most what this opportunity had meant to her.

"Well. At least you've not had to separate them. They live for one another, those two."

"If I'd had the money to send them both, I would have; it's coed, that school. I used to have dreams about it. For years I used to think, I'm so stupid, I didn't think fast enough, I should have asked for a place for both of them—but they were babies, it was impossible to imagine they'd be, be as they are."

"And all the money's really lost, is it? It's gone? Cause you could make no small use of it here, is what I'm thinking. It must be thousands."

"It was never money, really. He gave it to the school in one sum all those years ago, with the condition that it guaranteed her a place and holiday boarding, money for books and uniform and all. Use it or lose it. Except no one would be stupid enough to lose it."

"*Kerida*, you did your best, truly, I saw how hard you tried. She'll grow up a good girl. You didn't exactly have a silver spoon in your mouth and look at you."

"She'll never have any more than this, now."

"I know that hurts. And I know it isn't what you wanted. But it's not so bad here. And there's those of us fighting to make a difference, doing what we can in our small way. I keep my eye on your Annie, you know that. I'll not let go of her till she knows what's what, I know how to teach that girl. You have my word."

Marianne flushed. "I didn't mean—Miss Moz, sorry, I know the school here is good and you're a wonderful teacher, I wasn't saying—"

Moz hushed her, firmly.

"I didn't take it like that, I know exactly what you meant. Believe me, I wish we could do more than we do. It keeps me up at night, trying to find ways to get these kids all they need, to teach them all they need. It's a hard life here. But—we're not doing so badly, and most importantly she has you, setting her an incredible example of love, of how to make a real family. Maybe, I don't know, maybe you could make it a gift? Maybe they'd agree to take another child instead so it's not wasted, what do you think? If you called them and explained. Or let me call them, if you like. There's got to be a little girl already in England who needs a place. We could make sure it helped someone. It's only June now, if they're on the mainland already it's not too late for them."

Marianne nodded, barely hearing. There was no other girl. Her heart was full to bursting. Annie—her sprite, her charm, her beloved. Annie had stayed. It was unthinkable. Her body did not believe it, still taut with ten years of accumulated sorrow. A decade of waiting to lose her child to the world.

12

Inside, the Rockhopper was a strange fusion of a backpackers' beach bar and a rural English pub that had seen better days. In the 1950s, someone had imported a stock of disused Yorkshire pub furniture including one entire dark mahogany booth, high-sided, complete with stained-glass paneling. This now sat on the sandy linoleum at the far end of the room, usually serving as table of honor for Island Council members, or WI meetings. The rest of the pub's tables had come in the same shipment but many of the seats had broken, substituted over time with a mixture of stacking tubular school chairs and white plastic picnic stools. The low ceiling was strung with old fishing nets, and from these hung storm lanterns in clusters, strings of festoon bulbs, and occasionally some fresh or dried flowers tucked into suspended jam jars. On the walls were an assortment of tortoise-themed artworks, and several huge clip frames filled with dense photo collages of the sort Charlotte associated with undergraduate dorm rooms or family kitchens, and featuring many of the people in attendance.

"Are you going to be everywhere?" Charlotte asked Levi, who was on the bar, pulling a pint. Curling postcards had been tacked to the wall behind him, and notes of various currencies.

Charlotte had escaped from Elsie again who had, delightfully, revealed not only a beloved pet tegu lizard, acquired through some sort of questionable customs seizure, but a lifelong love of reptiles in general. Although she had then gone on to describe the mechanism of the jukebox arm.

"This is where I work. And I live upstairs, remember, because some FFA tortoise lady is sleeping in my bed."

"I'm not sleeping in your—oh, give it a rest. At least here you wear clothes."

"I know that must be a disappointment. Let me guess. White wine and soda? Cosmopolitan?"

"I can't tell if you think you are insulting me. I'm not a drinker. Fizzycan, please."

Levi clinked some ice cubes into a glass, and filled it with lemonade from the bar tap.

"Thank you. Listen. Do you have any idea why your minister seems to have taken against me?"

Levi set her drink on the bar, garnished with a neon cocktail cherry on a toothpick.

"Garrick's old-school. He's been taking care here a million years and we all got time for him. He ain't about preaching or praying, he rolls up his sleeves and works as hard as anyone else here, and he knows everyone's worries, he knows farming here ain't easy and we ain't got much, even pulling all together as we do. Losing one cow can finish a family for the season, no matter that Island Council'll come along and get them a new one. Island Council ain't exactly loaded in the first place. We ain't had a vet on the island for a long time, and now a beautiful young woman comes, and I don't want to make you big-headed or anything, girl, but you pretty flashy here, big news, all your degrees or whatever, latest training, and then the rumors say you here a whole year but you ain't going to treat real animals. You can see Garrick'd wonder, someone somewhere spending a lot of money, and what's in it for his community to have you here?"

"So you're saying not only Garrick will hate me, but everyone will hate me."

"I said there's a problem, and people think you the solution. Go be humble, tell Garrick you want to learn about Tuga from him, that you're not just here to take, you want to help."

"But of course I want to help, that's my entire reason for being here. Preservation of island ecology is crucial to the future of the whole planet. You have a threatened species here that deserves close study—any study, actually—and I've been given the responsibility of paying it the attention it deserves."

"Whatever you say. And just remember if it's my attentions you need—"

"I'll bear that in mind."

Levi grinned. "You do that."

Charlotte turned her back on the seemingly ubiquitous Levi, and scanned the room.

Dan was approaching again, and Charlotte searched for another escape route. Joan was dancing with Saul, and so Charlotte picked up her lemonade and made her way back to Garrick, to act on Levi's unexpectedly wise counsel, ignoring Garrick's faint look of displeasure as she neared him.

"I wanted to say," she began quickly, "I'm aware that there's a huge amount I don't know about life here, and it's important that you know my research isn't just surveying for its own sake, but in order to help, for the future. Maybe you might be able to introduce me to some of the older islanders so I could ask what they remember of the gold coins, and understand a little bit about the history of their wider cultural significance? I thought it would be quite meaningful to start my interviews with Martha Philips."

Even before she had finished speaking, a burst of Levi's laughter made Charlotte flush. When she looked over he was shaking his head, and actually tearing his hair. Garrick's habitual frown had deepened into an expression of unconcealed irritation.

"I don't know how you plan to spend your time here, Dr. Walker. But I will say that my wife has exhausted herself preparing for this fellowship, and so far you have not convinced me those energies have been well spent."

Dan joined them and she had no opportunity to escape. Couldn't he see his existence was a humiliation? And now he'd probably witnessed a completely incomprehensible dressing-down.

"Our new Fellow was just telling me she looks forward to interviewing Martha. She is apparently not simply a veterinarian but a whisperer."

"Oh no. No, Garrick, sorry, that's my fault." Dan turned to Charlotte. "I'm so sorry. You said something on the boat and I thought it was so charming that I let you think—I should have explained."

"Explained what?"

"Martha's a tortoise, she lives at Grand Mary's. I'm sorry. Garrick, truly this is my fault, don't blame Charlotte." Unexpectedly, Dan bowed low before Charlotte. "Will you caper, milady? By way of apology."

Charlotte cast around. Levi was resting his chin on his fist at the bar, eyebrows raised.

"A caper! What is it I'm meant to say?"

Dan remained in his bow and looked up at her. "You say, 'I will, sir.' And then you curtsey, and dance with me."

"In that case I won't, sir. I make it a principle not to dance with men whose fiancées are overseas. And especially not to caper with them."

Saul Gabbai had just handed Joan Williams back into her chair and appeared at her elbow.

"Sound principle. Dance with an old married man instead." Saul bowed. "Will you caper, milady?"

Charlotte curtseyed, casting an arch glance at Dan, who had the grace to look embarrassed.

"I will, sir," she said, and took Saul's hand. As she moved away, she heard Dan trying to explain once more to Garrick that it was she who had been the victim of a prank, not the pastor himself, but it wouldn't matter, she felt sure. The damage was done.

13

The walk to the clinic took a long time in the darkness. The Rock-hopper's bluegrass faded, replaced with raspings and creakings, and by sudden, unidentified rustling in the low wild roadside taro. His mother had taught him that if you lay quietly enough, by night you could hear the jungle growing. This had anthropomorphized the huge plants and made Dan, as a boy, feel keeper of a great secret; they animated, not quite sinister but certainly ravenous, reaching out tendrils and suckers while he dreamed, a doubled nocturnal world. *Jack and the Beanstalk* had seemed quite reasonable to a child accustomed to magical overnight growth, for plants changed visibly, evening to morning, in the humid Tugan dark. Now the beam of Lusi's spare head torch was diffuse and pale across the stony track, while his own white LED lanterns were still in cargo. He remembered this thick, hot blackness, feeling it wrap around him.

He went wrong twice, turning the first time into a farmyard, where the high scent of steaming goats' manure caught, not quite unpleasantly, in the back of his throat, and the second time into what seemed to be a mechanic's yard, before he found himself at the low white gate of the clinic garden. In his pocket was the key, given to him earlier by Saul with much ceremony. There were not many keys on Tuga.

Dan looked for a long time at the unremarkable building ahead of him—whitewashed, L-shaped, a roof of corrugated iron, windows frosted with peeling privacy film. At one side was a driveway of biscuit- and cream-colored crushed shell, leading up to the covered ambulance bay, in which was parked the only ambulance. This too had a key, of course, but as with all other vehicles it remained, for safekeeping, in the ignition.

The Benjamin Cole Centre for Family Medicine, known simply as the clinic. Exam room, hospital, laboratory, operating theater, pharmacy, delivery suite, morgue. It was for this—just this, all this—that he had come.

The following morning Saul was surprised to find the clinic lights on, Taxi audible on a loud portable radio in the foyer declaring that cargo had now been processed, and anyone might go to Customs House from mid-morning to collect whatever they'd shipped. "Some o' you cattle people going to be mighty disappointed this day," Taxi went on over the opening bars of the next track, "sounds as if the cold storage failed for the Brangus bull semen, but you're to see Elsie and she'll tell you more. I'm thinking"—here it became clear that the upcoming song was "Shout" by the Isley Brothers—"that all this might make you wanna throw your hands up and . . ."

"*Paz, kerido.* You're up early."

Dan was on his hands and knees before the bottom shelf of the hall cupboard, rummaging.

"Haven't slept. Where's the instruction manual for the Reflo-tron?"

"Who needs the instruction manual?"

Dan's face was shining with sweat, and his white shirt, the same he'd worn last night at the Rockhopper, was rumpled, and no longer clean. He looked, Saul thought, like a little boy crouched in fer-ocious concentration over a train track. Dan sat back on his heels.

"Me. I had a play-around but I want to know I've not missed a function. Is there somewhere we keep all the test strips? Who cleans here? Some of the storage is in a right state."

"Several places. But—" Saul was distressed by the battered card-board boxes and spilled paperwork in his hallway, only an hour before his first patient would arrive. And he did not need to be reminded that Queenie cut corners with some of the housekeeping. He had been managing a string of contract doctors, often doing the work of two, and had bigger fish to fry than worrying about the state of the lockers. One did not conduct surgery in the back of the cupboards. Deep into her eighties, Queenie Lindo-Smith had been the hospital cleaner since before Saul had come back from medical school and she no longer found bending particularly easy. If asked to get on hands and knees, Saul feared she might never again get up. She preferred a slow push of a mop, or to knit in the waiting room, keeping the patients company. This was more helpful than it sounded—Saul's clinics ran late, and waiting times were long. Queenie defused mounting irritation, and she had never missed a day of work, which was more than could be said for Calla and Winston, the two nurses. Saul had been called out twice in the night, once to a baby with a high fever that wasn't responding to paracetamol, and the second time, just after his body had given in to sleep, to a teenage boy who had cut his foot open on a rock on the beach, in some drunken tomfoolery. Nonetheless, he had pictured himself behind his own desk before Dan arrived, inviting him in for a handshake, a welcome speech, an orientation through the kingdom. This disruption to his expectations was—disruptive.

"Clinic starts soon. Might be best to put all that away."

"Oh. Sure. Are the nurses late?"

"They don't start till ten."

"I thought the first patient's at nine?"

Saul passed by and went into his own office, leaving the door open behind him. He had a headache.

"They've got animals. And gardens. Everyone's happier if they can set it all straight before they come in. Have you slept at all?"

"I got excited."

"Go home and have a shower. Sleep. Let's meet for lunch and talk properly."

"Are you sure?"

Saul was sure.

"OK, I'll be quick, that gets my run in, as well. Not that this is ideal attire." Dan grinned. "Let me shove all this back in."

"Shove away," said Saul, and thought to himself, oh, well. He had been wrong to expect Dan to remember more than he had. The boy had been a teenager when he left, impressive, driven, and determined, burning with anger at his father and pity for his mother, suffocating, desperate to escape it all. He had not recalled Tuga's particular needs and ways because he had been what teenagers are: self-focused, self-obsessed, fighting for space to construct an adult self. That hard work had been done somewhere far away and now this adult man was back, jovial and committed, Saul could see, but more FFA than islander. Well, that was a disappointment but not the end of the world. Saul had overseen a hundred FFA orientations before, and this one, at least, would be the last. One day soon he would get some sleep.

14

It was early—the kitchen curtains had not been designed for light exclusion. Levi was audible outside, sawing and sanding, singing along to what Charlotte already feared might be his only album, *The Best of the Pogues*. When she peered out of the window she experienced a troubling flash of disappointment that he was wearing a T-shirt. Was it simple Pavlovian conditioning, that Levi's relentless innuendo meant that merely seeing him now made her think of sex? He was without shame, possibly without social boundaries. He was also wearing a pair of flowing lavender and peach tie-dyed trousers, and mauve plastic clogs. Still, the beauty of his torso was indisputable.

She made two instant coffees and went out to join him in the yard. Levi was bending over his workbench, from which rose the smell of burning. When she approached she saw he was writing RAFFLES on a slice of tree trunk the size of a dinner plate, sawn off from a huge log that lay behind him.

"When's the raffle? If the prize is an air conditioner, I'm buying all the tickets."

Levi did not lift his head but looked down at his handiwork, and after a moment added a small love heart on either side of the word.

"Hello?"

"It's a headstone for Rebecca's special piglet. It got out and mangled its leg in a vermin trap, Walter found it last night." He blew on what she now saw was a grave marker. "Had to put it out its misery."

"Oh no, poor little girl, the one whose mother left?"

"My niece, Maia's my sister. Rebecca asked if the new vet'd come give the sow and the rest of the litter a once-over, she's worried the mother's upset about her little'un. I said I'd ask."

"Of course I will. But I'm really not meant to be seeing patients, I'm not insured to practice here."

"Rebecca ain't going to sue you."

"I've not worked as a vet since I qualified."

"Right, so you're not a very good vet. That's OK, you still a vet round these parts. I ain't asking you to give it a heart transplant, just do some stuff that looks professional, reassure a sad kid."

"That I can do. But I don't remember anything about pigs. I haven't even got a stethoscope, it's still in cargo." Charlotte set down the coffee she'd brought him on the workbench, and it slopped over the edges.

Levi grinned. "No worries about the kit, you can just go interview that sow, Dr. Dolittle, just like you got planned with Martha. Ask her what she thinks about Tugan independence or such, you know, find out if she got anything on her mind. Atta girl."

The sun was remorseless and the sky was without a cloud, and so Charlotte stayed in the shade of the banana palms that wound down the track. She passed a laden donkey, driven by a teenage girl with long plaits who said a shy "*Paz*, Dr. Vet," without looking up, and a man in a string vest swinging from a harness up a palm tree, who stuck his machete into the side of the trunk, tipped his baseball cap, and called down, "*Ke haber*, Vet Lady." Charlotte smiled and raised a hand at each greeting, and continued down towards Harbour Street and Betsey's, on her way to Walter Lindo-Smith's.

Betsey's Cafe was slightly set back on Harbour Street, with room at the front for two aluminium tables, beneath red umbrellas advertising a brand of ice cream that Betsey did not sell. What Betsey did sell was whatever she was in the mood to make, or had bought in from Marianne Goss, who baked the cakes, muffins, and sandwich bread. The coffee itself was grown by families on the moshav, a farming collective in the north of the island, who also supplied the butter and milk.

The exterior of the low building was painted a pale pineapple yellow, the interior wallpapered with psychedelic daisy heads in shades of umber, cantaloupe, and gold, over a floor mosaic tiled in similar shades. At the walnut-laminate coffee bar stood a row of rattan bar stools, opposite which was the coffee machine, stacked crockery, and a long glass shelf high above displaying knickknacks—a teapot shaped like a rooster; a biscuit tin shaped like a rosy thatched cottage; a few potted orchids; pride of place a sepia photograph of some stern-faced young people in a pink, shell-encrusted frame. The opposite wall displayed nothing but an expanse of the dizzying wallpaper and, at its center, a single cuckoo clock. Charlotte was put in mind of a 1980s suburban kitchen, an impression that deepened when a woman in a floral housedress and white frilled apron stepped away from the window and embraced her, kissing her warmly on both cheeks as if she were the first guest arriving at a party.

"Hello, Charlotte Walker, I've been wanting to meet you, I'm Betsey Coffee. Well, Smith. Would you look at that, the demons have dropped half Annie's stuff in the muck. Marianne will have their guts for garters."

Betsey returned to her post by the open window and Charlotte followed her eye towards the water. Near the dock she could just see a large trunk standing open. A boy and a girl were pushing a rusty, overloaded wheelbarrow up the curve of the street, a trail of items fallen behind them in the dust.

"What are they doing?"

"Unpacking Annie's trunk, it's been sitting there since the ship unloaded it again. She lives clear on the other side of Lemon Tree Valley and we're none of us allowed to help. Marianne says to Annie, 'If you're old enough to make decisions, you're old enough to sort out the consequences.' I reckon they couldn't catch a donkey. Ice coffee or hot? No more chicken soup, I'm guessing."

Charlotte had understood almost no components of this speech, rich with information though it seemed to be. She searched for a way in.

"Iced, please. Annie's the girl who was meant to be on the boat?"

"That's right, going to boarding school in England. It's been ten years planned. Is a chance most could only dream of here, the money was put down years ago by someone who owed Marianne, that's a story in itself. English schools don't open their doors to Tugan kids every day, and Marianne's been saving for that berth pretty much since the plan was made, but Annie doesn't care a fig, she wants to be on the island more than she wants an education. 'I'm staying with Alex and that's that,' she says, and poor Marianne says, 'Well, if you're staying with Alex then so be it, you and Alex can ruddy well sort out the mess you've made, too.' She's only small and a scrap of a girl but, *guay de mi*, she's strong-willed, that Annie Goss. And in truth Marianne was wild with losing her."

Betsey returned behind her counter and switched on a deafening coffee grinder, so Charlotte looked up the hill. The children had set down the wheelbarrow and were staring rather despondently up the steep curve of the road where the cobbles gave way to a rutted dirt track, not Charlotte's road but a smaller one that ran in the opposite direction, towards the Lakes and the *montaña* at the center of the island. The two children stood head to head in earnest discussion and then swapped, Annie lifting the handles and Alex guiding the front. Each was in grubby denim shorts and identical white cotton vests. Alex wore plastic sandals, and Annie was barefoot.

Betsey wrapped two muffins in a clean tea towel and handed them to Charlotte together with two cartons of guava juice from the freezer, frozen into squashed rhomboids.

"It would have been a cruelty to separate those two, in truth. He'd have pined himself to death. Like a hound. Do me a favor, *kerida*, and pop those into the trunk as you pass. Just for goodness' sake don't let anyone see you do it."

15

"We take this opportunity," said Garrick, looking about him with much gravity, "to remember the worthy contributions Raffles made, the love and the cuddles, and the funny things she did. May the memory of Raffles bring comfort to those who loved her, and may she live in your hearts, and in your deeds, and in the stories you tell. May peace be upon us, and upon all communities. And indeed, upon our piglets."

Charlotte, standing off to one side, took the opportunity to glance down at her notes. Had she detected a gentle touch of humor in humorless Garrick? Rebecca had earlier made it clear that she expected a service not unlike the one she'd seen on television for a British royal, and had also expressed the belief that there was no such thing as heaven and that, now dead, it was all over for Raffles. A funeral was for the living, Rebecca had explained earnestly, and Pastor Garrick had told her the right thing was for the living to do good in Raffles's name. Charlotte would imagine this was all cold comfort for a six-year-old, but the thought of an everlasting void did not seem to bother Rebecca.

Earlier, Charlotte had crouched in the pigpen, a borrowed stethoscope in Rebecca's ears as she taught the little girl to listen for the difference between the racing heart rate of the six piglets and the slow, steady beat of the sow. "Her pulse is less than half that of her babies," Charlotte had said, drumming the beats on Rebecca's palm with her fingers, and Rebecca moved between each bristled chest, delighted, and had then caught Charlotte at a vulnerable moment by looking up, long-lashed, to ask shyly if Charlotte might later say a few words over Raffles, in the manner of a visiting dignitary. Everything about this request was pure horror to Charlotte, for whom public speaking was about tied with karaoke, bungee jumping or life modeling, the mere contemplation of which could bring her out into a cold sweat. Pure horror, and on this occasion utterly unavoidable. Now her big moment was approaching.

The deceased was already interred, Levi's headstone in place upon the small earth mound at the bottom of Walter's vegetable patch, between the okra and the compost heap. Rebecca held a mauve calla lily and a Polaroid photograph. The demon twins were there, still in grubby vests, joined by a woman with thick, straight blonde hair, loose to her waist, who from the similarity was either Annie's sister or her mother. She stood in between Alex and Annie with a serious expression, holding hands with both. Joan Williams watched her husband with solemn reverence, her pallor striking beneath a vast sun hat. She looked gray, almost translucent, and kept glancing at Charlotte whenever Garrick paused. Charlotte began to avoid the odd intensity of her gaze.

Garrick went on, "We remember Raffles with you, Rebecca and Walter. Now, as I understand it, our new, ah, visiting vet would like to say a few words."

He gestured for Charlotte to join him at the graveside and she felt her face flame, embarrassment dwarfing any horror she might otherwise have felt to hear herself inaccurately described as "the new visiting vet." On a piece of paper were five sentences, which had taken her an hour to compose.

Had she gone into clinical practice she would by now have euthanized innumerable beloved animals, and would have spoken words of comfort to all their corresponding humans, for it was virtually a daily occurrence in a busy vet's practice. As it was, she had absolutely no experience of managing bereavement and knew next to nothing about humanism. Piglets were about her only safe ground. She stepped forward and cleared her throat, her eyes fixed on Rebecca.

"You know, one of the reasons I wanted to be a vet is because animals love with open hearts and no conditions. They teach us absolute acceptance. They teach us mindfulness, to be absolutely now, and present." Was this true of piglets? Probably. "Your daddy has told me how you took care of Raffles, and I saw today how much you know and understand what your pigs need. You had a love for Raffles that rose above your differences in species and I've got no doubt that if you want to be a vet when you grow up, just like you told me today, that you can do it."

That was surely enough. She had acquitted herself and could stop. But something was happening, a drama of some sort. Joan Williams had fainted, and Garrick had rushed to her side. Levi stood beside them, circling his hand for Charlotte to keep going, keep talking.

Then she saw Dan. It was inconvenient, the way her stomach lurched at the sight of him. She had not seen him arrive but there he was, kneeling and fanning Joan with what seemed to be an actual palm leaf. Charlotte recalled herself to Rebecca, who was glancing between her father and Charlotte with increasing anxiety.

"Your love rose above your difference in species," Charlotte repeated slowly, while panic flowered within, for she had said all that she could possibly offer. Her mind kept coming back not to the piglet but to Rebecca's mother, gone for who knew how long. She remembered the scene on the dock.

You must think I am a monster, to have just run away like that, Lucinda had written. *Haven't I always supported you in everything you do? . . . Why are you so untrusting? Can't you accept that sometimes my motivations can be private without being malign? . . . What are you doing to your life, WHY ARE YOU THERE? . . .* "And it will rise above time, too, and above separation. After all," she risked, forcing aside the insistent fragments of her mother's email, "just because someone isn't physically there doesn't mean we have to stop loving them. Or that they stop loving us." Oh God, she thought, that bit's all wrong for all those bloody rational humanists. Never mind. "I believe that those we love stay close to us, and the way that we keep them close is by loving them. It's true not just of people who die, but those who leave us for a time, who have to go long distances, even though we know they will definitely come home one day. Your mother must be incredibly proud of how beautifully you take care of all her animals while she is away. And when she is back, you can show her."

Was this too on the nose? It seemed worth reminding them all, Rebecca foremost, that this was not a funeral for the mother. *It feels like you've died*, Lucinda had written, and, *do you understand you are trapped there for <u>months</u>? What if something happens? I can't get to you even if you need me, can you imagine how that feels to a mother?* Rebecca nodded fiercely, and turned her face into her father's legs and began to cry again. Walter lifted the little girl and she buried her face against his neck. Charlotte felt she had misjudged with her ad-libbing, and cursed Levi for making her go on. She watched as Levi and Dan carried Joan Williams, conscious now but still wilting between them, through the garden and into the Lindo-Smith bungalow.

After a moment, Walter suggested that Rebecca might be ready to put her flower down for Raffles and the little girl slithered from her father's arms and ran to seize Charlotte's hand, gazing up at her with adulation. Walter gave Charlotte a grave nod of approval. The island saw. The island heard. If it had been a test, Charlotte had passed it.

16

Suddenly, it was very hot. Till now the heat had been a pleasure, the sort to warm the bones, to lift the heart; a summer-holiday warmth that was soporific after lunch but tolerable most of the day. Walking home from the Rockhopper the previous night, the air had been cooled by a sea breeze, salt and kelp and black frangipani that Charlotte had sucked greedily into her polluted city lungs like a tonic.

But today the breeze had dropped, and an entirely different sort of weather had descended. She had read about and yet still not understood the humidity that was possible during Island Close. How to explain the kind of air that felt like the touch of clammy unwelcome hands pressed against every square inch of your burning skin? That it felt as if not she but the air around her was sweating? She wanted to submerge herself, like a newt, in a frigid pond. She wanted to shave off her sweat-stiffened hair to free her scalp. She would make devil-pacts for an electric fan. The Rockhopper would have ice, but to get there she would have to move again, and movement was to be discouraged. Since dark had fallen it seemed, if possible, to have grown hotter.

Charlotte lay down, experimentally, on the bare wood of the porch. After a moment she went briefly to the kitchen for a tea towel and a bottle of water from the fridge and returned to the porch to lay the cool, sodden cloth over her face, separating every limb into a starfish. Then the whine of a motorbike startled her, and she raised her head an inch.

"Levi?"

"Sorry to disappoint."

It was Dan Zekri.

"I thought you might be hot. But I see"—he peered down at her, spread-eagled on the porch with a wet towel on her head—"that you are coping just fine."

Charlotte cast off the cloth and sat up, piling her damp hair high upon her head. She was fairly sure she had sweat patches down her spine, and she was in a small pair of boxer shorts printed with love hearts. But then Dan had seen these pajamas before.

He was carrying a cool box, which he set down beside her on the deck.

"Would you like a beer?"

"Is it cold?"

"Very."

"Can I also have one for each armpit?"

God, she loved his laugh. What a disaster. It was important he go away very soon. She watched as he knocked the caps off against the side of a step, and handed her one. They clinked bottles.

"Have you got a few minutes? I really need to talk to someone trustworthy." When she didn't answer he added, "About a work thing."

Charlotte flopped back down and put the icy butt of the bottle to her forehead. "Sorry. Don't do humans. Not my sort of animal."

"Please. You're not from the island, and more importantly I trust your judgment. I need to confide in a friend."

"We're not friends, Dan."

"Ouch." He gave a long exhale. "That's my fault. God. I am sorry. I'm embarrassed. I owe you several apologies, and I can't even figure out where to begin with some of them. I just—I do really want to talk to you about how I . . . If I make you a promise to grovel properly in a minute, can we pretend just for one brief digression that I'm not a total idiot?"

Charlotte smiled, despite herself. She left a silence for Dan to continue.

"I need to betray a medical confidence. Do vets have a Hippocratic oath, or equivalent?"

"No, as it happens, we do not. But whatever, I gave the eulogy at a pig's funeral this morning so all bets are off at this point. Do you know this is my first beer?"

"Of the day?"

"Of my life. I am uptight and inhibited. And I am mostly teetotal except when in extreme emotional distress, when I drink vodka. But this is very nice." Charlotte took a deep swig, and then coughed. A pale velvet flower drifted down from one of the frangipani trees. Dan picked it up and closed it in his fist, and inhaled.

"It's hard to even know where to start. I knew moving home would be a culture shock. If nothing else, I've come from a teaching hospital with, like, sixty critical-care beds. But I grew up here, you know? I expected to readjust my expectations. The health budget is stretched, we place drug orders six months in advance and still sometimes stuff doesn't show up, or there's a medication you need and none left in the pharmacy, so you're going through old medical records to find whoever was last prescribed it, and asking some old man if he wouldn't mind going through the back of the bathroom cupboard. It's bush medicine. I've been swotting up again on spider and centipede bites—actually maybe you know about that stuff too," he added, as Charlotte sat up abruptly, casting about for any venomous centipedes that might have joined them on the porch, "but anyway, I've been trying to get up to speed with the major active conditions, needs, histories, and I found out that someone's dying here, or rather, someone has a disease that is—possibly curable, with invasive treatment, and this person doesn't want it because it would mean months away from the island. England, almost certainly. And Saul isn't pushing her, he's providing palliative care. I confronted him and he made it sound like I was an ignorant FFA, he said, 'I am not sure you remember how we do things here, we honor the patient's wishes, we don't bulldoze,' and then I swore and he said, 'You are going to need to recall yourself, *ijiko*,' and then he had to race off because the man never stops running from pillar to post."

Charlotte moved to sit down beside him, on the steps. For a moment they were silent together, and he watched her face, quiet while she was thinking.

Eventually she said, "Patients must refuse treatment in world centers, too, with all sorts of different motivations. Quality-of-life decision. Religious beliefs."

"But not wanting to leave the island, that's such a stupid reason." Dan dropped the flower and flexed his hand. "She's just—she's making the wrong decision. I've come home to help. I can't help people if they won't help themselves. She was born in England, this patient, and I'm just suggesting she take up her rights to NHS treatment in the UK, as the British citizen that she is, go for maybe six months, a year, and take her chances. Staying here is suicide."

"But it's Island Close now anyway, isn't it? There's no way off?"

"I know, so now until Christmas there is absolutely nothing I can do in any case. It's just given me such a—it's a reality check, I guess, I just worry I don't have it in me to do this job, now I'm actually here, and Saul is exhausted, he's basically been on call for forty years. When you stop and think about it, it's completely insane. Do you know until recently the clinic shared the ultrasound machine with the sheep farmers?"

"Wow. Now I'm really glad I'll have nothing to do with lambing. But would the treatment work? If she had traveled?"

"It would be a very long shot," Dan admitted. "But a shot, at least."

Charlotte remembered their journey here. Her own comparatively trivial sickness, her own comparatively trivial uncertainties. She imagined making it in reverse, watching a familiar island recede, without knowing you would ever return.

"Maybe she wants to spend whatever remaining time she has here. Maybe she doesn't want to die far from home. And if she's a woman you respect, shouldn't you respect that choice?"

"Huh." Dan looked at her. "That's exactly what Saul said. I don't know—I just know I don't want to be a worse doctor for coming here."

"On the contrary, you'll have to become a better doctor. It would make sense to be scared."

Dan glanced at her, and if she hadn't known he was engaged she would have sworn she felt it again—a mounting energy between them. A spark of something. A connection. That scared her, Charlotte thought, unable to articulate it without feeling even more vulnerable, or idiotic. The utter inaccessibility of another's emotional truths. The light years of distance between expressed behavior and the dark inner recesses of thought. She had felt so safe with him. Now he was dangerous.

"What scares you?" Dan asked, and she looked away.

"Oh, everything scares me," she said lightly. "Public speaking. Public spectacles of all kinds. Neurotoxic peptides in spider venom. My mother. Doing my work badly. Failing the species I'm committed to saving. Sleepwalking through my life. My own bad choices, primarily."

A knocking sound began in the garden, first one, then another, and then a creaking, loud enough to make her pause, delighted. "Geckos!"

"The lover-girl gecko. They're this big." Dan lifted up the cap of the beer bottle.

"Yes. One of your three hundred and seven endemic Tugan species."

"She's very loud for someone so small," Dan said. "I've always wondered about that."

"It's not just one, it's both of them; that's a duet you're hearing, a call and an answer. Part of an extended courting ritual that goes on for days."

The noises went on, a rusty gate swinging back and forth in the blackness.

"Romantic. I never knew that. Like Marco Polo."

"Yes, well." Charlotte drained her bottle. "I think it's probably the only Tugan courting ritual I'm interested in."

"I should have told you about Katie."

"It would have been good manners, yes."

Dan set his beer bottle down on the step, between his feet.

"I don't quite know—it never came up at the beginning, when you felt so awful, and then by the time you were feeling better it was somehow too late. It meant something, getting to know you, it was—you were, I don't think you know how much you helped on a journey I was, not dreading, exactly, but fearing. It was a distraction—no, that sounds exactly like what I didn't mean, I didn't mean you were a distraction—your seasickness and then getting to know you . . . I didn't want anything to change about the way we were spending time together or make it awkward or whatever, and then it seemed presumptuous to think that you would even care anyway. Or is even that too presumptuous to say, I don't know. Probably you didn't care. Sorry, I am making this awkward. Maybe you're one of the things that scare me. Did you?"

"Did I care that you have a fiancée you never mentioned when we spent weeks together talking?"

"Yes."

"I don't think you get to ask me that."

"You're right, you're right. I'm sorry."

"It's OK. I'm not really in a headspace to be . . . I came because I was missing fieldwork but also I needed to be somewhere with no drama, for a while. Just quiet. Well, quiet apart from the geckos."

"Thank you."

"For what?"

"For being—elegant."

She looked down at her bleach-stained pajama shorts and laughed.

"I'm sorry to break it to you, though, but small islands are drama factories. It's one of our major industries. Tuga de Oro does a really good line in gossip. For example, Raffles."

Charlotte hung her head and covered her face with her hands. "Was I awful? I really did my best. That poor little girl, I just wanted to make it right for her. Was I too earnest? Was it embarrassing? Just thinking about it makes me die a bit."

"No, no, not you. You were wonderful. Precisely earnest enough. Especially considering Raffles wasn't even in there."

Charlotte's head snapped up.

"What?"

"Nope. Mound of earth from the veg patch, and Levi's wood-slice monument thing on top. This is Island Close, in case you hadn't noticed. You don't waste good bacon." Dan leaned forward and clinked his bottle against Charlotte's. "Welcome to glorious Tuga, Dr. Walker."

17

Ten years earlier

When it happened, Sylvester had been sitting outside his shop with a pint of grape Fanta, enjoying the breeze and the bustle. It was Shop Day, two days after a ship's arrival, and Harbour Street was closed to cars, bikes, and donkeys, and instead was thick with pedestrians. The previous boat had been a washout, and this cargo was expected to compensate for many disappointments. Flour had been scarce again. Strawberries had come, and broccoli, and tinned tomatoes. Island Council was very excited about some new waste-treatment chemicals. Vitali Mendoza had ordered a circular saw. There had been a Coca-Cola drought longer than any since the 1980s, but now the syrup came in in great barrels, rolled into the Rockhopper under the greedy eyes of Caleb dos Santos and his friends, teenage boys who were rumored to drink little else from breakfast onwards. The bigger children had felt keenly the lack of chocolate. Mac and Rachel made sweet jellies from dried figs, or pineapple candied in dark coconut sugar, but these were widely considered not to count as proper treats.

Some new vehicles had come on shore. There was a small tractor for the moshav, one Land Rover for the meteorology station operators, and another, older but serviceable, for the clinic. This had been lent to the visiting optician, Martin Blackburn, who had also been newly off-loaded, back for his second tenure, until the next ship. He didn't actually need a car as he saw all his patients at the clinic, but this time he had written in advance specifically asking for one, and as he was returning as an unpaid volunteer, accommodations had been made. Here he was in fact—idiot!—trying to turn into Harbour Street on Shop Day. Sylvester and various others shouted. Martin could not have seen that Marianne Goss was crossing the road behind him for he looked panicked and the huge car lurched suddenly into reverse. Sylvester dropped his glass and began to run. They had meant to stop him going forwards, not to send him plowing backwards into pedestrians. For the rest of his life, Sylvester would hear Marianne's scream as her buggy slammed over on its side and disappeared, between the huge wheels.

Fists pounded on the Land Rover's roof, on the windows, on the windscreen. It was women who filled the street on Shop Day, and wrathful, sickened, mobilized women who were now hammering on all sides of the car, which in panic began to inch further backwards. A collective baying rose, as if from a pack of hounds. Martin's shaking hand tried the gearstick once, twice, and finally he found first gear and moved forward. Sylvester's body told him what to do and he launched himself at Marianne with strength he had not known for a decade. He spun her round, and held her. No mother should see what surely lay in the horror of the road.

But what he saw was Miss Moz righting a mangled buggy in which was still strapped baby Annie, sprayed with dust, gravely silent, wide-eyed, unscathed. The front wheels of the pram had ninety-degree surrealist folds in them. The back wheels had entirely detached, crushed beneath the Land Rover. Moz dragged what remained to the pavement—a frame around a miracle. Sylvester released his grip on the young mother and turned her again, this time to see.

Marianne was shaking violently. Her teeth had begun to chatter. She was a good girl, Marianne, and took such serious care of the babies. She was only eighteen, after all, and she'd not had a good time of it, till Ruth fostered her. Moz surged back out of the crowd and enfolded the teenager in her strong arms.

"Shhh, look, she's fine, look here, Annie's absolutely fine. Lovey, *kerida*, leave her be just there for a moment, look, no you can't, *kerida*, you're not fit to hold her yet." Here Moz held tighter to Marianne, who had lurched forward and was trying to snatch Annie from her seat, though the straps were still taut across her chest and Marianne's shaking hands could not capture the buckles.

"She's absolutely right as rain. You're the one who's had a scare, you need a moment, she's best where she is while you just, just give it a minute."

"Yes, yes, I see," Marianne was repeating, "yes, I see," but she had fallen to her knees and her hands still scrabbled with the clips, clawing for her daughter. In the end she buried her face in the baby's lap. The listing remains of the buggy gave an ominous creak and Sylvester grabbed for the handles to hold it steady. Nobody else moved.

It was then that they all noticed Martin Blackburn, who had stepped out from the driver's seat and was standing beside the car, one hand on the open door as if for support, the other clutched in his hair. The women rounded upon him, shouting. Such language, Sylvester thought, he'd never believed possible from island mothers. They would tear him limb from limb. Fists pounded upon the side of the Land Rover, punctuating torrents of invective. They began to close in upon him. Martin raised his hands, as if under arrest, and emitted a sort of whimper.

"I—I, it was the crowd in front, you see, I hadn't, I didn't realize I couldn't drive this way and—"

The voice of Miss Moz rose above the others, head-teacherly, enforcing discipline.

"You haven't said you're sorry. They will need you to apologize."

"But of course, of course I am deeply sorry. Of course! Of course." His voice was patrician, booming even in apology. He began to rotate, as if to address each of the women in turn. "I am so sorry. So sorry. Terribly sorry, I hadn't realized that . . ." On he went. He'd only just arrived on this last boat, along with the Land Rover itself, and would still have to see each one of these incandescent mothers for an eye test before he left again, thought Sylvester. Poor sod.

Betsey Coffee approached with a square of masapan and a saloop into which she'd stirred three sugars, and soon Marianne had calmed and was nursing Annie on a bench, beneath the shade of a walnut tree. Miss Moz stood guard over the girl, tall as a sentry, arms crossed, formidable. The baby, who had looked almost impossibly tiny in the moments after the accident, an ethereal being lashed with padded straps into the huge black mangled wreckage, looked instantly larger and more solid when she was encircled by her mother's thin arms. She was not newborn; she was a plump, hearty lass learning to sit, to babble, to grasp.

Marianne took small sips of the lavender saloop, occasionally setting it down beside her to rest her hand across her daughter's warm back. After a while she began to hum an old Ladino folk song to the baby, softly, and without self-consciousness. Mother and baby became an incongruous oasis of tranquility, while around them the shaken witnesses were not yet ready to disperse. Deep breaths were taken. Looks were exchanged. They patted one another on the back; they squeezed one another's elbows. They milled. They felt overwrought; relieved; united. They would rehearse it, first with one another, and later each would carry it home to those who had not been there. *I really thought—I could have sworn—for the rest of my life I'll see—*

It was Ruth dos Santos that Marianne would want; Ruth, who was suited to crisis management and had, for example, managed her foster daughter's mysterious pregnancy with characteristic dignity. No one ever heard a word of censure, nor a passing worry. "We like to keep busy in our house," was the most she would say, firmly moving on. No further mention of an earlier hope to get Marianne to a cooking school in Ballymaloe, where there'd been a chance of a year's job as a kitchen hand, with full board, if they could only find the money for her berth. Instead an elegant pivot, new plans for a household that would have not one but two unexpected arrivals.

Ruth had had some trouble, since her own baby. It had been a long, hard labor, and these last months she'd suffered crippling back pain that kept her home, mostly in bed. Marianne generally discouraged visitors, which was unusual for an island on which problems were normally shared, and anyone ill cared for by the community. But from what she reported of Ruth's progress, there was widespread expectation she'd be up and about fairly soon. She was needed—indeed, expected—on the Island Council. Ruth's back must be reasonably comfortable today or Marianne would not have left Alex at home with her, and that too was a blessing. Moz gave Marianne's shopping list to Sylvester, and someone else had gone for Dr. Gabbai, who appeared and said he'd run Marianne and the baby home, where Ruth could take care of her.

The mangled buggy was loaded into the car, and Sylvester said he'd send one of the mechanics round to take a look at it later, and see what might be done. Shop Day resumed. In the end nothing had happened, except an almost-tragedy.

18

Not for the first time in her life, Marianne Goss was at war with Grand Mary. Most Tugans had been at war with Grand Mary at one time or another, apart from possibly Joan Williams, known to be saintly, with whom it was impossible for even someone as cantankerous as Grand Mary to have a falling-out. Joan even visited Mary every Thursday morning, stopping at Marianne's to collect a bag of fresh fig rolls, disappearing with them inside Martha House for as much as an hour, and emerging looking tired, but with no visible wounds or scratches. Joan said that Grand Mary "liked to be kept up to date," whatever that meant, and this was an arrangement so long-standing that even Garrick did not remember how it had begun. No one else went inside that house unless paid to do so.

Mary Philips was in her eighties, bad-tempered, capricious, small and slight, erect as a pine. Far younger elderly than she were accompanied to Sylvester's or for a saloop at Betsey's Cafe, aired at hops if they were sprightly, or for slow walks if they were not. As the oldest person on the island, Grand Mary was Island Elder, yet actively resisted all attempts to be helped. She organized her own standing orders from the farmers and the fishing boats. Marianne baked her bread and cakes, for which she was promptly and fairly paid, and a quiet girl rode all the way from the moshav and did the kitchen and the laundry while Mary was out running errands, terrorizing the island in her little red car. Those who wished to feel helpful instead felt rebuffed.

Layered beneath their concern, there was also a less admissible sense of grievance (ugly, Marianne admitted) that not only did Mary refuse to need island charity but that, with all her money, she didn't take care of them a bit too. It was hard to quell resentment when a donation box stood on the shining bar of the Rockhopper, another by the till in Sylvester's, a third in the entrance hall of the Old Kal—coins for the new playground, for the clinic, or the schoolhouse—and Grand Mary Philips had never been seen to drop in so much as a penny.

Now Annie and Alex had upset her somehow—the specifics of it had been lost in the fever pitch of Mary's rage, and Marianne had only the gist. Mary had been in the old cemetery, a strange place for anyone to be, let alone Mary, who had long ago laid claim to its last remaining plot, though she did not have much competition for it. The new cemetery was meticulously maintained, and visited regularly, which probably was Mary's objection—even when she was dead, she didn't want visitors. Here was crumbling and overgrown, and she would have to lie beside the pirate, Benjamin Cole, infamous for stealing a yacht in Cape Town and, when he could have sailed his prize anywhere in the world, had instead brought it home, where he was drowned in an Island Close storm just a mile off the Tugan coast, punished for hubris and chutzpah.

Marianne had no idea why Annie and Alex had been there in any case, for the tree reached long arms over the strange wild marigolds that grew nowhere else on the island but in a blazing ring around the pirate's grave, and all the island children whispered that in those western branches lived a dybbuk hungry to possess the body of anyone who scrambled within its grasp. Even reckless Annie wouldn't risk it. Mary had not known the children were up the eastern branches of the vast, spreading tree, and either she had frightened them or they had frightened her, or both. Mary wanted Marianne to give her word—"absolutely ensure and guarantee"—that the demon twins would never climb that particular sycamore fig again.

"As the whole of Tuga now knows," Marianne had said, with some fatigue, "I can't force Annie to do anything. I will try," she'd added, seeing Mary's color rise. But rather than pity, Mary had unleashed a stream of abuse directed at Marianne, Alex, and Annie, in particular. Marianne had said, "I think maybe it's time you go," and Mary had risen, queenly, and said, "That child of yours is a wild animal," and Marianne had said, tired, "Don't I know it," and closed the door. So that was probably a weekly white loaf and a lemon cake gone, as well.

Now, exhausted, Marianne had put the children to work preparing carrots and potatoes. When asked to give her own version of events, Annie stopped, gesturing around her with the peeler.

"She's batty," Annie said, "honestly, she's mad as a boiled bat. Of course we was scared when she started speaking, she was lying down in that spot, you know, where she's going to be buried, and it's all long grass so we couldn't see her, it was like she was a ghost or something. And she's shouting at us and bashing the tree with her walking stick and saying we was to get down right this instant and this was to be her final resting place after all, so she had every right to be there, except she wouldn't have no rest there if we were going to be 'clambering around above her head for eternity.' Which when you think about it is a stupid thing to say. But we didn't, because she would have whacked us with that stick. Alex was so scared he almost climbed into the dybbuk side. But we got quite high up the other way and just stayed there, and in the end she gave up and drove off, and come here. I thought that cemetery was closed. Ain't no one ever there."

"It is, it's full, that's why we've got the new one. There's one space left that's Mary's. What do you mean, 'ever' there? How often are you two there?"

Annie ignored this question and bit the end off a carrot.

"Why does she even want to be in that crumbling old place? The new cemetery's much nicer, and not full of dybbuks and pirates and spooky things. I don't suppose it matters once you're dead, but it's much nicer for the people who visit you. Maybe she knows no one would want to visit her."

"I have no idea why she wants to be buried there. And I don't know what she's doing trying out her own plot, either; I agree she's batty, but she's also not someone to mess with."

Annie pouted. "I ain't scared of her."

"I am," said Marianne and Alex, together, and then laughed. Marianne took the heap of chopped potatoes from Alex's board, and the scantier pile of carrots from Annie's, and slid them into the soup. Look at her, she thought. Her beautiful, ferocious girl.

"Keep an eye that doesn't boil over," she told the children. "I'm going to see to Ruth."

19

It was a strange thing, to let go of ambition for a while. In the life of a chelonian, a creature that might take three weeks to digest a heavy breakfast, twelve months is not significant. Charlotte was here and soon she would be gone, and in that time very little would have altered for Martha or for any of her free-range tortoise cousins. But however endless this fellowship might feel when a mosquito got into her cottage at night, or when she was trying to get online to check her email at the post office, a year was a very short time in which to become the world's expert in gold coins. She should have begun the work immediately, if only to leave time for trial and error. Launching the survey of a relic population was new to her. Jungles themselves were new to her. Camera traps were new-ish; really of all the many components of this project, it was only PIT-tagging in which she had extensive experience, and that was hardly complex when the animal to microchip was the size of an upholstered footstool. During the years of her PhD she had developed the dexterity to tag delicate young newts without killing them; huge lumbering tortoises would be easy targets. Charlotte had always been ambitious; a rare opportunity to learn and stretch and pioneer should have fired her up.

But a creeping island lassitude had wound itself around her, by stealth. The heat alone was immobilizing and, to anyone not born on the island, physical, outdoor labor was near impossible for the middle third of the day. In the mornings she sat beneath the ceiling fans at Betsey's drinking iced mango juice, often setting down the work she'd intended in order to listen to Taxi on the radio announce the incoming weather, or a birthday, or sometimes merely completing a private conversation he had begun earlier with a passenger in his cab. Rainstorms and wedding anniversaries made up most of the news, though on one occasion Taxi had interrupted almost a solid hour of Barry Manilow to report that Nicky the bull had escaped from the moshav, going on to suggest that anyone passing through the southwest of the island should carry ranch ropes. It was radio as soothing as *The Archers*, and only fifty percent comprehensible.

She went for evening walks along the coastline, idly collecting shells to identify, and these piled up in a rattan basket at the center of her kitchen table, their accretion marking her days. She bumped into Dan Zekri at least twice a day—indeed, she bumped into everyone at least twice a day—and so through attrition had semi-forgiven him. They met for coffee and walked several times together on the beach, and she did her best to dream about him breaking up with his fiancée as infrequently as possible. Dan taught her to recognize the clumps of wild mintberry that grew almost everywhere on the south of the island; later Levi taught her to spit the seeds, though she could not match his velocity or precision. She dried some of these pods in the sunshine, wondering if Tugan mintberry would ever like to grow in a pot on a north-facing kitchen windowsill in Regent's Park.

Before coming, Charlotte had understood that the Tugan public library contained all of the island's agricultural and settlement histories, as well as several accounts of visits by explorers, before and around the time of Darwin. Any of these documents seemed likely to include records of tortoises, from which she might start to sketch a picture of population changes, over time. Indeed, the supposedly numerous island histories had been part of the lure of the fellowship. Charlotte had pictured her own iron barrel key. Late at night she would sit at an acre of pitted antique iroko, as the warm yellow light of a brass lamp fell upon her pages, a reading room that she later realized she had lifted wholesale from the pages of a novel.

Housed in a shipping container left high on a hillside after its previous incarnation as a store for unprocessed sheep fleece, the reality of the Rupert Whitten Library proved to be five thousand musty volumes, mostly crime and romance novels from the late 1980s and early 1990s. There was no iron barrel key because there was no lock, the door held shut with a length of gardening twine. She had hoped to find *Tuga de Oro, My Home, My People*; *Five Seasons on Tuga: Smallholding Against the Odds*; and most particularly the three volumes of *Tortoise on the Hillside: A Military Vet Remembers Tuga de Oro*—all treasures the British Library had listed as Missing. None were here. The Tuga de Oro section had six books in it, four of which she had already read, one of which contained local fables, and one of which was in Ladino.

At the Rockhopper that evening she'd confided her frustration to Dan, who was equally preoccupied with professional frustrations of his own. For his part, Dan was still at loggerheads with his uncle about their underuse of the nurses. He had not managed to convince Saul about the additional training sessions, nor about an idea he'd had for a nurse-run clinic for repeat prescriptions, to ease the doctors' burden and make time for high-level planning. Saul said he was dreaming if he imagined Calla and Winston would want more work, not less. (Charlotte, who had several times been reading at Betsey's during what seemed to be a ninety-minute lunch break for the two nurses, was quietly inclined to think Saul knew best on this one.)

And so it was a surprise when Dan then revealed that Tuga de Oro did have the library she imagined—one that had natural light and comfortable chairs, and was free from the oily scent of damp sheep. Martha House had an archive going back sixty years, including firsthand accounts, several handwritten. This was Grand Mary's private collection. But when Charlotte wrote for permission to visit she got no reply.

In desperation, Charlotte approached Grand Mary in the street. It did not go well.

"It's no more business of yours what's on my bookshelves than what's in my smalls drawer," Grand Mary quavered and Charlotte backed away, taking this unwelcome image with her. Mary raised her stick. "And you're not to interview my tortoise."

Charlotte made no reply, but stomped once again to the Rockhopper, because there was nowhere else to go except Betsey's Cafe, and she'd been to Betsey's twice that day already. Levi was cashing up, and Charlotte sat down at the bar.

"Why is she so grumpy?"

"You're lucky she didn't actually throw something at you. She split my eyebrow once, with a mango."

"She threw a mango at you? That's awful."

"A friend and I were getting somewhat friendly in her orchard."

"Ugh, you should be castrated. But what I don't get is, *why* she's so mean? I just want to see what she's got. Presumably if she's hoarding all these amazing histories it's because she cares about the island, and I'm trying to help. And I don't think that tortoise of hers is on top form, from the little I've seen."

"It ain't personal, I promise you; she'd be much worse than that if she had it in for you. Why d'you need to bother with Mary, anyway? Does it matter that she's got a few books you want? I thought the whole point was to go counting gold coins and sticking up all your sexcams?"

"It is, I will. Not sexcams."

"It's all they do, they're at it like rabbits, tortoises."

"They're at it like tortoises. Except they're not, because I've not seen a single one yet, apart from someone's pet on a front lawn. I might as well have popped to the ZSL Reptile House."

"That ain't going to change if you spend the whole of Island Close mooning around Out the Way beach with Zekri."

Charlotte shot him a withering look.

"It's just so tantalizing that all this data's just sitting there. It's so unusual, a relic population that's entirely unstudied, a huge cache of papers basically unstudied. Even those nineteenth-century explorers who were all over the place, you know, not many have ever been to Tuga, not many accounts have ever been published. Imagine having read every single one."

"Imagine." Levi lifted a bin of melted ice and poured the water carefully into a potted ginger plant.

"What? What is that tone?"

Levi paused with the empty bin in his arms.

"I feel bad breaking it to you, but all of life ain't in books. Let's say Grand Mary dies tomorrow and leaves you her library, just you, and you go read every word ever written about the island, not just the tortoises and your own vet stuff or whatever, but all of it. History, geography, family trees, captains' log books, missionaries' letters. All the cargo coming in and out. Are you then the world expert on Tuga de Oro?"

"In academic terms, yes, I would be."

"Right. But, would you *know* Tuga? Would you know more about Tuga than, say, Rebecca?"

"Your niece Rebecca? You are being fatuous."

"Well, as it happens I don't know what 'fatuous' means, but I can take a guess. I'm just saying, didn't you come to do field research, anyway? I thought you wanted to get your hands dirty, track some real live animals, not just read letters about old dead animals. And maybe along the way, I don't know, don't you want to have a bit of fun?"

Charlotte frowned. Levi was now holding a jar of crimson cocktail cherries and she took this from his hand and tipped the top of the syrup into her soda water before handing it back to him.

"My idea of fun is reading historical accounts from which I can impute fluctuations in the Tugan tortoise population."

Levi tipped the rest of the cherries into a stainless-steel tub, covered it and put it into the fridge. Then he began to stretch his neck, first one side, then the other, regarding her as he did so.

"You a sad case. Grab your glass, I'm locking up."

Charlotte slid off her seat and followed him while he closed the wooden shutters, waiting outside while he carried bags of rubbish to the wheelie bins at the back. A hollow noise made her smile.

"Geckos," said Levi, washing his hands under the outdoor tap.

"I know. Endemic lover-girl geckos. They sound like creaking bedsprings," she said, and then blushed.

"See, Dolittle, you've nailed the local wildlife already, you don't need Mary. You know they're known for having near the greatest variety of sexual positions in the animal kingdom?" He wiped his hands dry on his jeans and grinned at her in the darkness. "That's a true fact. Want me to walk you home?"

"Absolutely not."

Charlotte checked for her torch, and then turned into the steep track behind the Rockhopper and up, into the back of the Mendoza place. She heard his soft laughter, and his footsteps ringing as he climbed the iron staircase to the roof. When these fell silent, the geckos sang on.

20

Charlotte had been in the garden for at least fifteen minutes when she heard whispering, and so the children must have been there longer, watching from the avocado branches while she attempted the only yoga class she'd thought to download before traveling to Tuga. With repetition it had become deeply tedious, and yet somehow no easier. But Levi was out fishing and the garden would be quiet, so she had ventured into a shady patch to try again, in pursuit of the yogi's mental tranquility. Then the same tree from which Levi had first sprung began to make strange noises.

When Charlotte approached to investigate the rustling, Annie Goss had jumped down, and was now wiping grubby hands on the back of her denim shorts and grinning, unabashed. Alex swung down next.

"Alex said I had to let you finish your rituals," Annie explained, as if Charlotte had been performing a Wiccan spell. "You're good at that balance-y one."

"I'm trying. I think my shoulders need to get stronger. Also I find yoga very boring."

"We're trying to free-climb the coconuts. I could teach you," Annie offered. "It's good for shoulders. Or you could start with a looped rope, if you liked."

"I don't love heights," Charlotte admitted. "FFA, you see."

"We get shouted at by the grown-ups for climbing but we don't mind."

"Levi Mendoza was up a tree when I first met him. That same tree, as it happens."

"Levi doesn't count as a grown-up," said Annie, with admiration. Alex nudged her. "Oh yes. We came to ask you, can you come and see our goat?"

Charlotte rolled up her mat. In theory she had another seventeen minutes and a savasana to go, but mental tranquility seemed a lost cause.

"I'm not really a practice vet."

"Oh please, you have to." Annie looked stricken. "Mum's called for Mac's Rachel and you know what that means."

"I don't, I'm afraid. Who's Mac's Rachel?"

Alex spoke, for the first time. His voice was high and melodic, unbroken, and full of distress.

"She's ruthless. It'll be Kidda for the chop if you don't save her."

"Kidda?"

"We were quite small when we named her," said Annie, defensive.

"Kidda the Kid. Got it."

"It's fine, we really don't mind if you're still just a practicing vet," Annie implored, and Charlotte hid a smile. "Anything's better than Mac's Rachel and her Axe of Doom."

Charlotte dropped her yoga mat on the porch and went into the kitchen for some water. The children followed. Annie collapsed into a kitchen chair and Alex stood close beside her, like an attending valet. Charlotte took a bowl of cut melon from the fridge and set it before them, together with two glasses of the local pineapple juice to which she had become addicted. Then she sat opposite Annie on the end of her bed, and was about to reach for a piece of melon when she saw the bowl was already empty, the glasses drained.

"The thing is, I'm here to study your tortoises. They're very rare, they only exist this one place in the whole world, and they need attention if we are going to protect the species from extinction. And

I'm only visiting for one year, so I've got to spend as much time as I can gathering data. I'm not here to take the vet's job."

"But we haven't got a vet."

"Everyone here seems to take very knowledgeable care of their animals," said Charlotte, but in return she received the withering look she deserved for such an idiotic and patronizing statement. The island should have had a permanent vet posted here decades ago. She felt duly chastened. "Of course I'll come. Who usually looks after sick animals?"

"Farmers do it themselves, mostly, or if it's really bad they call Mac's Rachel, who's a midwife and a herbalist, and she knows a lot. And Council sent a man to agricultural college for a year in England so he knows some animal stuff but he's mostly busy on the moshav. Basically, no one. Lots of animals get killed that a vet could save, Mum reckons. Two doctors for humans, but not a single soul to care for the beasts. It's a very cruel arrangement," Annie finished.

Charlotte opened a packet of plantain chips from Sylvester's, and watched as these too were disappeared.

"What are Kidda's symptoms?"

"She's had a cough for a few weeks but it's got much worse today, and she's doing this weird neck-stretch thing now, and yawning a lot."

Charlotte had a thought. "Does Marianne know you're here?"

They shook their heads.

"Oh, then I shouldn't, really. It's meddling, a bit."

"It was all her idea, she really wanted to call you, I heard her telling Alex's mum that she wished she could ask the visiting vet. Honestly. She said, 'I wish I could call that lovely new vet who is visiting but I can't because she is only here to practice. Oh, if only someone on the island could save my Kidda!'" Annie was wide-eyed as she performed this shameless fiction.

"Fine," said Charlotte eventually, won over by a child with such enterprise and tenacity. "I'll come. But you have to understand, I'm not much use, I've got barely any kit, no drugs, no equipment. There's almost nothing I can do except have a listen and a look."

"We have an answer to that, we thought about it. There's a vet's cupboard at the clinic."

"Is there?" Vaguely, Charlotte recalled a conversation with Elsie Smith about a cupboard, which had segued into cupboards in general, their construction, the merits of various hinges.

"Whenever a visiting vet has been they get a room at the clinic, the one at the side that has its own outside door, you know, so animals don't have to go through the people spaces. And then, when the month's up, they end up feeling sorry for us and leaving everything they brought in that vet's cupboard, even some expensive stuff, my mum says."

"When did the last vet come?"

The children frowned at one another, thinking. "We were . . . six? Seven, maybe?" Alex ventured.

"Right. Well then, I don't think I want to go scrabbling around in the back of some dusty old cupboard, to be honest. Let's first just go and see Kidda and listen to her chest and find out what's what."

The demon twins seemed to consider this acceptable. Charlotte went to pack her bag while they dashed out of the door and up the track to the road, fishing their bikes from the bush into which they had dropped them. She felt a pang for the Royal Veterinary College's teaching farm on which she'd trained, where the animals were handled so frequently by inept new students that they all but examined themselves. She thought with longing too of her battered copy of *Farm Animal Medicine and Surgery for Small Animal Vets*, a wonderful sort of idiots' guide, intended for the busy city vet to panic-skim in the bathroom when unexpectedly confronted with an alpaca, or a chicken. Every textbook that might help her was thousands of miles away. There was nothing for it but to have a go, and try not to kill the goat.

There was no call for Mac's Rachel, nor her axe. Kidda had lungworm, Charlotte guessed within moments of seeing her, grateful to her diligent former self. She felt almost nostalgic for that girl she had been at college, late nights spent at her desk while her contemporaries were playing darts, or stealing traffic cones, or falling in love. Charlotte had spent those evenings filling notecard after notecard in the yellow light of an anglepoise lamp, highlighting, reciting, remembering. Keeping up had been effortful, but now seemed worth the effort.

Kidda was a sweet-tempered animal who submitted to examination without complaint, and Charlotte stroked her rough caramel flank with immediate affection. Marianne sat in a plastic chair in the yard holding the goat's collar, and Kidda rested her head in Marianne's lap like a huge dog while Charlotte took her temperature, and listened to her chest. The animal was lethargic and underweight, had a persistent wet cough, a high fever and a slightly increased respiration rate. But it was when Charlotte saw the thick nasal discharge she felt an unexpectedly powerful surge of certainty and triumph. One could run Baermann fecal testing to confirm the presence of the parasite but it was an easy test to do wrong. Best just to get on with treating, as far as she recalled. It turned out that all she had forgotten was the rush of pleasure that came with solving a problem, and helping an animal.

Annie was likewise triumphant. She dragged Charlotte down to the clinic, where Saul unlocked the vet's office with much apology that he had not offered access before. Joan had warned him not to presume.

They found a quantity of both fenbendazole and ivermectin in the famous cupboard, expired, but not by long enough to matter. Charlotte took a cursory inventory and saw sufficient equipment for most emergencies, as well as a portable ultrasound that looked almost new, a cauterizing machine, and a very old, very large microscope. The pharmacy was limited, and several drugs that ought to have been refrigerated must have perished long ago. With surprise she saw that the ACP, ketamine, and a terrifying quantity of pentobarbital were lined up on the open shelves alongside anti-inflammatories and worming tablets, and so before investigating further she dragged the spinning office chair over to the cupboard and stood on it to put the controlled substances on the highest shelf. Saul Gabbai held the chair steady and looked somewhat embarrassed at this lapse, nodding his approval.

When she climbed down, Saul declared that she should henceforth treat the vets' exam room as her own. They had internet access at the clinic, he said, abandoning his tone of formality, and so she was also welcome to come just for the computer. He'd be honored to furnish her with her own key. This was not the iron barrel key of her fantasies, and the key ring was a knitted donkey, boss-eyed, the name of the island embroidered across its saddle. Charlotte accepted it.

There had been widespread hope among islanders that they would eventually persuade Dr. Charlotte Walker to run a clinic. Now, news began to spread that not only had she visited a sick animal but also taken ownership of the vets' cupboard. Before night fell, she had been asked if she might look at a cow with a poor appetite; some piglets that sounded as if they might have coccidiosis; a Labrador with a persistent yeast infection in both ears. To each of these she had had to assent, pleading that the hopeful owners might at least give her until the next day. She did not say, *I am more familiar with the invasive newt species in British waterways than I am with basic mammalian medicine.* She did not say, *I will be sneaking back into the vets' room to try and get onto VetNet, to study until the small hours, and to panic.*

"What'd you expect, telling them all you're an animal doctor?" said Levi. "Now you're a sitting duck."

"Someone's already brought me a duck," Charlotte told him, in despair. "A beautiful Cayuga with a sticky eye. I'm not a farm vet, I've got tortoises to save."

"So you say, Dolittle." Levi bit his thumbnail. "And I know what you brainiacs all reckon, but round here, gold coins just ain't top of everyone's list."

"They should be. Islands are some of the most biologically diverse places on earth, their ecosystems are disproportionately important."

"You sound pompous as Garrick. Important to who? We got needs, right here. I'd say our sick ducks are more important than our tortoises."

"Locally, perhaps. Not globally."

"Right. But we don't live global, right here. We live local as it gets. There is only local, here. And you know something, those tortoises ain't going to feed no one during Island Close, or if a boat don't come, or we have a major hurricane, or the taro fail. They ain't going to put milk in the seventy-two coffees you drink a day. Those eggs everyone's always leaving on your porch, they ain't tortoise eggs, is all I'm saying. If we had hard times, I'd fry up the last gold coin on Tuga, and I wouldn't think too much about it."

"Of course *you* would," said Charlotte, disapproving, but she was left feeling uncomfortable. She thought of Rebecca Lindo-Smith, tending to the family's single sow with the serious care of a child twice her age. She thought of Alex and Annie, nervous and hopeful while she worked, of how much rested on the shoulders of that one, slight, caramel goat. She had come to make a difference. She had come to help. At sunrise the next morning, she started farm rounds.

21

Charlotte's muscles now reminded her why all those vet students had lived in the gym—Herculean strength and endurance were required to treat large animals. Bending, lifting, reaching, straining, crawling, hiking between homesteads (getting hopelessly lost several times), and all of it in the sweltering heat. She had been jostled and stepped on by sheep. Her thumb had been pecked by an irritable rooster, and her index finger had been nipped, not gently, by the needle-teeth of a calf still *in utero*. She had made only three farm visits, but had been forced to eat lunch with the family on each.

The following morning, after yet another sunrise wake-up, an aching and exhausted Charlotte had gone back to bed, with the new innovation of a pair of leggings tied around her face against the sunlight. With the extra precaution of a pillow on her swaddled head she had not heard Elsie's knock, and by the time the noises in the room had woken her she removed this blindfold to discover a silhouetted giant looming in the doorway, and screamed. Elsie screamed. Then the situation clarified, and each subsided.

Charlotte got hurriedly to her feet, barking her shin painfully against a cabinet door that stood open. Seeing how many kitchen tasks she could accomplish while technically in bed had become a sort of personal challenge in the quiet evenings, a variation on the game of Twister, and the previous evening she'd forgotten to close this cupboard while drying and putting away the saucepan.

"I did more exercise yesterday than I've done in a year, and I had a bad night's sleep," said Charlotte, to explain why she'd still been in bed. Here she noted Elsie's utility belt, and recalled the subject of their previous conversation. "Actually, do you have any idea what I can do about the windows in here for some privacy, and to block out some of the light?"

Elsie brightened, and immediately produced a tape measure while Charlotte retreated to the bathroom. When she came out Elsie had rolled up the sleeve of her boiler suit, and was printing numbers on the back of one arm in large, painstaking digits.

"You leave them windows with me."

"Thank you. Can I help with anything, would you like a coffee?"

Elsie pulled out a kitchen chair and turned it backwards, straddling the seat. She had left her heavy work boots outside and Charlotte was touched to see her yellow and black Snoopy socks, from which one toe protruded.

"No thank you. I'm here on a surprise mission. I know when you first came you had some confusion about Martha being what she is, a tortoise an' all." Elsie crossed her arms on the back of the chair, watching Charlotte while she made the bed and smoothed down Joan's intricate quilt. "But Grand Mary's asked you to come and look at Martha. Give her a once-over."

"Wow—I'd love that, but she's changed her tune. Do you know why, did Joan talk to her?"

"You stitched a torn udder at the Spencers' yesterday, nice, neat work apparently. Goat's much happier."

"How does Mary know? That was only yesterday afternoon."

"Was on the radio this morning," said Elsie, as if this ought to have been obvious.

"I see. Is the goat already happier? I'm glad, that's good news. I'd love to meet Martha."

"She was Mary's grandmama's tortoise, and she'd probably been with someone else long before that. We don't keep 'em as pets, as a rule, but I don't suppose rules was the same in those days. Martha's a-hundred-and-fifty-odd, she's older than rules."

Life expectancy of gold coins was believed to be between seventy and a hundred years. Elsie rolled her sleeves back down over brawny forearms and, buttoning the cuffs, "A hundred and fifty if she's a day," she went on, "And she's bigger'en any gold coin you'd catch out in South Jungle as well, twice the size. They do well at Martha House."

"Martha House is where she lives?"

"Grand Mary called her own mansion after her tortoise an' all. She does as she likes. Will I take you? It's a good time, Grand Mary's out. She's as likely to change her mind tomorrow, she doesn't like meddlers. Or most folks. Best we go while we can."

Martha House was one of the central oddities pointed out to Folk From Away, a three-story Georgian townhouse, a terraced house without a terrace, rising up on a tropical island that elsewhere was breeze block, corrugated metal, pallet wood, palm thatch. Mary Philips had commissioned it on her fortieth birthday, and her specifications had been precise and eccentric. For the years of its construction the house had been a swarming hive of activity, with most of the island's craftsmen and workers employed to make reality of her vision. An architect came from London, a young Regency obsessive who made an adventure of it, bringing his wife and children to Tuga for six months, during which he was harassed and browbeaten by Grand Mary, and his small boys enjoyed a raucous sabbatical from their prep school, and from shoes. Once completed, the newly christened Martha House fell almost silent. Tugan homes were secured against animals, not intruders, but Martha House had tall cast-iron gates, their intricate leaves and flower heads the flora of cooler climes, and these were always closed. More Tugan were the perimeter walls, low enough to step over, and these offered islanders ready access to Martha herself, who was always on ponderous patrol within. She would often present herself to passersby to be stroked and petted, and fed titbits of all sorts that would horrify Charlotte, had she known of them. Misanthropic in all other areas, Grand Mary had to accept Martha's totemic status among islanders.

Elsie led Charlotte around to the left, where three tortoises were close together in the shade of a mulberry tree. As Elsie had described, one was almost twice the size of the others, more like an Aldabra giant tortoise than any image of a gold coin that Charlotte had previously seen. But her markings were unmistakable, each broad, brown-black scute peaked with the distinct, bright disc that gave the breed their name. Her huge shell was dull and scratched all over but the gilded spots gleamed still, as if a child had daubed her with metallic paint. Martha's coins looked closer to aged bronze than gold.

The two smaller tortoises were mating, the female with her front legs in their food tray, the male thrusting in slow motion with loud hisses and grunts, his snake-head high, his snake-mouth open. Beside them Martha was grazing, impassive. Charlotte and Elsie stood back politely, watching. The huge shells creaked, like hinges.

"Does he mate with Martha too, do you know?"

"Oh, yes, he has a go most days. That's Dusty, he was brought to be Martha's mate, and that's Goldie, underneath him. They're newer, those two, and they're more of a couple, I'd say. Mary had them caught about twenty years ago. I don't know their ages."

Charlotte squatted down and unzipped her bag quietly, unpacking her camera. Martha was far bigger than she'd thought possible, and it was obvious now she would need different equipment merely to take her measurements, let alone provide veterinary care. She had not expected to treat tortoises. Her role was to study nature, not to intervene with it. But Martha was another story. Whatever the rights and wrongs of it, Martha was a pet, and a very old lady deserving of a health check.

Charlotte had a set of bathroom scales and a baked-bean tin in her rucksack, the beans sold to her by Mac with the reverence of a man dealing in the finest Beluga caviar. Standard practice with medium tortoises would have been to zero the scale with the tin on it and then, to prevent escape, to balance the tortoise on its plastron on top, legs pedaling pitifully in the air for a brief few seconds while she took an accurate reading. But even Dusty and Goldie were far too big to balance on a tin like a stick puppet, she realized now, casting her eye over the mating pair. She guessed Goldie to be around twenty-five kilograms, and Dusty about ten kilos heavier. She could probably pick them up and step with each of them in turn onto the scales.

Martha would be a different matter. Her carapace looked almost three feet long and Charlotte doubted she could lift her weight, even if she could get a purchase on the huge shell. Martha could easily be eighty or ninety kilos. In any case, Charlotte and Martha combined seemed likely to exceed the maximum weight limit of the bathroom scales, even if she could somehow suspend her. She would need large-animal walk-on scales, of a sort that seemed unlikely to exist on the island. She made a note to ask some of the farmers.

On the way they'd stopped at an honesty stall for a small watermelon, which Charlotte now took from her bag and hacked into rough pieces. That seemed to mark the end of romance as Goldie grew tired of humoring Dusty, breaking free with surprising agility to approach a chunk of fruit. A moment later Dusty followed and the two snapped and gulped, side by side. Martha remained where she was, and Charlotte observed her, frowning. Then she took the remaining half a melon over to the huge tortoise and set it down between her thick front legs. Only when it was almost touching her beak did Martha seem to awaken, and began to eat with slow snatching movements, juice and pulp dripping down her small sharp chin.

"I wonder how well she can smell," Charlotte mused to Elsie, who was standing at a respectful distance, legs apart, arms crossed behind her in a stance that was faintly military. While the tortoise ate, Charlotte scratched the small head affectionately, and ran her hands over her shell. Martha liked a chuck under the chin like a cat, Elsie told her, going on to say that her own pet lizard was soppy as anything and enjoyed exactly the same, and while doing this Charlotte examined Martha's face. Her beak, which should have been razor-sharp, looked soft and crumbly beneath the gloss of melon juice. There was a telltale cloudiness in her eyes that indicated cataracts.

Charlotte looked around the garden. They had a big shallow pond, as well as a concrete shed that stood open on one side. Underfoot was only lawn of seashore paspalum grass, apart from the gravel path that ran from the gate to the front door of the mansion. Charlotte studied Martha's feet.

"You need a pedicure, my darling," she told the huge animal, frowning at the nails, which had become painfully overgrown. Even jungle-dwelling tortoises like gold coins spend a lot of time climbing and digging, and many years of a captive environment on a soft terrain had not worn down Martha's nails as nature would. They would need cutting, and while describing the procedure to Elsie, Charlotte realized with a tug of professional pride that she would not trust anyone with this task but herself. But oh God where's the quick, she thought, with a flash of anxiety, peering closely at the dark-pigmented toenails, undifferentiated in the bright sunshine behind her. God help me if I cut into the quick and accidentally give some horrible systemic infection to an old, beloved and, most importantly, endangered tortoise. Aloud she said, "Presumably someone on the island has canine nail trimmers. But I actually think I'd need bolt cutters, for Miss Martha."

Elsie affirmed that she herself had bolt cutters.

"But you'll have to check with Grand Mary," she told Charlotte, with a look that said it was by no means certain that this would be well received. "Rather you than me, wanting to operate on Martha."

Levi was digging at the end of the garden, a tray of seedlings beside him, which he was lifting out one by one with surprising tenderness. Charlotte stopped to watch.

"Do you ever plant flowers?"

"Can't eat flowers, Dolittle. These are cantaloupes."

"If this was my house I'd grow bright pink bougainvillea all up that side of it."

"Would you." Levi sat back on his heels and grinned at her in a way that made her suddenly suspicious.

"What?"

"Nothing. You're all about home improvements today." He nodded towards the house. "Like what you done with the place."

Charlotte narrowed her eyes, and carried on towards the door. She was exhausted and hungry. She had stopped at Betsey's Cafe, where Betsey had guided Charlotte lovingly away from thin-sliced local tuna cured in Tugan citron—nothing special, Betsey told her, just everyday Tugan fare—and instead insisted upon bringing her Heinz baked beans on toasted taro bread, a special, she confided, that wasn't even on the menu board. Tinned beans in Island Close was an indulgence, and she'd not be willing to serve it to most. But nothing was too good for the new vet, after a morning taking care of their beautiful Martha.

While grateful, Charlotte did not like baked beans, which reminded her of prep-school lunches, and she wanted to find her copy of *Tortoise Medicine and Surgery*, a book she'd specifically ordered for this fellowship but had so far not yet opened. She felt sure Martha needed a beak trim and certainly some dietary supplementation, but wanted to establish her course of action before approaching Grand Mary. When she opened the door she discovered the room was mired in gloom. Elsie had been in, and had painstakingly gaffer-taped compost bags over the kitchen windows.

She could hear Levi laughing, and she wrenched open half the door and stuck her head out.

"Actually it's perfect, it's *exactly* what I asked for."

She withdrew her head with as much dignity as she could muster, retreating into the new cave-darkness of her small home, like a tortoise.

22

It was the wrong season for renovations. The weather was hot and wet, and if you got halfway through a job and found you were out of blind rivets, or were short six feet of guttering, then more fool you. All supplies had to be sourced on the island, or else done without. But Walter Lindo-Smith was being overpaid to do up the old Cole house for Dan Zekri, who had a fiancée coming at Island Open, and whose time in England had made him grand. Walter's wife, Maia, was away working for a family in London, her emails full of all the ways in which mainlanders were spoiled and impractical, and a touch of this appeared to have afflicted Zekri, who seemed to need a kitchen bigger than the Rockhopper's. But the sooner Walter had his debts paid, the sooner Maia might come home.

"We don't need anything fancy," Dan had told him, before going on to list several fancy improvements, the fanciest of which was a new extension off the small kitchen to be Katie's consulting room. Some scrubby *Lantana camara* would have to come down, no loss in a kitchen garden, and a pretty good pomelo tree. The tree was a shame.

Levi and Walter were digging taro when Zekri had found them. He hadn't quite settled, old Dan, and Walter felt for him. They'd lost touch in the years he'd been in England but Dan had been in his class at school and Walter had always felt easy with him. Dan had been more studious than the rest, not above japes, but desperate to prove, Walter thought, that he was nothing like his father. Still, however well he'd done over there, Dan would have an uphill battle convincing Tuga he could fill Saul's shoes.

Dan had arrived at the taro field on foot, red with heat and effort. "I know, I know, I should have caught a donkey," was all he'd said, wiping his forehead on his T-shirt, clearly embarrassed, so there'd been no need to josh him about whether he'd been waiting long for the Tube, or got stuck in rush-hour traffic. Then he'd asked them to help with the house.

"She's a physiotherapist. Rehab, massage, you know. I want her to arrive and find a room ready to go. She's stayed these months to do an additional course in women's physio, postpartum, et cetera, she takes it seriously. So what do you think, can you do it?"

Walter and Levi exchanged looks. Levi spoke.

"Tempting as it is to rip you off, *haver*, it's too much money. Half of that and Walt and I start Sunday."

Dan had broken into a relieved smile and then insisted about the payment, saying he had set it aside for the house and in particular Katie's consulting room, and the boys were just to do the job as well as they could, and if there was a lot of money left at the end they would talk.

"I thought," Walter said then, and as he was a man of few words the others both stopped and looked at him, "ain't we sorting out a room in the clinic? A therapy room. Saul's called me about painting it, fixing up the window. I'm already planning all your shelves at the clinic, too, for your boxes. I want the work, Zekri, don't get me wrong. But it's twenty feet from your new room, as you plan it, to the clinic. She need two rooms in twenty feet?"

But apparently she did.

"General physio stuff at the hospital, and her women's physio at home. More discreet that way."

Hauling sacks of tubers into the truck, Levi paused. "Why's women's physio different from men's? Is that, like, naked massage?"

But Dan had just climbed in the back of the truck and collapsed on top of the taro, and demanded a ride home, wondering aloud how he had forgotten the kind of heat that could make your bones sweat. Two days after that, Walter put the boat in dry dock, and they started on the house.

23

Marianne had set the dough to prove when Annie appeared, very dirty.

"Where've you been, *mi vida*? Where's Alex?"

"In the jungle, helping Dr. Vet pack up. I came back early because I'm hungry."

She might have said, *I was drawn back to you, Mama, to a rare moment when I might have you to myself.* But instead she sat on her mother's lap and put her muddy arms around her shoulders, her muddy cheek against her mother's neck. Marianne stroked the bent, narrow back, feeling the pearls of Annie's spine beneath her hand. She closed her eyes and breathed in her daughter.

"Where've you been all day? You smell like the bottom of a swamp."

"Helping Dr. Vet with her tortoises, in the interior. She's found some now, finally."

"Helping or getting under her feet?"

"Definitely helping, I don't think she knows what she's doing at all. She'd probably get lost and die without us." Annie sat back to look at Marianne. "We had to show her everything."

"What did you do about lunch? And since when did you take up volunteering?"

Annie was combing dirty fingers through her mother's long golden hair, feeling it slip between the rough pads of her fingers. Her own was always dry and tangled, because she resisted brushes wherever possible. Petting her mother was like stroking a magnificent glossy tiger, strong and sleek. She turned a silken strand around her finger.

"She makes us sandwiches. She's going to pay us to be her assistants."

"I bet, else you'd not be doing it. Are you charging her fair? You ought not to charge at all, you know; she wouldn't take anything for fixing up Kidda. She's not charged anyone for anything. She spent nearly a whole night on the floor of Winston's barn with that first calver and Betsey said she only took a cup of coffee at the end of it."

Annie grinned. "She'd not find a single tortoise without us, I reckon. She'd been out loads and ain't found even one till we took her; she was all in the wrong places but now she found twenty-three, and that's just so far. We worked one good big one out that was under a log she hadn't even spotted. Then we hold them while she tags."

"How do you tag a tortoise?"

"Two ways." Annie was swinging her legs, and speaking with new authority. "She injects something into it, so we hold it still while she disinfects and then sticks in the thing and then checks that it works, and she's gluing a code thing to a bit of their shell with something in these glue-gun tubes, can't remember what the stuff's called. It's colored. 'Lake Blue' for the boys, 'French Rose' for the girls. She uses a cotton bud with a tiny bit of acetone, and then we do the glue bit—epoxy!" Annie exclaimed, in triumph. "It's called epoxy. We do that first so it can dry while she does the injection. The code says what day she tagged it and some other stuff. Data," she added airily.

"She's coloring the tortoises?"

"Mama." Annie looked stern. "Of course not. It's a tiny dot to hold the numbers on, and we don't go near the growth rings. It was meant to be just a recon to see where we should move our trailcams, but then we found so many we were hours out there. You know you need to point cameras north?"

"I didn't know that, you've become quite the scientist. Maybe I should drop her another cake round."

"That's a good idea—toffee banana, please, because she'll give it to us."

Marianne had not expected to be impressed by Charlotte Walker when she'd come to visit the goat. The whole island believed they knew that Dr. Walker was sweet on Dr. Zekri, and until she'd seen her at work Marianne had been inclined to think the other woman somewhat pathetic, exasperated by the hopelessness of her obvious infatuation with Dan Zekri, who had a fiancée coming, and in any case had always had an untouchable quality, combined with a sort of aloof innocence that made him positively dangerous. Now Marianne had softened towards Dr. Walker, and felt that Dan himself was not helping the situation.

Dan Zekri's return worried Marianne for other reasons. She did not know if Saul would hand over Ruth's prescribing when he retired, or whether Marianne could still come quietly to the clinic every Friday morning for the little blue pills, always enough for a fortnight, because it was understood that sheets of pills were easily lost, and likely to need replacing.

Without medication, Ruth had constant pain, and drank. On moonshine Ruth was a hazard, a danger to herself, and a source of acute misery to Alex. The little blue pills made Ruth the opposite—vacant and pliable, often affectionate—and Marianne was at least able to care for her. Saul knew what had happened all those times they'd tried to stop the pills. Saul had seen the carnage of it, the chaos, and knew what it had done to Alex. He and Marianne now had an understanding that the little blue pills, even in slightly unconventional quantities, were the best they could do for Ruth, under island circumstances. Dan might see it differently.

"Do you want to know why you point cameras north?" Annie demanded again, louder, aware her mother's thoughts had drifted from her.

"I'd like to know why it's gone first bat and no sign of Alex," Marianne said, gently pushing Annie off her lap and standing up. "I need you to help me with these buns. Go on, hop in the shower."

Annie took Marianne's hand.

"Come talk to me?"

"And who's going to do the buns for Betsey Coffee?"

"We'll do them together afterwards, Mama," Annie promised, tugging on Marianne's arm and pulling her through the back door, though they both knew that by the time Annie was washed and in her pajamas, Alex would be home and then no such thing would happen. Marianne would do the buns alone, late at night, when both children were asleep. But she followed Annie out, round the back to the outdoor shower behind its screen of sugarcane, taking up her position on the wooden bench beside it. One by one, filthy items flew at her—a grubby vest, shorts damp with jungle mud, graying knickers, an overstretched hair elastic knotted with loose hair. Marianne gathered these into a bundle and set them beside her. In a moment, she knew, Annie would demand that her mother wash her hair, and Marianne would grumble that a big girl should be doing it herself, brusque, to disguise the poignancy of knowing that this degree of physical intimacy between them must surely be near its end. Each time she worked the suds into her daughter's scalp was likely to be the last, she knew, and she would look down at that small head beneath her hands, a perfect head, filled with its own huge, unknowable thoughts, and feel struck again by the impossible magic of it. For reasons of her own, for complex motivations, or because she knew what she wanted, or perhaps because Marianne had failed, her baby had stayed. The realization was a daily grief, and a daily miracle.

24

Walter and Levi had begun clearing the garden and pegging out the new room. It was hot, dirty work and going slower since they'd disturbed a hill of etrog ants a few days ago, and had to mess about with leveling and poisoning. The vet had been along in a state of high excitement about these ants, photographing the dispersing creatures with a huge zoom lens, slowing progress down still further. "Don't mind us, Dolittle," Levi had said, standing back with his arms crossed while Dr. Walker crouched in the dust with her camera, plastic bags tied around her feet against the bites. "Ain't no one here has any real work to do." But it had been Levi who'd stopped Walter's first bucket of boiling water, leaving the angry, massing insects alive until Charlotte could see them, Walter had noted, watching Levi watching Charlotte.

"What makes Zekri think they'll see his girl when they don't see him?" Walter asked now.

"Zekri don't know his arse from his elbow since he come home," said Levi, dismissive. He'd seemed oddly underwhelmed by Dan's return.

"She's ten years younger than him, I know that," said Walter. "The old biddies won't like someone too young, telling them what to do. They managed till now without physio-whatever."

"Island's filling up with English women."

"Is that so bad?"

Levi grunted, but made no other reply. He was bent over, hacking at a pomelo root. Walter got back to work, and a while later the new vet passed again on the far side of the road, riding bareback on one of the donkeys. Charlotte was presumably one of the invading English women of whom Levi disapproved. Walter hailed her and she grinned and lifted her bag to indicate that she was on a call-out again. That moshav calf, most likely. He'd heard that morning that an animal had got a rusted tin can stuck on its foot near the taro fields.

Even at a distance, Charlotte was a different woman from the one who had disembarked at Island Close. She had come to them stiff and brittle as a dry starfish. A few months on, she had more shape to her face, and some color to her cheeks. As she held the reins, her wrist was colorful with bracelets that Rebecca and the other adoring little girls had made.

Personally, Walter had time for this Charlotte Walker from London, who had arrived just as he was contending with a devastated six-year-old and a hurting heart of his own. After the piglet debacle, she came to visit Rebecca, asking for a lesson on island plants. One time she borrowed his daughter to take shopping, to help her identify local fruit, and it made Rebecca feel purposeful and important, and for a few hours he got back a calmer girl. Which was something because Rebecca was acting out all over the place, tantrums and biting even, sometimes, refusing to speak to her mother when they went out to the post office to call her, sucking her thumb again, which he did not tell Maia, for it drove her wild. Yet for Dr. Walker, Rebecca was full of enthusiasm, full of the giggles he missed at home. Yes, he felt, this new vet was an overall good thing. Let the hordes of English women invade, if they lightened Rebecca's thundercloud.

Spotting Dr. Walker, Levi called out some characteristic obscenity, and Dr. Walker shook her head and then raised a middle finger to him without halting her donkey, but Walter saw what Levi could not, that she had smiled after she passed, and the smile had stayed with her as she rounded the corner. When the sound of slow hooves had faded, Walter glanced at Levi, who had stopped work and was leaning on his shovel, looking after her.

"Oi. *Badjanak*."

"Yup. What?"

"You need help?"

Levi snapped back into motion and began to attack the rubble and roots with renewed fervor.

"I got it. You fill the truck."

"Not with this. With that." Walter nodded his head at the vet's retreating back.

Levi exhaled.

"Not your usual type."

"What, you mean classy and intelligent?"

"Your words. But yes. This is big. I like this for you, you know. She'd keep you in line, that's for sure. And you been passing some time with her, now that I think about it."

" 'Passing some time.' Who are you, Grand Mary? I ain't going to stand here all day gossiping with you like we salooping at Betsey's—get on with it, *badj*."

Walter laughed and went back to filling rubble sacks. But a moment later Levi stamped on his shovel again and said, "You know who likes 'passing time' with her a little too much is Zekri."

"Zekri? What, Dan? You standing in his girl's new office right now. He ain't no trouble to you."

"No matter he got a girl; I tell you, you wouldn't think it from the time he spends making up reasons to consult a veterinarian. He delivered a stuck cow with her or something the other day, like he's her nurse or something. All of a sudden he wants to go see Out the Way beach, needs to walk out to Priestess Creek, like he's FFA—and funny, it ain't been one of us he asks on all those hikes."

"He's been away, like, twenty years or something, he's allowed to want to see some places, and your girl's allowed to make some friends, doesn't have to be he's messing." Walter wiped the sweat from his face and neck with a dusty bandana. "I agree about calving, though, he won't make friends getting into what he don't know. Saul stays away from all that if he can help it. But ain't no one letting Zekri do any doctoring, so he's got time on his hands is all."

"She don't need friends like that, I tell you. She's into him and he's loving it, and it ain't going to go well when this massage girl arrives."

"Well, all I'm saying is she's lucky to have such a concerned friend in you, *badj*," Walter said. Levi spat out a mintberry seed, and turned back to his shoveling.

25

There were times, usually at the end of a bad day or when she thought Alex was upset, when Marianne would tell stories about the old Ruth. He could see her coming with them, bearing them deliberately towards him like a platter of biscuits on a tray, a certain expression on her face of loving concern or the bright, managed calm of the psychiatric nurse, depending on what had just taken place in the moments before. Then he would know that she was about to launch into some tale or other of wonder.

There was a note of inauthenticity to these stories and Alex invariably hated them. Maybe she would wax lyrical about the times Ruth left work early to take her camping up the *montaña*, just the two of them, because she was so exquisitely sensitive to the days Marianne was overwhelmed at school. Or she would describe Ruth's instinctive generosity about Monty, a huge old collie who'd been six or seven, and the way Ruth had settled Monty to sleep with Marianne from that first day, though until then he'd never missed a night draped across the foot of Ruth's bed. "She loved him, and I know she missed him, but she loved me more," Marianne would say, misty-eyed, "and she made Monty my dog, because I needed him." Every day Monty waited at the school gates to escort Marianne home to Ruth's house, but it was Ruth who'd trained him to do it. She was loved and respected like nobody else, Marianne would insist; she was the linchpin of the community, the ultimate authority on pretty much anything. The whole island saw Ruth as the best person in a crisis, the best person if you were in a sticky corner, the best person to see the dark humor in hard times. The best, the best, the best. Ruth had been like Saul Gabbai—known and needed by all. Well. That seemed improbable. Alex didn't exactly see them all lining up to visit his mother now.

It couldn't all be true. Maybe none of it was even true. Wasn't that just what you were meant to say when someone died, and no reality remained to puncture the fantasy of all this perfection? Except in Ruth's case she hadn't died, and there remained a reality that did not remotely resemble these fairy stories.

When Alex protested (he had been known to put the pillow over his ears, to jerk away from the hand that reached to stroke his cheek), Marianne would look briefly crushed, and would say softly that she just wanted to paint a picture—that was what she always said—to paint a picture of the person his mother had been. But what good did it do him, all these colorful portraits of the woman he'd murdered, coming into the world? Giving birth to Alex had undone something in her, and almost every day since then she had taken opiates, or drunk. On good days it was true that she hummed mildly, and cooked and cleaned and managed the family's laundry and appeared, at least in these small ways, to be functioning. But Alex was eleven now. That meant it had been eleven years since his mother had left their compound. The truth was that his mother was broken, and it was he who had broken her.

26

When the children were in school Charlotte worked alone or sometimes with Elsie, whose amateur herpetology turned out to be impressive, and who proved herself strong enough to flip a huge tortoise, if need be, and gentle enough to soothe the creatures agitated during their short periods of restraint. Charlotte needed a car really, but FFA were no longer allowed to borrow cars after a long-ago incident, and though she had tried a bicycle for an afternoon it had not been a success. On the days Elsie was wearing one of her many other professional hats, Taxi would take Charlotte and all her equipment to the periphery of South Jungle.

Listening to Taxi in the taxi turned out not to be very different from listening to Taxi on the radio, for he kept her informed of the day's likely precipitation and humidity, passed on any notable island news, whether or not Charlotte had ever heard of the protagonists, as well as updating her on the welfare of any animals she had recently treated with a thoroughness that suggested he kept a running list. On these journeys Charlotte found herself enjoying both a break from the terror of Elsie's jolting motorbike, and the perfectly Tugan logic of commuting to an isolated tropical jungle in a black hackney cab. Taxi had the cabbie's skill of timing an anecdote to the precise length of the journey.

"Do you know who I had once, in the back of this cab?" he had asked her last time, grinning at her in the rearview mirror, his few teeth on proud display, the deep brown of potato-skin. Cilla Black was playing, and Taxi had stopped singing along and turned down the volume to ask. The possibilities were limited, Charlotte thought, scanning through the islanders. Presumably everyone had reclined on these sheepskin seats at some point.

"Only another animal researcher, I swear. Twenty year ago, now. Came and left on the same boat, so he only had four days to find his birds. RSPB, if I'm not mistaken, or they were who sent him, paid for him to come all that way and go back four days later just to go poking about. He was here counting the crake nests up the cliffs just past where the Boatmen's Memorial is now, though of course in those days, may they live in our hearts, they was all still with us. They nests just inland from the seabirds so they can steal the eggs, you see; they're cheeky, those Tugan crakes. Not too many of them, though, so their thieving's no problem to the seabirds. Anyway, along come this skinny little chap from the RSPB, asking me to take him over close as we can get, and I pick him up dressed like he's hiking Kilimanjaro, Indiana Jones hat and boots and sticks, the whole business. Reckon he felt a bit foolish when I pull up ten feet away, all his hiking gear on to walk ten steps"—here Taxi paused to laugh, a process that seemed to involve closing his eyes, though they were rounding a particularly tight hairpin bend—"and he's at the Rockhopper eating jump chicken stew each night, he wants local dishes, see, asking everyone if they'd seen a Tugan crake, saying how he wants to see at least one before ship out, he's on borrowed time, they're rare, he says, endangered, he's aching to see one, it's a privilege to see one, on and on he goes, and finally Johannes Zekri leans over and says to him"—here Charlotte was left in the dark for some time, as Taxi was so overcome by the hilarity of his punch line that he wheezed and coughed for several moments—"ahh, so Johannes leans over and says to him, '*Haver*, you seen more of 'em than anyone else these last days, just look down at your plate.'"

Charlotte waited, uncomprehending.

"And of course the RSPB chap's sitting there looking just like you's looking now, so Johannes kind enough to enlighten him, 'What'dyou think jump chicken is, *haver*? If it's a privilege to see 'em, I reckon it's even more privileged to eat 'em!' Oh, we had a laugh that day." After a pause Taxi sobered, thoughtful. "Felt bad when the man cried, did Johannes. But then he went off in a sulk and had his own back on us, that joyless fool, because soon letters is coming from England making it a crime against the Crown to eat Tugan crake. It's a shame, Dr. Vet, I tell you. My mother's jump chicken stew was something else."

Today she had no need of Taxi, as she had a new colleague. Dan Zekri had been unusually quiet in the Rockhopper the previous night. His uncle's inability to relinquish even partial control was frustrating, and the island's refusal to get behind Dan as any sort of physician, let alone the imminent chief medical officer, was wearing him down from irritation to a franker despair. It did not feel good to be a medic barred from practicing medicine. He had taken a full inventory of all equipment and its condition, was studying the health budget expenditure and projections, and had thrown himself into administration and plans for the future—he was designing and assembling a set of clinical boxes. Saul knew where everything was, but organization of equipment was not instinctive for anyone else, which would slow response times if someone had an asthma attack, or went into diabetic ketoacidosis. A hospital was not a kitchen cabinet; it was insufficient for Saul to just "know" that the catheters were kept in the bottom drawer of the spare office. And so it was necessary work and would make emergencies safer, especially if a doctor was delayed and a nurse was temporarily in charge. These new boxes would contain all the necessary kit and medication, as well as printed instructions and flowcharts. Dan was excited about his boxes, and enthused to Charlotte about them, with pride that she found touching. So far he had begun on Minor Suture, Burns, and Cardiac, and had drawn up lists for Asthma; Chest Drain and Respiratory: Adult and Child. But it would be nice to see an actual patient sometime this decade. For what, he asked, uncharacteristically theatrical, had he been called back?

"Even the patients who deign to see me want to pop into Saul's office afterwards to discuss what I've suggested."

"We do." Nicola Davenport had materialized behind his shoulder, returning her empty glass to the bar between them and patting Charlotte on the arm with affection. "*Ke haber*, Dr. Walker. I am all for the young'uns learning but it's best to be on the safe side when they're new, don't you think?"

Dan laid his head on the bar, and Charlotte heard herself inviting him to come out the following morning to spend the day surveying. Had Levi been within earshot she would have felt unable to ask, but Nancy Gabbai was behind the bar that night and Charlotte did not feel the same constraint. Dan had already attended a tricky calving with her as they'd been at Betsey's together when the summons had come. He may as well keep her company for what was likely to be a particularly long, slow day. "You might quite like it, for a change. Vets don't need consent, you see. It's all very illiberal. We don't need our patients or study subjects to choose us or even like us, we just need to run faster than they do."

27

For Charlotte, unlike Dan, work was full of satisfaction and was going well. The focus of it steadied and settled her, and in the quiet evenings she wrote her mother long emails full of passion and detail, offering up proof that her absence was academically legitimate, and ecologically urgent. The more she could persuade Lucinda of the significance of the gold coins, the more likely it was her mother would forgive. She did not yet dare imply she had reason beyond the tortoises for being on Tuga de Oro, nor did she mention her increasing, and increasingly joyful, workload with the island's ducks, sheep, and cows. Instead she described Martha, who after some research she was convinced was underweight and probably mal-nourished, expending more energy than she needed on cropping the grass because her sense of smell was shot, and her vision was imped-ing her ability to seek out a wide range of plants. *Elsie and I managed to trim her nails without killing her*, she wrote, *and I've designed a supplementary nutritional program, so she's now getting lunches that would put the Selfridges salad bar to shame.*

Her mother was at least replying now, on subjects beyond her own devastation, and had begun to ask about the island. How was the food? Who were her friends? Who had she met? This new, more reasonable Lucinda almost immediately deflated Charlotte's own anger, and in its place rose a tide of baroque guilt. It now seemed clear to her that it was ungrateful and inconsiderate to have snuck off, in a way that had not been obvious in all the months she'd been planning it. The lie about her father had dominated everything, and had made her defiant. *You must think I am a monster,* Lucinda had written, and it had lodged. Charlotte could not explain that something did indeed loom in her own night-fears, huge as a shadow-beast, not her mother per se but her mother's disapproval, the monster-nightmare of her childhood. *I'm sorry, I should have told you about the fellowship,* she wrote, contrite the moment Lucinda began to ask about the weather. On the other hand, whenever she glimpsed the polished walnut in her washbag, she was reminded with absolute certainty that, had she shared her plans in advance, she would not now be on Tuga.

But when she wasn't anxious about Lucinda, her mind was full of tortoises. She was convinced they played a greater ecological role on the island than anyone had yet acknowledged. This week she had decided to add an individual tracking study, to characterize the diet of the gold coins. No one had ever been exactly sure what they were eating, and knowing would go some way to clarifying the nature of their contribution to the Tugan ecosystem—their grazing on non-native plants, for example, their impact on leaf cover, and especially their role in endemic and non-native seed dispersal. This would involve following specific tortoises for long periods to record everything they ate—her current plan was up to twelve hours continuously. Perhaps ten different animals on ten different days, assuming it was feasible at all in such dense jungle.

Charlotte was excited precisely by the intense focus of such methodology, and by the meditative slowness of following and monitoring a single ponderous animal through a small and now increasingly familiar patch of jungle. It was coming to feel like hers, here. Even the path was hers, cut back, beaten back with effort, and a technique of trial and extensive error. She had started with hedge clippers (inefficient, finicky) and was now a dab hand wielding a machete. She had stashed a few belongings, including a hammock, and since Elsie had identified two trees fit for purpose had become adept at lashing it between them. On days this lashing went well, she felt herself a veritable Robinson Crusoe. *Ha,* she would think, addressing her fellow vet students, who had, she was certain, believed her a fey, impractical, city girl. *Ha. Watch me wield my machete. Watch me lash my jungle hammock.*

She had been energized by the thought of the solitude. She had planned the music she would listen to, the lunch she would pack, and the two bottles of frozen coconut water from Mac's Pantry out on Lemon Tree Road, which she hoped would defrost by precisely the time she felt in need of them. Very little concerted thinking or intellection would be required to follow around a tortoise. It permitted space for imagination, reflection, and the pure pleasure of tortoises, alone in the busy racket of the teeming forest. She was not a botanist, and so she would make not a written but a photographic record of each plant eaten, to identify it later. Just a camera, and her own attention. But then by accident she had invited Dan, and now she was waiting on the porch with her kitbags and an acute case of butterflies. Not since the ship had they spent so many hours alone together.

She heard the wheels up the track, and stood. Usually Dan was in a pristine white shirt and chinos, but he stepped out of the Land Rover in a surprising pair of combat trousers and work boots. The second surprise was that he was holding two cappuccinos in cardboard takeaway cups.

"Did you just pop to Starbucks?"

Dan gave a sheepish grin. "I went to a wholesaler for a load of stuff to ship before I came home and a few of these cups just somehow . . . found their way into the trolley." He handed her both coffees and began to load her bags into the back of the car. When she was beside him in the passenger seat and the car lurched into motion, he went on, "I don't know, it symbolized something to me when I was away; it made me feel like I was in a movie, or something. Standing in a huge queue of other commuters, so many people there that you need your name written on the side of the cup. Drinking coffee in the street, too important to stop and sit. Not Tugan. Urban. I realize that just exposes how Tugan I actually was. Am."

"I used to feel that way in my first few surgeries. Like I was playing a vet in a film."

They had reached the end of the Mendoza driveway and were back on the main track, and Dan accelerated. He was happy, Charlotte realized, watching him. Coffee cup in one hand, steering with the other, grinning at her. He looked as excited as a little boy given an unexpected holiday from school.

"Ah, my first surgery was the greatest feeling in the world. Bilateral tonsillectomy. What was yours?"

"Neutering, in an animal shelter. Big ginger tomcat, lovely affectionate animal. Then I did about seventy spays and neuters in a fortnight."

"God, you put our access to shame, you vets. I'm not sure I've done seventy of anything, yet. I won't make any of the obvious castration jokes."

"They would be beneath you," Charlotte agreed. "It was a pretty amazing placement. And a total liberation to start out without having to worry about owners. No one ever warns you about owners when you're at school and you say you're an animal lover and you want to be a vet. Everyone says, 'How lovely,' or if they know a bit more they say, 'Oooh, isn't it very hard to get in?' But they never say, 'Remember you'll be dealing with anxious humans forever.' In a shelter you don't get insecure men demanding you give their bulldog silicone prosthetics. That's a more complicated procedure than just popping them out, of course; I've never actually done it. No one who cares that much about appearances would let a student do their dog's plastic surgery." Oh, shut up, she thought. Why are you talking to him about testicles?

Charlotte turned away and looked out of the passenger window, down the steep drop that fell beside the winding road as they climbed. The thick vegetation and the height of the old trees hid the almost sheer gradient beside her. She rested her chin on her hand and studied the tops of the fruiting palms.

"Taxi has been dropping me just past Priestess Creek and we can walk the rest, see who comes to say hello, who gets to be the lucky one today. They're quite friendly, which is precisely not the point of my observing them, by the way. I'd hoped to be more ignored than I am."

It was as they tramped deeper into the interior that Charlotte understood the intimacy inherent in the collaboration of it, and that by allowing him into her fieldwork she was in some obscure way allowing him to see what was truly important to her, pointing out the parts of herself that were essential. It was not the same as having Annie and Alex here to command, and not at all the same as having Elsie, who could keep up a constant stream of chatter even if her companion had long fallen silent, or possibly indeed fallen into a creek. Elsie and the children worked for her. Dan was a medic and a fellow scientist, and it mattered to her that he found her impressive, and was duly impressed by the quality of the study itself. He stirred her competitive streak. *Why?* she thought, scathing. Did she think any man had ever left a fiancée because he fell in love with another woman's research project?

They had reached her unofficial base camp. Here she had left a wheeled cooler containing her hammock, dry clothes wrapped in tarp, her machete, a bottle of sun cream, some toilet paper and hand sanitizer, epoxy in different colors for coding tortoises, and some snacks in tiffin tins, in the hopes it would all remain unmolested by pests and weather in between visits. It served as storage, seat, and desk.

"So how do you want to do this? Would you like your own tortoise to track? Or would you like to share one?"

Dan was competitive too. "I want my own," he said instantly. "I want to work. I want to do."

"That means no breaks, though. No stopping, if yours wanders miles from mine."

"That's fine. Just give me my orders."

Charlotte fitted him with a small camera on a neck strap, and a notepad and pen. Now they had arrived, she felt reassuringly businesslike and had decided that her initial instinct had been right, it would be nice to have Dan here. Nice, and nothing more complicated than nice. They discussed protocol, exchanged walkie-talkies, wished one another good luck. Dan would take the first tortoise they encountered so that Charlotte could check its code, if it had one, and get him started. They would spend much of the day ahead in silence anyway—one could not sit chattering near animals if one meant them to feel unobserved.

As it turned out, after the first half an hour they saw nothing of one another. Once Charlotte had found Dan his subject, a big broad male of about forty, it had taken her some time to find another. She then came across three in a neat row beneath an old fallen jackfruit, as if shelved there, but by then she was far from where she'd left him.

In late afternoon they met back at base. Charlotte herself was sweaty and tired, but was startled by Dan, who looked as if he'd been living in the jungle for a week. He had ripped his trousers and cut his cheek pushing his way through a coral cabbage. His hair stood on end, gelled with muck. He had obviously been in the creek, for he was sodden, a tideline of black filth around his knees. He had a wild look in his eyes.

Charlotte's tortoise had had a lazy day, sunning itself with two companions in the small discs of intense sun that penetrated the jungle canopy, following this light, or shifting occasionally to graze on tamarind leaves, going twice down to bathe in a shallow pool that stood encircled by trees that she could not identify, their trunks wrapped thickly with wild vanilla vines. Despite Dan's invisible proximity, Charlotte had passed the day as she'd envisaged, spending long, quiet hours breathing in the scent of forest clearings, orchid-spotting, picking ripe, fragrant vanilla pods, imagining herself to be Jane Goodall.

Dan's tortoise had turned out to be a daredevil psychopath, he told her, pouring the last water from his canteen over his head, drying his filthy face on the bottom of his filthy T-shirt. It had not been a tortoise at all, but some sort of rampant troll-beast. It had barely stopped crashing about all day, barely stopped grazing, had mated with four other tortoises—none tagged, by the way, so lots more out there, she had work to do—had made a point of leading Dan back and forth across the creek so that it was impossible for him to do anything but plunge in after it. At one stage, he was certain, it had been stalking a skink with a look of malign intent in its eyes. That was interesting, and unexpected.

"Tell me more about the skink business."

"Later. I'm finished. I've been running all day, it's forty degrees. I've not had lunch, I've not sat down, it's worse than Friday night in the ER. You're not seriously going to do this again tomorrow?"

"No, I thought I'd do these at a rate of one a week. Did you hate it?"

"I didn't hate it." Dan grinned. "I loved it. I've been playing commando all day. I swear it was creeping up on that skink, till it was spotted."

"Tortoises don't eat lizards."

"This one would have spit-roasted a goat, given half a chance."

She handed him a bag of Mac's dried pineapple from her backpack, and began to put away her kit. "I'm glad you've had a good day."

"Streuth, I'm ravenous. A great day. I've had a great day. The best since I came home. Thank you."

He threw himself into the hammock and crossed his arms over his chest, closing his eyes.

"I've been thinking all day, you know. It's bliss out here, it is usually impossible to be alone on Tuga." He fell silent for a long time, and Charlotte wondered if he had fallen asleep. But after a while he said slowly, "I do know that this is home for me, according to most people's definition of home. It's where I'm from, and I've come back in a very definitive way. But Saul never misses the opportunity to tell me I am FFA now, and I think today I realized that it's been getting to me more than I admitted. It makes it hard not to question what I'm here for, you know? If I'm actually just FFA then I could be anybody, or rather they could have hired anyone to do this job, and so what did I actually come back for?" He opened his eyes, staring upwards into the canopy. "But maybe I just need to be more patient about the changes I want to make, I realized that as well, and be a bit humbler with Saul. Endure the discomfort of not knowing."

"You had an epiphany in the jungle."

"Maybe."

"People here are rooted in a way I deeply envy."

"Really? But you've lived in London all your life—you're rooted. You're a proper Londoner."

Charlotte breathed deeply, and for the first time on the air caught the penguin-scent of noddies nesting, high and invisible, somewhere nearby. She could spend her life learning this jungle, she thought, and not meet a tenth of its inhabitants. There was a slow cracking sound and then a crash, as somewhere a heavy palm bough fell.

"It's hard to explain. It's about knowing who you are and how you fit, isn't it. I always had this sense—you know, my mother used to travel loads for work and whenever she was away I felt like it wasn't home anymore, it was just this big empty container for a lot of stuff, and me with a random nanny. And when she came back she brought it all to life again. I got homesick for her, when she was the one going away."

"That's beautiful, though. A person as home."

"Well. Maybe. Or scary, because she kept needing to travel and I never got used to it. Even as an adult I hate being alone in that house, and I know how pathetic that sounds. I don't know. I don't feel that way here, for some reason; I love my little cottage. You know what it is, it's the rootedness in one another as well as a sense of place. There's just such—*certainty* on the island. Wake up, let's go."

Dirt had settled in the creases of Dan's face, in his eyebrows, down his neck. His attempted wash had cleared only a streak here and there. He groaned, and hauled himself from the hammock.

"I get its appeal. But it's worth remembering that a lot of what you see as certainty is lack of choice. People are here, together, for generations, because they don't have any alternative."

"What about you? Don't you have an alternative?"

"That's harder to answer. Technically, yes. I can afford it, and I have transferable skills. Morally, perhaps not. I'm needed in a very precise way."

"But if you'd not come back another FFA doctor would have come on contract?"

"Yes, and we will need another one next year when Saul retires, if he ever actually unclenches. There's meant to be two of us, just in case one gets ill or goes out fishing or drops dead. But there's always been at least one Tugan doctor since the community here began, even if that person was barely qualified. Or sometimes not qualified at all. It's tradition. There's a girl of about fifteen who's bright and has expressed an interest—do you know Chloe Ben-Ezra? My aunt Moz is working hard to get her some A levels and on the way to medical school, maybe South Africa, assuming she can get the grades. But even if Chloe manages to get off the island and manages to stick it out, she won't qualify for a decade, so at the moment apart from Saul the only possible person who could take my job is me. Literally in the world."

"That is completely insane. It's an unthinkable pressure."

"I mostly didn't think about it. Then Saul turned seventy, and my aunt Moz sent a few spicy emails about how tired he was getting, and the guilt began to be harder to ignore."

"You're the chosen one."

"Yes, and that's all very special, but I sometimes think I could stand a bit less specialness. Things can be special in a bad way. And then again, the part of me that enjoys all the specialness feels threatened when people call me FFA."

"Stick with me, kid," Charlotte told him, accepting the camera he handed her and switching it on to scroll through the first few images.

"On my patch you're only as special as the tortoise you track. Wow. This is like battlefield photography."

"You see? Mine was special!" Dan protested. "Unique, in fact, as you can see. It was carnivorous. Or—lizard-ivorous."

"Not sure what you'd say, lacerti-something, maybe. Reptivo-rous. You know, if it turns out to be true it will actually be unique, and if we publish you can be first author."

They smiled at one another, complicit in the joke, complicit in the day, and, perhaps, in their parallel ambitions. Each recognized in the other an earnest commitment to the work for which they'd come, and the pressure to do it well. Dan offered his hand to agree this deal and Charlotte accepted it and shook it briskly. Then she turned away and began stuffing the remainder of her belongings into her bag, suddenly irritable. He had no business being funny, nor in expressing what appeared to be a genuine appreciation for her reptiles. It was all a bit too special, in a bad way.

28

Alex dos Santos appeared in Charlotte's yard, on his bike. He stood high on his pedals and circled round her, without dismounting.

"*Paz*, Dr. Vet Lady. You wanted, please," he told her. "It's Grand Mary, she says come now-now."

Apparently he was to be her ride; Charlotte sat on the seat with her hands on the delicate shoulders of an eleven-year-old, feeling apprehension as they bumped down the track. Yet Alex had perfect control, despite the overhanging branches, despite the potholes and rocks that seemed to appear from nowhere like a game of Space Invaders; despite the beautiful dappled zebu cow crossing the road on the far side of a blind corner. They arrived at Martha House and Charlotte dismounted, exhilarated. It was humid and her T-shirt clung to her back and chest. She leaned against the gatepost to compose herself.

Martha herself was moving across the lawn at a surprising rate, huge, bandy log-legs carrying her at speed towards her food bowl.

"Cabbage!" Mary said gleefully, making Charlotte jump. She had been standing just the other side of the pillar. "Look how she runs for it. Gained weight already, I reckon. Doesn't look a day over a hundred." Mary began to laugh, a terrifying sound, like a gate loose on its hinges.

"I came as soon as Alex found me. What's happened to her?"

"Martha's fit as a fiddle. Come inside."

Charlotte followed Mary up the long path to the house. On the way she couldn't resist pausing beside the food bowl, where Martha was snatching and tearing at a cabbage leaf. Even in a matter of weeks, her beak had sharpened.

"She's looking perky."

"I told you," said Mary, accusing, gesturing with her stick for Charlotte to get a move on. It was as if this improvement was despite Charlotte rather than because of her. "Come in, quick. I don't need busybodies seeing you."

Inside, Charlotte was taken not to the library, as she had hoped, but up the steep staircase. Watching ancient Mary take this stone ascent was hair-raising but it was obviously an established technique, hand over hand on the banisters like a ninety-year-old abseiler. Behind, Charlotte assessed the angles and wondered if she was strong enough to catch a falling body, but in the end they made it up to the first floor without incident. Mary stopped outside a closed door, hand on brass doorknob.

"It's your help I'm wanting, not your judgment." Mary glared, and Charlotte's heart sank. Every vet meets deliberate cruelty, neglect, the owners who lie about injuries, or fail to call until it's too late to save a suffering creature. She might not have been in London practice, but Charlotte had heard enough stories. Behind the door could be anything.

Mary turned the handle with kissing noises, and a moment later Charlotte felt the familiar pressure of warm fur winding itself about her ankles. She bent down to stroke a huge violet-gray British Blue cat, feeling with pleasure the lithe, solid little body beneath her hand, the spine arch and flex beneath her fingers. Then she caught up.

"A cat!"

"What diagnostics," said Mary drily. She closed the door and went over to a small armchair, lowering herself into it with effort. Immediately the huge cat leaped up on to her lap, a thick glossy rug over her knees.

"But, how did you get it here? It's illegal."

"Never you mind how Virginia got here. Can you take care of her or not?"

"Cats were eradicated from the island in the 1970s, weren't they? There are fines and penalties and—"

"Yes, yes, they've all got their little knickers in a twist about the birds, but if you report her she'll be murdered, and you'll probably be the one to have to do it," said Mary, quite reasonably. She stroked a gnarled hand down the huge back, and the gleaming gray fur beneath it rippled.

Charlotte immediately saw the truth in this. Non-native mammals were a threat to fragile island ecosystems and, with the exception of farm animals and a quota of domesticated and working dogs, were no longer allowed on Tuga. The number of cattle, pigs, and sheep were tightly controlled. Goats, those reckless destroyers of flora, had to be fenced or tethered. Cats had wrought damage to the endemic birds, many of whom were flightless or ground-nesting, and thus easy prey. A conservation law in 1981 had removed the final house cats from the island. The right thing as a responsible veterinarian, a conservationist, and most importantly a citizen, however temporary, was to report this one. But—Mary had a strong point. Charlotte had no particular desire to euthanize a beautiful, healthy cat. And the customs officer herself kept a red tegu lizard.

"What's been the matter with Virginia?" she asked warily.

"Her claws are getting long, and I don't trust my eyes to do them anymore. I want them clipping."

Charlotte thought for a moment.

"I'll do it if you let me into your library."

Mary beamed with triumph, and Charlotte felt a growing certainty that she'd been had.

29

Saul was missing Moz when she knocked on the door of his office and entered, sitting down heavily across from him in the patients' chair. She was delivering tea and an admonition. He could feel the latter coming, like a warm front.

He saw her now in duplicate. Once as she sat before him in a cloud of pale-gray curls, an expression of disapproval in evidence behind her cherry-red glasses, and again to her left, in the wedding photo framed on his desk. In this image, not much bigger than a passport photograph, the young bride had flowers twisted into her fiery red hair, leaning forward, eyes closed in laughter though she had not let go of his hand. Because she was bending, the bride-groom beside her looked tall in the photo and, at twenty-six (the unimaginable age of that fresh-faced boy, white linen shirt, freshly clipped four-inch flat-top, borrowed conch-pearl tie pin), Saul had indeed wanted to feel bigger than he was. He was marrying the tallest woman on the island, and the most beautiful, and the most brilliant. He was small and slight and only newly returned to Tuga, hungry for work, intimidated by the two senior doctors, both men in their fifties with decades of experience, and worryingly long careers still ahead before either would make way for Saul.

Saul Gabbai finished medical school and worked as a junior doctor in Luton for only as long as it took him to find a berth home—eighteen months, not so bad in the end. The Island Council had wanted him to do five years more in England. With two senior medics far from retirement, Saul would be most useful to Tuga de

Oro if he stayed put, gained a clinical speciality, and waited to be called.

But Saul had not wanted to stay one moment past qualification. He did not, he wrote back to them, want to specialize in anything but the job ahead, best learned, surely, by doing it. He did not attempt to explain to them how little he had enjoyed being Tugan, and a man of color, in 1970s Luton. He did not describe the daytime mockery, the nighttime fear.

Fermoza Williams, Moz since her own babyhood, had been sixteen when he left and was twenty-four when he returned, already teaching at the school, already beloved by her pupils and, her brother Garrick had told him, courted by several contemporaries. But she'd waited. "Mostly waited," Moz had shrugged, and Saul had burned with jealousy and demanded she confess everything and then marry him, and she had laughed and said he had no right to ask such questions when he'd been away so many years, but condescended to marry him nonetheless.

Saul looked often at this photo, two young people, their former selves, captured on the day that he considered his adult life had begun. She did not believe him, but if possible she was more beautiful to him now, in her familiarity. Then she had been an enigma, and the idea of all her inaccessible thoughts had tortured him. Now she continued to surprise him, but he no longer felt threatened by her separateness. She had always been a commanding presence, an authority figure even as a teenager. She knew things. She led. Saul had wanted to follow. Much of his growth, he felt, sprang from Moz's generosity, and wisdom. This belief she dismissed as foolishness, as she dismissed much else.

"You're doing health checks all morning, I read the schedule."

Saul assented, and lowered his gaze to his lap. Here came the admonition. It was a relief to know what he had done.

"*Guay de mi*, of all the trivial wastes of time, on top of everything else you're juggling. What's the point of Dan if he's not doing the health checks, at least?"

"Most of them protested."

"Your nephew appears to be becoming a hobbyist veterinarian. He shouldn't be poking around in jungles with a woman who isn't his girlfriend. And you know what? If you're determined to kill yourself working like he's not here, I'll take him for the school. Hand him over."

"I can't force patients to see him. And poking around in jungles is better than the trouble he causes here, messing about with all my kit, and his crackpot schemes to train Winston into a Band 7 nurse practitioner, asking for all his paperwork and qualifications. Winston, let me remind you, who has never left the island, and whose entire nursing education consisted of a few days of first aid from an army doctor twenty years ago, and a lot of subsequent ad hoc. The subsequent ad hoc has been the best education he could have; Tugan nursing doesn't require paperwork, it requires common sense. What's he building up their CVs for? Who here needs a CV?"

Moz produced a Thermos of tea from her string bag, which she nonetheless withheld until she had finished her speech. "Retire! Then Dan'd be the doctor and that would be that. Let him train Winston to become a juggler, or a tightrope walker, it won't be your problem."

"I can't yet, he's not remotely ready. He caused total chaos in the diabetes clinic this morning; he asked Ettie and Mercy to just 'hop on the scales,' and I had Ettie weeping and Mercy in my office screaming that she'd never been so insulted. I told him, 'You can't just go around weighing women. The older generation expect you to tell them they've never looked better and then to make an informed estimate.' Actually Calla and Winston are the best at that, to be fair to them. See, that's not a skill you can put on a CV."

"What did Dan say?"

"He was pigheaded about the whole thing. He said that was 'not a reasonable way to be expected to practice medicine.' He's come home priggish. He wants to give public lectures on nutrition and exercise."

"Well. I don't know what is or isn't a reasonable way to practice medicine but it is my recommendation that you make it between him and his patients. No one will ever accept him while there is a beloved, familiar alternative. Why wouldn't they prefer you? You've taken beautiful care of them since the Stone Age. You know them, you understand them. And it is because you are such a wonderful doctor that he's not going to be able to grow in your shadow. For everyone's sake, make him space, *mi vida*, let him make his mistakes in the saddle, he'll learn soon enough. You also came home and wanted to revolutionize everything, if you recall. And you cannot know how cross with you I will be if you die before you've retired."

"I'm not saying it's an optimal approach, obviously"—Saul was still on the subject of the diabetes clinic—"obviously in a dream world we would be charting their weights over time, calculating medication to the kilo, but he has to have some sensitivity and understand context. If they never set foot in the clinic again, that's worse than a bit of a guess. Better not to scare them off, that's what he doesn't understand. I've not killed anyone yet, calculating by eye. And I promise, I'm retiring this year."

"So you say, and yet the phone goes on ringing." Moz thumped down the Thermos and stood to go, brushing down her skirts. "I don't like the weather one bit, by the way. This Island Close has been too quiet. The season's not finished with us yet, you mark my words."

Saul came round from behind his desk to embrace her. She had always teased him about this, his inability to say goodbye to her even for a matter of hours. He hated to see her moving away from him. "How far could I get, on Tuga?" she would ask him, but she failed to understand that physical distance wasn't the point.

"Never die," he said, into the warmth of her neck. "You must promise me."

"You need to take five minutes away from this clinic for a haircut, at least, *mi alma*." Moz stroked his head fondly. "I promise I shall do my very best."

30

Island Close was the hurricane season, months during which the seas were near-impassable for a thousand miles all round. Every Tugan shipwreck for a century had foundered between June and late November, a passing whaler or an intrepid fishing vessel destroyed by the winds above and the rocks beneath. Many men had died within sight of the harbor, but some of the shipwrecked sailors had been rescued, and stayed to make a home on the island. It was a joke, among their direct descendants, that a reverse natural selection had brought a glut of men to Tuga who suffered some combination of misplaced bravery and poor judgment.

The hurricanes themselves usually passed further north, but the rough seas and the humidity came each year without fail, for a week or a month or three, and with them the rains. And now, with dry season almost upon them and the Island Open ship already on her way from Southampton, Taxi took to the airwaves to announce the formation of a new tropical storm. Not a big one. A few showery days, a few days of wind, then clear skies again. But overnight the tropical storm engorged into a hurricane, and the islanders began their well-rehearsed preparations, clearing gutters, testing branches, picking fruit, checking stores, bringing in the animals.

"Thing is, Dolittle, I just don't trust to your prep."

Charlotte scanned the list Levi handed her, scribbled on receipt paper from the Rockhopper's till. *Wrench*, it read. *Gaffer tape. Plastic sheeting. Bin bags. Baby wipes. First-aid kit.*

"Where am I to get any of this stuff? What do you intend me to be wrenching?"

"Don't you go wrenching anything. I'm saying I want you familiar with what's in the house. If you do need any of the storm kit, look in the metal lockers in the bottom of the larder. Water's in those two big cans at the back of the larder as well. And take this."

He disappeared and returned with a cardboard box, which he set down beside the sink. She peered in and saw tinned tomato soup, a box of cereal, another, larger torch and batteries, four wrapped packets of biscuits, and a jar of Mac's fig jam. She was touched, and so did not feel she could tell him that she had about thirty jars of jam in the house now, fig and mintberry and mango, glossy starfruit syrup. She never charged for veterinary services, and islanders found other ways to express their gratitude. It was likely she would never again need to buy eggs while she lived on Tuga, for they appeared now on her doorstep in quantities to supply a custard factory.

"You are being very attentive. It makes me nervous when you're nice to me."

"I'm being nice to my house and its contents. You're contents. It will be fine, it's still just a tropical storm for now; one night, start to finish, I reckon. Now listen. This is not a major deal, this hurricane—"

"You just said it was a tropical storm."

"For now. But you are not going to be one of the idiot FFA who gets themselves killed by stupidity, you hear me? You will be in this house from six p.m. until told otherwise, you will not go outside, you will not open the windows."

"Yes, sir."

"If the power goes out, if the water stops, you stay put."

"I stay put."

"If you hear noises outside and you want to go investigating, you don't, you stay put."

"Jesus, yes. I've seen enough horror movies. I stay put."

"Someone comes by and says, 'My cow's having trouble with its whatever,' what do you do?"

"Well, that's a potential medical emergency, so—"

Levi made the noise of a quiz-show buzzer. "Wrong! That was a test and you failed. You ain't risking your life for a damn cow, even on Tuga."

"I stay put."

"Good girl. Now don't stay put just yet, I need you to hold the storm panels up for me. Come."

Charlotte followed him outside. The wind had picked up slightly and there were ragged clouds, still white, whisking through the sky. The sun beat down on the hot yard. From the workshop Levi dragged three huge polycarbonate sheets and Charlotte stood where he directed her, holding them in place as he began to affix them over the windows using holes she had just now noticed around the frames. When they finished Levi went to check the guttering, and instructed her to close the wooden shutters on the small upstairs window and to pack her books and papers in plastic, just in case the roof sustained damage. Before he left, he paused.

"You could go somewhere else, go stay in Town maybe. Lots would have you."

"Thanks. Betsey offered, and Elsie, and Joan, but I'd go mad locked up with Garrick. And Dan said I could go there. Don't worry, I'll stay, it will be an adventure."

"Zekri said you could go there."

"Yes, he didn't think I should be alone up here."

"I bet he didn't. I finished off his love shack just in time, you'll be very cozy. When are you heading down?"

"I just said—" Charlotte started in irritation, and then resolved not to rise to Levi's provocation. Instead she closed him out, remembering this time to slam both halves of the stable door at once.

Before the winds, the rains came. Water poured through newly secured gutters and their outlets became pounding torrents. There was respite from the hot yellow sun, and everything had darkened to gunmetal and smoke and pewter.

In the front yard of Martha House, Martha herself was looking glossy and black, washed clean of dust, her dull scratches disguised by the water that ran in sheets over her huge shell. She seemed to like it—rather than retreat into her private hollow, she extended her neck out long and serpentine, and lifted her small pointed face, eyes closed, jaw gently working. Soon she would be closed into her low concrete shed, safe from falling debris until the storm passed.

By lunchtime a river ran through Harbour Street, down which floated palm fronds and torn plastic bags, milk cartons and disintegrating newspaper and crushed beer cans. The water was gray and opaque, like the sky. Town did not, in this weather, resemble a paradise postcard, rather an abandoned English seaside resort through which someone had swilled a hundred thousand polluted gallons. FFA could be identified from their attempts to fight the weather—they wore boots, long trousers, and plastic coats in which they steamed and sweated. Locals wore flip-flops and as little clothing as possible. Dan had not been aware of his own remembering, yet he too had instinctively dressed in shorts and a singlet of his father's. He passed Levi Mendoza and Walter Lindo-Smith, shirtless and barefoot up ladders side by side, performing their final checks on the upper windows of Customs House, having already taken down its swinging clock face. Dignified and upright, Aunt Moz cycled slowly past him through the deepening filth, a plastic bag tied tight round her wild silver hair. For the moment everyone was out, but it would soon be time to batten down the hatches.

Betsey emerged into Harbour Street, pushing an outraged crab through her doorway with a broom. "Shoo! You want to go in the pot? You big enough. Out." The crab waved and skittered, and eventually slunk around a corner. Betsey greeted Dan with a nod. "Nothing," she called, when he began to cross towards her, "nothing left. Unless your mother needs, that's different, for your mother there would be something left. Lusi got what she needs?" Dan assured her that his mother was well stocked. Betsey nodded her approval and withdrew, and a moment later the storm shutters closed on the cafe.

Dan had joined Saul on his traditional pre-hurricane rounds, reading the riot act to whomever they considered most likely to do something foolish while the winds were high. No driving. No farming. No one on the beaches. You'd have thought these admonitions unnecessary, Saul told Dan as they drove back from the moshav, but they remained an essential part of the job. Some people had lived through so many hurricanes they believed themselves inoculated. Taxi reinforced this message by playing "Take Me Home, Country Roads," and reminding them all to return to the place they belonged.

Of late there had been tension between the two doctors on various issues, ranging from their use of combined-formula proprietary drugs, to which larger items ought to be stored at the back of the ambulance bay. This public-health intervention of Saul's touched upon a tender point between them, because Saul had been disparaging of what he called Dan's obsessional attempts to launch some public-health programming of his own—counting steps; nutritional awareness; opening a conversation with the Island Council about a possible tax on processed food and fizzycan imports. Diabetes was rising on the island, Dan noted, and could one day create an avoidable pressure on the annual health budget. Saul himself sat on Island Council, but had never felt it necessary to restrict the islanders' access to refined sugar, like a parent putting the biscuit tin up out of reach. They were not children, and could make choices as private citizens.

"But explain how is this different?" Dan asked him, reversing into the bay. They had gone out in the ambulance mostly to check the battery wasn't flat, but also to add gravitas to their message. "Surely if you take that approach, then it's also a private citizen's right to walk his dog in a hurricane."

Saul shook his head.

"No. No one's dinner is a public threat. What people eat or don't eat I can suggest, gently, in an appointment, and I do—all your posters and drives and initiatives are conversations I have, but I have them privately, quietly, one on one, I don't go making people self-conscious. And at the end of the day I'm not going to start making a noise about something that's their own private affair. Your example of walking a dog in a hurricane is totally different, that's a public threat and I'll tell you why. You and I are the only medics in thousands and thousands of square miles of empty water. No backup teams. No safety nets. Not much will make you feel more vulnerable than that, if you stop to think about it too long. Whenever the contract doctor's been an idiot these last years, since I turned sixty, I've found myself thinking, *If I have a cardiac incident or I split my head open, then it's this fool who takes care of me.* You can't lose sight of the reality that the most acute public-health emergency the island could face is something that puts me, or you—or worse, both of us—in needless danger. I do not want us out in an ambulance in a storm if I can help it. Not for some idiot who took it upon himself to walk his dog. You take care of this island by taking care of yourself. And of me, for that matter."

"Roger. On that note, have you considered taking up jogging, Uncle Saul?"

"You are a cheeky so-and-so," Saul told him, but the slight tension between them had dissipated. "I'll admit your boxes aren't a bad idea. Let's check the oxygen regulators and then go home."

31

Now it was past six and Charlotte was doing as Levi had bidden her, and hunkering down. The storm panels distorted but did not entirely obscure the slender frangipani and the heavy, spreading avocado tree, which Levi had earlier stripped and cut back. The sky was the color of iron. Humidity thickened the air. Charlotte was to stay downstairs, Levi had said, and so her laptop had moved from upstairs desk to kitchen bed, ready for what she had thought of as a quiet evening scrolling through cam-trap images. She now realized the night would be anything but quiet. The incessant white noise of water was like rushing blood in the ears. The whole island seemed awash—the rush of the swollen river and creeks, the thunder of the falls, the roar of brown torrents through straining gutters. Beneath it she thought she'd heard a pounding at the door and opened it to find Levi, soaked through. In the tangerine porch light the dripping wax tapers of flowering ginger seemed to glow behind him. Rain ran in rivulets down his face, plastering his hair to his cheeks.

"*Ke haber.*"

"I thought no one was meant to be out." She was bellowing.

"No, I said *you* ain't meant to be out."

"What are you doing here, you're not coming in?"

For a moment Levi's expression altered and Charlotte wondered if she'd hurt his feelings. Then he laughed and shouldered inside, slamming the door behind him and shaking his hair like a dog.

"You want me to spend a hurricane in a shack on a roof? Don't worry, Dolittle, you're safe from me. I'll sleep on the sofa." He was standing on the doormat peeling off wet clothing. His sodden T-shirt fell to the floor with a slap. He leaned forward, using a clean tea towel from the cupboard to scrub dry his face and hair. Charlotte watched, unable to look away. Say what you liked about Levi, his physical beauty was undeniable.

She glanced away, embarrassed.

"You eaten?"

"Not yet, I was going to have one of my ninety-two million avocados. Stop taking things off."

"Then maybe get me a bigger towel?"

Charlotte opened the chest of drawers and threw him a bath towel, which he caught, and wrapped around his waist. A moment later he was dry and dressed again, sorting through the contents of a huge backpack. She took up her laptop from the bed and shifted to the sofa, feigning concentration while at the same time listening to the sounds of Levi moving through her kitchen—his kitchen—with familiarity. A stack of tiffin tins had appeared, which he was emptying into dishes. The taps ran, and she heard the snick of a knife through vegetables. She went back to studying her footage but stole glances at him intermittently, thinking that she would not have invited him, but that it felt oddly comfortable to have him here. Charlotte had never before encountered anyone to whom she exposed her authentic and unfiltered self, and yet her ease with Levi was instinctive, and irrepressible. His silent proximity stirred and comforted in equal, and equally confusing, measures.

After half an hour Levi called her to the kitchen table, on which he had laid out plates of shredded duck in tamarind and watermelon, chicken skewers, spicy green beans, and sweet coconut rice parceled in banana leaves. These were Tugan dishes, he explained, and the imposed stasis of a hurricane was a good time to sit properly and appreciate the local food. They had nowhere else to go, after all.

"Avocado ain't a meal. Annie Goss cooks more than you."

"I'm busy," Charlotte said defensively.

"Something wrong when you too busy to sit down to enjoy a dinner."

"But this isn't dinner, this is a proper feast. Who actually made all this?"

Levi was putting chicken skewers on her plate with a pair of tongs. "I ain't *actually* just a pretty face, Dolittle. And I like to eat." There was a smile in his eyes, and she could see he was proud to have surprised her. He was, she thought, such a pretty face.

The duck was one from the moshav, the chicken from a farmer on the east side who Charlotte had visited, one of several who now brought her eggs. The rice was a cheat, Levi said, and couldn't be said to be truly Tugan because rice had to be imported. He stole his tamarind from Mary's huge old tree at the back of Martha House, near the wall. Charlotte spooned more of everything onto her plate with pleasure. "It's *delicious*," she told him, seriously. "Who taught you to cook like this?"

"It's decent is all, it ain't so impressive. My dad cooks a lot. Why, who taught you to eat toast in the street?"

Charlotte gave a sudden laugh. "You've just described my mother precisely. Half an English muffin in one hand while she's flying out the door. '*Ciao ciao*, darling!' Her housekeeper cooks most nights, or I don't think she'd ever eat sitting down."

As she had periodically these last months, Charlotte tried and failed to imagine her mother on the island. Tuga was not a place of pashminas and kitten heels, of Nicole Farhi and juice fasts and starched white shirts. Her mother was phobic about the sun's aging properties, and liked rustic only when hyphenated with something that effectively negated it. Rustic-chic. Rustic-luxe. Then she had another thought.

"Have I met your parents?"

"I don't know, Dolittle, you tell me. You been over to Conch yet?" Levi took the banana leaves from her plate and his, wiped them clean, and began to tear them into strips.

"What, they're on the island?"

"Yup, moved out to Conch about ten years ago. They like the quiet."

"Quieter than Tuga."

"Very funny, Dolittle. This the big smoke, compared to Conch. You can walk from this house to Town, for one thing. Shout long enough and chances are someone would hear you." Levi was weaving ribbons of leaf together on his lap below the table, with a look of concentration.

"But if I'm shouting it's because I want someone to be able to hear me."

Levi straightened. Then he tossed into Charlotte's lap a tiny box made of banana leaves, and stood and began to clear the table.

"You got it in you to shout, Dolittle? Or you too buttoned up?"

Charlotte ignored this.

"What's Conch Island actually like? I've read about it and it sounds—a bit eccentric. Like, how can Tuga not be remote enough? The world's most isolated island is too busy, you have to find an even smaller island off the island?" While she spoke she was turning over the bright green cube in her hands, surprised both by its intricacy and the apparent ease with which he had made it.

Levi set down his stack of dishes on the counter and began to rinse them, speaking over his shoulder. The taps were loud, outside the wind was picking up, and she had to strain to hear him.

"Twenty-five people full-time out there. No running water, no power. Totally collective property and animals, just like Tuga at the beginning. No money allowed on the island, barter only. It ain't my scene, but my folks are into it. They'd have done it years earlier except me and Maia needed to be able to get to school. Listen, Dolittle, I'm cleaning these fast, then we fill the sink with clean water just in case, OK? Don't dump dirty stuff in it."

"God, OK. Conch sounds totally bananas. Are the animals vaccinated? I'm so fascinated. Don't you find this just totally fascinating?"

"Dolittle, it's my life you're talking about here; this ain't some anthropology seminar."

"You're right, sorry."

Levi relented, seeing her contrition. "They're good people. Happy. Quiet. Homebodies. Dad's a carpenter, and my mum works the Conch gardens with her pals there. Upstanding citizens, foodies, obsessive tavla players. Good people. Nothing like me, in other words."

"You're good people," Charlotte protested, realizing as she said it how deeply she knew it to be true. Levi had a purity to him, an inability to dissimulate, and a kindness that was palpable no matter how much macho front he put up. She trusted him.

"Ah, thanks, Dolittle. It's OK, my folks love me even though I ain't brought home a PhD in newts, or whatever. What about you? Your people overachievers, like you?"

Charlotte picked up their glasses and brought them over, leaning beside him while he put away the clean dishes. She was about to begin upon the usual anecdotes, to present all the ways in which Lucinda was remarkable and had compensated for the smallness of their family with devotions above and beyond. But for the first time, Charlotte felt the omissions in this speech as the untruths they really were. With Levi she never felt the need to reconfigure her thoughts into more acceptable dimensions before speaking them aloud. She loved her mother with a desperation that bordered sometimes on panic, but she saw, too, that this was not quite as it should have been, that Lucinda might somehow have freed her from it, had she chosen to.

"I'm always scared to make my mother angry. So instead of telling her I was coming I literally ran away. Like I'd stolen something."

"Seems to me a grown woman don't need her mother's permission to take a job."

"Yes, well, you'd think. You might have hit on the issue, though:

I'm not entirely sure she knows I'm a grown woman. Or maybe I don't. It never seemed to make sense to leave home when I made no money as a postdoc and my mother had this huge empty house, but now I think—I don't know. I don't think it's done either of us any favors. My father is a whole other story."

Levi dried his hands and then took a bowl of lychees from the fridge, a gift to Charlotte by a family whose dog she'd attended after it had stepped on a shard of glass. He moved to the sofa, put his feet up on the coffee table and regarded her, the bowl on his lap. She watched him split each fruit with his teeth.

"In case you hadn't noticed, I ain't going anywhere. Pass me an empty something?"

Charlotte handed him a plate for the mounting pile of peel he had balanced on one knee.

"My whole life I was obsessed with finding him, trying to find clues in tiny things my mother said. But it was all with this overriding sense of rejection and, like, he doesn't want me, so screw him. And the thing is, for all I know he still might be awful, I have no idea, but I now think he probably wasn't some grand villain because it turns out she never actually told him I existed. I think now I was so bloody naive, she's the ultimate control freak and having someone else involved would mean sharing me, so of course she'd never tell a man she was pregnant if she could help it."

"Not naive," said Levi quietly. "She told you that your whole life. Why would a child expect an adult to lie? So it was there as fact, as you grew."

Charlotte, who had been in a state of self-blame about this perceived naivety since last year's awful Christmas party, felt surprise, and a surge of unexpected gratitude. "That's true," she said, realizing that it was.

"So now is she talking? She told you any more about him?"

Charlotte shook her head. "Nothing. Not if they loved one another for years or if it was a one-night stand, or what he did or what he looked like or where he's from, nothing. She just got defensive that I thought her lying was a big deal. All I know is what I've pieced together. Once when I was little I asked if he was from London and she said, 'He's from about as far away as you can get,' and another time she said, 'The ends of the earth.'"

Levi offered her a peeled lychee. Charlotte took it, and paused.

"I've literally never said this to anyone before, you're going to think I am crazy."

"You think he's from Tuga de Oro."

Charlotte sat forward. "How did you know I was going to say that?"

"You're looking for something here, Dolittle, I feel it. You're restless."

"I'm *not* restless."

"I ain't judging; we all got our stuff, believe me."

She bit into the fruit, and then set the glossy seed on the plate with the peel. Then she flopped back on to the sofa cushions and closed her eyes.

"The thing is, it's on so little supposition. My mother says I am 'fixated on superimposing a heteronormative dyad over a happy childhood,' and thus I am 'an agent of my own patriarchal oppression.' She says one devoted parent should be enough for any child."

"I understood zero of that, Dolittle. Speak in English."

"Sorry. It's how my mother argues me into submission. I'm trying to get my head around this new reality. One devoted parent, no paternal rejection, just neutral absence. She says he never knew. Except at the same time I have this faint memory of someone coming for tea when I was really small, maybe four or five, I don't know. So maybe there are other lies, and I have no idea what to believe anymore."

She fell silent for a moment, remembering. Lucinda had had a visitor, or maybe visitors, and whoever had come had handed five-year-old Charlotte a polished walnut shell, and inside she had found the smallest doll's house she had ever seen, and a tiny tortoise within. Then the sitting-room door had closed, and a child

159

usually supervised and fussed over had played for a blissful hour alone at the kitchen table, inventing a world inside a walnut.

"All I know is someone gave me this toy and I was allowed to play with it that day, but after that my mother had this strangely violent antipathy to it, and kept trying to throw it in the bin. Hold on." Charlotte disappeared into the bathroom and returned with something in her hand. She passed Levi the walnut, glossy with varnish.

"I thought Tuga was the name of the tortoise who lived inside it, you know, because it was carved in between the hinges, and then years later I went to a lecture on isolated oceanic island farming practices and Tuga de Oro came up and I remembered—this. It's lived in the bottom of my washbag for years. And when I mentioned the island to my mother she hadn't heard of it—but also she went mental and started going on and on about what a hovel it is, how awful, and how no one in their right mind should ever think of coming here. It was so irrational, like, why should she have such strong feelings about some random place, unless she was trying to put me off? And how can somewhere you've never heard of be a hovel? So now I think, maybe he did find out about me somehow. Maybe he came that day."

Levi's rough fingers immediately found the catch. The walnut lay open in the palm of his hand and he studied it, in silence, for a long time.

"What do you think? It's beautiful, isn't it. It made me wonder if maybe he had a special affinity for tortoises."

Levi handed it back to her. Then he stood unexpectedly and loped up the stairs, taking them two at a time, into the creaking bedless bedroom in the roof.

"I thought no one was meant to be upstairs tonight," Charlotte called.

"No, I said *you're* not meant to be upstairs tonight!"

Levi jogged back down with a shoebox, which he laid gently on Charlotte's lap. She lifted the lid.

Inside was a series of white cardboard jewelry boxes and inside each, in a cloud of clean sheep's wool, she found a walnut. Each had a polished hinge and contained a miniature home like her own nut: one for a mouse, one for a little donkey in a neckerchief, several for tortoises. Each had the word "Tuga" scratched in tiny letters between its hinges. Charlotte looked up at Levi in disbelief.

"But, but—you *can't* have made this, you can't! I've had it since I was a child, it's not *possible*—"

"My father."

"Your father made this? But wait, Levi, seriously, this is unbelievable. Does he sell them in London? Oh my *God*, did he have an affair with my mother and then come back to England and give me this?"

Levi laughed. "Cool it, Dolittle, you're safe; I ain't your sibling or whatever. No more upright, faithful man walks the earth than Vitali Mendoza. And in any case, my father ain't got a passport, he never left Tuga for one day in his life, unless you counting Conch. He makes these for the market and for the gift shop, local handicrafts and whatnot. A few, not millions. Tuga ain't exactly got a thriving export market, except stamps, and fish. He'd make you another, if you asked him. He made Rebecca one with a piglet."

"Oh my God," Charlotte said again. She could not take her eyes from the box. It was uncanny, as if a dream had coalesced suddenly to solid form. She ran her fingers over the miniatures. They were something and nothing, and yet they came to her as further proof of her own connection to the island. Her heart was pounding in triumph, and something else—a closing-in on something, perhaps. She had not been wrong.

"I ain't saying they were Tugan, but any person gave you this has been on the island. You can put that on your list of clues. But what I'm thinking is, most Tugans live and die without ever leaving, there's not many can afford to travel. Ain't it likelier someone just visited here, and bought this?"

"Maybe. I don't know. But how unbelievably weird that your dad made my favorite toy in the world. Honestly, I have treasured this since I was little, it's part of why I fell in love with tortoises. Your dad sort of, sort of—led me here."

They were staring at one another, smiling stupidly. Then there was a sudden fizz, and the house fell into blackness.

32

Charlotte sat very still, and waited.

The temperature of the room rose almost instantly as the ceiling fan above them slowed, and stopped. She could not—literally could not, she realized, raising it experimentally—see her hand in front of her face. This cosmic darkness remained for only a few seconds before Levi turned on the bright beam of a small torch, and used it to find his way to the kitchen table. When she rose to help he gestured for her to stay put, and a moment later he had found candles and lit them in glasses and holders round the room. Levi moved in and out of the pools of warm light, intermittently visible. Even with the windows covered, the air shifted slightly; the candles flickered.

"Now you're getting the authentic Tugan experience."

"When will it come back on?"

"Oh, this is it, now. If we're lucky they'll sort it out tomorrow, maybe the next day. You'll have to wait a while to get back to"—he sat down heavily beside her and peered over her shoulder, shining the beam of his torch on the pile of papers at their feet—"'Integrating telemetry data at several scales with spatial capture–recapture to improve density estimates.' Don't spoil the ending for me, now; we're doing that for my next book club. Jesus, girl."

Charlotte laughed and swatted at him and somehow found, though she had been pushing Levi away, still she had not quite let go of his wrist; that somehow her hand had then slipped into his, resting together on his thigh. Her breath caught in her throat.

Levi looked down at their fingers, interlaced. Charlotte followed his gaze. She said softly, "I'm glad you're here."

This did not encompass all she felt.

His rough thumb was slowly circling her palm. He had beautiful hands, she thought, recalling with new vividness all the places she had imagined them. But as he began to draw closer, she placed the flat of her palm on his chest, a gesture of instinctive intimacy, and yet stalling him at arm's length. Her mind was racing.

"Wait. Tell me, tell me about what you just said, tell me more about your parents."

Levi clutched at his hair and groaned. He stood up suddenly, moving away from her, and she felt a wrench at the abrupt distance between them.

"*Guay de mi*, you're killing me, Dolittle."

He threw himself down on the floor on the far side of the coffee table, an arm over his face as if in bright sun, or the beam of a searchlight.

"This is really how you want to spend our time, drawing family trees?"

When she didn't answer he went on, "I don't know. They solid folk. Whenever I messed up as a kid they gave me the benefit of the doubt. Unconditional love."

Charlotte moved back while he was speaking, out of the candlelight. "You're lucky," she said eventually, from the safety of her shadows.

Levi cleared his throat.

"Well. No false pretenses here. What I know about love you could fit in one of those walnut shells." He closed his eyes, and Charlotte wondered if he intended to fall asleep there, on the floor. She did not want him to retreat. She did not want him farther away.

Charlotte held her breath as long as she could, then let it go. And then she rose and crossed to the other side of the coffee table and sat down quietly. A moment later, when he hadn't moved, she lay down beside him on the floor, flat on her back as he was, staring up into the darkness together as if they were stargazing. She was aware of his bare shoulder beside hers, not quite touching. The humidity had risen.

"You could have told me if you wanted your house back tonight, I'd have gone somewhere else."

"Sorry you missed an excuse to go to Zekri's."

"You know that was exactly not what I meant."

Levi rolled onto his side and raised himself onto his elbow, looking down at her, and she stared up at him without moving. He smelled of juniper and woodsmoke, his hair still damp with rain. He was very still, watching her face, waiting.

Levi didn't move. He stayed where he was, steady above her, his face a question. Charlotte felt her body's answer, unequivocal and entire. She reached out for him, pulled him down to meet her, and found herself laughing aloud with pleasure and release when finally he kissed her and she felt the heat of his back beneath her hand like sun-warmed stone. His fingers ran down the side of her jaw to the nape of her neck. Then there was urgent pounding at the kitchen door and a second later it flew open with a bang, as if someone had kicked it. The white beam of a huge torch fell upon them and she was dazzled, and raised an arm over her eyes.

"Charlotte! Are you OK?"

Levi sprang up.

"Everything fine here, *haver.*"

Charlotte scrambled to her feet and stepped out from behind him.

"Dan? What are you doing here?"

"I thought you might be frightened when the power went down, I didn't know if anyone had— Obviously I wouldn't have worried had I known you were in such—ah, *capable hands.*"

Was he sneering? Charlotte's face flamed. She found herself stumbling away from Levi, putting a conspicuous distance between them.

"No one's in anyone's hands, Zekri. It's my house. I'm in my house. What's your excuse? As I recall, you were the one all over Tuga yesterday with a bullhorn telling us no one should be driving in the storm."

"I'm the island medic, I have a duty of care."

"Ain't no one here's needing your care."

"I can see that."

The wind gave a gothic howl, and Charlotte retreated to the shadows.

"It's not safe out there," she managed. She felt her cheeks burning.

"He got here just fine," said Levi, and at the same time Dan said, "I'll make my way back."

The door slammed.

Charlotte watched Levi, his jaw set, following the beam of his torch as he moved through the room, extinguishing candle after candle. She sat down slowly on the bed, watching the dancing circle of light shift as he crossed to the sofa. Then she heard the springs creak as he lay down, and a moment later the room was in blackness. She stood, hesitating. Levi said softly, "I tell you something, girl. I don't know what games you playing, but I think I'm going to fold right here."

Charlotte lay back down in confusion, and a new misery. When she woke in the morning the winds had dropped, the skies had cleared, and Levi had gone.

33

At the dock the Brassy Ladies were in full swing, the Spencer sisters on cornets, Miss Moz exuberant and expressive on the French horn. The children were ready with platters of fig jellies and had been more or less successful in restraining themselves, though here and there were gaps in the concentric circles of sweets, like the missing teeth in several of their own smiles. Rebecca Lindo-Smith had been chosen to scatter frangipani petals, and had a flower tucked into the elastic of each of her plaits (Walter's hairdressing had come on, these last months). Determined to prove to Marianne that enterprise was possible even in the absence of a boarding-school education, Annie and Alex had set up a stand selling their own homemade postcards, painstakingly drawn and colored, and bearing the legend, "Welcome to Tuga de Oro! The best plaice in the world!!!!"

Elsie had completed the on-board customs checks. The sky was clear blue, the humidity of the last months unimaginable now that it was finally December and the good weather had returned. The first lighter was in, and passengers began to step ashore. The island was Open.

Through various cries of "What, ho!" Dan Zekri was suddenly seen to vault over the wooden barrier and run up the dock. A ripple of low talk went through the crowd. This was their young doctor breaking the rules after all but, from her place at the front, Lusi Zekri sensed that the spectators approved the devotion it suggested. There was a widespread curiosity about Katie Salmon, and the climate she might bring to the household of the future chief medical officer.

Dan reached the end of the dock, where a young woman with a bright pink backpack flew into his arms. Here she was, thought Lusi. The moment of truth herself. She had long resolved to love this girl, whatever form or fashion she might take, and here came her first opportunity. She shifted her handbag from one arm to the other and peered, looking her future daughter-in-law up and down from beneath her sun hat.

Katie stood barely above Dan's shoulder, Lusi saw. She had fine, light brown hair, tied back in a sensible ponytail that blew across her cheeks in the sea breeze, and no makeup on a wide-eyed, clear-skinned face. Lusi watched as the girl turned and lifted a huge bag with surprising ease. Beside her Dan duly sprang into action to help her, but not before Katie had made it an astonishing distance down the dock carrying both her backpack and a duffel bag that seemed as heavy as she was. Independent, thought Lusi, approving.

They came closer. Katie wore a white cotton shirt, light jeans, and very battered brown hiking boots, with glittery purple laces. When Dan brought her over, Katie was beaming, and seemed positively to bounce with each step despite the rucksack, and then Lusi found herself tightly hugged by thin, strong arms. Not very tall herself, she was unused to grown women smaller than she. Lusi hugged back, and then Katie released her. She pushed her pink sunglasses into her hair.

"I am so happy to be here. My goodness, how lovely, you look just like Dan."

"Oh, *kerida*." Lusi was suddenly overcome, her voice not as steady as she'd hoped. "We are so pleased to have you, I can't tell you. Was that your first time at sea? I hear you didn't get seasick."

"First time at sea," Katie said, "but it was great. The beginning of the adventure." She was looking around at Harbour Street and began to point at shop after shop, naming each, their wares, and their proprietors. "I've studied," she explained, when Lusi expressed admiration, and some surprise. "I asked Dan to annotate a map for me."

"Katie likes to hit the ground running," Dan said, reaching to tuck a strand of Katie's flyaway hair behind an ear, and Lusi was moved to see that he too had tears in his eyes. Then the band launched into "It's a Long Way to Tipperary," and Katie was presented with the sweets and flowers, bending to talk to each child with the ease and confidence of Princess Diana, Lusi thought. She had a lovely open manner, a lovely open face. Natural.

After a time Dan extracted his fiancée from her small admirers and Lusi followed them back through the crowds, towards Up Yard, where Dan had left the car.

"I popped round a chicken soup, with some fufu, and chejados in a biscuit tin," she told Katie, when they reached the car, and then said she was going home. She wished to be welcoming, but also to give the young couple time alone together after a separation of many months.

But Katie seemed genuinely disappointed, as she had been expecting to come first to Lusi's house. It was an island tradition to honor the parents of those recently returned, and "Dan and I will have every day together now," Katie said, opening the passenger door for Lusi, "so I'd really love to come over. Gosh, it's as beautiful here as I hoped it would be. I feel very lucky."

Lusi felt lucky too, a rare sensation, and said so.

Beyond the fact that Katie was a physiotherapist and loved kite-surfing, whatever that was, Dan had furnished his mother with few specifics. She was young, Lusi knew, this girl who had finally captured her son's wary heart. At first, that youth had worried her, but she had not liked the sound of Camilla or Laura or the other one, each more suitable on paper perhaps, the same age as Dan, doctors too, but when he'd spoken of those women Lusi had heard something in Dan's voice akin to awe, or perhaps it was closer to angst. An imbalance, in any case, and they'd not worked out, in the end.

This one, this Katie, seemed to shore him up. He sounded calmer, somehow. More settled. He phoned home more often, the calls often at Katie's instigation. She was medical, too, but their points of communion seemed to go beyond simply the professional. Her son might be remaking himself as an Englishman but Lusi knew he had a Tugan soul, and he seemed to be reclaiming a part of it with Katie, kayaking, foraging, getting out of the city. Lusi began to hear less about jazz clubs and fancy food, and more about camping holidays and day trips to windswept English beaches. This child-sized woman apparently pitched tents and started fires, and even from thousands of miles away, Lusi had been inclined to approve of her. And then, long after Lusi had accepted the island mother's proud sorrow, this girl had not only encouraged Dan to move home, but had worked the miracle by offering to come with him.

It had therefore been Lusi who had suggested the old Cole place, Lusi who had suggested Dan renovate it so that the walls gleamed with fresh whitewash and the kitchen was twice the size and better equipped than any she herself could have dreamed of. No matter. She could never envy the woman who brought her son back to Tuga de Oro. As a possible insight into Katie's future assimilation, the new vet had given Lusi no little angst, going around asking everybody if they knew any old family recipes for cooking tortoise, and wondering if Sylvester sold acetone nail-polish remover. Sylvester had, miraculously, produced from beneath the counter a dusty, serviceable sachet of non-acetone remover wipes, but Charlotte had apparently said no, thank you, these were not "fit for purpose," and had gone away disappointed. A girl that fussed about her manicure would not last long.

Dan had made money in England and now Lusi, intensely frugal on her own behalf, intended he spend it. Katie would need active and early support to build an island life. She would need wooing, and Lusi would woo with ceiling fans and a deep freeze. British girls didn't move to Tuga very often.

But so far this other British girl had little of the FFA about her. She surprised Lusi by asking to drive the ancient Defender that had once belonged to Johannes, and straight from Up Yard she took herself, directed by Dan from the back seat, on a whistle-stop tour of the island, negotiating over sand and gnarled roots as if she'd been driving off-road her whole life (which it later turned out that she had). They went through Lemon Tree Valley and out to the Lakes and all the way round across Princess Creek, after which Katie then navigated back to Town without further direction. Lusi turned and raised her eyebrows at Dan, who was positively incandescent with pride.

In Lusi's house they drank saloop, and Katie continued to be surprising.

"It's not really my sort of flavor," she said, with refreshing frankness, setting down the teacup, "but I know saloop is important here so I'm sure I'll learn to like it. Do you like it?"

Lusi, who had never before considered the question, found herself admitting that in fact she preferred coffee but no one ever offered it to her.

"You'll have nice coffee in our house, Dan is a very good barista," Katie told her, and Lusi felt a sharp stab of envy. It would take her time to know her adult son. Teenage Dan had not liked coffee, before he left. She forced herself to suppress this rising competitive energy, for it did not represent the elegance on which she had determined.

"I don't think Dan has told me much about your family. You grew up on a farm?"

"Yes. I moved from Bristol to a farm in Wales when I was six. My mother joined a cult."

Lusi paused, saloop at her lips. She couldn't help but shift her gaze to Dan, but he was looking only at Katie. If he felt his mother's eyes upon him, he did not respond.

"I lived on their farm till I was eighteen. It was a bit complicated. As cults go, I suppose it could have been worse but it wasn't ideal. I learned a lot, though, even if it wasn't very enjoyable. I've been driving a tractor since I was a child. I can start a fire with a bow drill."

Lusi nodded, unable to reply. So much was other. Bristol; Wales; kite-surfing; cults. Katie filled the silence.

"My mother is still there. I didn't get to school very often but I did some online courses, and then one day I went away to study physiotherapy and never went back again. It wasn't a very healthy place to be, really. Before he left England Dan offered to go with me to say goodbye, and I did consider it, but us going there wouldn't turn her into the sort of person who'd suddenly care about good-byes, so in the end we didn't. I don't think she will miss me much. She takes a lot of drugs, and has a lot of dysfunctional sex."

Lusi nodded again. Would she nod forever? Possibly. Now that she thought about it, Dan had said something about a complicated family setup, independent very young, self-motivated, but Lusi had not wanted to pry. She began to calculate. Katie was only twenty-five now—seven years ago she had escaped from a cult.

In the abstract all this foreignness might be threatening. But Lusi didn't feel threatened, she felt hopeful. The girl was forthright and forthcoming, competence embodied. Lusi would not exactly be gaining a daughter, she saw, for this girl did not invite mothering. Indeed she almost repelled it somehow, for her self-possession was extraordinary. But she did invite ease, and a sort of Quaker egalitarianism.

Dan stood, and announced that he was taking Katie to see her new home, and thanked his mother, kissing her warmly on both cheeks. Katie bobbed beside him in a cheerful curtsey, and invited Lusi to please join them for coffee in the morning. Lusi put her shoes back on and went next door to tell Saul and Moz the good news.

34

Dan and Katie had left his mother's and were back in the Defender heading to the old Cole place—their own house, finally, for some much-needed time alone—when Uncle Saul appeared in the rear-view mirror in the ambulance, and turned on the siren. Dan pulled over and Saul hurried to the window, introduced himself to Katie, and segued immediately into a heartfelt and urgent plea for them to join the biosecurity team dealing with the Island Open cargo. It had to be now, this moment, as fast as they could get back to the lighters and onto the ship. Something had gone wrong.

It was just as well Katie liked to hit the ground running, Dan thought with a kind of despair, as he drove back in the direction they had come, for he had barely reclaimed her when she was swept from him by unstoppable island forces. But far from disappointed, Katie was almost gleeful that their reunion had been hijacked by a turn of events so classically Tugan. This enchantment with bureaucratic idiosyncrasy would make her the perfect FFA.

Harbour Street was closed but Saul declared it an emergency, so Dan parked at the water, where they climbed back into a lighter, returning to the ship from which Katie had only just disembarked. Saul led them down to the hold, where they found a very dirty and extremely irritable Charlotte Walker, wearing a white coat and stabbing her finger at some writing on a clipboard. She was speaking with great animation to a man who appeared to be the captain. Dan heard her before he saw her, and felt a kind of panic that she continued inconveniently to exist, now that Katie had arrived and his torments on that front were supposed to be over. He had known Katie and Charlotte must meet—everyone on Tuga met, sometimes twice a day—but he longed for Katie to be securely restored to her place in his understanding of his own life before it happened. He was also feeling a rising sense of guilt about whatever was unfolding on this ship, because this was supposed to be his responsibility. Several weeks ago, Saul had asked Dan to take over the superintendence of cargo and Dan, who had felt relief at the thought of a job he was finally able to accomplish without objection from islanders, had nonetheless asked to be let off working on this first ship, to be free to greet Katie. Then the hurricane had interposed, with its attendant drama, and Dan had all but forgotten about the surge of public-health administration that was engendered by the arrival of any vessel. Obviously when Dan said no, Saul had palmed off this inspection to Charlotte.

"But I've already said that," Charlotte was saying loudly. "Either I condemn every single vegetable and fruit on this ship, or you'll do it my way."

"What's going on?" Dan asked.

"She told him there are flies in the hold," said Saul.

Charlotte spun on her heel at the sound of Saul's voice echoing through the low corridor. A sequence of expressions crossed her face when she saw Dan standing with Katie, but then she appeared to recall herself.

"Sorry, I didn't *tell him* there are flies in the hold, there *are flies* in the hold. As a minimum the ship needs to be properly fitted with fly traps and LED zappers, and they should have sprayed two days out of Uruguay and two days away from Tuga."

"Is not protocol," said the captain sulkily.

"Well, it will be protocol when I've written my report," Charlotte snapped. To Saul she said, "You know, I was not exactly top of the class in my Public Health module but God, I know enough to recognize a bloody mess when I see one, and this ship is a mess. And obviously I said yes when you asked for my help because I cannot think of anything more important to an isolated island than biosecurity. I've literally come to work on island conservation, I get that, but I cannot"—here she rounded again on the captain, who had been attempting to sneak away—"I cannot be asked to do a job and then do a shitty job. I won't do a shitty job. It makes me wild to think of what would have happened if I'd not come down here. Do you not actually care? Do you just let in a new random invasive species to colonize vulnerable island habitats with every single arrival?"

The captain reassured her that he did care, that it was not his regular practice to create ecological catastrophes at every port, but that what she was asking was not a reasonable request. They had been at sea a fortnight, and he had promised his own crew shore leave.

What Charlotte wanted them to do was to empty and inspect every tray of fruit in the hold, repacking what was acceptable piece by piece to take ashore, condemning and disposing of anything contaminated. Saul knew that she was right. The last thing the island needed was the introduction of non-native flies. That was, after all, the whole point of the inspection. But at the same time he had the irrational sense that roping in fastidious Charlotte Walker had somehow led to the appearance of these flies. No other inspector, himself included, had ever had such zeal—crates were stacked floor to ceiling in a hold the size of the Old Kal. It would be many hours of work and a lot of produce lost. Saul wondered whether he would have been so meticulous, and felt relieved that he had outsourced a particularly difficult inspection. He was also feeling preemptive sorrow for the now-threatened punnets of chestnut mushrooms, of which he had been dreaming for weeks.

Katie stepped forward and crossed to Charlotte. "Katie," she said, extending a hand. Charlotte indicated her blue surgical gloves, and instead offered a minute arc of a wave with a hand that held a biro.

"We're here now," Katie said. "We've come to be your team. Put us to work."

"Well. I won't worry now I'm in such *capable hands*," said

Charlotte, thrusting at Katie a pair of gloves of her own, and Katie smiled back at Dan, who felt briefly queasy.

And that was it, for hours. Dan and Katie and Saul and a thunderous Charlotte formed a miniature production line, turning over sweet potatoes under bright torches, stacking and sorting broccoli, while the ship's crew went ashore to do what was also vital to Tuga de Oro—for rare day visitors to spend their money in Betsey's Cafe and the Rockhopper, to buy souvenirs for their children and stamps for their uncles and moshav knitting for their wives.

"I wish I'd known this needed doing down here when we were all those weeks at sea," Katie said cheerily, slitting open the plastic wrap on a tray of apples with a fuchsia penknife that had been, startlingly, already in her pocket. "I was basically the only passenger who didn't get seasick, it would have been great to have something to do."

35

There were many things Charlotte felt she would have liked to find, waiting for her at home. A shower that actually had some water pressure. The vast, arresting kitchen bed magically restored upstairs, so that she was no longer lurched into wakefulness by the intermittent helicopter whirring of the ancient fridge two feet away from her head. A dog to curl up with—a sleek, long-nosed whippet, perhaps, or the huge, steady reassurance of a wolfhound.

What she did not need to find was Levi digging again, this time a series of enormous holes next to her front steps and down one entire flank of the house, so that her perfect little Tugan refuge now resembled a building site and, for some reason, smelled like a farmyard. She had been trying—trying so hard it was pathetic, she feared—to win Levi's forgiveness. The degree of discomfort she felt that he had moved away from her had taken her by surprise. It contracted her chest when she thought of it. He had not yet spoken to her with any warmth or even much interest since the hurricane fiasco, and Levi without a single obscene or even a suggestive comment was a somber being. She missed him. She missed talking to him, she missed being near him. She missed his common sense, his opinions, and every day had felt the absence of his usually ready smile.

Now, overwrought and exhausted, Charlotte was already on the verge of tears, furious with Captain Rodríguez, Saul Gabbai, Dan Zekri; furious with the flies, and furious especially with that smug and maddening Katie Salmon, with her practicality and her *helpfulness* and her relentless *good humor*, not to mention her excessive sea-hardiness. Nonetheless, she tried to compose herself and sat down on the steps beside Levi, to try one last time. He seemed to be connecting his holes into a deep trench, and to be filling this trench with what smelled very much like sun-warmed goat dung. Beside him was another full wheelbarrow. The front steps were covered with a fine layer of dust.

"What are you doing?" she asked lightly.

"Painting my nails, Dolittle."

"Planting something?"

"Seedlings in from the ship. Don't need 'em now, but I ordered them months ago and they'll die if I don't get them in, so—" He stopped talking, and looked up at her, steadily. "Can I help you with anything?"

Charlotte was stung, and after a day of what had felt like extended humiliation, trying to focus on vegetable inspection while Katie and Dan canoodled, it was close to the final straw. She had been longing for solitude all day, and now even her beloved little refuge was polluted. In the heat, the smell of the manure was overpowering. She drew herself up.

"Yes, actually. I didn't see your seedlings on the import list."

"I ain't got time for all that, I had a friend bring them over, he's crew. How's that your business, Dolittle? Tortoise work slowing down, you joined the police force now?"

"Saul put me in charge of biosecurity of this ship."

"It ain't weed, if that's what you're worried about. Or weeds."

"All non-native imports need declaring. You can't just go rogue and make random individual decisions to plant whatever you want, that's just not how islands work."

Levi sat back on his haunches, and pushed his hair from his face with a forearm, his hands encrusted with dirt. He looked up at her, dark eyes narrowed.

"You know what, Dolittle, I ain't got the time for this, or the energy. I'm sorry if it ain't all to your satisfaction, if you haven't been able to come to Tuga and teach us all *how islands work*. Best you get on back to London and let us primitive islanders get on with screwing up our own place, OK? Because at the end of the day, you get your little knickers in a twist about how we ain't committed to planting enough native plants, or whatever, but in the meanwhile we got bigger fish to fry, right here, we got our own real lives. Maybe one day a ship don't come, or two ships don't come, or someone come on shore with a virus that kills half our elderly who ain't never been exposed to it before, or a hurricane blow the roof off the schoolhouse and we gotta pay for a new one. So if I'm planting something here that, by the way, I happen to know ain't going to spread anywhere I don't choose to put it, ain't going to invade anything, whatever, forgive me if I didn't see the need to prioritize the paperwork, I had some other stuff to do. It's bright pink bougainvillea, by the way, to climb up the side of the house. Want to go back and report me now? Or you just want me to throw them in the compost, would that make you feel better?"

Charlotte, who had felt a mounting pressure in her throat during this speech, now found herself entirely unable to answer. She shook her head, rose, and went inside, where she turned on some very loud music so that Levi would not hear that she was crying. All in all, it had been a very bad day.

36

Dan had left her bags in the car and he had carried her, his light, laughing Katie, over the threshold of the old Cole house and straight up the stairs to bed, where she had been gratifyingly enthused by his attentions, and gratifyingly responsive to his own needs. Other silences might sometimes fall between them, other differences of temperament or outlook, but he and Katie had always been sexually compatible, not least because her own frankness and ease made possible his own.

He had always felt a sort of disbelief, watching Katie move through the world. She seemed almost not to understand embarrassment, rendering it a pointless feeling in her presence. She was never self-conscious, and so far proved impossible to shock, for she worked on the simple assumption that all human feelings have been, and will be again. Her own aspirations were quiet ones—monogamy in a house she hoped never to leave; a belief in God, which Dan, raised a Tugan atheist, found alien and charming; a steady career doing good in a community small enough to build meaningful relationships. She loved children but never wanted her own, a conviction that had surprised Dan when he'd learned of it, and later he had understood that this surprise was mostly because of the ways in which she herself seemed childlike: the high voice; the affinity for pink and sparkles; the pencil case filled with glitter gel pens, so that her case notes resembled the diary pages of a twelve-year-old. Her determination to bestow the benefit of the doubt; the way that her face remained in a preparatory smile of appreciation as she listened to a story, often before comprehension had dawned: these things too made her seem younger than she was.

Katie seemed to Dan the embodiment of wholesomeness and what he thought of, nebulously, as "family values." Yet when she spoke of her upbringing she made casual, unblinking reference to orgies and overdoses; to car theft and internecine feuds in the farming collective of her childhood. These memories were related without apparent distress and mostly without judgment, but they came up in conversation rarely, and only when prompted by an immediate relevance. She had formed, it seemed, in opposition to them.

In general Katie was not a talker. If she had a hard day at work she did not want to come home and analyze it but preferred, she once told him, something that took her out of the prison of her head and into the playground of her body. This could be kite-surfing or circuit-training, though her preference was often sex. Regarding the lithe, strong, responsive body in question, Dan was both happy to facilitate, and impressed by a woman with the self-knowledge to have found a way out of one of life's darker corners. He himself was a talker, he came to realize, and occasionally he wished for a partner who took an interest in motivation or subtext, her own or anyone else's. He had not mentioned the children thing to his mother, and when intermittently it bothered him, he was very quickly distracted from it. Katie wished instead to improve the lives of the children and mothers already in the world, and that seemed a sufficiently valuable commitment for which to sacrifice a family of his own.

Now, with Katie back in his arms for the first time in almost six months, he felt he had been returned to sanity from some sort of island fugue. Perhaps sexual frustration had been all that had been wrong with him. Charlotte had been near, Katie had been far, six months was a long time, and that was all. Katie's wisdom had been far away, along with the rest of her. He should have known to pay less heed to his busy and destructive brain, which of late had cooked up all sorts of sabotage and scandals. He had been wrong to be temporarily seduced by the fantasy of a woman who would whisper with him through the night and laugh, and listen. If Katie wasn't an elaborate conversationalist, if she did not believe in touching with talk, in closeness through understanding, it was hardly a grand flaw. There were other intimacies. He should learn to live more fully in his body, which responded entirely to this woman who lay beside him, at ease with her rhythms, at home in her certainty. He wanted to hike with her and climb with her and sail with her and sleep with her. In short, he wanted a life with Katie. He lay back, in what was now their bed, on their faded rose-sprigged sheets, the ones that had been on her bed when first she'd brought him home in another life altogether. On the bedside tables the same framed photographs of one another in brass frames; above them her black-and-white print of nuzzling elephants that had hung in the same position in their old flat. Katie made right the oddity of these precisely transplanted objects. He felt at peace, for the first time in weeks. On the window ledge stood a jug of the wild calla lilies he'd picked on the roadside to welcome her home and as he fell asleep he gazed at their silhouette and thought with pride of Tuga's beauty, of her clear skies, her sweeping beaches. He was lucky, and now Katie had come and he had all he could possibly need.

37

A few weeks after Island Open, Garrick received a note.

Garrick. Come at four p.m. this afternoon. Urgent. Mary Philips

Moz handed the letter back to Garrick.

"I don't know how you can stand going there every week, Joanie, that woman is without charm. Who's she to go summoning people, what if they had somewhere else to be?"

"I'm not sure she'd consider that a problem," Garrick told her, folding the letter and putting it back into his shirt pocket. Joan refilled Moz's cup from the squat brown teapot.

"Does she write to you like this?" Moz demanded.

"She doesn't write to me." Joan gave a placid smile and sat down again. "I just pop by on a Thursday morning."

"But why?"

"Oh, I'm sort of a—a news agency. Or a town crier. I've told you, Mary likes to know what's happening."

"If she bothered to be nice to other people here, she wouldn't need a weekly news bulletin, she could get her gossip at Betsey's Cafe like the rest of us. I don't know how you got yourself into it, honestly. She's a vile old crone." Moz thunked two coconut sugar crystals into her tea with the tongs. "Do you know what she's given to the school in all the decades I've been asking her? With all her money and nothing at all to do with it, she's given not one penny. Not a pack of coloring pencils. All those children sharing a single computer, everyone else giving and giving who can hardly spare it, Island Council with less in the bank than she carries in her handbag, and she doesn't care that we've had no new schoolbooks since the donor gave that last load five years ago. She should be ashamed to show her face."

Then to Garrick, "So will you go? I suppose you must."

"I must take responsibility for the needs of all the flock," said Garrick, rather pompously, and Moz mumbled something about Grand Mary being more wolf than sheep, and then lost interest and began to ask Joan whether she should be using a size-eight needle to bind off on a brioche stitch, or a size six. Garrick was eyeing a second slice of *pastel de nuez*, when Joan nodded towards the clock. He rose to his feet without enthusiasm, and reached for his baseball cap.

"Steal something expensive," Moz called after her brother, helping herself to the cake.

It was many years since Garrick had been inside Martha House. Inside, the high-ceilinged hallway was light and cool, reminiscent of the reception rooms of Customs House, where, if the committee could ever mobilize without Ruth to direct them, there would one day be the Tuga de Oro Museum. Mary stumped ahead of him and he followed, suddenly curious about this formal and increasingly shabby anachronism into which his wife disappeared every Thursday morning. Joan would be familiar with these now-chipped black-and-white floor tiles, the botanical drawings in thin gilt frames, and over there, above a blush-shaded, tassel-hung table lamp, a small charcoal portrait of a marble-eyed and presumably long-dead Persian cat. Garrick had been to England; while in London he had been inside other, far grander homes: Regency stucco, ornamental oranges, tall steps of Portland stone, towering columns, old servants' bells. He had lived, though others might not know it of him. But this was not England. A transplanted facsimile was uncanny.

Mary led him, as he'd hoped, to the library. Here were the fabled bookshelves floor to ceiling, their treasures behind tall glass doors, protected from the ravenous destructive island elements. He had been brusque when Charlotte Walker had tried to speak to him about this private collection, not wanting to mention that the Williams household alone were its beneficiaries, for Joan often came back from her visits to Mary with a book she had been quietly permitted to borrow. No one else took too much notice of Mary's reputedly unsurpassed collection of local writings. Paperbacks were portals; most ordinary Tugans did not see much sense in burrowing still further into Tuga when they might travel elsewhere between the pages. They had no need of their own island history, nor an anthropological study of their own wedding rituals, nor a record of their own farming calendar; they were too busy living it. Betsey's book club would much rather read about handsome Argentinian polo players. Taxi and Sylvester shared a passion for the biographies of famous cricketers.

It was an unwelcome development to find that Charlotte Walker herself had been invited to this mysterious encounter and was already sitting prim in a wingbacked linen chair, a notebook open on her knees. She looked slightly manic, he thought, and wondered what had preceded this meeting. Mary had never before been known to relent, when asked a favor.

Mary sat down heavily in an armchair, and Garrick took a seat on the edge of the sofa.

"I've changed my mind about this library," Mary said, without preamble, and without offering them a drink. "It's never been properly catalogued and Dr. Walker has agreed to make a list of what's here, in exchange for limited access to the texts. While we have a scholar here, she can make herself useful."

Charlotte's mouth opened and her pen raised a little, as if she was about to ask for permission to speak, but then she lowered it again and said nothing.

"I'm not having an FFA left to her own devices," Mary went on, "so you have to supervise. I don't want her in my house without your eyes on her, do you hear?" She spoke to Garrick like a schoolboy whose detention she was enforcing, and as if Charlotte wasn't there at all. "Make sure everything goes on the list, and stays where it should."

It was money alone that gave her this authority, Garrick thought. Money that insulated her against need of anyone's kindness or goodwill. Her vast fortune had been accumulated very fast and in some opaque business that had taken place off-island and many years ago. Various theories circulated. She had traded copper. She had pulled off a con. She had smuggled or money-laundered, or trafficked captive women. She had been the secret mistress of a millionaire, this last dismissed because no one could imagine Mary attempting to please anyone except herself. In the absence of a single concrete fact it was all just as likely, or unlikely.

"I shall have to run it past Joan," Garrick said, but Mary flapped a hand back and forth, as if shooing away a fly.

"Joan will say yes. She'll clear your diary."

Charlotte had been mute throughout this exchange. Perhaps, having achieved her victory, she was afraid to jeopardize it. Her eyes were narrowed with focus, and she was scanning each shelf that was close enough to read.

"Monday," said Mary. "Come at eight."

Garrick's irritation was further enflamed when he went home later, longing for a quiet talk with Joan, only to find his wife looking ashen with fatigue, and yet deep in conversation with an unknown woman, who turned out to be Dan Zekri's recently arrived fiancée. She seemed friendly and cheerful enough, and had come with gifts of Marks & Spencer's tea, and shortbread in a tin shaped like a London bus. But she outstayed her welcome and asked far too many questions, presuming an intimacy with the islanders that Garrick found distasteful. She mentioned Ruth dos Santos, whose situation was certainly none of her business. Garrick and Joan quietly coordinated a network of neighbors who checked on Marianne, who helped with the heavier work in the garden, or found errands for the children, lightening Marianne's burden wherever they could, but

Ruth and Marianne were both intensely private, and the Ruth that he remembered would not have wished her troubles to be aired to this small, presumptuous Katie person. When Garrick said something to this effect, Katie had merely shrugged with easy acceptance, and gone on to ask Joan for assistance arranging a space for people to gather to perform something called Zumba, and that was the final nail in her coffin, where Garrick was concerned. The introduction of newfangled religious rituals was the last thing Tuga needed.

He'd had quite enough of all these various meddling FFA, behaving in new and unpredictable ways, all of which seemed to exhaust his endlessly tolerant wife. He would talk to Moz about whether a volunteer might be found to take over some of Joan's community responsibilities. Joan needed rest, some peace and quiet in which to recuperate. But Joan had been thrilled when she learned that Charlotte had been granted access to the library and she did, indeed, tell him he must do it. She added quietly that he needn't worry, she would clear his diary.

38

Recently Charlotte had lost her focus. She had allowed herself to be discombobulated, and as a result her research had slipped. But now she had brief access to Mary's library, and would not allow a single maddening Tugan to distract her from making the most of it. Not Dan. Not Levi. Not any of the dotty and irritating farmers who called her far too late to their veterinary emergencies, described an incomprehensible local condition ("real bad case of *guzanikos*, Dr. Vet"), and then wasted hours more of her time, making her stay for a barbecue. *Effing Tugans*, she thought, taking childish relish in the profanity of which the effing Tugans themselves would disapprove. She would seize back control of her time, and her mind. She would make headway with the tortoises if it killed her.

A suspicion was forming, some instinctive thesis taking shape, that the korason palms might be dependent upon the gold coins for not only dispersal but propagation, for she no longer thought it a coincidence that these endemic trees now grew only in tortoise territory. Tortoises were known dispersal vectors for many seeds, but she had begun to wonder if their digestive enzymes might not be essential for the korason seeds in particular to germinate. Germination was slow; any experiment with digested versus non-digested seeds would still have to be running long after she had left the island. She planned to email Kew Gardens to see what might be done in London, but first she wanted to learn what she could about the historical distribution of the korasons, versus the historical distribution of the gold coins. Mary's collection offered the only possible records on the island.

In the meantime she read papers about the germination of seed-lings from dung samples, and late at night in the vet's room investigated tortoise dung samples of her own, trying not to see it as a metaphor for her personal life. In the Rockhopper Levi would be humorless and unreachable behind the bar, while the unbearable Katie Salmon had a caper with every island man that asked her, and Dan looked on with nauseating admiration. Charlotte would have enjoyed telling all of them that she preferred to stay in with piles of reptile feces.

On Monday morning Charlotte and Garrick converged at the gates to Martha House. Charlotte was holding a lemon cake, wrapped in cellophane.

"What is that?"

"It's for Mary."

"She won't like that one bit."

"Why? Marianne says she orders one every week. I thought no one on the island paid visits empty-handed?"

"Unless you're visiting Mary. It's presumptuous. You wouldn't take a lemon cake to Buckingham Palace."

"Maybe I would," said Charlotte crossly, thrusting the crinkling package into her bag and shifting the straps back up her shoulder. She felt nervous with anticipation that something might yet go wrong.

Their exchange was cut short by Mary, whose quavering voice could be heard demanding that they come around, she had opened the French doors to the library. Charlotte made a detour to greet Martha, who was half in, half out of her large shallow water bowl in a shaded corner of the garden, huge dinosaur legs immobile, her body and shell tilted at what did not look a particularly comfortable angle. Her small head lifted up and out at the approach, inquisitive and serpentine. Charlotte studied the animal's expressive face and felt Martha's steady gaze, studying back. Supplementing her diet had reduced her need for endless random grazing, and there was no question that she had more energy. Charlotte bent to tickle the loose skin of Martha's neck and to sneak her a cube of raw butternut squash. Then she returned to Garrick's side, and they carried on around the building.

Grand Mary had opened all the glass cabinet doors and had begun arbitrarily to pull out some of the lower books. Precarious stacks of hardbacks rose on the previously clean-swept stone floor, and in the sunlight the air swirled with dust. Now she stood in the center of the room, like a sorceress in the eye of a storm she had summoned. A neatly ironed pile of cloths and an orange feather duster lay on a small side table. Charlotte coughed. Garrick reached for his handkerchief.

"Make a list, that's all, and do it fast. Then we see. Anything you want to borrow put here, so I can look at it." Then, to Garrick, Mary added, "You make sure nothing goes missing. I blame you if it does. And dust them before you put them back. It's time I had a list, it's important for the future."

"Yes, of course," Garrick appeared to spring to life, "if you plan to leave it to the island, which would be—"

"Who's leaving?" Mary snapped and shuffled out, mumbling something about coffee midmorning. Garrick and Charlotte stared at one another in heavy silence.

"Well. Do you make a habit of stealing books?"

Charlotte glared at him, though not even old misery-guts Garrick could dampen her rising joy.

"Very well. Then I do not see that this exercise in fact requires my active participation. I shall be in the doorway with work of my own."

He disappeared into the yard beyond, and moments later Charlotte heard the scrape of a chair as Garrick turned his back to the sun.

Charlotte felt the same stirrings of surprise she'd felt the last time she'd been in this library, and wondered once again about the strange old woman whose capacity for empathy seemed never to have enlarged, despite the worlds she must have traveled, the lives she must have lived between all these thousands of dusty pages. Charlotte's eye had been drawn to the shelves of battered Penguins, their muted pumpkin spines stretching for what must amount to two meters, maybe three—all worn, all seemingly read, many of them first editions simply by virtue of how long ago Mary had begun her collection. Charlotte thought of the sorry and swollen titles in the public library, mostly accumulated when rare tourists abandoned or donated what they'd brought. Three copies of *Gone with the Wind*, and no Dickens. She'd have packed all her paperbacks, if she'd known.

She moved on from the Penguins and found herself facing the Tugan section. Alone, finally, with the hidden treasures for which she had traveled, quite literally, halfway around the globe. She knew that Cook had tried and failed to land in both 1771 and 1775. In 1836 the HMS *Beagle* had also been unable to anchor in the treacherous waters and had gone on to St. Helena, taking with it the young naturalist Charles Darwin. That was tantalizing, though it had been a foolhardy attempt, for it was July, and already Island Close. But one naturalist or another must have made it on shore and written about what he'd found. Here were histories the British Library listed as "mislaid"; bound and loose-leaf collections of letters; stories and diaries and personal accounts; mimeographs of a long-defunct island newspaper published through the 1930s and 1940s. Charlotte ran the tips of her fingers along dusty spines. No one had touched any of them for decades. On one shelf Mary had collected the logs of fishing boats recording each catch, each storm, each small repair. Charlotte's months on Tuga had taught her more than she'd realized, for in just a few words she could see these ancestors with their weather-beaten faces, hauling in nets hand over roughened hand, roaring out that wonderful, twisting melody, a Ladino sea shanty, in a minor key. Late one night Sylvester had played one on the accordion, sung with an unexpected clear beauty by Elsie, and much of the Rockhopper had then joined in with equal enthusiasm, if not equal talent.

Charlotte picked up the top volume on one of Mary's teetering piles and found, in tidy copperplate, in brown ink, recipes for a traditional Tugan wedding dinner; she felt in the tight loops and flourishes all the angst and hope of the mother as she wrote, documenting the feast with which she would launch a daughter's future. And even this cookery book might hold clues. Gold coins had regularly been eaten in the early years. Indeed, it was probably as a food source that they'd been brought to the island in the first place but no one she'd asked had known, nor seemed to care, particularly. All Charlotte could surmise was that someone had carried the gold coins' earliest ancestors to Tuga, probably from the Amazon Basin, home now to the yellow-footed *Chelonoidis denticulatus* and red-footed *Chelonoidis carbonarius*. To the best of her knowledge, no gold coin tortoises remained outside of Tuga, and the small population was a true relic. But when had they come? How many? How had their grazing altered the ecosystem over the centuries? How central were they to Tugan korason, and how many were needed to maintain a healthy botanical status quo? How had their numbers expanded and contracted over the years, and why? Somewhere here, surely, lay the answers to the lineage and history of these tortoises. And—it was hard to extinguish even the most unlikely hope—maybe as she read, she might even uncover a clue to her own mysterious lineage.

A shadow over his papers made Garrick raise his head.

"I need you. They've all got weevils, or something, it's horrible."

"What has?"

"Oh, just come, please! One whole shelf of manuscripts. That right wall is intact, as far as I can tell, but the lower shelves on the left have got something terrible going on. Oh, just get up!"

"What are you talking about? Stop shouting, for goodness' sake."

Garrick squinted up at her, shielding his eyes. Martha, who had come to stand beside him like a dutiful coffee table, did not like the shouting either. Her shell creaked as she shifted hugely, and with small dips and bobs her head began slowly to retract into the loose folds of her neck. Charlotte placed a soothing hand on her warm carapace.

"Show me," Garrick said.

"I am. Look."

Charlotte extended towards him a thick volume bound in gilt-stamped dark green leather, and he took it.

"Not over your—lap," she finished, too late, for he had already opened the covers and a rain of ashy fragments drifted down on to his trousers, and on to a half-written sermon. A second later what remained of the pages detached from the spine and fell with a soft whump.

"My God. How much is like this?"

"A whole shelf so far, but then I stopped and came for you. Oh, God, what a waste." She was actually wringing her hands. "Entomology's really not my thing, I've been looking to see if I can catch one red-handed but I really have no idea what sort of pest has done this—"

Garrick rose, and began brushing the dust and paper fragments from his dark trousers.

"It's probably silverfish, it will need treating. She should have let me in here years ago."

"I didn't know you'd ever asked. Shall I get Mary?"

"Not yet, hold your horses, let's figure out the size of the problem. We can sort it out."

The problem was considerable but confined, at least for now, to one set of shelves. Mary had earlier threatened them with a coffee break and so they were working against the clock, trying to ascertain the extent of the damage before she returned. In the end they managed to identify precisely where it began and stopped, laying out the volumes in neat rows. Charlotte wondered if there was any large newspaper lying around, to which Garrick replied that if he had possession of anything so precious as a broadsheet, he would not go wasting it on silverfish.

They agreed to isolate the infested books from those that seemed intact. Any cataloguing or rearrangement was now impossible. Nothing could be moved unless to quarantine the clean from the infected; everything would need checking, dusting, laying systematically in the sunshine.

"Well, now you can't stop until you've fixed it," was all Mary said when they told her. She thumped down a tray, on which was a small cafetière, two not very clean cups, and no milk. Charlotte was ravenous with adrenaline and angst, and thought with sudden gratitude about the lemon cake still in her bag. She waited impatiently for Grand Mary to retreat. Garrick said Mary wasn't to go to any trouble, he would go home for coffee and elevenses, and Mary told him sharply that she had already gone to quite a lot of trouble as he could well see, and there was good coffee right here. Garrick sat obediently back down on the sofa, and poured out two cups. Mary withdrew.

"It's priceless, all of it."

"It's about damage limitation."

"Shall we call someone? Who's best with pest control?"

Garrick shook his head. "I don't trust anyone else to do it. I don't want someone coming in here and soaking it all with insecticide."

"I'll go to the clinic, I'll have a look online. The sun should do something, I'd imagine. Kill the larvae."

"Yes. But what else will it do?"

"We'll have to just hope."

And on they talked, staccato exchanges in their new camaraderie, a temporary truce called now they were united in battle against a common enemy. They shared Charlotte's lemon cake outside in the shade, and Charlotte explained the need to be meticulous about fallen crumbs, guarding Martha against excess sugar. Garrick nodded his approval, and checked beneath his chair.

Charlotte met Martha's steady dark gaze, and felt understanding pass between them.

"Sitting in London, it seemed so obvious that the gold coins needed urgent study, to protect the entire island's ecosystem." Charlotte addressed this to Martha, who gave an appearance of listening, her head cocked, her eyes fixed upon Charlotte's face. Also watching Martha with a fond expression, Garrick gave no indication he was paying attention, but Charlotte went on, mostly to herself. "I know you think I've got my priorities wrong but it's not just species preservation for the sake of it, that isn't the way conservation works anymore, or it shouldn't be. It's truly because I think their extinction would have island-wide consequences for local stakeholders—for humans. I think the korason palms might need the tortoises, for one example. But then just when I think, right, today I'm going to the jungle, then I think, well, there's also the farms, the dependent livelihoods, the beloved dogs, and that's all work that needs doing now, today, yesterday if possible. And the biosecurity! And now a whole cultural resource, literally being eaten. Everything here is so—high stakes. There is so much to do." She glanced up at Garrick, who was stroking his chin in the manner of an ancient sage.

"To be needed is one of life's honors," Garrick intoned, with a distinct note of disapproval. He appeared to believe Charlotte had been complaining, rather than observing. "Work of meaning. We are called to help."

"I know. I like helping, that wasn't my point. Though I must say, to be 'called' sounds religious."

"Called by conscience," Garrick corrected.

"Is that the god of humanism? Conscience? I'm not sure I want the responsibility of creating my own ethical system all the time."

"My conscience is my unfailing guide in all affairs," said Garrick pompously, frowning, and with that dissolved the fine threads of connection that had begun to pass between them while they worked. Charlotte stood, and Martha began to turn ponderously, to return to her wallowing pool in the shade, and some fresh tamarind leaves. Garrick was looking after Martha, meditative. Then he rose to follow Charlotte back into the library.

"Did you say that you think the korason trees need the tortoises?"

Charlotte picked up a duster. "I think they might, to germinate, I'm not sure. Endozoochory."

"So you're saying we need tortoises in order to make saloop."

"If I'm right then yes, exactly."

"Oh, I must say I think that sounds fanciful." Garrick crossed his arms, marking a firm close to the conversation, and regarded the stained and peeling wood of the now-empty shelves. "Perhaps while it's all out, Mary should get Levi Mendoza in here to see if he can get the doors to fit better."

Charlotte exhaled, louder than she'd intended. Fanciful was precisely what science wasn't. "Fanciful" was just an old man's word for science practiced by a young woman, whose conclusion he disliked. And Levi was just about the last colleague she wished to add to this silverfish-fighting squad.

"What?"

"Nothing. Nothing. Just—why is this entire island obsessed with Levi Mendoza?"

"Who on earth is obsessed with Levi Mendoza?"

"It's Levi this, Levi that. He's the bartender, the landlord, the odd-job man. He's the most—*ubiquitous* man I've ever met."

Garrick looked at her shrewdly. "You don't need to sit at the bar drinking fizzycan every evening."

"It's to get a sense of the island," said Charlotte, somewhat hotly. She was surprised Garrick noticed anything she did. "And in any case I don't do that anymore."

"Indeed. That is probably wise. Shall we press on?"

39

There followed an unexpected week during which Garrick, who had looked forward to a few days of his own quiet work and reading in the sunshine, had been forced to roll up his sleeves. The books each needed assessing, airing, wiping, the shelves swept and dusted with a dry insecticide that then needed to be hoovered away again. Garrick and Charlotte developed a system, taking turns on this tedious production line, though it was an unspoken agreement between them that only Charlotte climbed the ladder. Charlotte relented a little, forgiving Garrick a degree of his pomposity when she heard him speak, at exhaustive length but with undeniable sincerity, about his desire to help the island.

"I don't know if you realize the unique series of cultural forces that shaped the secular egalitarianism of this island," he told Charlotte, who had read a great deal and so did, in fact, realize. "My founding Tugan ancestors were radicals, who demonstrated that reason and humanity are sufficient for an ethical, fulfilling life, without recourse to the supernatural."

"Yes," said Charlotte, who wished to avoid giving offense with accidental ignorance, and so avoided any direct response. "Hand me up the sprayer thing?"

"I'm no monarchist, you know," Garrick went on, "and I am pro-independence, in case you had wondered, although we've had self-governance since the departure of the last administrator, but I don't believe we will ever again have an entirely independent Tugan republic without a perpetual recommitment to our founding values, to our own interdependence, if you like. The past holds valuable lessons for the future."

The crisis with the silverfish seemed to have energized Garrick. He had been reading, he told Charlotte, about the use of ozone for pest eradication, and also about scanners. They lived in the tropics; bugs would come again, or moisture, or perhaps even one day a hurricane that razed the whole structure. The glass doors had been insufficient and the books were not disturbed with enough frequency to catch nascent problems. But the greatest threat was Mary Philips herself, capricious enough to build a bonfire if the fancy took her, contrary enough to revoke their access once she realized how much pleasure it was bringing. And as for later years, she had said often enough that she was leaving all her worldly possessions to Martha. They would have to be canny with Grand Mary.

"We must get it all on floppy disk," Garrick had said, frowning with uncomprehending disapproval when Charlotte failed to hide her smile at "floppy disk," and once it was scanned they could pursue other ambitions. He wondered whether she would spend some time with him at the Rupert Whitten Library, taking seriously that neglected and underfunded public resource in the same manner. She had occasioned a catalogue, after all. But if that became home to the "floppy disks," for example, more scholars might come. It was high time Tugans had a library of which they could be proud.

"It reeks," Charlotte told him. "And it hasn't got any windows."

"Yes, well. Not everywhere can be the Bodleian, Dr. Walker."

But this was said with better humor than usual, and Charlotte felt he had paid her a compliment by seeking to extend their collaboration. It did not seem the moment to point out that where Tugan volunteering was concerned, her dance card was already full of ailing livestock, and illegal cats.

40

It was remarkable how readily Katie had slipped into the rhythm of his Tugan life, which was surely all the reassurance Dan ought to need. She was up at dawn to swim or cycle before he had woken and then came ravenous to breakfast, wolfing down three poached eggs and a whole avocado on toast, her wet hair buttoned into a fuchsia microfiber-towel turban thing that otherwise lived on the radiator of every bathroom he'd shared with her. Her cheeks would be flushed with exercise, her eyes bright with enthusiasm for the challenge of the day ahead. She had a drive and hunger in her, for food, for experience, for knowledge. From the beginning he had loved being one of the things she wanted.

At eight they would step outside to meet Saul at the clinic, where Dan had begun to implement a few small changes. He tried to do this gently, so as not to provoke Saul. He'd scheduled a series of disaster planning meetings for the nursing staff, and added the rarely used ambulance to Queenie's list of cleaning jobs. Mornings were supposed to be for appointments, not that many people were making them, and then a coffee break at eleven a.m., and lunch with Katie at home from twelve-thirty until one-fifteen, unless they were making house calls. Dan took as many of these house calls as he could, for patients hid their disappointment better when Saul was far away in Town, rather than in the next room. Clinic ended at five, when Saul locked the doors again and set out for his regular rounds, none of which, apparently, could possibly be taken over by Dan. In the evenings Charlotte often let herself into the vet's room, Dan knew, but since Katie's arrival he was always sure to have left the building long before she came. He took as many of the emergency calls as Saul would release to him. He ran farther and more often, to reinforce his own community fitness messages, and to clear his head.

Katie insisted that they go to everything. She had not missed a hop at the Old Kal. She was a startling and terrible dancer, a fact Dan had known and forgotten. But Katie participated in all the traditional dances, and as a result was known by everyone in the room before the first of these nights was over. Dan was torn between mortification and admiration and wondered if his mother was experiencing a similar ambivalence, for she had more than once brought them each glasses of punch and suggested they might like to take some air. By the second hop he had prepared himself, reconciled to the fact that wherever there was dancing, Katie would dance. What he hadn't considered was that by then she had already been at work for a week, beginning upon their backlog of physio referrals, and was sparking connections of her own. Katie was whirled away from him, praised and cosseted and interviewed and sometimes challenged, but in all cases a subject of ferocious interest and examination. Dan stood against the wall and watched her, while the island swarmed. He had been offered congratulations for her on a daily basis. The key to contentment with Katie was straightforward, it seemed, and simply involved staying away from Charlotte.

"I've just come back with some iron tablets," Dan called, from the yard. He had popped in to see Isadora Davenport at home that morning, who was pale, and feeling weak and headachy. Dan had taken a blood sample, run it back to the clinic to analyze it himself, and now was returning, not much later, with the simple prescription. It was hugely satisfying to have the means to resolve a problem so fast and so entirely, knowing the old woman would feel better within days. There was something to be said for the simplicity of being a one-man general practitioner, phlebotomist, lab tech, and pharmacist.

"Come through here, Little Doc." Anwuli was standing in the doorway of her small barn, across the yard from the kitchen, her skirts tucked in her wellies, waving to attract his attention. "Isa's here, with Dr. Walker."

Of course Charlotte was here. She was everywhere. She had been at the moshav when he'd been there last Thursday, he to see a baby with a rash, she to see a lamb with paresis and ataxia, which she had diagnosed with a presumptive atlanto-occipital joint infection. By the time he arrived Charlotte had given the lamb an injection of dexamethasone and now after only four days of procaine penicillin it was well on the way to recovery. He knew all about its progress, because he had run into her every day since. She had also successfully sectioned triplet lambs (without calling him), and been positively high on the triumph even though, by her own admission, the stitching had not been a thing of beauty. And here she was with yet another recumbent sheep, whispering sweet nothings into its ear while drawing up a huge syringe. Isadora was sitting beside her on a stool in the corner of the pen, her stick across her knees, watching intently. Isadora and Anwuli had eight ewes, and could not afford to lose any. This one was heavily pregnant and in a bad way.

"Calcium borogluconate," Charlotte said when she saw Dan leaning on the gate. She seemed oddly perky for a vet kneeling over an animal that looked, to Dan's eye, half dead. The ewe's head was down, her expression glazed. "I'm fairly sure Cher has hypocalcemia. Milk fever. Watch this."

The sheep didn't even flinch at the injection, which seemed to Dan, used to injecting considerably smaller volumes, to go on for hours. But before Charlotte had withdrawn her needle the nostrils had begun to twitch; within moments the sick animal had lifted her head. They all remained silent, watching as the ewe got to her feet, swished her tail, urinated, and trotted back to the other side of the pen, where the flock of seven stood, impassive. Within moments Cher was indistinguishable from the others.

Charlotte was smiling to herself, still kneeling, packing away her instruments. Anwuli squeezed her shoulder.

"Would you look at that. Magic. Now, can you do that to Isa, Little Doc?"

"Ha ha, yes, wouldn't that be nice." The wind was rather out of Dan's sails. "Thankfully no milk fever for Isadora. These are your iron tablets, they should help with the shortness of breath, and the headaches. Not with dairy, please, so don't take them on a cup of tea or a saloop." To Charlotte he said, "So you're having absolutely nothing to do with lambing, then."

"Oh, it's only ad hoc." She was wiping her hands on a rag, but her eyes were blazing with pleasure and triumph. He watched her as she left the barn, and heard her singing as she washed up in the yard. For a theoretician, she was spending an awful lot of time on the farms, and it appeared to suit her, however little it suited him to see her everywhere. Then he noticed both old ladies were frowning at him, and recalled himself.

"Vitamin C helps absorption," he said brightly, "so some of Anwuli's etrog cordial to wash them down is perfect. You'll be as skippy as Cher the sheep in no time."

41

Ten years earlier

For a long time Martin Blackburn stood in the darkness of the yard. Two small, low houses were adjoined here at right angles. They were painted pale plum and robin's egg, respectively, but dusk had muted them to gray, so all he could see was that their slanted roofs were corrugated metal. Like a slum, he thought, or like living in a shipping container. Noisy in the rain, in any case, worse even than that hideous island thatch. Hellish.

The yard between them seemed to him a pitiful place. In the shadows he could not see the lush garden, nor the heavy fruit trees beyond it, nor the rich colors of the climbing spiderflowers, surging forth pale curling tendrils up the gateposts even as he stood beside them. Their night-scent filled his nostrils, but anxiety made his breaths shallow, and he did not notice the sweetness of the air. The buggy he had damaged was upended by the open front door, where someone had already begun upon an attempt to fix it. All of this— two cottages and the clean-swept dirt space between them—it would all fit within his own redbrick family home.

It had been a year and a half since he'd been in Tuga and it was as he remembered it. If anything he found it less believable this second time. The accents! There was still a picture of Queen Elizabeth II on many living-room walls, each in those god-awful frames they were all so proud of, decorated with chips of seashell. The tea dances. The hops. The aversion to what they quaintly called profanity so that even the dark, brawny men at work on the fishing boats would bellow, "*Guay de mi!*" if their catch got away. The Tugan independence movement was a joke—where did they think they'd be without British infrastructure? British healthcare? British education? And the British taxpayer, come to think of it, for Martin would not be surprised if a load of subsidies were needed to keep this infernal place even nominally functional.

The pub, if you could call it that, a hodgepodge secondhand furniture warehouse hung with stinking old fishing nets and serving whatever they had. A bewildering ethnic mix, another hodgepodge, that had been described to him as a few British traders, some Dutch or possibly Brazilian merchants (how could they not know the difference between a Dutchman and a Brazilian, for Christ's sake?), and then some Nigerian slaves and random passing Americans. Rarely did anyone seem to descend from just one of these groups, and surely by now on such a small island they were all marrying cousins, and where would that end up?

Back in London he had dominated dinner parties with his Tugan stories, describing the moonshine brewing in the pantries, the washing lines between mango trees hung with endless island-spun garments, or football kits representing cities the barefoot children would never visit, had probably never heard of. The dated hippie socialism. The generosity that bordered on aggression. His bags had been stuffed with local handicrafts, which he had then distributed liberally to his children, his cleaning lady and receptionist, together with some sort of printed guff about the local artisans. His youngest child had taken to a tortoise made in a walnut shell, until it had been chewed by the dog. Antimacassars. Christ, how did people live like this? Black rooftop water tanks heated only by the sun. Bugs and creepy crawlies and biting things, and the terrifying isolation and claustrophobia when all around the sea roiled and there was no way on or off, just water and sky and the purgatorial emptiness of that unbroken horizon.

Now he knocked, though the door stood ajar, and hearing a noise of assent he stepped inside. He had forgotten, if he'd ever known, that Tugan guests remove their shoes.

Marianne's arms closed more tightly around the baby at her breast. On the scrubbed-wood table were flowers, cakes, masapan, gifts, and tokens as if there had been a birthday. Or a bereavement, he thought. At the sight of the infant he felt a sudden contraction of fear in his bowels.

"I almost killed you. I can't stop seeing it. The pram flipped on its side. Christ."

"Not me. You almost killed Annie."

"Annie." Martin made an odd, strangled noise. "Ah. My eldest daughter is named Annie."

Marianne raised her head and looked at him for the first time. He was staring down at the draining board, where some white cotton Babygros were soaking in a blue washing-up bowl of diluted bleach. Marianne pulled her robe closer around her, though it was nothing he had not seen before.

"Well," she said. "So's your youngest."

The sweetness of the island girls had been the only reason Martin Blackburn had agreed to come back for this second visit. The weather was pure glory, but he was rarely left alone to enjoy it. The atmosphere was parochial and oppressive. He detested being greeted by name by strangers as he moved about his business in the town, and found their accent so peculiar that for a week, rather than the equally inexplicable "*Paz*," he had genuinely thought they were all saying "Pants." He was irritated by the way that even the most trivial information seemed to pass by immediate osmosis between island-ers, like so many jolly and accommodating Midwich Cuckoos.

He'd worked longer and longer days, seeing more and more patients in order to discharge his obligations as fast as possible, and had tried to bring forward his departure date only to discover that he was scheduled to stay a month because that was how often the boat called. He had taken to scanning the unbroken horizon for the ship's approach, like a castaway. Tax write-off or no tax write-off, he had cursed the colleagues who had persuaded him to join this charitable mission.

And then, with only days remaining, he had seen Marianne, a somber, beautiful girl hunting for clams on the sugar-white sand of Out the Way beach, and had slowed his pace. He stopped beside where she crouched, her golden hair so long it hid her face, and brushed the wet sand. Bending, he had picked up a gleaming silver shell from which frilled black lips emerged, expanding and contracting elegantly, and offered this to her. Marianne had snatched it from him and hurled it out to sea, in disbelief that he was ignorant enough to pick up an animal plump with poison. He'd admired her island wisdom and said she had saved his life. "I insist," he had said, "that you keep me safe until I leave."

She barely spoke. Barely looked at him, most of the time. Yet she had taken his request seriously, shown him creamy pink avocados and how to pick them ripe; she had shown him the swollen purple globes of flowering bananas, scornful when he had marveled at all that to her seemed unremarkable. He ate what she fed him. She was seventeen, an incomprehensible two decades younger, and yet she could climb and swim and fish and knit and whittle, could start a fire with almost anything, could card wool. She knew when the tide would be high and would strand them, entirely alone in a moonlit cove, where he had laid her down like a mermaid on a bed of silver sand that glittered and shifted with skittering ghost crabs, among the dry heads of fallen sea hibiscus flowers. Her conqueror, he felt himself an island king. It had not occurred to him that there would be other things, the universal things, that she would not know. Afterwards, they had to walk waist-deep in the seawater to get back to the main beach, and her face in the moonlight had betrayed the salt water's sting. "Nothing ever happens here," she told him. "Now, you've happened."

Marianne had been on his mind this last year, in rush-hour traffic, or when he heard screaming from within the house before he'd even turned his door key. The two-year-old was getting molars and most nights his wife was ratty with sleep deprivation, pushing away his hand before it had touched so much as the waistband of her flannel pajamas, and the rest of the time fixated upon the seven-plus exams, or berating him about equitable supervision of Annie's violin practice. One day, he had heard himself explaining that it was good to have consistency in ophthalmic readings, and surprised his colleagues at the See the World Foundation by volunteering to pay a second visit to a remote and impoverished island that most could not summon the energy or time to visit once. The berth was long booked, they'd told him, but no optician had wanted to take it.

On the crossing he had been near-feverish with thoughts of Marianne. That morning he had been whistling—actually whistling!—as he drove though the hot streets. And then there she had been, glimpsed in his rearview mirror, a tired sea nymph pushing a buggy. He had panicked, and the gears of the Land Rover had not been as he had expected. People had been shouting. Then he had almost killed her.

Now he said, "I came back thinking I might see you. And then there you were with—it was a shock. I changed into the wrong gear and—" His gaze had slipped away from her and fastened on Alex in the cot behind her, swaddled and sleeping. He gave a dry swallow, glancing between the pair of babies. Marianne followed his eyes.

"Ah." He swallowed again. "My God."

"I nurse him sometimes. His mum took—takes care of me. She's not very well, just for now."

"I see. So not—both yours."

"Not both yours, you mean."

"Ah. Well. Yes, that too. Ha. God. I am terribly sorry. I presumed you had the matter in hand. Naive of me."

Marianne stared at him. In her arms Annie had gone slack with sleep, but she would not put her down in her usual space, beside Alex.

"I assume nobody knows, do they? No one knows? No, no, of course not, sorry, shouldn't have asked, you're a good girl, you understand how it is. They can't know, I'm afraid. No one can know, and now I can give you a little help and we will just say it's all because of the accident. What do you need, for her, you know, to set it right, ah, once and for all?"

He named a ludicrous sum, more than twice what her mother would be making in a year, on a cruise liner. Did he really have that sort of money? She took a breath, but before she could speak, he tripled it. Her heart was pulsing at her throat. She was thinking.

Marianne knew of the Fabian Academy. When she was eleven they'd started a pen-pal program with Tuga de Oro, and for two years she had exchanged letters with a girl named Dolores, who had dutifully told her all about boarding school in Kent, and asked stupid but well-meaning questions about whether Marianne had electricity, or plumbing, and whether she wore a grass skirt. At the Fabian Academy, Dolores did drama and fencing and played something called Eton Fives, and she called her teachers by their first names, and she seemed very proud that the school had goats and ducks and a kitchen garden, though these were the least interesting of its attributes to Marianne, who knew goats and ducks aplenty, and who single-handedly worked a productive garden twice the size. Dolores's parents lived in Hong Kong, and she stayed at school most holidays, so Marianne knew that children could board there from overseas. She named the school. She named her terms. She offered lifelong silence. And just like that, her daughter had a future.

42

The Lindos were holding a birthday party for Cecil, who was turn-ing eight. Lindo celebrations had been held up at the Lakes for as long as anyone could remember, one of the many arguments in favor of investing in the crumbling path that led there, up and round Thursday's Peak, for there were many Lindos and therefore many family birthday parties. Nimbler guests wore packs and scrambled there through the steep bank of cinnamon trees, and up the rough steps carved into the east flank of the *montaña*. Those less steady on their feet could go the long way round by the dilapidated road and take the final stretch by donkey, though there was often some pressure on the donkeys on the way home. Many revelers were less steady on their feet after these parties than before them.

Cecil Lindo was a broad-faced, red-haired boy, small for his age, who could not be dissuaded from his attempts to attach himself to eleven-year-old Alex and Annie, however insistently they rebuffed him. Scornful Annie Goss was his grand love. Alex was the softer touch, however, and thus it was Alex on whom Cecil lavished stamps and driftwood carvings and masapan balls, as a likelier route into their company. But today even Annie was obliged to be nice to Cecil, forced to attend his eighth birthday party because her mother was friends with his parents and, more importantly, had also been commissioned to make the cake.

Dan Zekri, too, had come on sufferance, having hoped to spend the day with Katie—a hike, maybe, or a drive to the other side of the island. Anything but more of this empty, separate togetherness. At work he was often near her and yet they were never alone, never able to hold a sensible and private conversation, and as a result he had been feeling increasingly fraught these last weeks. He felt he was chasing her, following her to potlucks and parties, and waiting up later and later on the nights he had not the energy for community participation and stayed at home. It seemed unworthy to cast aspersions on her motivation: sunny, open Katie, who was incapable of dissimulation or falsehood. She had thrown herself into a new life in which the ailments of the islanders seemed to outnumber the hours in her day and was impatient to attend to everyone who suffered, to reverse an eternity of sciaticas and plantar fasciitis, of injury recoveries and arthritis. *Well, lucky her*, he thought, with a flash of ungenerous envy, *she actually has some patients*. She hounded Saul for more details, more background, more, more. But as time passed Dan was no longer entirely convinced that her enthusiasm for the island and its needs was matched by her enthusiasm for the fiancé who'd brought her to it, nor that she wasn't, whether consciously or otherwise, deliberately avoiding him. They had been six months apart, and now had not eaten dinner alone together since the first night she had arrived six weeks ago. Even Old Year's Night, when it was traditional for courting Tugan couples to watch the sunset at Papasiegas, had been spent, at Katie's behest, at the Rockhopper. He wondered if she also worried there might be silence between them. He wondered, too, if in fact this side-by-side busyness was all they'd ever had, its oddity and emptiness masked by two demanding hospital schedules.

In this state, he was particularly keen to avoid Charlotte Walker. Each time he saw her he felt destabilized for twenty-four hours; he wanted just a night at home with Katie, to set right between them what felt increasingly askew. Yet here they were at another community picnic and Katie was off over there on a blanket in the sunshine, sharing a bottle of wine with Betsey and the Spencer sisters, and hadn't so much as glanced in his direction for an hour.

He had imagined, he realized, that once she came they might spend long evenings discussing her first impressions of the island, her insight into its people. He had looked forward to relief from the loneliness of being a Tugan among the FFA and an outsider to the Tugans, to having someone with whom he could acknowledge all that was maddening here, all that was charming, all that was troubled or broken and that might, with work, be fixed.

But this would always have been a fantasy, only enabled by their separation. It had never been in Katie's nature to spend long evenings discussing anything, and so it was dangerous to have constant proximity to another woman who offered just that connection, just that insight, just those pleasures. He needed Charlotte to go home. Next Island Close could not come soon enough.

Marianne Goss was sitting alone on a rock in the shade, carefully peeling an apple. Dan sat down beside her. He remembered Marianne as a schoolgirl, still a child herself when Dan had sailed for England and university. People had worried about Marianne then, he recalled. Not a happy home, somehow, though he had forgotten the details. Marianne has grown into a serious, quiet woman, not yet thirty and mother to an eleven-year-old whose paternity was obscure, and possibly itself not a very happy story. Two eleven-year-olds, really, when Ruth's back pain left her unable to care for Alex, which seemed to be most of the time. He made a mental note to ask Saul about Ruth's current situation, when they were back in the clinic.

"*Ke haber*, Doctor." Marianne was watching Alex and Annie as they tried to scramble to the top of a spreading sugar banyan, no doubt, even on his birthday, trying to shake off Cecil. Dan followed her gaze upwards.

"Fearless girl you've got."

"She's a devil," Marianne said, without taking her eyes from her daughter.

"She's a wonder, too."

"Well. Whatever she is or isn't is nothing to do with me, I've realized. They come out as they are. I just have to—I don't know. Hold firm at the outer limits. Keep her alive until she's old enough to make better choices. She's been entirely herself since she was born, I don't know how I thought I would get her onto a boat to school if she didn't want to go, she's not done a thing she didn't want since she could sit."

"You tried pretty hard, from the sound of things."

"Well." Marianne shook her hair out of her eyes, pushing it from her face with the back of her hand, and then returned to peeling. "I wanted—I wanted her to know enough to choose. You've studied in England. How bad is it, that she didn't go to that boarding school?"

Dan considered the best way to answer this, and before he could answer she went on, "I can't even tell her what all the things are that I wanted for her, because I'm too ignorant to know what it would even mean, to get away, to have an education. I wanted her not to be ignorant."

"I guess," said Dan slowly, "I guess whether it's a loss depends on who she is, and the life that she wants."

Marianne spoke with such simple honesty that he decided to reply in kind.

"For me, I knew I wanted to be a doctor and that would never have been possible if I'd stayed. I somehow knew I wouldn't be happy within the limits of what was on offer to me, without that chance. I feel—" He started to say that even now he felt trapped, but knew he could not, not to a woman who had never left Tuga de Oro and probably never would. "It's about having choices, I guess. It opens doors."

"That's always what everyone says, they're always on about doors. She can't yet know the doors she's closed. I don't think she understands what they're trying to say, she's never known a door that doesn't open. There's not a locked door on Tuga." Marianne began to eat the green curl of peel from her apple.

"You weren't tempted to go with her, just to get her there? Do what Maia's done, work in England while Annie was at school?"

"Right. And who'd look after Ruth dos Santos if I went? And Alex?"

"Of course. Sorry, that's true. But . . . eleven to eighteen at an

English boarding school. She'd have become a totally different person. Is that what you wanted?"

They looked together at the child up the tree, one skinny bare leg dangling, one knee bent up under her chin, straggled hair hanging loose about her sunburned face. Annie was shouting down instructions to the others. A group of children listened below, rapt. Dan tried, and failed, to imagine her neat as a pin, buttoned into an English school uniform and duffel coat.

"Not everyone wants that academic path, it's not . . . inherently better. Would you have left the island at her age, if you could?"

"In a heartbeat," Marianne said fiercely, and in her face he saw a flash of Annie's temper.

"Me too, actually. So maybe you can trust she knows herself, too." He was remembering himself as he spoke, and realized he believed what he was saying. He had known his own mind at Annie's age. Already he had been motivated to prove himself a better man, a bigger man than Johannes. "If we'd both definitely have chosen to go, and at the same point she chose to stay, then maybe you have to just trust her. It's possible to know yourself at eleven, we did, and from where I am now, I don't even know anymore. I used to always think, you know, more, further, up, out. But there's also something beautiful about knowing who you are and where you're from, too. Rooting in. When I was away I tried so hard to be English it was embarrassing, and yet somehow being Tugan was always the first thing anyone noticed, or asked about. And now I'm back I'm made to feel like FFA."

Marianne began to slice the peeled apple into a fan of thin slivers, shaking her head in disagreement even before he'd finished speaking.

"You're not going to get me to feel sorry for you, *Doctor* Zekri. You've traveled the world, you've come back with a real career and a load of money, a good woman who's followed you halfway round the globe. You have the sort of life that most here can only dream of, you're not weeks at sea away from your own children just to pay to fix the roof again, or like Maia away from Rebecca a year, looking after some stranger's kids instead, cause one boat sank. You're not all night worrying whether to fix the truck so you can get in the taro or buy fertilizer so there's taro to get. A berth's not three years' salary for you like it is for most of the island, so you can settle in your big fancy house, have a brace of kids, and one day, if you want to go travel or live somewhere else, you can take your kids and just—go. Anywhere."

"Katie never wants children."

Marianne unsettled him, with her refusal to politely ignore the economic and social inequalities between them. He had said it, he realized, because he wanted to show her that his life was not as perfect as she believed, but it had been a petty instinct. Of course she was right. His worries were trivial compared to the life of a single mother on the island, his concerns all for the pursuit of personal fulfilment because his fundamental needs were met, and would always be met. He did not have to expend energy worrying about the failure of his crop. He had a job for life, his comfortable salary and pension guaranteed by the Foreign, Commonwealth & Development Office. For the rest of his life he need never fear hunger, and nor would his sons and daughters—though he wasn't on course to have any.

He had long ago decided not to talk to anyone about Katie's opposition to having children, knowing that the information would be passed around the island as surely as a cold carried in from a ship. There were no career women here; no one, male or female, pursued ambitious and deliberately child-free personal goals. They were, as Marianne had only too eloquently reminded him, consumed in the business of sustaining their collective island existence. Anything else would be, at the very least, fantastically interesting gossip. And here he was baring his soul to Marianne Goss, of all people, who didn't even seem particularly interested. His own future without children had been an abstraction from their busy life in England but was, recently, a fact to which he kept returning.

He remembered Katie that night, a third or maybe a fourth date, smiling as she spoke, so sunny that he had felt her almost emitting light, a delicate woman in a rosy gingham dress like a little girl's party frock, leaning forward over her pink cocktail to tell him lightly in her sweet singsong that life is pain, and the world is dying. She would do her small part to honor that dying world by caring for the bodies already in it, but she would never add another body, no more suffering, no more need. They had been at a party and her fingernails had been painted bubblegum, and her iridescent, strawberry-colored eyeshadow had fallen onto her cheekbones like fairy dust. He had not heard, he thought now. He had not listened. And Katie was not a woman to repeat herself. It did not feel abstract any longer.

"Well," Marianne said, "some people don't. Certainly there's enough babies in the world."

Dan was watching Annie Goss, who had clambered down from the huge tree as soon as poor panting Cecil had managed to climb up. She snatched up a hot dog from the trestle table and began tearing at it with small white teeth. She was laughing at something Alex was saying, bent double, and she covered her mouth as a half-chewed piece of bun and hot dog threatened to fall. She was beautiful, Dan thought, having never before considered her. Vivid and captivating and unpredictable. Funny and also deeply serious, a child in whose eleven-year-old face one might sometimes catch glimpses of a future woman. So very much a person, and an interesting person. For a moment he imagined her his own daughter, and felt a surge of protective pride at her charisma, at her bravery. He imagined guiding and encouraging her, helping to shape who she became.

"The thing is," Dan said, "I think I want to be a father."

"Then you're in a mess, aren't you."

Marianne said this without malice, but without much warmth either. She seemed older than he was, and tired. She had set down the knife and her hands rested in her lap.

"The truth is, if you'll forgive me, most don't get all they want.

Some do, maybe, though I don't know those sorts of people. I hoped Annie would get a chance of all she wanted, that she could spread her wings and—I don't know. Maybe, as you say, all she wants is right here with me and Alex, maybe it's enough, and I hope so, and I'll give anything I can to make it so. But then the worrying, did you do the right thing at this point, at that point, wanting to start all over with your baby and do it all again, but better. But your Katie Salmon must love you, to come here, of all places, halfway round the world and where there's nothing, so maybe you'll find that's worth as much as a family. You better sort it out, though. Especially if there's someone else you planning to have all those babies with."

"She's nothing to do with this," said Dan, without thinking, and grasping only too late what he'd admitted. Marianne gave him a long look, from which he understood that it had not been a coincidental comment.

The understanding that he would not have pursued Katie much further than was convenient fell first lightly, like a trickle of falling sand through an hourglass, and then with a hammer blow. It was, or had been, nice, comfortable, appropriate. The sex was regular, and athletic. The consistency of her enthusiasm for Tuga had made him lose sight of how exceptional it was that she'd come so willingly, and with so little persuasion. But he now saw that, had the situation been reversed, he would not have followed Katie to a far-off, isolated homeland, however beautiful the beaches, however balmy the weather. It had been right because of circumstance, but circumstances were a shaky ground on which to build a lifetime, and six months on Tuga without her had changed him more than he'd acknowledged. He was home, but Katie wasn't home, for him. Marianne Goss could see him, or perhaps could see through him. He just hadn't seen himself.

43

"Little Doc." Taxi was coming at speed towards the picnickers in an odd limping skip. Dan scrambled to his feet, relieved to have an excuse to move away from Marianne.

"Can't find Big Doc. You gotta come with me now, I brought the ambulance close as I can get it. Nicola fell down at the Breaks, reckon maybe something broke, or twisted, or something, she can't stand and she got a load of pain." Taxi was dwarfed by a large pink high-vis vest he had added to his outfit, presumably to indicate he had come in an official capacity. Beneath were a Barry Manilow T-shirt and denim shorts, which suggested he had been on air.

Dan began to jog down the hill, with Taxi hopping at an increasing distance behind him. Seeing them, Katie stood and started to run, falling into easy step with Dan despite her flip-flops, and they made their way to where the ambulance juddered in a black cloud of diesel, the engine left idling, the door open. Dan kicked a jungle roach from the footstep and climbed in, after Katie. Taxi caught up with them, and clambered back up into the driver's seat, panting.

"You wanted us running, so I ran, but I reckon running don't feel any good, Doc, I'll tell you." Something black and winged was crawling across the dashboard and he gave it an expert smack. "From here best to go over the top," he added, pulling the ambulance hard up the hill. Dan tried to give Katie a glance of warning for the drive ahead, but she was looking only at Taxi and he could not catch her eye.

They screeched from the clearing. Taxi accelerated round the corner and up the track, rarely used, that followed the pass over the *montaña*. Dan hung on grimly to the handle, wishing for seat belts. This was not the route he would have taken, for it was steep, and prone to rockfall—he would have gone all the way back down and round. Between them Katie had her hands braced against the dashboard, alert and surprisingly sober for someone who had been drinking white wine in the blazing sun for hours. Dan wondered why he had never thought to test-drive the ambulance at speed, for there was an ominous series of clunks from the back, and a clattering sound. Then there was a louder scrape, and two bangs.

"Oh, boy." Taxi was frowning in the rearview mirror, slowing. Not slowing enough, Dan felt, for someone looking only backwards. "Someone not secure the back doors."

"*What?*"

"Didn't you have everybody out cleaning this ambulance, telling them all it's dirty? That's your clean stretcher, off down the hill."

"Oh, shit."

"Little Doc, that's no language for a public man."

"Well, stop, for crying out loud!"

Katie placed a calming hand on Dan's knee, which in his current state of agitation provoked the opposite effect. Why, when she was manifestly such a good, nice person and, more importantly, almost perfectly suited to him, was he so irritated? Why was he struggling to imagine the rest of his life? She was serious, athletic, intrepid. More to the point, she, unlike ninety-nine percent of the women he'd ever met, actually wanted to live on Tuga. He resisted the urge to throw off the small hand.

"All right, all right. I can't see it no longer, Doc. Oh, that's gone way back. Waaay back."

Dan leaped out before the ambulance had come to a complete stop and began to sprint down the pitted track after the rickety stretcher, which, complete with neatly folded Tugan knitted blanket and newly washed pillow, was squeaking and rattling its way down the mountainside at an impressive and increasing speed. It would be impossible to catch but this did not stop him trying, aware that in this direction eventually lay the high cliffs, with only the razor-sharp coral of the reef far below. This was the only stretcher for thousands of square miles and he cast about desperately, wondering if he could lasso it with a vanilla vine, like a cowboy. Then ahead the road made a switchback turn and the stretcher continued forwards, and crashed to a stop in a mintberry bush. Dan slowed, gasping, the sharp scent of crushed mintberry filling his straining lungs.

Taxi came ambling up behind him. "That was OK, Doc. You fast like lightning. A good advert for your Couch to 5k, I'd say."

Wordlessly Dan began to extract the stretcher, which made a terrible grinding noise as he hauled it out from between the cracked branches. He began to push it up the hill towards the ambulance but then, feeling a wheel might come loose, thought better of it and asked Taxi to reverse the rest of the way back. Katie had remained placidly in the front. Dan showed Taxi the stretcher's wheel brakes, and Taxi peered at them with interest, and suggested that Winston and Calla might benefit from such a lesson, as well as some orientation around the catches of the ambulance itself. The stretcher restored, and doors tightly secured and then rechecked, they set off up and over the hill again, only to be confronted near the crest by three large gray cows who stood impassively, blocking the way, staring at the ambulance. Dan felt near hysteria. He wound down the window and began to bellow.

"That ain't going to work," Taxi told him. "Those cows only answer to Bert."

Dan leaned over and pressed the horn, which did nothing. Katie giggled. Then she reached up and turned on the siren. The cows leaped as if electrocuted, and disappeared.

"Let's leave that on, Doc. That'll tell them we're coming, won't be much longer."

"I guess it's a good opportunity to see if we can get all the new protocol actioned, test out the clinical boxes," Dan said, thinking aloud. "If it all goes as it should, it will be a good day for the team."

"Hardly a good day for Nicola, though," said Katie, giving him a look of sanctimonious rebuke. The irritation was mutual, it seemed.

Dan opened his mouth to reply that if Nicola was treated in a clinic that he'd managed to modernize with the creative use of a few plastic storage bins, it would be a good day indeed to have broken her leg, as opposed to any of the previous days this year, or indeed ever. But then he closed it again, not trusting himself. Taxi looked between them with a frown, and Dan fixed his gaze on the road so that at least one of them was looking at it. They hurtled over the crest to find Nicola.

Nicola was a tall, cheerful woman in her late fifties who ran a small sheep farm with her second husband, Hugh. She was in good health, and though she saw Saul sometimes for cholesterol checks she had managed to stay off statins. She was not cheerful when they found her, still on the ground, holding her ankle, her face buried into grass.

"It's really hurting," Nicola's daughter, Chloe, told them. She was kneeling beside her mother, stroking her back.

"We're here now." Dan crouched beside them both. "We're going to make you feel better."

"Where's Saul?" Nicola moaned.

Katie knelt and took Chloe's hand. "Saul will meet us at the hospital," she said soothingly. "Don't worry, he's on his way."

Which was true, Dan thought, but exceedingly annoying nonetheless. He could manage a broken bloody limb, for goodness' sake.

He dosed Nicola with morphine, and splinted her leg, talking through every stage, partly to reassure Nicola and partly to include and calm Chloe, who had long wanted to be a doctor. Taxi drove them all back to the clinic in the jouncing ambulance, where an X-ray showed a break across the medial malleolus, and an angle Dan wasn't at all keen on. He set up a ketamine infusion and manipulated the ankle until he was happier with the position, and by then Saul and the nurses had arrived. A second X-ray looked much better.

Saul squeezed Chloe's shoulder.

"Dr. Zekri's done a great job, look at that. It's all exactly where it needs to be to heal properly. Are you going to be the first to sign your mum's plaster? I hear you took beautiful care of her, you're doing stellar medical work already."

Chloe looked teary, and anxious.

"We were running," she told Saul. "We're going quite far, now."

Nicola turned woozily to Dan, and lifted a limp hand.

"We've been following your leaflet, Little Doc; it's been going so well, the jogging." She was slurring from the ketamine. "And then today I just—plop! Down." She giggled. "I feel a bit . . ." but she was unable to convey this final insight.

Dan, by contrast, knew precisely what he felt. Moments ago he had been enjoying some quiet pride that his reorganization of the equipment had made for a smoothly managed minor emergency. At this revelation he simply felt discouraged, in anticipation of Taxi's next radio bulletin. It duly came, with the evening news.

"There's a new fashion for extreme sports on Tuga de Oro," Dan heard, in despair, "and I know you'll all join me in wishing Nicola Davenport a speedy recovery from her jogging injury, after a heroic attempt at Little Doc's Couch to 5k. Sign her cast with a happy thought." Bruce Springsteen had begun in the background and here it was, Dan thought wearily, the sucker punch, "Maybe us Tugans just weren't 'Born to Run' . . ."

44

When the vet knocked on the door of Ruth's kitchen, Marianne was giving the children supper in an atmosphere of tension. They sat side by side on a rough wooden bench, small hands clasped together beneath the table, on which four untouched soup bowls lay on an incongruous waxed Provençal tablecloth of yolk-yellow, printed with leafy bunches of black olives, and resting cicadas. There was thick silence in the cluttered little room, and Charlotte wondered whether she had interrupted a scolding. Annie leaned her head on Alex's shoulder, whispering something low. Then Charlotte spotted Ruth herself, passed out on the sofa behind them. Though it was warm, someone had tucked a cotton blanket over her sprawled legs.

"Come in, Dr. Walker," said Marianne briskly. "If you're here we may as well put her to bed."

Marianne roused Ruth enough to get her standing, and the older woman reeled between them. Her chin was on her chest, and she seemed unable to open her eyes for more than a fleeting moment, as if dazzled by the low light. She smelled strongly of patchouli, and urine. She began to mumble, something about needing her oils, and Marianne said she'd get them but be good now, and just put one foot in front of the other, Ruthie, my love. Ruth seemed able to follow this instruction, though her weight bore heavily upon the two women flanking her. Once they'd negotiated into Ruth's room, Marianne gave a small, guiding push, and Ruth crashed heavily on to the bed. She did not stir from where she fell, and Marianne spent some time trying to straighten out the odd angle of her neck. She stroked Ruth's long graying hair back from her face, and spoke softly. Charlotte looked away. The room was stifling with heartbreak.

By the time they returned to the kitchen, Alex and Annie had moved apart and were slurping soup, deep in a dispute. Alex had instantly brightened, with his mother out of sight.

"Mango and chocolate chips and marshmallows and strawberry jam all smushed," Alex was saying, and Annie said fiercely, "All of those separate are my best but together they would be my *worst*."

"You can't know what your worst is until you've tried it," said Alex reasonably. "Can she, Dr. Vet?"

"I will never try it as long as I live, it would be a waste of Mama's strawberry jam. Nobody puts jam with chocolate chips, it's the worst idea you've ever had in the history of the world, and you have had some very bad ideas."

"Speaking of your jam," Charlotte said quickly to Marianne, noting how crestfallen Alex now looked, "I was wondering if you were baking tomorrow morning?"

Both children instantly brightened.

"She is," Annie announced, before her mother had a chance to answer. "That's why deciding about fillings is so important. When can we come back out with you?"

"Soon, I promise, now I'm finishing at Martha House. Please can I have something to bring to Garrick tomorrow, in that case? It's our last day at the library together. I'm sorry it's short notice." Charlotte managed to resist the urge to add, "But until basically yesterday I thought he was a pompous ass."

"Garrick likes savory, I might do you some cheese and chive scones if it's for him. I start at four a.m., one of the children can drop it at the Rockhopper before eight with the bar's order, would that work? Teeth and bed, you two, if you've finished. Get on."

Alex and Annie were on their feet and darted out of the kitchen door with the synchrony of a single being. Through the window

Charlotte heard their laughter, and could see them disappear next door into Marianne's house. Marianne let out a long breath.

"Are you all right?" Charlotte asked softly.

"That depends on what you mean by all right, doesn't it."

Having sat down for barely a moment, Marianne stood and briskly began to clear the soup bowls.

"What I want no one can give me—Ruth better and proper work in Betsey's kitchen, or a cafe of my own maybe." Marianne paused, holding a stack of dishes against her hip. We are probably the same age, Charlotte thought, with disbelief, and a flash of gratitude and guilt at her own immense and almost innumerable privileges and freedoms.

"Don't judge on what you saw, Dr. Walker, tonight was a bad one. I stayed too long at Cecil's picnic, she was alone all afternoon. It's better for me not to leave her."

"But you have to be able to go to a picnic—"

Marianne gave her a pitying look. "It ain't like that. People need looking after, you look after them. It was Ruth who taught me that, and she didn't teach me by telling, she showed me by getting on and doing it, taking care of me and everybody else besides. Someone needs help, you help. Something needs doing, you do it. It's not someone else's problem and there's no—there's no time limits. I can say it's inconvenient, I can say I want this, I want that, but it's Ruth who suffers. I keep telling Alex, Ruth is worth the rest of the island put together and then some."

She put the crockery into a plastic tub beside the sink, and carefully poured the remains of the soup from a saucepan into a tall glass bottle, scraping out the pan until it was almost clean.

"I know what I'll do for you tomorrow, I'll do you her spiced coffee cake. That's a Ruthie recipe through and through, Garrick'll recognize it too. It's important people not forget who she is, really."

She took something from the fridge and handed it to Charlotte, who stood holding the dense parcel, embarrassed. Whatever she'd been given, she felt sure Marianne could not easily spare it.

"Take this, thank you for your help just now. I need to go and check those demons before Alex falls asleep in Annie's bed and I can't shift him. I need him to stay here tonight and keep an ear." In the doorway Marianne paused and, despite the clipped tones, her eyes had filled with tears. "I'm just doing what I can to keep her safe. She's the best woman I know. I can still often talk to her, or sometimes. It's not just, just what you saw. Goodnight, Dr. Walker."

Charlotte left Marianne's house with what turned out to be a slice of frittata wrapped in wax paper, and a feeling of helplessness that she could only alleviate by doing something useful for the island. She had been working hard to treat animals ad hoc, it was true, but to make an impact she must leave Tuga better prepared than she'd found it. She couldn't help Ruth dos Santos but she could help Ruth's goat or dog or chickens and, most importantly, she could ensure that the next time any of these animals sickened there was protocol in place to treat it, even after she had gone.

Back at the cottage, she sat down to begin a list of drugs, ranked in order of priority (color-coded, with highlighter), ready to brandish at Saul. Her new goal was to see it all here before she left, and not just here but organized into kits she planned to construct for the most common veterinary crises, a concept shamelessly ripped off from Dan's clinical boxes. It seemed a system she might even operate remotely, from London, if she recorded and photographed it all, and left Elsie in charge of keeping everything where she left it. Compiling these would be a huge task, but the thought of it energized and excited her. This was a legacy that would make a difference.

She had already scribbled an inventory of the pitiful vet's pharmacy, but now sat down with the World Veterinary Association's list of essential medicines for livestock, as well as the one for small animals. These pulled together all the basic vaccinations and drugs that formed a bare operational minimum, and someone else had already done the hard work of choosing formulations that were effective, well priced, and readily available. She had only to cross-reference the WVA suggestions with what they already had, and to make a list of queries for Saul about what she might command from his own stores. Many of these drugs would be largely useless without a veterinarian to prescribe them, but it still seemed better to have them on the island than not. It was doing, versus not doing. She would leave knowing that the WVA minimum requirements for safe and ethical animal care were met on Tuga de Oro.

45

The following day Charlotte stopped at the Rockhopper early, where the chairs were still upended on the tables. This morning her mind was still ferociously busy. She was determined to overcome the awkwardness that had characterized most of her interactions with Levi since the hurricane, but for now her only weapon was to counter his irony with a sort of idiotic, tin-eared positivity.

Levi greeted her with an unsmiling nod, but from beneath the shelf of bottles behind him he produced the cake from Marianne, and thudded it onto the bar. Charlotte unwrapped the tea towel and the greaseproof paper within.

"This smells incredible."

Levi peered into the open parcel. "Ruth's spiced coffee cake. What's the occasion? First threesome with Zekri and his masseuse?"

"What the hell is wrong with you? If you must know, it's a thank-you to Garrick. We've cleaned the bugs, and I've found some promising texts, so I might be able to plot population shifts over time thanks to him, or sort of thanks to him, and he was the one who found *Tortoise on the Hillside,* which I've literally dreamed about. Today's our last day."

"So now you get to hide away up there at your little desk and see if anyone a hundred years ago wrote a letter about a tortoise. Sounds great."

"I know, it is great!" Charlotte dumped her bag on a bar stool and sat down, inhaling the warm scent that rose from the open package. The cake smelled like nutmeg and allspice and something else. "German Christmas biscuits," she said aloud. "And I'm tracking korason palms dispersal too, now, not just tortoises. And I've come up with a great plan for the vet's clinic. A brain wave, last night. Basically, I am a genius all round."

"If you say so. Coffee?"

"Yes, please. You know Mary's got a load of recipe books? Not that that's much to do with what I'm doing, although now I'm checking them for korason fruit harvesting as well as, like, tortoise stew, but I find it very moving, honestly, you should see them, all these handwritten annotations and amendments. It's such a vivid way of remembering that these were real families, eating real meals. There's one from a hundred and fifty years ago that says, 'Thomas did not care to eat this a second time.' I love that."

"Thomas should have made his own damn dinner in that case."

Levi moved away and began lifting the chairs down from the tables, and didn't speak again until she heard him call, "Oi, Zekri. *Haver*, Walt's got booby eggs, if you pass by for lunch."

Charlotte turned to see that Dan was in the doorway, looking unexpectedly disheveled. His white shirt was rumpled and his hair was askew, standing up on only one side, as if he had been clutching at it. He was casting about the empty Rockhopper as if scanning a crowd and, though she was the only customer, he seemed to startle when he saw her. Levi returned to his place behind the bar and leaned forward with his chin on his fist, glancing between the two of them. Dan came over.

"*Paz*, Mendoza. Charlotte, I've been looking for you, can we talk?"

When Charlotte nodded, Dan took her wrist and drew her away to the far wall, beside the jukebox. Aware of Levi, Charlotte was about to suggest they step outside when Dan cut her off.

"I've been awake all night, I'm sorry, I've been looking for you, I just came from your place, I had to tell you straightaway. I would have come to tell you last night but I wanted to finish the box first—I've ended things with Katie."

From behind them Charlotte heard the chinking of glassware. Levi was emptying the small dishwasher beneath the bar, polishing condensation off the glasses with studied care. From his expression she was pretty certain that he was in earshot. Her heart was pounding.

"You've ended things with Katie and—made a box for it?"

"No, no, I've been trying to finish off my last box all night, I've just come from the clinic. It's over with Katie. Two unrelated sentences. I didn't have anywhere else to go so I thought I'd sleep in my office and I just . . . didn't get round to sleeping." He was emitting pulses of manic energy, like a threatened sea creature. "But wait, no, that's not what I needed to tell you right now, listen. I had to find you, I can't wait till— Listen, I have a clinic starting any minute and, I know it's sudden but I need to—I'll tell you later but, Charlotte, honestly, I can't spend the day not having told you, I feel like it's all been for this. There is something between us, you and me, I know you know it, and I've not been free to tell you how I feel until literally today, right now. I can't stop thinking about you. I'll come to London if you say so, I just want—" He had been standing slightly too close to her but now was backing away as he spoke, moving towards the door, throwing the words over his shoulder like a man about to miss a flight. "Don't say anything— meet me at the beach at six. Out the Way beach at six."

Dan shouldered out of the door, tripping over the doormat as he went. She wondered for a moment if he was drunk, a suspicion not allayed when she heard him bellowing, "I'm not drunk, by the way," from the yard outside.

Charlotte watched him as he receded, frozen by her awareness of Levi's gaze. Then Levi said softly, "Would you look at that, Dolittle. All your little dreams have come true."

46

Garrick spent the morning grilling Charlotte about methods of digital preservation, and Charlotte spent the morning pretending to an authority she did not possess, while at the same time wondering why she felt such turmoil, and no small degree of relief that a day of work had interposed itself between Dan's speech and her own obligation to respond. The two conversations went on contrapuntally and did not impede each other's flow; aloud with Garrick about megapixels, and in silence, with her own heart, words like "connection," "soulmates," "rebound."

For months she had imagined precisely such a declaration, but it had been a safe fantasy, constructed upon the firm and absolute belief in its own hopelessness. She had never had to consider a reality with Dan Zekri; only the dream of a reality, in soft-focus, and excluding any truth that was remotely inconvenient. It was surely this, she thought, that made immediate clarity impossible. She did not feel unbridled joy because she simply needed to *think*. Dan Zekri was single. Single, and wanting to meet her at sunset at the beach.

And all the while Levi had been there, watching, polishing pint glasses, impassive. Dan did not parade around shirtless in the heat, sinking white teeth into whole mangoes as if they were apples and heckling her like a 1980s construction worker. Dan did not emit an inconvenient pheromone that stripped her of filter or social restraint; in his presence the first thought in her head did not become the first words on her tongue. He did not gallop off on a moral high horse at the first sign of a complication; he did not remain maddeningly unmoved by subsequent overtures. Dan did not shrug at life; he worried and questioned. Dan wore collared shirts and spoke softly and stood when she approached; he opened doors, had traveled, read books, had prospects. Dan was complex and clever and passionate, and now, apparently, willing to upend his life and follow her to London, though it was hard not to feel that a grand romantic gesture ought not, ideally, to involve the sacrifice of an entire island's healthcare system. Dan had imported a younger fiancée and then apparently just dumped her, such that Katie was now dumped, literally as well as figuratively, upon a remote South Atlantic island with no hope of escape for months.

All of this went on, churning below the surface, while Charlotte and Garrick discussed scanners, and which among the eldest schoolchildren might, with proper training, be entrusted with the mammoth task, once they had circumnavigated Grand Mary's inevitable resistance. And meanwhile she could not fritter this final morning. There were still treasures to be found here—just yesterday she had unearthed a copy of *Famous Tortoises* by venerated Peterhouse scholar Justin Gerlach and who knew what else she might find, given half the chance? The silverfish had guaranteed her access, and wasted so much precious time. Focus now was both essential, and impossible.

They were double-checking one another's lists when Joan appeared in the open French doors, a slight figure in loose dark robes and a straw hat, a wicker basket over her arm—like a character in a fable, Charlotte thought. All morning she had felt so jangled that she could barely contemplate eating, and had entirely forgotten the wrapped cake in her own bag, but then Joan produced two small white china plates and placed a piece of cake upon each, and she found herself ravenous.

"Coconut and passion fruit," Joan said, when Charlotte admired it.

"It smells incredible. Is it a traditional Tugan recipe?"

Joan gave a soft smile, and then shook her head. "Nigella," she whispered, and then giggled.

"Stay, Joanie." Garrick was on his feet, pulling over a third chair. But Joan was adamant she had other plans for the afternoon, she had to press on, was late, really, and would see Garrick at home. She turned to Charlotte.

"But would you join us for supper? I've wanted to ask you."

Charlotte said she was afraid she couldn't, she had other plans at six, and Joan picked up her basket again and stood back, regarding them.

"Another time, perhaps. I'll leave Mary's slice with you rather than look for her, if you don't mind. I must say this makes a perfect tableau. Two scholars, hard at work. It is just how I've been picturing you this week. I shall treasure it," she finished, with surprising warmth, and then disappeared. Her soft voice could be faintly heard a moment later in the garden, taking her leave of Martha.

Charlotte watched Garrick, watching the door. Then he busied himself brushing crumbs from the tabletop into his cupped hand, newly conscious of the tortoise, who had been known to venture into the library for company, and for the starfruit chunks that Charlotte smuggled in for her. Before them on the table Charlotte regarded the white china plates. Joan had also brought real cotton napkins, worn, but lovely. These were cornflower blue, their edges embroidered with lemons. Charlotte felt a sudden affection for all of them, for all of this. It was from all this wholesome goodness that Dan had come, and Levi. It was in them, and of them. In her too, perhaps, in some way.

"Did Joan make these?"

Garrick frowned at his napkin as if he'd never seen it before, turning it over.

"I suppose so, yes. Joan and Moz. They often do that sort of thing together. For the gift shop too, as well as knitting all those mice."

"They're amazing, truly. They're like the sort of delicate beautiful thing you'd find in Liberty's for hundreds of pounds. Imagine being able to make the world more beautiful like this, just little pockets of beauty for no reason. I can sew up incisions but it's not very decorative, my work."

"They've been embroidering for forty years together. Like to keep themselves busy. They'll teach you, if you wanted to learn."

"It's lovely that your wife and your sister are such good friends."

"It's not uncommon here, you know, none of your fast-paced disposable city friendships."

Charlotte decided to let go this slight, because she found she was taken with his idea that while she was on the island she might be able to acquire Tugan life skills. She saw herself in her next few months drifting through the Mendoza garden beneath a huge straw hat, a trug over one arm, gathering in her own lush produce to the amazement of the islanders. Then home at Island Close and a new, richer, slower life rebuilt in London, a hand-knitted sweater cast over a kitchen chair in an intricate Tugan pattern, or serving home-ground saloop when she came in from the lab, the warm island soul awakened within her even as she moved through cold gray London streets. Tugan flowers would bloom along her windowsills, in her own glazed pots, maybe even a huge korason palm in one corner, if she took home viable seeds from her gold coin fecal samples. And it would not be an appropriated cultural identity, not like all those embarrassing younger colleagues who came back from three-month placements in Argentina in ponchos, clutching gourds of yerba maté. Dan Zekri had offered himself as the ultimate Tugan souvenir, a bombshell too unsettling at present to consider. In any case, wasn't there still a chance, after all, that she herself was half Tugan?

She looked at Garrick, who was squinting once again into his notebook. This ceasefire between them might not last, and time was running out. In many ways he was the obvious person to ask.

She said, lightly, conversationally, "You know, I'm pretty sure my father must have been Tugan."

She had expected this to land like a missile, but instead Garrick's heavy brow merely contracted.

"I highly doubt that. Who was your mother, when was she here?"

"She was never here, she must have met him in London. But—I'm more and more convinced. From stuff she said and just—intuition, I suppose."

Garrick thought a long while.

"I understand why one might be drawn here if one felt—without anchor. And I'll concede you have been rather taken up as few others are. But that doesn't make the connection hereditary. Tugans barely travel, we'd all know."

"It's not wishful thinking, if that's what you mean. I'm not some lost soul wandering the globe looking for any old appealing identity to assume—"

"I in no way intended—"

"I really think I'm right about this." Her voice rose. "Of course I want it to be true, because if it turns out I'm wrong then I'm back to square one, I'm back to literally nothing. That, that *nothing* was there my whole childhood, and 'Oh, poor Charlotte Compton-Neville doesn't know who her dad is,' 'Charlotte Compton-Neville spends Father's Day making cards for the driver,' but it's not just the question of narrative, it's—"

"Compton-Neville," Garrick repeated, in a voice that was strangely hoarse. He cleared his throat, took a sip of water, and tried again. "Compton-Neville. But you're Walker. Compton-Neville was your father's name?"

"My mother's. I never knew my father, that's precisely what I'm telling you. Walker was my stepfather's name, I was little when she married him so my mother changed mine too."

Garrick frowned, opened his mouth, closed it again, and his face resolved into what she imagined was professional impassivity. He looked like a carving, she thought, until, after a long time, he spoke.

"Your mother is Compton-Neville. I see. I see. What is your mother's full name?"

"Lucinda Compton-Neville. She was briefly Lucinda Walker when she married my stepdad, but she changed it back after they divorced and I kept Walker because it was just easier. Listen, please don't tell anyone about what I said, I don't want to start rumors and obviously I'm not one hundred percent certain, but things have added up, and if you can just help me to think—"

Garrick stood up abruptly, jostling the table, fumbling for his baseball cap.

"I am stepping outside. I will be back shortly."

47

Hot and bewildered, Charlotte closed all the curtains against the blazing sun and sat beneath the ineffectual ceiling fans in partial gloom, wondering how on earth she had managed to offend Garrick just when relations between them had begun, fractionally, to improve. He was not deserving of spiced coffee cake. She had offered up her deepest confidences and he had barely replied, had just blundered off, and wasn't he meant to be a bloody pastor, and thus quite literally concerned with pastoral care? She had confessed her childhood feelings of shame and rejection and he had, with impressive irony, left her feeling ashamed and rejected.

She did not want to risk seeing Dan before six, and so she worked on through the afternoon, hungry and claustrophobic and cross, with no clearer idea of what she wanted, and no idea if Garrick would even come back and end their final day with civility.

He returned just as she was packing up to leave, stepping through the heavy curtains like an actor appearing, rather furtively, onstage, and looking strangely rumpled and sweaty, as if he'd spent the intervening hours walking in the heat. He was holding a bag from Sylvester's, from which he produced two cans of cold ginger beer and, after taking his usual seat, he wiped these with one of Joan's embroidered handkerchiefs and gave one to Charlotte. She took this as a peace offering.

"Fizzycan."

"Thank you."

Garrick frowned down into his ginger beer, so that all Charlotte could see was the top of his cap, his face hidden beneath the brim. She waited, sensing something was coming. Garrick cleared his throat.

"Charlotte, I do believe I have understood who your father is, if you would truly like me to tell you. When you said your mother's name I, I—I think you are not mistaken. But I must have your word that you will never tell a soul. Not a soul. It could cause great hurt."

Her heart had begun to hammer in her chest for somehow, from the moment he'd spoken her name, she had sensed what would follow. Of course Garrick could tell her; who held the community's darkest secrets if not the minister? It had seemed unknowable, and yet in seconds she would know it. Her stomach turned over. She could not speak, but she nodded.

"Very well. Very well. Your father was my dearest friend in the world, my *haver*, Johannes Zekri." He spoke each word so slowly, so quietly, that time itself seemed to have slowed. "You must be twenty-nine, thirty? Yes, yes, I thought so. Johannes and I went to England together, I had a conference in London, and some important fundraising for the island. Joan had been, had had, several illnesses and Johannes traveled with me. And in London Johannes met your mother. Lucinda Compton-Neville. The name just brought it back."

Charlotte released a small, involuntary sound, and covered her mouth with her hand. From his pocket Garrick produced a clean handkerchief and this she held over her nose and mouth, her eyes closed, though no tears came. The handkerchief smelled of lavender water and she tried her best to deepen her breathing, though she had begun to shiver violently. She could not look at him. This was the secret that her whole life had seemed concealed like the face of God; inaccessible like the inside of another's heart. No secret now. Just a sad and sordid truth, like any other.

And if she hadn't talked to Garrick! If not for this conversation then what, tonight, at the beach? At this last thought her mouth filled with water, nauseated. Dan's father was her father. Was that what had drawn them together? Beneath everything, a connection that was not a natural chemistry or a shared sense of humor, but genetic similarity, shared sibling temperaments? It was intolerable to know; it was unthinkable not to know.

"It must be a shock, I am sorry. Probably it wasn't what you wanted to hear, no doubt you've heard things about Johannes . . . people said a lot of things about him. And he wasn't a good—he wasn't good to Dan's mother. He wasn't suited to home life. You know, we have customs here, traditions, and especially in those days, but not everyone is good at being married. And we were—" He paused. "Would you like me to go on?"

Charlotte had remained as she was, face bowed into his handkerchief, frozen but alert to each word. She said, "Please."

"You know, I pride myself on not speaking negatively, or in a way that might damage a person even if, even if what is said might in fact have truth to it. Johannes was constitutionally incapable of— conjugal fidelity. His actions did not give Dan an easy childhood, and Dan is very angry and as a son that is his right. After the accident, Joan and I, we mourned Johannes, and we mourned most that he would never get to set it right with Dan. And if you could have met him—I am sorry, truly sorry, that you will never meet him. You have come all this way. It was brave to search. Brave to seek. I can tell you one thing of which I'm certain, Johannes had no idea about you, because he would have told me. I am telling you this, Charlotte, because I believe you asked me."

"I did," she managed. "Thank you."

"Please, may I ask again that you keep it to yourself? Lusi couldn't take . . . It would be hurtful to a lot of people. If you have any questions please bring them all to me, anything you want to learn or understand. Today, if you have time, or another day perhaps, when you've had a chance to think. But he's dead now, and I wish to guard what remains of his reputation. Others must not judge him all over again."

The carriage clock on the mantelpiece began to chime the hour. Somehow it was six p.m., but Charlotte made no move to stand.

"I've got nowhere to be," she said softly. "I'd like to hear."

48

It had been obvious since they left Grand Mary's house that Garrick did not want her to come home with him for dinner. Perhaps, having pieced together her identity (having made a bonfire of her own tranquility of mind, possibly forever), Garrick now wanted to escape from his best friend's sordid love child. Certainly he could not look at her. Probably he wanted to whisper to his wife in private about what he had discovered—but here her conjecture ended, because a pale but smiling Joan opened the kitchen door and welcomed them both in.

Charlotte did not want to go for dinner with Garrick any more than he wanted her to come. She wanted desperately to be off this godforsaken island and safely at home in London with her mother's arms around her, weeping for the shame and pity of it all. Lucinda had had some sort of liaison with possibly the least suitable man on the planet, as a result of which her father was a dead, philandering Tugan fisherman. Charlotte's imagination gave Johannes as few teeth as Taxi, twisting his grin into a permanent licentious leer. She had been ready to discover herself Tugan in some way that might explain her, draw her disparate parts into a whole that made sense. She might be part Nigerian; she might have Sephardi ancestors from Dutch Brazil. She might even have had a whaling ancestor, about whom she could make horrified conservationist jokes.

Not this. She felt spent and exhausted, wrung out, and now had an urgent need to avoid Dan Zekri, the existence of whom added a nightmarish tint to the discovery. She had not been able to think of a more effective place to hide from Dan than at the Williamses' dinner table, for given his fervor that morning, she felt certain he would go to her house, once it became clear that she wasn't coming to the beach. She was frantic not to see him—ever again, if such a thing were possible.

Charlotte had not been inside the Williamses' house since her first week, when Joan had invited her over for coffee to talk about the island, and the fellowship. Joan said often that she did not wish to impose on Charlotte's time, and so while she was always friendly when their paths crossed, they had not made a subsequent social arrangement.

Charlotte understood the room differently now. A sturdy pot of beef stew bubbled on the small stove, and on the table was a platter of potato cakes. Joan had made the potato cakes and the stew, and had grown the vegetables it contained, had sewn and embroidered the napkins and the cushions and the seascape hung above the fireplace. Vitali Mendoza had made the table and chairs, but Joan had painted these chairs and embroidered their cushions, had stuffed the two footstools, had woven the palm-frond basket full of logs. In the old days, she told Charlotte, she would have split the logs too, but now they left that sort of work to younger friends. She seemed delighted to see Charlotte but her face looked waxen, and once they were all inside she sat at the table and just for a moment rested her head in her hands. Garrick began to mutter that perhaps all this was best postponed, that dinner parties were not really the order of the day.

"Oh, I'm absolutely fine, I'm tired, that's all. Now I have willing helpers, I shall exploit them. Come sit with me, Charlotte."

"If you're not well enough, Joanie—"

"Nonsense," Joan said, quite loudly. "Charlotte will do me good, I insist. Come here, come here."

Charlotte sat beside her and Joan held out her hand. Charlotte took it, looking down at the dry, pale fingers that lay upon her own, and at the strangely ostentatious gold ring with its rich celestial pattern, its frame of glittering diamonds. Garrick hovered behind them, frowning, agitated.

"Your ring is very beautiful, Mrs. Williams."

Joan withdrew her hand and looked down, smoothing her thumb over the glossy royal-blue enamel. "I'm glad you think so, it really is, isn't it. I always thought it is like the Tugan night sky. Garrick, can you serve Charlotte some stew, and yourself? I'll just have a potato cake and a little butter. Cooking never does much for my appetite. Now tell me." Her eyes were shining. It was a trick of her face, Charlotte thought, that Joan Williams often looked as if on the verge of tears. "Of course I want to hear all about your work at Mary's, but first I want to know how your patients are."

Garrick, emanating disapproval, did as he was bidden. Joan and Charlotte talked about the collie pups due at Mac and Rachel's, and then about horses, about which Joan knew a surprising amount, and which she missed, she said, on Tuga. She had ridden a beautiful bay hackney as a teenager and had not seen a horse since she was last walking in Regent's Park—but here memory seemed to fail, and she left off the recollection.

Joan ate almost nothing, Charlotte noticed, but she seemed to take pleasure in every bite that Charlotte herself took, so that she felt obliged to keep eating, though she also had little appetite and indeed was fighting surges of nausea, whenever she thought of Dan. Once or twice Joan seemed to slow, and when Garrick excused himself and went to the bathroom Joan exhaled heavily and rested her head for a second time in her hands.

"Are you all right, Mrs. Williams?" Charlotte asked softly.

"Mmm. Help me to the sofa, Charlotte, and when Garrick comes back we shall ask him for a little of that beautiful cake you brought us, and to make some sweet saloop. Perhaps one day he will teach you the traditional Tugan saloop recipe."

"I'd love that," Charlotte said, wondering why on earth the pastor would want to start giving her cooking lessons. She offered Joan her arm and Joan stood slowly with Charlotte's help. She seemed to have aged twenty years during dinner. They walked together to the sofa and Joan sat down abruptly. Garrick emerged, surprised to see the two women had moved.

"Time for you to go to bed, I'd say, Joanie."

Charlotte was inclined to agree. Joan looked clammy, she thought, and gray.

"Thank you so much for dinner, it was wonderful. If you don't mind I won't stay for saloop, I'll get going and leave you in peace. It's been wonderful, thank you."

"It has been wonderful, yes. Really wonderful. I hope you'll come often now. Ah." Joan smiled, but her face began to twist. "Ahh, ahhh." This last sound faded to an odd whistle, as if a balloon were deflating. Her head fell forward and she slumped over the footstool.

"Joan!" Garrick sprang across the room but Charlotte was already there, heaving her into the recovery position.

"Help me lift her."

"Do something, oh, do something! She needs Saul!"

Charlotte went to stand.

"No, not you! You stay with her, you're, you're medical!" Garrick gave a last agonized look at Joan, who was unresponsive, the whites of her eyes visible. "Just wait, Joanie, just wait there, I'm going for Saul, I'm getting Saul."

Charlotte was left with Joan. Medical she might be, but this was far beyond her expertise. She checked Joan's airways, she listened for breathing and heard nothing. She began rescue breaths, but had done only three when Joan gasped and shifted, so Charlotte took her hand and began to talk, slow and continuously, words of reassurance. Saul was coming, Joan was to hang on, Garrick would bring the doctor, Garrick would be back.

Garrick returned with Saul, and Dan. Charlotte was kneeling over Joan with her limp wrist in one hand, taking her pulse. Startled, she locked eyes with Dan for a fleeting moment, and then looked away. It was many hours past six.

Saul came to kneel beside her.

"Exactly what happened?"

"She seemed tired and pale, and then about fifteen, twenty minutes ago she seemed to flag so I was going home, and then she collapsed. She stopped breathing for a period and I started rescue breaths but she gasped and breathing resumed, so I stopped, and then you came. Pulse is sixty-three."

Between them Joan began to stir again, distressed. Her head was turning now from side to side, her eyes open, seemingly without focus. Garrick did not approach but remained in the kitchen, looking stricken.

"Joanie, it's Saul, we're here."

Her hand was flailing and Saul grabbed it, firmly, and held it to his lips. "Joanie, we're all here."

After that Joan came round quickly. Within moments she was already struggling to sit up. Dan and Saul were kneeling on either side of her and she slumped against Saul, gray-faced and sweating.

"We're going to put you to bed now, and find out what's going on."

Joan gave an indistinct noise of assent.

Charlotte was backing towards the door, to give them privacy. But hers was the face on which Joan seemed to focus.

"Charlotte," Joan whispered suddenly, her first cogent words, and so Charlotte stopped. She set her bag down again and went and knelt in front of Joan, and took her hand.

"I'm sorry," Joan managed. "Not very—hospitable. Will you come back?"

Charlotte reassured her that she would, she would come again soon. Dan was near her and she could feel his eyes fixed on her face, and the burning of her own cheeks. He had shaved, she noticed, and the morning's wild look had left him. She would not, could not meet his gaze, though his hurt and confusion reached her nonetheless. Charlotte squeezed Joan's hand once more and then retreated. Dan and Saul carried Joan into her bedroom and Garrick followed, wringing his hands. Charlotte cleared the food from the table, stacking plates in the sink, finding smaller bowls for the leftovers. She washed up as fast as she could and then let herself out, before Dan could reemerge. Never again, she thought, as her adrenaline slowly receded and her claustrophobia returned, never again would she set foot in a place that did not have an airport.

49

North Beach was empty, covered in black seaweed as Charlotte had not seen it before, black ropes and fat swollen bladders in a mucky tideline of crushed shells and debris, and a strong scent of seaweed on the air. The beach was steep, the sand darker and coarser than elsewhere on the island, and the palms grew almost horizontally out towards the water, thrust forward like lances. Someone had hung little woven baskets in some of the trees—for long-ago candles, maybe. A crisp packet and two empty Fanta bottles lay beneath the canopy of a low sea hibiscus, surrounded by a scattering of cigarette butts. The sun had gone but it was still light, and the sand and air felt damp. Charlotte kicked off her sandals, dropped her bag, and sat. There was the sound of the sea, the wind, and the dry susurration of the palm fronds. At the water's edge she shouted an expletive, not very loudly, but then tried again just once, from the bottom of her lungs.

She had come specifically and deliberately to cry but discovered, now that she was here, that nothing happened. It had been a romantic idea, to sit in solitude and weep while the heedless waves crashed before her and the sight of the vast empty water reflected back the truth of loneliness, despair, indifference, and perhaps the triviality of individual human suffering. But instead she felt only a great fatigue, and a sense of purposelessness. No further urge to shout. No grand sorrow cracked and opened in her, promising catharsis. She had searched her whole life for her father and had found him, and in doing so had found—nothing. Trash. Her mother might have lied, but she had not been wrong. Charlotte should not have come to Tuga. She sat so still that the ghost crabs she had scattered soon resurfaced, resuming their busy traffic from hole to hole, from miniature dune to dune.

Someone sat down beside her, and the crabs took fright and vanished. It was Levi, in his tiny shorts, and carrying a holdall from which spilled various ropes and thick, pastel-colored elastic bands, the accoutrements of a 1980s aerobics class. In the wind she had not heard his approach.

"*Paz*, Dolittle."

"How did you know I was here?"

"I didn't, I came here to work out. This is my beach, remember? I showed you."

"Oh. Yes. Sorry for stealing your beach. There aren't many places to be alone on Tuga, I'm discovering. Lonely, yes, but alone is a bit trickier. Don't let me stop your workout, I'll go."

"My house, my beach, all yours, *havera*."

He stood to leave but she grabbed for his hand and pulled him back down beside her.

"Don't. Don't go, I'm glad you're here."

Levi dropped his bag and lowered himself again, surprisingly yogic and agile. Together they looked out at the water. She felt him next to her, waiting.

"I can't actually believe this is my life. It's all such an unbelievably sordid mess—but the thing is, I came looking for it, and now I feel actually ill, I can't—" And here came the tears, hot and fast, a burning mass in her throat that made it hard to speak. The unexpected comfort and relief of Levi, the immediate expansion of her heart at the sound of his voice, had come upon her like all she hadn't known she needed. Levi's presence had brought forth everything she'd hoped the beach might draw.

"It makes the most terrible revolting sense and I am just so angry with myself for being so fucking childish. What did I think I would find here, a new life? A daddy to make it all better? Something that somehow explained all of my stupid choices, how incapable I actually am of engaging with other humans?"

"What happened?"

"I solved my great mystery, I was right, clever me, my father is from Tuga. Was." She gave a tight, bitter laugh. "Johannes Zekri. Garrick told me."

"*No.*"

"Yup. You can't tell anyone. No one, not one soul. He and Garrick went on some trip to England, Garrick didn't know about me, obviously, but he knew all about Johannes meeting my mother and"—her fists were clenched, knuckles white—"literally, she just picked up a nothing random stranger—"

"So Dan's father is—"

"I know."

"*Guay de mi.* Wow. *Wow.*"

Levi touched his shoulder to hers, and she leaned against him. That single point of contact between them, his arm against hers, felt like the source of all her remaining strength. Levi's shock, too, was somehow consoling.

"I mean, no wonder my mother didn't want me to know, and no wonder she's been so mental about me being here, it's just so horrible and sad and—I just literally want to go back in time, I just—"

From his gym bag Levi pulled a flowery peach and lilac flannel printed with repeating unicorns, and handed it to her. Charlotte managed a weak laugh at the sight of it before pressing it over her face with both hands. Her shoulders heaved. Levi waited.

There was the first bat, brown-black and silent as it crossed the still-pale sky, the island's sign to all roaming children to put down the tools of their play and run home for supper. Dusk would soon come and the bats would mass and scream in the huge old jackfruit trees behind them, but for now the only sound was of the leaves and waves, and Charlotte's breathing, shallow in her chest. Levi felt her arm against his, in turn. His mind was working hard and fast, following the ramifications of all that Charlotte was struggling to assimilate.

That she loved Dan was obvious. All this shame and rage, all the tears he longed to kiss from her wet lashes, it was because Dan was swept forever out of reach.

While this came to him Charlotte laid her cheek against his shoulder. On the sand her hand found his, and interlaced her fingers. After a moment of stillness she lifted her head a little and turned to look at him, her eyes red-rimmed, her face a question.

His resolve wavered as Charlotte moved closer, and when he inclined towards her she rested her temple against his. She was electric and she drew him, but she was alight with pain and needs he knew he could not meet. She had loved Dan. What she did not need was intimacy sought for consolation. She did not need cheap, which was, inevitably, how she saw him—he himself had told her often enough that was what he stood for, and he could not blame her for having listened. Levi was not a man who turned weakness to his own advantage. Everything had changed. He lifted a hand to her cheek and even in the cool breeze felt it hot, beneath his palm.

"Not a good idea, *kerida*," he whispered, into her hair, but was unable to stop himself from stroking her face beneath his thumb, from breathing in the scent of her. Then he disengaged himself and stood. A huge, pale rock lay beside him on the beach and Charlotte watched as he picked this up and hurled it, like a shot put, deep into the water.

"*Guay de mi*, come, Dolittle. Don't test me. You need to go home, have some proper dinner, go to sleep. I'll give you a ride."

She drew her knees up to her chest, making herself very small beside him. "You're right. You're right. Bad idea, thank you. No. I'll stay here, I think."

"I'll wait for you at the road as long as you need."

She shook her head.

"Levi, I wasn't—"

"It's OK. We're *haverim*, you and me. I'm here, I'm easy, I ain't going anywhere."

He was not easy. He was in pain, somewhere around the solar plexus. He shouldered his bag, and stood over her, awkward, and then turned back into the jungle and made for his bike. He felt emptied of hope and filled, instead, with a sense that something he might once have reached for, worked for, striven to be worthy of, in the days when it had been a fair fight, had slipped forever beyond his grasp.

50

"She's tired today, isn't she."

Betsey Coffee closed the door of Joan's bedroom softly behind her, addressing Garrick and Moz. She had taken in a sweetened saloop, lovingly prepared in the cafe and carried over in a tartan Thermos flask, to be decanted into one of Joan's own teapots. A minister's wife must have an armory of teapots ready to deploy at any moment, and from Joan's collection Betsey had chosen her own favorite, white Meakin porcelain painted with faded orange poppies. This and two empty teacups she now held with professional competence, balanced on one forearm on a painted tea tray. Moz took it from her, adding the cups and saucers to an already full sink.

"Joan wanted the vet in to see her this morning, for some reason. She's had too many visitors," said Garrick shortly, and Moz frowned at him, but Betsey's robust self-confidence prevented her from fearing this might apply to present company. She nodded, full of sympathy.

"Well, it's Joan, isn't it, we all just want to see her on her feet again. Isn't that just classic Joan, inviting the visiting vet round for tea when she's the one feeling poorly? I'm sure Charlotte doesn't expect entertaining, now of all times. I've left some bits in the larder for you, I showed Moz before." She paused, her hand on the front door. "Speaking of visitors, I saw Katie Salmon as I was on my way up, she looked to be coming from here."

"Katie Salmon," said Moz, turning from the sink and drying her hands on an embroidered muslin tucked into her waistband for this purpose, "is an angel sent from heaven. I truly believe it."

"Well. Our Joan deserves no less."

"She's got a magic to her, that girl. Her hands, her manner, the whole package. Dan's lost his mind not to marry her."

"He'll come round," said Betsey comfortably. "I feel sure of it. He's been all over the shop, hasn't he, between one thing and another. He's all hung up on England, and Englishy things. Back home after so long, and his dad gone since he was last here. If they're meant to be, he'll come round."

"And if she leaves before he comes to his senses?"

"She's not going anywhere. She planned and trained six months and she's not throwing in the towel when she's needed, marriage or no marriage. She's told me, and she told Mac's Rachel." Betsey resettled her straw hat. "Anyway, you know as well as I do it's not that easy to get off the island even when you want to, how would she get a berth? She's here a year at least. Long enough to get Joan well again, and that's what matters most."

Betsey took her leave. She would resume her post at the coffee maker, where she could disseminate the hopeful bulletin that Joan had been quiet but smiling; pale, but keeping down the saloop, which Betsey herself had sweetened with coconut sugar and fortified with some ginger and cardamom, for nausea.

Betsey had been gone less than five minutes when Garrick and Moz heard the sound of an engine and the kitchen window darkened behind the lace curtains, as someone parked far too close to the house. Fatigued with social niceties, they exchanged a brief glance.

There was a loud rap, and then the kitchen door opened. Grand Mary stood erect, holding aloft the walking stick with which she had knocked. She looked like a tiny dictator about to address the people she suppressed. Together with a black peaked cap, she wore enormous black sunglasses that gave her the outsized, globular eyes of a fly.

Garrick rose.

"Mary. This is a surprise."

"Shouldn't be. Joan asked me to come."

Mary entered the kitchen, without removing the sunglasses, stick still held aloft, as if on guard for ambush. She needed no help walking, so was it a weapon? Moz wondered.

Grand Mary was only twenty years her senior and had left the island for a long period during Moz's childhood. She had gone away a fierce young woman and come back to Tuga like this, as far as Moz could recall, mysteriously rich, imperiously mannerless. Moz could not think of anyone she'd less like to find looming over her own deathbed than Grand Mary, horribly alive with her own particular poison.

Deathbed. The word dogged her, each time she saw her sister-in-law's gaunt face, white against her faded Liberty nightdress, a riot of English wildflowers with some incongruous beads, purple glittery acrylic daisies, stitched into a heart shape on the breast pocket. Joan herself had said it yesterday. *I am on my deathbed, Mozzy.* It sounded so Victorian, like something that ought to have been cast off with crinolines, and smelling salts. "Oooh, you're at death's door," Moz had countered, in her own mother's most scandalized voice, and Joan had laughed, painfully, and said in the same tones, "Like death warmed up," and then they had fallen about together until Garrick's head had appeared around the door, a rigid mask of disapproval, and when he withdrew this had worsened their fit of giggles. Joan could still bubble over with that hard-won precious laughter. How could Betsey Coffee be blamed for thinking she would get better?

"I think she's sleeping at the minute."

Mary sat down in a kitchen chair, and laid her walking stick across her lap. She glared up at Moz, jaw set into an underbite, blue penciled eyebrows raised.

"I'm here now, Fermoza."

"Still," said Moz steadily, refusing to be rattled by this condescending appropriation of her own full name. She had been teaching long enough, and was more than capable of handling defiance. "If she's asleep we can't disturb her."

But when she crept in she found that Joan had heard Mary's voice, and was anxious she be admitted. Who knew why; their relationship remained one of the island's mysteries. But what Joanie wanted, Joanie got. Moz led Mary in and closed the door. As a small private act of rebellion, she did not offer Mary a cup of tea.

Mary's car reversed at speed, and as the car moved away from the window, light returned to the kitchen.

"Joanie's crying," Moz hissed to Garrick, enraged. "Really crying."

"Should I, ah. Should I go in?"

"Oh, you are a useless lummox, how should I know? She's your wife. Do whatever you normally do when she's upset."

"Ah." Garrick inspected a loose thread on his shirtsleeve. "Crying's not really something she's gone in for, is the thing."

Moz washed her hands and dried them, took the fish out of the oven and slammed the hot tray onto the hob. She pulled off her apron. She didn't know why she'd even asked the question. Of course Joan would never cry on Garrick. Moz had never understood their marriage, she thought wearily, for the millionth time; the polite formality of it, the carefulness, Joanie's devotion to Garrick's every whim, attuned to his needs like an obsequious valet while concealing from him even the idea that she might have needs of her own. Not to trouble him, not to bother him, those were Joan's abiding and near-obsessional guiding principles. Why not bother him? Moz wanted to know. What's he saving all this grand energy *for*? Might he not feel some relief at the idea of his wife as a nuanced human person? But there'd be no changing it now. If Joanie was crying she needed strong arms around her, and those arms were going to be Moz's.

"I've always known Mary was pure poison but I'd never have thought she'd upset a dying woman," Moz said to Garrick now, one hand on Joan's door handle. Her brother was an old fossil, she thought, irritated; and grateful, as she was every day, for Saul's warmth, his willingness, his open heart. "I tell you something, we won't let her in again. I'll warn Saul and Katie as well. Joan is never to see her again as long as she lives. *Guay de mi*, I didn't mean— anyway. Turn the oven off for me, there, that knob there. It's your oven, Garrick! *Streuth.*"

51

"Oh, but we've been taking great care of her in here," Betsey Coffee was saying to Sylvester, who had come next door for waffles and had stayed through breakfast service and deep into the lunchtime rush. If anyone had urgent shopping needs he wasn't hard to find. "She has to stay, don't you reckon?"

Natalie Lindo was sitting at the table closest to Betsey's till, exhausted from a night up with a colicky baby, lured in for a saloop on her way to buy red thread.

"The vet?" she asked, interested.

Natalie and her husband kept only a few sheep, all of whom had survived the last six months with disappointingly robust health. She had to rely on others for her gossip about the glamorous Londoner who stirred up so much interest. Natalie's youngest was weaning, but when it stopped smearing her with everything she planned to make herself a copy of Charlotte Walker's neatly tailored cargo trousers.

"Not the vet. Katie Salmon. Come all this way and now Dan Zekri says he isn't going to marry her."

At the far end of the coffee bar with a saloop and a platter of banana pancakes, Anwuli Davenport looked up. Between them, Anwuli and Isadora had twelve nephews on the island, and woe betide any of them who discarded a woman the way Dan Zekri had thrown over Katie Salmon.

"I tell you, that boy came back thinking he the best thing since sliced bread. He had the cheek to show up on my doorstep telling

256

me he wanted to check my blood pressure and I told him, 'I changed your nappies, *ijiko*, and you ain't checking my nothing for nothing. As long as Dr. Gabbai's standing, I go to Dr. Gabbai.'"

"Why would she stay on Tuga when Zekri's left her high and dry?" Sylvester wanted to know.

"She's cured my sciatica," said Betsey, adoring.

"She's taught me how to lift boxes properly in the shop. She's got me doing Pilates and all."

"She ain't going to stay on Tuga to be your Pilates teacher," Anwuli said to Sylvester, withering.

"Enough," boomed Saul from his corner table, laying down a month-old copy of *The Times*. No one had seen him there behind his newspaper or, if they had, they'd forgotten him in all the excitement. Betsey, who had earlier served his toast and etrog jam and ought to have recalled herself, retreated shamefaced behind the coffee machine.

"Stop turning that poor young couple's troubles into a soap opera," Saul added, for good measure. But this had gone too far.

"Oh, come off it, Saulie." Sylvester spun his stool around. "We are worried is all. That sweet girl far from home and I know he's your nephew but Dan ain't done right by her. You don't bring a woman to Tuga with promises and all sorts, and then decide once she gets here that you change your mind."

"Shown himself in a poor light," agreed Anwuli, forking a pancake. "Now we know there ain't no trusting that boy." She took the remaining coconut syrup from Sylvester and tipped it into the dregs of her saloop.

Saul felt the return of his despair. Too young, too long away, Dan had never been an easy sell to the older islanders, but this Katie business had been the last straw. He was FFA now; had forgotten island decorum and kindness and manners; worst of all, he had thrown over the sweet girl who had danced their dances, listened to their stories, and eased their aches and pains. They had never laid eyes on her until Island Open; now they could not be without her. Katie was their physiotherapist; their doctor was Saul Gabbai, and that was the end of it.

Saul stood wearily, indicating that Betsey should add his breakfast to his tab and he would see her later, and left to see Joan, whose condition was not good. Then, inevitably, on to the clinic to wheedle with patients refusing to keep their appointments with Dan. Today was supposed to be a day off, but it did not seem he'd ever be allowed to retire.

52

Joan Williams died on April Fool's Day and was buried in the New Cemetery the following morning, a day of clear skies, unbroken sunshine, and a mute, collective shock. Nobody had known she was dying, and this concealment had the strange effect of making the outer circle notably less composed than the principal mourners.

Because the minister was the bereaved, his sister Moz led the service. It was she who gave the eulogy, too, who spoke of her beloved Joanie as the soul of the island, treasured friend and trusted confidante to all, of her open heart, her generosity. Joan's life's work had been to care for others, Moz said, and as she spoke she wondered why, when it would have filled Joan with modest pride, to speak this truth aloud nonetheless made her own anger rise. Joan had longed for children and it had not been possible, and Moz had watched as a series of miscarriages had made her abject with guilt at what she saw to be a failure of her own wifely duty, even as—on at least one occasion— they'd almost killed her. Joan became intent on a lifelong compensation, with a devotion to Garrick's daily comforts that bordered on fanaticism. It had been on her mind even these last weeks. *It was my fault, Mozzy,* Joan had whispered, only a few days before she died, *the truth is that I denied him a child,* and when Moz had replied quite sharply that she could hardly be said to have miscarried on purpose Joan had simply shaken her head, too weak to argue further.

"Joan first came to Tuga de Oro when she was six," Moz read, squinting through reading glasses at her own scrawls, though she knew this history by heart in any case, "as youngest daughter of the then

Administrator, Hector Swire. They'd been in Rhodesia, and found us somewhat lacking in dinners and balls. But they stayed on, and made the best of us. Joan loved Tuga from the first, and passed five happy years here. I remember how jealous I was at school that she could already tell the time. And then, being Joanie, she taught me.

"At eleven she was sent home to England, to boarding school, and did not see her parents again until she finished school and came out to join them for the final Christmas of their posting, after the bill of rights that year removed a British Administrator from Tuga de Oro and restored full authority to the elected members of Island Council. Where it always should have been." Saul began to clear his throat, warning her off politics. Moz, refusing to look at him, went on, "As fate would have it, my brother Garrick was on that same ship as Joan, coming home after university and a period strengthening his ties with the British Humanist Association. And if Joanie couldn't make a man believe in God then nothing ever would." This won a fond, if muted laugh. "The rest, as they say, is history. One can only imagine how the Swires felt when their eighteen-year-old daughter disembarked, engaged to a Tugan pastor. Joan has hinted that it was not exactly *the thing*. If nothing else I'm fairly sure her parents thought we'd all go to pieces without an Administrator nannying us and interfering where they weren't wanted, but whatever she heard from them, Joan was discreet about it, like she was in everything. Certainly Joan felt no longing for England and went back only once in her life, many years later, after the death of a beloved aunt." Moz took a steadying breath, for here came the harder part to read. It was like a school assembly, and she was needed at the helm of the ship. Some of her smaller pupils were in attendance, and it would not do to frighten them with an unrecognizable Miss Moz.

"Though raised with very different expectations, Joan gave her whole soul to making life here beautiful for Garrick, and for all of us. She was without pretension, without artifice, without edge. She was my sister," she said, unable to look anywhere but at the shaking paper in her hands, "my sister, sister-in-law, sister-in-spirit, sister in life. The greatest gift my brother ever gave our family was to marry her."

Moz embraced Garrick, and they stood together a long time. Garrick then thanked them all for coming, expressing his hope that they would forgive Joan this one concealment. It was, he went on, and this was the only time his voice broke, the only lie of her open-hearted life.

Having had her say, Moz now felt exhausted, and wobbly with the relief of having acquitted herself with sufficient composure. Whether Garrick and Joan had had their say was another matter. Their last days were spent in the sort of obsessive mutual consideration that had characterized their marriage. Moz had tried to withdraw herself discreetly where she could, to offer husband and wife the chance to speak openly. But if she sought to leave the room Joan would call her back, take her hand, grip her with surprising strength, and look between brother and sister with silent love and gratitude. Moz brought levity, which was her intention. She brought practicality, and she tried to set an example of fearlessness and particularly calm to Garrick, who, having comforted the dying for decades, seemed to have forgotten all of what he knew mattered in those final days. He spent hours adjusting the shutters so that Joan might sleep better, despite her protestations that she did not mind the chinks of light. He drove to the moshav for a particular coconut jelly, though anyone would have gone for him, and Joan was barely eating. He, who had abided quietly at so many bedsides, could barely sit at this one. Moz had watched with pity, and frustration.

In her pocket, Moz crushed the notes of her speech to a tight ball. Anodyne, she thought, anodyne and empty. Joan had deserved better, today, and always. She wanted to cry out, *I loved her and still I never reached her.* Who had she been, Joan Zinnia Swire Williams? What had been her truth? Moz didn't know, not really, and if Moz didn't then no one did.

*

"It's her right not to spend her last days saying goodbye to every Tom, Dick, and Harry, everyone sobbing all over her and whatnot," Betsey would say stoutly, though privately she was hurt not to have been an exception. But then Joan had left them all gifts, such thoughtful gifts, on a list that must have been pages long, its length and detail making clear that Joan herself had long accepted she was dying. Betsey wept over the Meakin teapot, reverentially delivered by Alex dos Santos in one of Joan's own baskets, and it went pride of place on the high shelf behind the coffee counter. Any Tugan worth her salt would know to whom that teapot had once belonged. Betsey moved her orchids aside, and even shifted her framed picture of Herb and Virginia Moore, a spangled, sepia photograph that was the only image of the infamous string of conch pearls, the loss of which had inspired the annual Pearl Day Picnic. Betsey recognized this teapot as what it was—a teapot of explanation, of apology, and of love.

53

Most evenings Charlotte hid at home, keeping her distance from the Rockhopper, and from whichever hop or barbecue might be commanding the community's attention. She was avoiding Dan, who had got the message, but shot her burning, plaintive looks that made her feel uncomfortable, and sometimes actually nauseated. Levi seemed to be avoiding her, in turn, though someone was training and tying up the bougainvillea plants, already two feet tall and thickening with glossy leaves along the flank of the small house. Whenever she passed she begged them, silently, not to flower until after she'd gone.

She did not have long left before Island Close, but the weeks stretched ahead interminably, and working helped. In addition to her patients and her research, she had begun a report for the Island Council, in which she hoped to argue that there was every justification for hiring a full-time salaried island vet. The improvement in the productivity of the farms would justify the cost, let alone the protection it would offer against future alien-species invasions, epidemics, and potential zoonotic transmission. This last point— guarding against a human epidemic that would overwhelm the medical resources—she hoped would encourage the British government to cover the costs. A lot of what she thought about while in hiding from Tuga was Tuga. The rest of the time she rewatched the movies she had downloaded on her laptop, wove wonky boxes out of palm leaves, and composed emails to her mother demanding her full history with Johannes, none of which she ever sent.

This evening she had a big old collie boarding with her, to spare the owners, who were a busy farming family on the moshav. They'd first brought Lobo to her ten days earlier with an enormous ruptured soft-tissue sarcoma on the back of his left front leg. Why they'd not brought the dog in long before it had reached this state was not a question she could ever ask and, in any case, she knew the answer. They were busy working, farming, living, surviving. They had six children under the age of ten. And they loved Lobo, who wasn't young, and they were scared of what she'd tell them. But on the X-rays there was no sign the cancer had spread, and so the prognosis was good. The dog was staying with her for a few days so she could change his dressings regularly, while the owners decided what to do. It was also for company, if she was honest with herself. She had volunteered with great eagerness.

Lobo was a working dog and liked to be helpful. Long before Charlotte would have known to anticipate a visitor he set up an early-warning system of pricked ears and a low growl, and then lifted his head and released a volley of sharp barks. They were sitting together on the floor beside the sofa, and Charlotte placed a calming hand on his back.

"Who's coming, Lobo?" she asked him, in a whisper. "Who do you think it is?"

Lobo whined. Then the door opened, and in walked Katie Salmon.

Charlotte and Katie had said a number of strangely awkward hellos in passing since their afternoon of cargo inspection, and had spoken brief and cordial words at Joan's funeral. There was some expectation that two new FFA young women should automatically befriend one another, but neither had sought out the other's company till now, and this lack of instant communion had been taken by many islanders as the most damning proof so far of Charlotte's designs on Dan Zekri.

Dan had implied that he and Katie had fundamental incompatibilities and that, even without his feelings for Charlotte, it would have ended. Still, Charlotte urgently wished his relationship repaired. She wanted them married; married and preferably relocated to Iceland or Greenland or indeed to any other land to which she herself was unlikely ever to go.

"Who's this?" asked Katie, whose neutral expression had lifted to delight at the sight of the dog. Charlotte patted the collie's flank.

"This is Lobo. Shhh, Lobo. He's boarding with me for a bit of inpatient TLC." She pointed to his bandaged forepaw.

"Can I stroke him, will he mind? What happened to him?"

"Yes, he's friendly, just loud. Soft-tissue sarcoma. The surface burst and it's hurting. The family live on the moshav, they were driving back and forth for dressing changes every day, but it's too far so Lobo's staying with me while they figure out what to do."

Katie bent over and took Lobo's long head in her two hands, scratching him behind both ears. Moments later she was forehead to forehead with the dog, nuzzling, accepting licks on her nose and cheeks.

"What's the decision?" she asked, muffled.

"Well. If I wasn't here then Mac's Rachel would have amputated, or maybe one of the doctors, I guess. And without a surgeon that isn't actually a bad option, dogs don't do badly on three legs. In an ideal world a specialist would remove the mass and spare the leg."

"Can you?"

"I'm not a specialist. I could have a go, but a new surgery without a proper clinic, without a veterinary nurse or anyone to assist— maybe a clean amputation isn't wrong to play it safe. It's complicated."

"All medicine on Tuga is a bit complicated."

"That is definitely true."

"Do you know they've never had a female doctor? I can't help but feel it shows in policy, somehow. Some stuff that's been left to slip . . ."

When she failed to finish the sentence Charlotte asked, "Can I get you a drink?"

"Yes, please." Katie straightened and then sat down on the other side of Lobo, lowering herself into a cross-legged position without touching her hands to the floor, her spine erect like a dancer's. She was elegant, Charlotte realized, surprised. She concealed this elegance, somehow, distracted from it with kitsch and sparkles.

Charlotte returned with Levi's bourbon, untouched since the night of the hurricane, and two of her many jam jars. Katie turned out to be a liberal pourer, and they sat together in the low light, the dog panting loudly between them. Katie put both hands on Lobo's shoulder, measuring the muscles beneath her palms, and then began to give him a slow massage.

"There are just such limited resources," Katie resumed, and raised her glass. "*Salud!* Like all that crazy import stuff, the day I came."

Charlotte touched her jar to Katie's.

"*Salud.* Yes, that was classic. 'Hi, you've just arrived and you've got a job in, oh, I don't know, dental hygiene. Could you inspect these nectarines?'"

This won a laugh and Charlotte relaxed, just a fraction.

"I had no idea you did that for every ship."

"I didn't, that was the first time. It's absolutely essential biosecurity work and Saul and Elsie were just sending out anyone they bumped into at Betsey's."

"It was quite a good introduction."

"You know they didn't have mosquitoes here until five years ago?"

"Seriously?" Katie uncrossed her muscled legs and extended them. They looked exactly as Charlotte's own had when she first arrived. A mess of welts and scratches, swollen mosquito bites scratched to bleeding and scabbed over. For weeks, each swim in the sea would bring the unexpected sting of reactivated constellations.

"They came on a ship exactly like those flies we stopped. And now the island has heartworm, among other things. You can't get rid of mosquitoes now they're here."

"You know, I think Saul . . ." Katie looked up at the ceiling, watching the slow turn of the fan, and for a moment her thoughts appeared to drift. There seemed something she wanted to confide, Charlotte thought, though perhaps it had just been the mosquito story that had unsettled her. "But also," Katie added, in a quite different tone, "what the fuck do we know about anything here?"

Charlotte laughed with small but distinct delight at the word "fuck," which she had not heard since leaving England. She missed the emphasis and informality of profanity. It was a pleasant surprise, too, to hear that Katie could be humble. She usually gave the impression of impermeable confidence, an alienating quality reinforced by the islanders' seemingly wholesale fondness for her. This was a side Charlotte had not been able to imagine.

"Nothing," Charlotte said now. "I know fuck all about any of it. Less than I thought I knew when I got here. I was busy judging Saul for neglecting the biosecurity side, but he's been one doctor taking care of everyone with no money, no backup, no infrastructure. The conditions he's navigated have been heroic. It's more like frontline medicine really, and we waltz in expecting hospital decisions, hospital outcomes. The truth is I can't even begin to imagine how Tugans ought to make their choices. I came here hoping to persuade everyone to be investing in a hundred-year ecological future when most people are trying to get through the week. I am a privileged FFA idiot."

"I'm not exactly Tugan, either. It will take a long time to separate my assumptions from reality."

And meanwhile it turns out I actually am Tugan, Charlotte thought, with no little irony, given the context.

"All I know," said Katie, leaning forward to pour herself another hearty measure, "is that I have to fight my own impulse to jump into things until I'm absolutely sure. It's one of the reasons it's so important that one of the medics is Tugan, so that long-term needs are perceived correctly, rather than superficial firefighting from a well-meaning outsider. But if I could choose I'd have a woman, finally, to break down some of this old-school shame and taboo."

"In an ideal world the vet should be local, too," said Charlotte, thinking of her own report, and keen to avoid this oblique reference to Dan.

Katie lifted her bag from the floor to her lap. A rare sky blue among Katie's magenta and lilac possessions, it was covered in reversible sequins that showed, in this orientation, the heroine of a recent Disney film. Katie unzipped it.

"Joan Williams asked me to bring you something. She left a long list of bequests."

"I didn't know."

"Yes. Mostly it's crockery. Yours is a bit different."

Katie took a small blackened copper box from her bag and set it on the coffee table, between their jars. It rattled when Charlotte picked it up, so she lifted its lid. Loose, inside, was the huge royal-blue and gold enamel cocktail ring. She felt a strange prickle at the base of her neck.

"Why?" she asked finally.

"She didn't tell me, and I didn't ask. But she was very clear that this was for you. Everyone else has been given teacups. I agree it's odd. She was in her right mind, if that's a worry."

"That is what I was wondering."

"Clear as day to the end, except a few moments here and there, but this wasn't one of them. This was definitely for you. It's from Tiffany."

"I don't think I should take this, I really didn't know her very well. She was lovely to me organizing the fellowship and everything and I really liked her, but . . ." Charlotte drifted off, looking down at the ring. It was impossible not to slip it on to her finger, just for a moment. A tiny diamond was missing from the pavé around the outside but the others winked, a circle of flashing light as she turned her hand to and fro. The enamel, with its gold stars, was pebble-smooth. Stroking it was strangely evocative. She took it off and put it quickly back into the box.

"You know I was at dinner at their house when she collapsed a few weeks before she died?"

"Was that the last time you saw her?"

Charlotte shook her head. "I went to see her once, she sent for me and we did talk about—real things—but that seemed to be how she was. No small talk, very . . . deep. I didn't assume it was me, especially."

"Dying probably puts an end to small talk," said Katie reasonably. "But either way, I think if she wanted you to have it you should take it."

"You're right."

She could not imagine wearing it. But she would put it in her washbag, where she would catch glimpses of it. She began to stroke one of Lobo's silky ears with a finger. Katie was still kneading his flank, and the dog lay in elongated bliss between the two ministering women. Charlotte thought back to her strange morning with Joan.

"She talked a lot about why they hadn't had children. The language she used, I felt so sorry for her. Owed him, failed him, let him down, all that stuff. Like it was something she'd done to Garrick, like it was her fault."

"She was from another time, in lots of ways."

"This whole island is from another time," said Charlotte, for once allowing her exasperation to surface. To speak freely was a relief, and she realized that she now felt precisely the sort of communion with Katie that the island had expected, and that she'd believed impossible.

"It is," said Katie simply. "Joan was very shocked that I never want children."

Charlotte glanced up.

"I'm sure you know it was one of Dan's reasons for ending things. He thought he was fine with not having any and then it turned out he wasn't. I assume you do." Katie was now looking directly at Charlotte with a level gaze, and Charlotte's heart began to beat faster. "Want kids, I mean. I don't know if you and he have talked about it. But I do think you should know I am staying. I'm not going back to England, I want to stay. It's nothing to do with Dan, I feel I should say that too."

Charlotte shook her head tightly, as if to dislodge something. "Dan and I are—I can tell you with my hand on my heart that nothing will ever happen between us, truly. Ever. Never."

Katie finished her second drink and set her jam jar down on the floor. She sighed deeply, and laid her head back against the sofa cushion behind her.

"Well. If that's true then I don't really understand. But it will probably help with the Poor Katie business. I'd prefer not to be Poor Katie for much longer. Either way, we will all get over it. People do."

"You're so . . . grown-up."

"Maybe. I'm not sure. I really love the work here, and I feel I'm needed. If I ended up muddled in a bit of gossip for a bit, it shouldn't really be important, I'm still going to stick it out. I feel sad, about Dan. I thought we would get married. But I know that one day I will stop feeling sad, that's how life works. Things pass. Gossip. Pain. I'll be your surgical assistant, by the way, if it would help Lobo, if you decide to go ahead with his operation. You could always try and remove the mass and then amputate if it's not going well, after all. I've seen some things, I've a strong stomach."

"You grew up—"

"—in a rural cult, yes. I can birth a lamb. And skin a lamb."

"I see." Charlotte looked into her untouched bourbon. "I've not had much call for the latter."

"No. You could do it, though, I imagine. If pressed."

"Of course. If pressed."

54

It had been a quiet month, though by Tugan standards, the island was busy. An oil tanker and a yacht had called as well as the ship, bringing supplies, distraction, and even a few tourists and day visitors. Dan Zekri had been managing biosecurity for these arrivals, which disguised the redoubled boycott of his medical services. Joan's death subdued the community.

Katie Salmon had begun teaching a Pilates mat class in the Old Kal on Wednesday mornings and another on the beach on Thursday evenings, both oversubscribed, for if her other good deeds were not enough, Moz had made it known how much comfort Joan had derived from Katie's competence and care. When the ship came in, Katie was first in line at Customs House, anticipating some important delivery, which suggested that the rumors were true—for now, she was staying on the island. Official berths were full, but the yacht could have taken her on to Cape Verde, after all, and from there she could easily have flown home. An exit had presented itself—they were a nice crew, and took two Tugans needing to travel, in the end. And yet, she stayed.

In the month since their breakup Katie was seen to be much more cordial to Dan Zekri than were many others angry on her behalf. But soon they would all have to forgive him.

"The end of an era is upon us, for our beloved Doc Gabbai is standing down," announced a mournful Taxi. Dan had no desire to know what song might follow, and quickly switched off the radio.

*

Now it was the morning of Saul's retirement party and Garrick had come over, as usual, for breakfast. Moz was peeling a bowl of kiwis at the kitchen sink, and the two men were sharing a pot of coffee and a jug of cream. Moz was giving them particularly hearty breakfasts at the moment, because she wasn't sure what Garrick was doing about lunch.

Saul was leaning back in his chair and patting his stomach. Today they'd had rice pudding with coconut cream and walnuts, followed by scrambled eggs and goat's yogurt, and Saul felt ready to go back to bed to sleep it off. Usually he went to work on a piece of toast with cashew butter and jam, for jam was a Tugan love-language, and Saul received a lot of it. Well. Tomorrow he'd be retired, and could go back to bed after breakfast every day if he chose to, or not get up for it at all. The thought sat oddly. He looked at the cluster of jars on the kitchen table. He wondered if they would all still bring him jam.

"Will the island let him do it?" Garrick was asking. He was spreading etrog marmalade on a fourth piece of toast, adding support to Moz's theory that this breakfast with his sister and brother-in-law was all he ate all day, until he returned to their house for supper.

"They'll have to let him do it, and so they will. Tonight he'll be CMO, and first responder too. He'll do a good job and they'll be forced to forgive him. And they'll forget all about me."

"I'm sorry to say I think that's unlikely," Moz put in, from behind him. She kissed the top of Saul's head and returned to what she was doing. "Though I do wish they would forget you just a bit. Just a day, here and there."

"Tugans have long memories for romantic misbehavior," Garrick warned him. "A jilting CMO. And she's rather the cause célèbre, Poor Katie. And poor Lusi, too."

"One bad decision ought not to indict a character," said Moz firmly.

Garrick frowned, setting down his toast and wiping his fingers with great care. "Do you really believe that? About a betrayal on that scale? I'd have hoped we'd all set him a rather better example of behavior than that."

"Oh, don't be so pompous, of course I do. To err is human, et cetera. Remember what a sweet little boy he was, always overthinking and doubting himself, but very focused, very hardworking, and that didn't make him popular at school. And of course he didn't always have the easiest time at home . . ."

Garrick was glaring at her and had begun to look wobbly, and so she reined in her implied judgment. They had argued about Johannes in the past, and now was not the time to be casting aspersions on the damage he had or had not inflicted upon wife and child. She began to sweep fruit peelings into a bowl for the pig.

"I thought you were waiting for Dan to settle before you retired," Garrick said, turning decidedly back to Saul.

Saul considered the dregs of his coffee, and decided against them.

"I realized he'd never settle until he was forced to take the lead." He hesitated. "In truth—in truth, I was waiting as long as Joanie needed me."

Garrick nodded. Somehow he had known this. He reached to pat Saul's hand where it lay on the table. Saul took his, and squeezed it, and the two men sat in silence together. Moz, about to bring over a platter of fruit, instead turned her back on them and busied herself.

"You will come tonight, won't you?" Saul asked. His voice was husky, and he cleared his throat several times. "It would mean a lot to have the, ah, moral support."

Garrick said of course, he would be there to give Saul the send-off he deserved after forty years of devoted service. In the meantime he had to get to the Old Kal for a meeting of the Island Close committee, and he wanted to drop in on a moshavnik whose daughter in America had recently had a baby. He would work, because sometimes his work was to bring hope, even when privately he felt none. After a moment they wiped their eyes, each on a handkerchief that Joan had embroidered for him, and on they both went, into the day.

55

"Have you got a few minutes?"

It was Katie at his office door, in a pair of light twill trousers the color of candy floss, and a Care Bear T-shirt. Dan had bought her the T-shirt. He had hung both items of clothing on many drying racks. He had peeled them off her eager body, more to the point. Her hair was damp, and so he knew she had just showered after a morning swim in the ocean. She was at once deeply familiar, and at the same time entirely altered by the complex new feelings that she engendered. Guilt, laced with resentment about the guilt. Shame. Relief. More shame, about the relief. Disappointment with himself for doing something that made him seem to be a man who would do such a thing. He nodded at her, one nod too many.

"Can we walk? I want to show you something. I brought coconut water." Katie raised two plastic bottles, unlabeled and warped by Mac's chest freezer, and handed him one across the desk. If this was going to be a grand moment of reckoning, it seemed unlikely that she would have brought refreshments. Somewhat reassured, Dan took his cap and sunglasses and followed her.

Together they crossed the garden that lay between the clinic and the old Cole house, as it was still known, despite the months that he himself had lived there. Of course in the eyes of the island, it was the house to which he had lured Katie only to abandon her. Dan had moved back in with his mother, leaving Katie the old Cole house until she could get a berth home. On Tuga that could be months, if not more than a year. Until then he was trapped at

Lusi's, enduring her kindnesses, her concern for his breakfast, his sleep patterns, his mental health, and his own guilt that he had let her down, though she staunchly refused to concede it. Many of his Tugan contemporaries lived with their parents, so it did not represent the failure it might have done back in England. But still. He craved privacy. It was not a valued Tugan commodity.

It was much better to see Katie like this, Dan realized, on purpose, as opposed to the one or two or sometimes the farcical three times a day they passed one another, in line at Betsey's Cafe, or on Harbour Street, or parking Up Yard, at the beginning of hikes they might have taken together. Between crossing paths with Katie and crossing paths with Charlotte, who these days seemed actually to rear away whenever she caught a glimpse of him, leaving the house had become a treacherous business. And this was all without the myriad encounters with other islanders keen to offer tuppence on his poor life choices. On the radio Taxi played Cliff Richard's "We Don't Talk Anymore" with suspicious frequency, on one occasion repeating what he seemed to consider to be particularly pertinent lyrics as he faded out the song, "And maybe that's something to think about for some of us thinkin' we can do better, not to come crying as we go into this, another sunny Tuesday . . ."

Katie led him in the direction of Lemon Tree Valley. This was not a picturesque and private walk through the jungle, nor was it towards the beaches, but instead a steady and unrewarding uphill climb on the dusty road, towards a settlement further south. It was steep enough to make silence acceptable between them, and together they kept up a good and well-matched pace, as they always had.

The road curved upwards around a small valley, on the other side of which stood three pairs of small cottages, unexpected blocks of color on the rising far flank. Katie took a few steps into the low scrubgrass and sat down neatly, cross-legged. It was a bright morning, and her eyes were hidden behind the pink sunglasses, her hair pulled back with a pink gingham scrunchie, printed with pairs of red cherries. In the valley below them, two donkeys were tethered, nibbling at mintberry bushes, in the shade.

They were—where were they? Not a beauty spot. In clear sight of the adjoining cottages where Ruth dos Santos and Marianne Goss lived, and at the curve of a rutted track behind them. Katie said nothing, looking out, and Dan sat and waited, and the minutes passed. She had a businesslike air, and he now assumed that she wanted to talk about the house or maybe the clinic, and a way to work together until she left. Maybe she needed help trying to secure a berth. Charlotte's boat, the Island Close boat, would be long full, but there were occasionally last-minute changes and cancellations: a passenger who'd booked two years ago now needing to stay. Katie and Charlotte might end up leaving Tuga de Oro together, he thought, and wondered for the hundredth time how he had once felt so certain of the affection of each woman and yet somehow, through his own doing, had lost both. He was surprised to discover how much his body missed the slight, self-contained woman beside him, and that his instinct was to reach for her hand. If they had not been right together, they had not been all wrong, either. Then Ruth dos Santos stepped out of her kitchen door holding a woven basket of wet laundry, a small caramel goat skipping lightly behind her. Beside Dan, Katie sat up straighter, alert, watching.

Ruth wavered, and then made her way to the long line and began to pin up items, very slowly. It was possible the first would be dry by the time she'd emptied the basket. Skirts and tops, Alex's red shorts, a whole line of gray rags flapping.

"It's Ruth I wanted to talk to you about," said Katie quietly. "I thought today was the right day. Tonight you officially become CMO of Tuga. From tomorrow you are making policy. Now look. What do you see?"

"Is that a trick question?"

"No. I mean, as a doctor looking at a patient. What do you see?"

Dan watched Ruth, and Katie, he sensed, was watching him. Whatever she needed, he wanted to get it right. As they looked, the small goat extracted a graying white sock and began to chew it, thoughtfully.

"Well. Look at her bending and straightening, and with repeated torsion. Like this, I see zero evidence of back pain. So, I'm pretty sure I see a physically able woman who is potentially feigning or at least exaggerating a chronic injury to sustain an opiate dependence. Is that what you're showing me?"

Katie hugged her knees to her chest, and rested her chin on them. After a moment she said, without turning, "It is a shame that's what you see. Because I see a woman elegantly battling extreme post-partum incontinence, alone in rural poverty, for more than a decade."

"*What?*"

"And I'm going to help her."

"Wait—how did you—"

"I just *looked*, Dan. I saw."

A breeze lifted the long line of rags.

"Have you read her notes from that time? I suspect fourth-degree tear. Or even fistula. She hasn't left the house since she gave birth to Alex."

"Fistula! Jesus. But, Alex is alive. He's cognitively normal, he's—"

"Certainly a fourth-degree tear, then. Look, I'm not a gyno, I just know that something during that birth caused terrible damage. But the thing is, she doesn't need to live like this. I've found a surgeon in London who specializes in repairing OASISes, and she's agreed that she'll see Ruth and potentially operate. I need you to write the referral so she can get funding."

"London! She hasn't been to Town in ten years, how are you getting her to London? Have you examined her? A fourth-degree—no one can live like that for a decade! Surely if she was incontinent she'd have talked to Saul?"

"She was too ashamed to talk to Saul. She tried to mention something in the first weeks but he seemed to suggest it would improve itself and then I think it just got lost in all the rest of what was a totally hellish birth all round. She was in genuine agony for months after Alex was born; that wasn't feigned, at the time. But I didn't need to examine her. I just asked her, Dan, and she told me."

"I've never seen a fistula, I don't work in rural Mali or—We section here, if it's needed!"

"Shh, please, she'll hear you, you're shouting. It was a shoulder dystocia, sectioning wouldn't have helped. Saul did well to get Alex out without broken bones or nerve damage, or asphyxia."

Katie never shouted. It was a quirk of her baby voice that it got higher and more singsong as the topic darkened. Dan had always found it maddening, and found it maddening now. Katie went on, "You don't need to be defensive, you weren't on the island, you weren't even a doctor yet. This is the reality of birth, here, or has been. You say you want to help. If you want to help, see."

Dan was screwing and unscrewing the lid of his coconut water. It had once been an Evian bottle, and he ran his finger round the plastic contours of the Alps. In fifteen years in Europe he had never skied, and now it was one of so many things he regretted. But at university the medics' ski trip had been prohibitively expensive and, in any case, he would have been too embarrassed to be a beginner. How arrogant to be embarrassed that one couldn't instantaneously perform a skilled task, without practice or training. But he had been a self-important young idiot. He did not feel self-important now.

If Katie was right, this was a catastrophic dereliction of Tugan medical care. However Saul had managed the birth—and he did not envy attending to an older mother in a Tugan cottage, the baby's head delivered and a shoulder trapped behind the pubic bone while the clock ticked down to irreversible asphyxia, then stitching up the resulting mess—Ruth should have been followed up at six weeks and then again, if she was still symptomatic.

"Please don't think I'm blaming your uncle," said Katie, when Dan had not yet spoken. "I'm blaming a system. He's been one man in charge of far too much, for far too long. He's exhausted and overstretched. There's been no consistency of care with all these contract

278

doctors rotating in and out, and if I may say, no interest in women's health. But the system can change. We can change it. Look, tragedies happen, and I don't live in cloud cuckoo land, I know there is a certain reality to life on an isolated island, I know there's never going to be a NICU, or a medevac helicopter. And so much is beautiful, that feeling of extended family, and the way everyone is accepted as they are, but the other side of that acceptance is passivity. Ruth's addiction is just sort of permitted, and Saul writing her these whacking great prescriptions whenever she says her back hurts means that, for Ruth, accepting her as she is condemns her to stay that way. She told him she had some pain, that's all. And I don't know if it was her shock or trauma or just her embarrassment, but in any case he took her at her word and didn't ask any more questions, or didn't ask the right questions, or have the bandwidth for any of it. Certainly he didn't scan. That was remiss. At some point I want us to build a program of postpartum care, because even if she is an extreme case Ruth can't be the only woman left compromised by a birth. But for now it's Ruth I'm dealing with. One thing at a time."

"This is horrendous. Horrendous. That poor poor woman."

"Yes," said Katie simply. "So let's fix it."

She stood up in a single fluid motion, without using her hands. Then she turned and was back on the path before Dan could follow her. He stayed where he was, watching Ruth, who had stopped hanging laundry and was standing motionless in the garden, looking vacant. He raised a hand in greeting, across the small valley, and Ruth saw him and raised her own, slowly, as if underwater. Behind her the children jostled from the house, and Dan watched as together they ran to Ruth, and Alex closed her hand around what looked like a little sandwich, before they dashed off to where their bikes lay, and were gone. Ruth remained where she was, looking after them. The hand that held the sandwich fell to her side, as if she'd forgotten it was there.

On the road Katie waited, and they began to walk back down together.

"If you want to try and get Ruth on that ship, you should talk to Marianne Goss. She'd have to go with her."

"Yes. Well actually, I thought if we could find a berth for her on that boat before Island Close, maybe Charlotte Walker could keep an eye on her."

Dan glanced at Katie, but Katie was looking at the uneven road that sloped away ahead. Was it his imagination or had she flushed while she said this?

"I'm sure she'd be happy to help," he said evenly.

"Yes, I thought so too. I'll ask her."

"But if there's a berth coming up so soon, won't you want to take it?"

"No," Katie said, without breaking stride. "I'm not leaving. Had you hoped that I would?"

Katie's own frankness drew out of him what it always had, an unintended frankness of his own. He nodded.

"I feel guilty for derailing your life. Seeing you home in England would be one way of knowing it was being put back together again. Your team. Your hospital."

She reached out her hand and touched his arm, slowing him.

"Dan, wait a minute."

He stopped.

"I am sad. And hurt. And embarrassed. I loved you. Love you. And I don't like drama. I was angry, and probably still am quite angry, because I've tried very hard to make myself a life of stability and then you came along seeming solid, and then ended up making the most—noise. Mess, in my head. I need calm."

Dan let this break over him, knowing he deserved it. The last was a particular source of shame to him. Brave Katie, who had fought so hard for her right to self-determination, who had battled so hard for stability. He had plucked her from her life like a passing tornado and landed her here two years later, and thousands of miles away, and still alone.

"But I've been thinking and the truth is, while I do feel sad, if I am being really honest with myself then some of it's about the wrong things, maybe."

"What are the wrong things to feel sad about?"

Katie gave him a small, bleak smile. "We are so similar, you and me. And that's been a nice thing. We live well together. We work well together. But I wonder now if it, if it maybe wasn't very brave of us. Of me. I don't know, I haven't finished thinking. The one thing I do know is that I'm staying here, I'm going to live here, and so you and I will need to work together. I feel sad, and a bit lonely, maybe. But I also still feel all the things I felt when you first told me about Tuga de Oro, and that is exciting. I feel needed here, I recognize my place. I had an instinct that I would like it here, like the work, like the community, and that's been true even in this very short time since I came. The best way I can describe it is that it's been like a, a calling. And that is more important than my discomfort at being around you."

"You're a remarkable woman," Dan said, meaning it, but Katie frowned and gave a quick shake of her head. It was empty to admire a woman you had recently discarded. He felt duly chastened.

"I will say this. It is mostly your fault, what's happened with us, but not all of it. I don't particularly want to be friends with you right now, but we do need to be colleagues, so if you do feel guilty then please can you use your guilt to give me that, and make it work. And help Ruth."

Dan nodded his promise, for a moment unable to speak.

56

Dan sat at his desk, writing and rewriting his referral for Ruth dos Santos. Each iteration bubbled over with inappropriately emotional language, defensive statements, apologies, or contained an implied or overt criticism of his uncle.

"Has been suffering for the past decade from . . ."

". . . undiagnosed since the birth of her second child, eleven years ago . . ."

In the end he wrote: *Please see this fifty-six-year-old mother of two for urgent repair of a belatedly diagnosed fourth-degree postpartum tear. Appropriate post-operative pain management will need to be considered, as the patient suffers a long-standing opiate dependency, begun at the time of the obstructed birth and as a result of its physiological and psychological trauma. Her quality of life at present is poor, and its improvement rests in your hands.* If it was emotional, so be it; he felt emotional.

And meanwhile his ex-fiancée would now forever be in his clinic—he couldn't help but think of it as his clinic—though he recognized that his proprietary feelings were both childish and wishful thinking. He had summoned Katie here, and now she would not simply leave again at his will. Nor in good conscience could he wish for her departure any longer, faced with the reality of her determination to fix what was clearly broken on Tuga. Katie was right. If Ruth had had no follow-up care, likely others hadn't either. He would call in every woman who had a child of ten or under. And what about endometriosis? Menopause? Osteoporosis? A climate in which stepping on the scales for the doctor was considered impolite was not likely to be one that would foster open menstrual discussions. Katie had shown him all she knew, and all that he still had to learn.

During their last months together in England, the trunks had lain open in their living room, slowly accumulating items to be shipped. Solar-powered storm lanterns, walkie-talkies, a twenty-four-pack of the mixed-herb seasoning that he loved on scrambled eggs; a Bluetooth-enabled ultrasound probe, a huge financial investment but an indulgent and potentially lifesaving innovation on Tuga, where, during his childhood, the only ultrasound machine had been the property of one of the larger sheep farmers. There were seeds for his mother, soaps and creams and perfume, some casserole dishes, two cricket bats and twenty balls, a toolbox. Most things could be ordered through the shipping agents and if ordered might arrive, eventually. But this packing represented the scale of the lifestyle change that lay ahead, and occasionally an item would stir up his ambivalence.

The coffee syrup, for example. He had found a wholesale supplier and bought four one-liter bottles of the caramel-flavored syrup that Katie liked in her coffees. Katie herself did not seem particularly distraught at the thought that Tuga represented the end of endless coffee choices, the end of frivolous consumerism and things that were chemically engineered to taste like other things. She liked caramel lattes, she told him, but she liked normal lattes too. "You said we'll be friends with the people who grow our coffee beans," she'd said, when he had frowned over these glass bottles, trying to stuff them in between the new towels and the old duvet. "Isn't that more exciting than a thousand flavors?"

Dan, who had unthinkingly known the provenance of every mouthful he ate or drank during his childhood and with hindsight found it monotonous and parochial, was inclined to think not. He wanted a thousand flavors. A thousand flavors was nine hundred and ninety-nine more than he'd had, growing up. He would miss global supply chains. He would miss pumpkin spice, and free samples, and ready, dizzying excess. Not to mention their local Indian takeaway, and urban foxes, and live football, and trains, and anonymity.

To shore himself up during these moments of panic, he had leaned upon what he now saw had been Katie's solid and unwavering conviction. She had never veered and only now did he wonder, considering the degree of isolation, the scale of the change, whether that was perhaps a bit peculiar. From the first she had never tired of hearing about Tuga de Oro. Other friends in England were interested in his island home, but their anthropological enquiries were always tinged with a slightly patronizing disbelief. Katie instead pursued clear lines of interest, asked technical questions about the community, the staffing rotations, the bureaucratic complexities of the relationship with the NHS, the ecological resources, the rainfall, family life. It had been Katie who had persuaded him that the island's lifelong expectation of his return was not his curse but his gift. Perhaps it was. And maybe it had been a gift for Katie, too.

57

The Pantry was a small roadside supermarket run by Mac, up the hill from Lemon Tree Valley. It was almost entirely vertical, a breeze-block structure the size of a public lavatory that had several times been extended upwards and now had shelves that loomed high above, like a university library. Mac used a long hooked stick to pull down diapers and toilet paper, kitchen towel and other soft items that would fall like coconuts into the waiting arms of a practiced customer. From his seat behind the narrow counter Mac could reach the cigarettes and booze; condoms; razor blades; the table salt and cinnamon and chili flakes. On lower shelves were toothpaste, de-odorant, bars of Dove soap, hand-stuffed packets of cassava chips soaked in oil and salt, and honey banana. Mac was in the yard out back when a little girl ran in barefoot and took a running jump, finding a toehold in the slatted face of the high counter so that she stood leaning over it, an Italian at an espresso bar.

"Gum!" Annie called, and without lifting his head Mac shouted, "Marianne expect a please from you, young woman."

"Please!" Annie slapped down her precious coin. She lifted herself on to her straightened arms, feet levitating for a moment like a gym-nast before coming back down to land on her tiny toehold. The soles of her feet were filthy, and peeling.

"I give it, *kerida*," said Mac, "if you don't spit it."

Annie expressed outrage at this accusation. She did not spit gum, she told him. She had never done it in her life.

In the chest freezer were homemade ice pops, mango and guava and soursop. A child who performed his parents' shopping with what Mac considered to be sufficiently good comportment might, on rare occasions, be afforded one of these treats on the house. Annie was a scamp and a rascal, and Mac was almost certain that she stole bubblegum and possibly cigarettes when his back was turned. Yet still he coddled and petted her. He was moved by the camaraderie between the twins. Regardless of what he gave one they would share it equally, however small, however seemingly indivisible. By way of experiment he had once given Annie a single purple Smartie, only to find her outside moments later, carving it on the dusty wall with a pocketknife she was too young to possess. True to form, he came back into the shop now and wordlessly opened the lid of this freezer for her, and she dived in and came up grinning with a lolly in each hand.

"You going to celebrate the old doc tonight, Annie Goss?"

"Yes. Me and Alex got plans, we getting sign-ups for our apple-seedling business. They ain't grown yet, but we taking subscriptions. We been collecting a load of seeds."

"You always got plans," he told her, returning to his stool behind the counter. "You got endless plans, you demons. Put me down for two. I want 'em six inches high before I'm paying."

But she was gone, taking ice pops, bubblegum, and coin.

58

The sky was palest pink, rose-colored clouds fading now to lilac, the pastel ending of a fiery sunset. Wending their way to the Rock-hopper, Moz had abruptly stopped the car on the flank of Obiuto Hill and pulled a crotchety and unwilling Saul to the cliffs to watch these last moments together, a private recommunion before setting forth into the exposure of public ceremony.

Saul was anxious about this evening in a way that had taken him by surprise, for usually he liked a party. But he had not enjoyed the relentless talk of send-offs and endings, of closing chapters, of going out, either in style or with a bang. These comments had dogged him ever since the posters had gone up, his own face enlarged and repli-cated in Betsey's Cafe, above the till at Sylvester's, and even as far out as Mac's Pantry, the text beneath inviting islanders to bring their memories, as if it were a wake. When he grumbled about this to Moz, she retorted quite briskly that she was a busy woman with no time for self-indulgence. She dared him to say such a thing to Gar-rick, left with only work after a real memorial service.

"You're alive, you nitwit," she told him, taking his hand. "And so am I. That's the whole point. Look at the sky, look at all this. Look at what we have! You're starting your retirement before it's too late, you've earned the right to sleep with the phone unplugged and so have I, more to the point. *Guay de mi, mi vida*, do it for your wife. Let's get this evening over with and get you retired, and go home to bed."

*

Saul Gabbai had been the doctor for forty years and, whatever their feelings about the chief medical officer elect, Tuga de Oro would see Dr. Gabbai out in style. Outside the Rockhopper were many of the island's cars, and most of the island's donkeys, who were having a celebration of their own, heads bent, nostrils flared, pink tongues busy over a series of Himalayan salt licks newly positioned by the vet.

That morning, Moz had sent the demon twins to pick flowers, and sheaves of mintberry were woven into the old fishing nets that hung from the ceiling, in between the storm lanterns and the string lights. The Rockhopper had a distinctive odor of sawdust and woodsmoke and possibly a hint of seaweed, from these old nets. Mintberry added a sharp, sweet scent that was somewhere between raspberry leaf and spearmint, which mingled with an unusual amount of eau de cologne on many of the party guests. Levi checked the fly screens and opened all the windows, and in doing so spotted the Gabbais' approaching car.

"He's coming," Levi called over his shoulder, as if it was a surprise party, and this announcement passed through the room, silencing conversation, and orienting everyone towards the door. Saul and Moz entered to applause.

"Remember you're alive," Moz hissed, and then cast her eyes around for Sylvester, who gave her a nod. Moz clapped her hands twice above her head, like a flamenco dancer, at which all of the smallest children pushed their way to the front, and Sylvester stepped forward with his accordion, Elsie, from the other side, with a penny whistle. Moz had been rehearsing this choir at school for weeks, and at her signal they launched into their own, personalized rewrite of "Thank U Very Much" by The Scaffold, complete with their own choreography. "Thank you very much for being our doctor . . ." Saul, as Moz had anticipated, began to cry. This represented most of the evening's formalities, and when the children had taken a bow she steered him purposefully towards a corner table, and a large glass of red wine. Those who wished to pay homage could queue up, as at a book signing.

It was standing room only by the time that Saul chinked a spoon against his glass for quiet, and began on the speech he'd been failing to write, in his head, for the better part of a year. He had done his best, he could say that, honestly. There had not been many mistakes, though it was true that there had not been none. There had been lows; nights when he had found his face slick with tears, Moz's warm hand upon his shoulder, her silent vigil beside him as he confronted the leering goblin of his own limitations. He had been one man. He had worked, in good faith, for forty years. And there had been so many good days. Saul took a breath, and began.

"Thank you all for coming this evening, I am so moved to look around and see so many I've had the privilege of caring for over the years. So many people I've had the privilege of delivering into the world, in fact. It has been my honor . . ." But here he had to stop for a moment, and attempt to refocus on his scant notes. He thought that he would remember all his life how it felt to see ranged around him the smiling faces of the men, women, and children whose health had been that life's work. Moz stepped closer, giving an almost imperceptible nod of encouragement.

"It has been my honor to be Tuga de Oro's chief medical officer for forty years. Forty years. I can scarcely believe it. Some days I feel I am still thirty-five. Other days, of course, I feel a hundred and thirty-five." He began to relax when this won him some laughter. "When I came back to the island I thought I knew it all, of course I came back when Robin Spencer was CMO and I finished my training under him, and Tuga set about showing me that first year how much I still had to learn. I've been humbled and honored. You have trusted me with your families and included me in your families and for that I am so grateful. And I can retire knowing that I am passing responsibility for the island's healthcare to my nephew,

Dr. Dan Zekri, who takes on the role of chief medical officer today and will, I know, do us all proud. And, see here, I'm not going anywhere"—he was ad-libbing now, obviously moved, and not quite willing to relinquish the intoxicating opportunity of reminding them he wasn't dead yet—"I'm not going anywhere, there's life in the old dog, and if Dan needs an assistant, or some advice, I shall be only too glad to step in now and again. Anytime, actually, and if anyone ever needs— But the main thing is, he is in charge now and he's going to do a fine job. A fine job. And now is the time to toast Dr. Zekri, and wish him well."

He was raising his glass but Dan came to stand beside him.

"A thank-you to Dr. Saul Gabbai first, I think," he said, and a cheer rose from the packed room. Saul asked if Dan would say a few words, and Dan demurred until Moz snapped that it was expected and so he should please just blooming well get on with it, because she was ready for her slippers. Dan cleared his throat. Saul had spoken with the confidence of a man who had earned his right to command attention. Dan had not yet earned that right.

"I won't keep you long, when I know we all want to get on with the business of celebrating a remarkable island physician. I just wanted to say—Uncle Saul, Dr. Gabbai, said just now that he thought he knew it all when he came back to the island. Well. I find that very reassuring and it means that maybe I am actually, I think I am actually a bit more, considerably more advanced than he was when he started, medically speaking, because I can tell you that I already know that I know absolutely nothing."

There was a ripple of nervous laughter.

"Absolutely nothing, truly. I've forgotten so much. I've forgotten the names of plants and insects here, and what they do. I've forgotten to go by donkey when I head out to the taro fields. I've forgotten not to swear, and how fast you have to move to buy flour when it comes in. I'd forgotten how quickly night falls and I got stuck at Out the Way beach without a torch and you can imagine how that went. But—but, I've learned a lot while I was away, and I worked damn hard—see! sorry, swearing—and I worked hard to equip myself to come back, and if I am not yet an experienced Tugan again I am an experienced first responder, I promise you that, and I'll keep learning and working and remembering. Give me a little time to remember the difference between cool poisonberry and hot poisonberry—"

"Check the stems!" called little Annie Goss, which prompted another wave of laughter.

"Thanks, Annie. Give me a bit of time to remember all the different branches of each of your family trees. It's inspiring and humbling to stand beside Uncle Saul, and it's been incredible to hear the esteem in which he is held by you all. I am as sorry as you are to see him retire, but rest assured that I will be here for you, and I will take care of you, and I will listen if you are generous enough to teach me. And Saul is standing down but it won't just be me in the clinic because we have our incredible and long-standing nurses, and a new superpower in the form of our physiotherapist, Katie Salmon. Who is committed to you all, and to the practice." Here he flushed but went on, obviously determined. "Katie and I are a strong professional team and remain united in our commitment to healthcare improvements here. And something I was told today made me think and I, I want to say this, too. We doctors are not psychic. We're not superhuman. We look, but we don't always see, and things aren't always clear to us even when they should be obvious, we bring our own preconceptions and biases and—so please come to me, please tell me things, please trust me. And if you don't think I am listening in the right way to you then say it louder, because believe me, I want to be made to hear. I want to help. Thank you."

The applause was tentative at first but then grew stronger, and soon was enthusiastic enough that he felt he had acquitted himself. He smiled self-conscious thanks around the room. Betsey Coffee was smiling back at him, her arm around Katie herself, he saw, who he had not expected to come, and who gave a small, defiant grin.

There were Anwuli and Isadora clapping, and inscrutable Marianne Goss gave him a nod. He was grateful for each reassuring backslap as he passed through the crowd. This was it. Everybody here was his to heal, to protect. *Do no harm*, he told himself, and moved towards the bar. *For God's sake, no more harm.*

59

The formal part of the evening was over and bluegrass was playing. Dan felt tired and unexpectedly emotional. He looked at face after face, smoothed and softened by the yellow light from strings of tiny winking bulbs, and shifting candle flames. They were beloved to him, these Tugan faces, worn by the sun and the wind and the unceasing labor of making a life, their lives, at the extremity of global isolation. Beloved, heroic, unsung. It was genuinely radical that they now had a physiotherapist, he realized and, understanding this, he could not wish Katie away. He longed to be worthy of a job that he had once considered beneath him. He was thinking all these things when he saw Charlotte approaching, and heard her offer her congratulations. It was the first time she had spoken to him voluntarily since he'd confessed his feelings here, in the Rockhopper, more than a month ago. When they bumped into one another she had, till now, refused to meet his eye.

"Thank you."

"You must be feeling very proud."

"Unworthy, mostly. I'm looking around and thinking, *I'll let some of them down.*"

"Maybe. You'll also save some of their lives. Deliver some of their babies. There's time for you to deliver some of their babies' babies, too. Lusi must be very proud, too."

"Some of my recent actions have taken the gloss off her maternal pride, but yes, I suppose."

Charlotte did not choose to pursue him down this conversational avenue, but neither did she move away. Instead she stood beside him and together they surveyed the busy pub. Betsey Coffee and Sylvester were poring over the jukebox, deep in a discussion about a record. At one table sat several farmers from the moshav, one of whom had called her out for a uterine prolapse after their only cow's twin calving, Charlotte told Dan, and it had been a disaster. Hours of fumbling, and though she had managed it in the end, she had definitely not covered herself in glory. Behind the moshavniks, Annie Goss and Alex dos Santos were spinning round and round on bar stools, high on fizzycan, way past their bedtime. Beside them they watched as Taxi bowed low before Elsie, and invited her to have a caper with him. Katie was dancing badly and exuberantly with Saul, a ring of others clapping around them, like a playground game, or a wedding.

"And your dad?" Charlotte asked carefully, averting her eyes from Katie. "What would your dad have made of tonight?"

Dan glanced at her in surprise. Charlotte did not tend to ask personal questions, unlike the rest of Tuga, who would ask about your digestion, given half the chance. But he was feeling unexpectedly sentimental, and the relief that she was no longer avoiding him made him want to talk. He said, with more generosity to Johannes than usual, "He loved a party, my dad. He'd have been right in the thick of it, not like me. My dad would be the one calling for karaoke and another round."

"What was he like?"

"He was—he was the life and soul of any party. He had these very intense blue eyes and very bright blond hair, you could always spot him instantly in a crowd. Funny. Irreverent. Completely unreliable. Broke my mother's heart over and over."

"Go on."

"I don't know. I worshipped him when I was little, I wanted to fish like him, farm like him, all of it. He had a limp from an accident when I was very small and I even thought that was cool. He used to drink London Pride, you know, the ale, he said it made him feel more of a Londoner. That was his grand dream, to go live in London."

Charlotte said levelly, "I think Garrick mentioned they'd been on a trip together."

Dan grinned. "That was a classic Johannes story. So, to put this in context, remember that passage off the island thirty years ago was even harder, even more expensive than it is now, if you can imagine. And it was all set up, they were going for something or other Garrick was doing, I don't know. It was the trip of a lifetime, anyway. And then when they were making their approach at Southampton, my dad got so drunk he slipped on the gangplank disembarking and fell before he'd stepped on dry land. He managed to give himself a concussion and break his leg in three places, and his hip. That's why he limped. He spent six weeks in Southampton Hospital, in traction."

"I don't get it. He spent six weeks in hospital? So how did he get to London?"

Dan was shaking his head, laughing, despite himself. He had always found this story an embarrassment, and somehow the epitome of failure. Tonight, for the first time, he could acknowledge its funny side.

"He never even made it to London. My dad's entire trip to England was spent inside the orthopaedic ward of Southampton Hospital. The nurses felt so sorry for him that he was a pet by the end, he stayed in touch with two of them. It was Garrick who went to London, and then collected him on the way home, still in a wheelchair, and loaded him straight back onto the boat."

Charlotte had begun to look strange. She had been taking small nervous sips of her water but now she held the glass in both hands, near her mouth but not drinking, and he saw that her knuckles were white with the strength of her grip. She made a small noise, as if she had cleared her throat at the same time as trying to say something. Dan wondered briefly if her water had gone down the wrong way and she was choking, but then she turned and walked, almost ran, away.

He remained looking after her, bewildered. For a moment a tentative friendship had once again seemed possible, but this odd flight was a return to how she had been all month. She hadn't left the Rockhopper, he saw, she had just fled from him. She was leaning over the bar before Levi Mendoza, who raised an eyebrow, and then poured what seemed to be a shot of vodka. Her face was really a very odd color.

Marianne was seated in the booth, sharing a plate of soft-shell crab with Betsey. She was ravenously hungry, having eaten dinner hours ago with the children. Betsey was scanning the room, commentating.

"Is the vet doing shots with Levi?"

Marianne looked. Charlotte Walker was indeed sprawled at the bar flushed, and slightly tousled. As they watched she banged down an empty shot glass, crossed her arms, and rested her forehead upon them, as if she meant to sleep on the bar. Levi said something to her, and without raising her head she shook it vigorously, side to side. Betsey and Marianne both stared.

"Well," said Marianne after a moment. "It's about time she let her hair down."

What Levi was actually saying was, "I ain't the one to rain on anyone's parade here, Dolittle, but don't you think you've had enough for tonight?"

Charlotte, looking down at the floor through the frame of her crossed arms, shook her head.

"No, Levi Mendoza, I absolutely have not. There is not enough vodka on this whole shitty island to get me where I need to go."

She lifted her head and glared at him, and Levi raised his hands in surrender.

"I am a grown-ass woman."

"I know it."

"So then another, please."

Levi poured another and slid it over to her. He had seen her talking to Dan Zekri and felt certain it was the wrench of her impossible feelings for Dan that had triggered this. His heart twisted with pity for her, and a sharp envy of Dan who did not deserve her love, and could not have it even if he did. Not to mention the fact that if she needed her stomach pumped later this evening it would be Zekri having to do it. She had drunk a lot, very fast, and was starting to seem messy.

After a minute Levi said, "You know what, Dolittle, you a grown-ass woman and I respect that, and you got sorrows to drown and I get that too. But this is my bar tonight, and I say you done pretty soon."

"I done, am I. I done." Charlotte pointed an accusing and distinctly wavering finger. "You done."

"Whatever you say, *kerida*." Levi poured another for himself and clinked it against hers. "I'll take this last one with you."

Garrick Williams approached Charlotte, his heavy eyebrows drawn together.

"Is everything all right, Dr. Walker?"

Charlotte spun around on her bar stool, looming at him so suddenly that Garrick took a step back.

"Oh, everything is fine. Thank you for your"—she began, inexplicably, to laugh—"thank you for your *very paternal concerns*." With each of these final words she slapped the bar, emphatic.

Garrick's eyebrows shot up, almost disappearing beneath the gray curls that were already growing wilder, without Joan's supervision.

"Dolittle was just saying she's about to head, Pastor, it's all good."

Dan Zekri came over, standing on the other side of Charlotte. She raised her vodka in his direction, and then downed it.

"Oh, you just what this situation needs," Levi said irritably.

"What's that supposed to mean?"

Levi dried his hands and came round from behind the bar. He took Charlotte's elbow. "I'm taking Dolittle home," he told Garrick and Dan, as Charlotte began to lean heavily against him.

"I think I need to go home," Charlotte mumbled into his arm, and then suddenly extracted herself and made for the door alone, raising an unsteady hand in greeting as she passed a fascinated Betsey and Marianne, and stopping briefly to rest her head against Elsie's starched-twill front, as if she were a wall. Then she had gone. Levi went to follow her.

"What a hero you are, Mendoza," said Dan. "Look at that. *Deus ex machina.*"

"Oh, *deus ex* my cock," said Levi, losing his patience entirely and springing forwards to shoulder past Dan, who was immediately enraged and so stood firm, blocking Levi's way.

"Do you agree that Mendoza is not a sufficiently upstanding character to check on the well-being of our vet and that under the circumstances"—good grief, thought Garrick, they were actually shoving one another now, heavy breaths coming between each word—"under the circumstances that should be the—ow, ow!—the responsibility of the *chief medical officer.*"

Without warning Dan threw himself at Levi and they fell into what looked to be a mutual headlock, on the Rockhopper floor. A captivated, horrified crowd formed around them.

Walter Lindo-Smith pushed his way forward to help, grabbing Levi and hauling him backwards. Garrick bent and heaved Dan to his feet by the scruff of the neck, surprised and gratified by his own resurgent strength. Dan wiped the sweat from his lip, looking sheepish, but still could not stop himself from glaring at Levi. Levi stood panting, Walter's big hands now resting on his shoulders.

"*Under the circumstances,*" Garrick boomed, as if from the pulpit, "I am going to be the one to see Dr. Walker home. She needs peace and quiet and I shall look very poorly, very poorly indeed, do you hear me, upon any man here who goes within twenty feet of her in the next twelve hours. She is in no fit state to talk to either of you.

No fit state. Shame on you. You are not to go anywhere near the Mendoza place until tomorrow."

Both men looked sullen, and Levi gave a sharp kick in the direction of a chair, muttering something about it being his own house. Garrick had a memory, as clear as yesterday, of each of them as Boy Scouts.

"Fine," Levi said eventually.

"Dr. Zekri?"

"Yes, all right. Fine. I'll go home." Dan took several steps backwards. "All right, all right."

"And let me remind you boys that you are *haverim*, and this performance is beneath you. Walk it off, Dr. Zekri. You assumed a public office this evening, and you have demeaned it within seconds. Poor judgment. Poor, poor judgment. Off you go." He gave Dan a little push between the shoulders. "And you"—he turned back to Levi—"get upstairs. Go on. Walter will mind the bar."

Levi raised his hands in defeat and then turned and jogged to the corner of the yard and up the ringing metal steps to his hut on the roof. Garrick broke into an uncomfortable trot, wheezing as he tried to catch up with Charlotte.

60

Charlotte had not made it far. Garrick heard singing in the shadows and approached to find her, nose to nose with one of the donkeys.

"Dorothy is another one who unexpectedly likes The Pogues," Charlotte said, without turning, "but don't even get her started on Cliff Fucking Richard. Riff Clucking Fichard." She had her arms around the neck of the donkey and began swaying with her, as if they were slow-dancing together at a hop. Garrick started forward in alarm. In the dark he was not at all sure that this one was actually Dorothy, and some of the others were known to nip.

Charlotte had begun to hum again and, most alarmingly, to weep.

"Why don't you leave, ah, Dorothy, and let me walk you home."

"Oh yes, you are a beautiful girl, aren't you, Dorothy. No more nasty *guzanikos* for you if Auntie Charlotte can help it, no, even though no one can bloody tell me if they mean cyathostomins or tapeworm or bloody liver fluke, and no one is willing to rotate a single grazing paddock, or compost their effing manure properly. Beautiful Dorothy. If"—she suddenly pulled away in disgust—"if you even are Dorothy. Who the fuck knows who anyone is round here?"

She swung around and was facing Garrick, unsteady. In the light of the storm lanterns he could see her smudged mascara, her swimming eyes. "Isn't that right, Garrick. Sooooo many donkeys, and only one ass."

Then she laughed for a long time at this, and sat down abruptly in the dust.

"You know at home I would say, 'I drank *all* the vodka.' But here it might actually be literally true. I might have literally drunk all the vodka on this shitty little island."

"I agree from all evidence it seems likely. I think you should go to bed."

She looked up at him blearily.

"Ooooh, *so paternal.*"

"Get up, Dr. Walker. Charlotte. Please."

"Yes, yes."

She was now on all fours, then clutching at the fence.

"Just trying to preserve a little dignity. My skirt is very short tonight, in case you hadn't noticed. I wore it with some prepid—prepid—that is a hard word. I wore it with some *trepid*ation because you know my dear brother Dan fancies me and that's"—here she threw up her hands in a pantomime of dismay—"just like, so awkward! I know, right? But then it turns out that Dan isn't my brother after all, so that's good, isn't it. No. Harm. Done. I can just put weeks of incest nightmares in the bin and go find him right now and tell him it's fine, now we might as well just go ahead and shag."

"Where are your shoes?"

"I really cannot begin to inform you of their whereabouts, my good friend."

Charlotte was standing now. She pushed off from the fence like a swimmer making a turn, and set off at a surprising speed across the car park and towards the road. Garrick shone the beam of his torch in an arc, and seeing no sign of her shoes he followed. The night was warm and still, and the rustling, creaking jungle became audible as the human sounds receded behind them.

When they were a reasonable distance from the Rockhopper he said quietly, "Maybe it's not advisable to be going and finding anybody just this evening."

"Thanks, *Dad*. Such super-duper paternal advice, pertaining to who I should or should not shag. Which is all so funny because—" She pointed an unsteady finger at him. "You, of course, have shagged my mum. I'm right, aren't I? I know I'm right, it literally couldn't be anyone else except you. S'strordinary information, that my mother has shagged a Tugan pastor. How many people can say that? Not very many, I'd say."

"Shhh," Garrick found himself hissing rather desperately, though there was no one within earshot but the donkeys.

"Oh yes, of course. We wouldn't want anyone here to think that such an esteemed minister was a shagger. Better to blame a dead dude."

"I am not a— This is not the time to talk about this. Can I take your arm?"

"Ow. Someone should really see to this road. You may not, as it happens."

Garrick followed her up the jungle road towards the Mendoza house, several paces behind. Charlotte was reeling, always threatening to trip and yet somehow remaining upright, and in motion. Garrick shone his torch ahead of her and she followed the disc of light, a drunken moth. When they reached the turning towards her cottage she sat down heavily again, in the middle of the road. All momentum seemed spent. She looked very young.

His turmoil seemed a thing apart, too big to be within him. Instead he writhed within it, a man inside a cloud of noxious shame and self-pity. He could not bear for anyone else to see it, and to risk what surely would be their total misapprehension of a single, ancient mistake. He was a good husband who had honored his wife every day, before and after that fateful London trip. He had come home chastened. He had atoned. And then over the years he had packed the mistake away, piling other, more respectable recollections on top of it in the attic of his memory. A life of service. A marriage of kind words and companionship. The nourishing and deserved esteem of all his fellow islanders. To guide their moral journeys with unwavering authority felt not like hypocrisy but re-assurance. They held him up as an example, and as they saw him, so he was. And he had barely thought of his mistake for years until, in Grand Mary's library, he had understood Charlotte Walker to be its flesh-and-blood consequence. His reputation was the cherished cornerstone of his identity without which, he felt certain, he would simply cease to exist. But now Charlotte knew.

"This is not a sensible context in which to discuss such matters," Garrick began now, a reflexive retreat into the emphatic rhythms of an ad hoc sermon, speech slow enough for thought to race ahead, preparing ground. "When I realized, after that conversation at Martha House, when I realized what must have happened . . . it was disappointing, a terrible shock to me, in actual fact, to discover that that *lapse* had had . . . the consequences that it did. Your birth, et cetera. And you must recall Joan was very ill, and it was essential that I protect her final weeks from avoidable pain. Essential. She had never known of that long-ago episode and it was right, you know, it was absolutely right that I not burden her with confession. And also"—here he found he had hit a stride, of sorts, an easier avenue down which to rush headlong away from the scene of his own misdeed—"and also, I can tell you this—Dan's father was my dear friend, and it came to me, it almost came to me in Johannes's voice, in that moment I absolutely knew he would have told me to say it, it's not the kind of thing I would even—you must understand, his reputation was in a poor way, it couldn't harm him. It was so much Johannes's behavior, in fact, not mine, in every way. He loved Joan, he understood her pain that we hadn't had a child, and so much of what made her who she is—who she was. And then of course he had been in England, it fitted the—your—chronology . . . it was right," he finished. "It was absolutely the right thing to say under the circumstances."

Charlotte was looking up at him while he spoke. The mockery had left her face, and she appeared to be listening. Then she said softly, "Dad, I need a wee."

"Can't it wait?"

"It cannot."

She disappeared into a bush, and Garrick closed his eyes wearily.

From within the rustling leaves she called, "Do you know what will happen now? Knowing my track record in this godforsaken hole, I will be stung on the ass—sorry, sorry, on the donkey—by some horrible invasive arachnid that just arrived on a plum, or maybe by one of those literary bookish silverfish, or maybe by a feral Persian cat, and I will need to call my brother the doctor. Humiliations never cease. Seize? Seeds. Whatever. But wait, no. The doctor's not my brother, the minister is my dad. It is so hard to keep up."

She reappeared. Her skirt was twisted the wrong way round, but she was at least decent.

They had reached her cottage and he opened the door. Charlotte went in and immediately slammed it shut behind her. Garrick turned to go, but before he'd left the porch the top half of the door reopened.

"Dad, am I grounded?"

"Drink some water, and go to bed now."

"I will. Also, may I say that however *disappointing it is* that I exist, so sorry about that, you did actually bring me that walnut Tuga tortoise toy when I was little so let's not pretend anymore that you didn't know I was born, OK? It was really great, I loved it. Almost as good as having a father."

"Go to sleep now, Charlotte."

"*Special affinity for tortoises.* Fuck you."

The door banged closed again, and the sound of her humming receded, so Garrick assumed that she was going into the bathroom at the back of the cottage. She would probably be sick. He sat down heavily on the front step, leaned his head against the small banister and closed his eyes. He would wait here for ten minutes, until he was certain she had passed out, and not reemerged to go searching the island for Zekri like some inebriated haunting dybbuk. He had

WELCOME TO GLORIOUS TUGA

no idea what she was talking about—walnuts and toys and tortoises—he truly hadn't had the first notion of her conception until that cold, sick dawning in Grand Mary's house when she'd said her mother's full name. He had never even been back to England since then, how could he have visited and brought Charlotte anything? His ache for Joan, which for the last month had been like a band around his chest, grew suddenly into a powerful longing to see Johannes, the only person in whom he could conceivably confide any of this, and the only one whose trickster wherewithal and creative ingenuity might have somehow extricated him from this sense of horror. Garrick needed his friend with such force that he felt the unfairness of it like atmospheric pressure. Johannes. *Haver.* How could he do *this* without him?

61

Footsteps rang on the iron steps, as someone made their way up to the shack on the roof. There was a pounding on the screen door and Dan appeared, bringing with him a wash of bright sunshine, just as a naked Levi was getting back into his unmade bed.

"Jesus, Mendoza. Pants, maybe?"

"*Paz, haver*, you're in my actual bedroom. How's the face?"

Dan tilted his chin to show a bruise beginning, lilac and mauve, along one side of his jaw.

"That ain't done flowering, you should see a doctor."

"If you know any good ones let me know."

Levi grinned. "You know I went easy on you."

Dan was still in the doorway, smacking his palms against the wood of the doorframe, as if testing it for soundness. He had put himself together that morning with the care of a penitent before a judge—crisp white shirt, dark trousers, polished shoes, a face clean-shaven, even over the blooming bruise. His many judges would see him contrite, sober, respectful. To Levi, he was able to return an embarrassed smile.

"You tell yourself whatever you need. Listen, I don't know what happened last night, I'm sorry."

"It's fine, *haver*."

"It's not fine. I behaved badly, I don't know what got into me. Of all the nights . . ." Dan came in and sat on the edge of the bed, head heavy in his hands. "And I don't know what on earth was going on with Charlotte. She was suddenly talking to me again, for the first time since . . ." He rubbed his face, fatigued. "You know, I went round there last night. I swore to you and Garrick that I wouldn't and there I was, banging on her door like a wild man. I just wanted answers, but I've got no right to ask for answers, she's told me how she feels loud and clear. I'm truly ashamed of myself."

"You get your explanation?"

"No. She must have passed out. She probably feels pretty terrible this morning, I've never seen her drink like that."

"Full of surprises, that one."

"I think I was feeling, this is meant to be the first day of the rest of my life, CMO now, taking on this mantle, and it was like, if I don't take a chance with Charlotte I will regret it till the end of my days. Island Close isn't far off and then she leaves, and that's it. It's for the best now, probably, though I'm sorry for you, too. I got it, last night. I didn't really know how you felt about her, I thought it was messing about, you know? Until you—"

"We old friends, *haver*," said Levi quickly, interrupting. "Don't stress it."

"Probably the best idea for both of us is to just stay away from her for a bit, get some breathing space, you know? Till she leaves."

In bed, Levi sat up a little, readjusting the pillow behind his head. "You going to be busy enough, taking a beating from all the grannies who saw you brawling at your own party, like you Benjamin Cole. That's a month of work right there."

Dan shook his head, laughing despite himself. "It's not like I was exactly flavor of the month to begin with."

"Don't sweat it, they stuck with you now," said Levi reasonably.

Dan stood to leave, and as he did noticed the huge window, opposite the bed. The sea was a glittering topaz beneath a cloudless sky.

"Look at that. You have the best view in Tuga right here, from the roof of the Rockhopper. You'd never know from the yard down there."

"Yeah. It ain't so bad here, for a time."

"Well." Dan briefly studied his own reflection in the glass of the open window, lifting his chin, wincing as he tapped his bruised jawline. "At least you'll get your house back. Right. Hell. I've got to go to work, to get ready for my zero patients."

He moved towards the door and then stopped, regarding Levi where he lounged, naked among the rumpled sheets.

"I'm truly sorry."

"We're cool. You worry about what needs worrying about."

"What, you mean like the catastrophe of my professional and personal life?"

Levi grinned. "No breakups, no fistfights, and just like that, today will be a better day."

Dan gave a sheepish salute and then left, pulling the door shut behind him. A moment later there was a ringing of metal as he descended the fire-escape stairs outside and, shortly after that, the squeak and slam of the Rockhopper's main front door as Dan Zekri went in to order a morning coffee, and to face the music.

Levi tossed the covers back. He stretched deeply and with satisfaction, then stood and went over to the broad teak wardrobe and threw open both doors. Charlotte was crouching inside it.

"Jesus Christ, why not ask him about his holiday plans for next summer while you're at it. Help me down."

"No can do, I just promised to stay away from you."

"Levi!"

Levi laughed and lifted her down easily. She was wearing a T-shirt of his that said *The Pogues* in an arc above a peeling green shamrock, and nothing else.

"God. My knees may never recover."

"Come back to bed now, Dolittle. Rest your knees. Or don't."

Charlotte gave him a push in the center of his chest. When he fell back on to the sheets, he took her with him so that she landed on top of him, in his arms. With a hand behind her head, he flipped her over in a single motion so that she lay on her back and he was above her, looking down. A surge of pure and wordless happiness rose, fresh and clear as a spring.

"So that's some interesting new information for us this morning. Our friend Zekri went round looking for you last night, after he swore blind he'd leave you in peace. Perhaps he ain't a gentleman after all."

Charlotte suppressed a smile.

"What? What's that look?"

"I know he came round, I was there. I heard him at my front door. My not-even-remotely brother Dan."

"Huh." Levi rolled off, and on to his side. He propped his head up on one elbow and regarded her and she gazed back steadily. "More interesting information. So why didn't you let him in? Your not-even-remotely brother Dan? Nothing in the world to stop you now."

"Nothing in the world. Except that I was halfway out of the window on my way to you."

While she was speaking Charlotte idly ran her fingers across his brows, his lips, tracing the lines of his face, learning him anew.

"As I say, all fascinating. So after all it was my door you were pounding on"—Charlotte covered his mouth with her raised hand, laughing, but he carried on speaking, muffled—"me who you were forcing to do tequila shots to catch up with you—"

"Not forcing!"

"And me who you were—"

"All right, all right!" Charlotte turned and hid her face with the crook of her elbow, and Levi dipped his head and nosed her arm aside to make her look at him. "Yes. OK. All right. I concede. Just stop talking."

"Gladly."

"Wait, no, one second." Charlotte wriggled away and got out of bed again, and Levi crossed his arms behind his head and lay back, watching as she paced.

"I actually don't feel that hungover, how is that possible?"

"Still drunk. And last night I fed you Alka-Seltzer, and Angostura bitters with honey. No messing, Dolittle, you had a hell of an evening. Suddenly you got a father who ain't dead."

Charlotte came to a stop in front of the window, dark against the light behind her.

"A father who isn't dead. Garrick. *Garrick.* Can you literally believe it? The world's most pompous hypocrite. I think I'd have preferred Johannes Zekri. It's his hypocrisy that is so unbearable, the lecturing and the holier-than-thou business and then lying through his teeth to save his own arse. What kind of a man slanders his dead best friend?"

Levi crossed the room and stood before her, and she reached out her hand for his. He stepped closer and began to study her face intently as she had been studying his, considering each feature in the morning sunlight.

"Stop doing that. I do not look like Garrick! Do I?"

"I never thought of Garrick as my type before, but maybe—"

"Oh, stop it. God. I do feel a bit green, actually."

"Seriously, though—something maybe in the chin, or this line here." Levi was still gazing at her with new gravity, and now ran a finger down first one cheekbone, then the other. He stood back again, squinting, not mocking but tender. "I do see something. Not your eyes, though. They're all you. But definitely—structure, and those dimples. Now I see it, how crazy. The evidence right here in your face." He bent to drop a light kiss on each browbone, releasing her from scrutiny, reclaiming her as herself. Charlotte shut her eyes and breathed in the heat of him. He was pleasure and comfort mingled, though all else beyond this room seemed a wreckage.

"But none of this changes who you are, you know that. Johannes, or Garrick, or Cliff Richard, or whoever. This ain't the definition of who you are, unless that's what you make it."

"I know. You're right, I know. If anything—" Charlotte paused, turning over his words. Levi had understood what she herself had not seen, until now. That her search for her father's identity had been a longing to define and understand her own identity, her own loneliness. "I think this has to set me free from the belief that it matters. I am an adult, now. I have to define myself. Whoever myself turns out to be."

"Will you tell your mother you've worked it out?"

"I just have no idea. At some point, maybe. I need to—assimilate this, I think. Work out what to do with it, before I can talk to anyone. And I think I may need some toast. And maybe a nap."

"I'll bring you something up from downstairs, you can sleep here. I'll go to work."

As he was turning she reached for his hand. "Stay. Levi."

"I've got to get home." He grinned at her. "I've got a bed to shift upstairs."

"You're kidding me. Now you'll move my bed, when I'm leaving in three weeks." She sobered. "I can't believe it's almost Island Close, I can't believe this has all come out now. Do you think someone might swap berths with me for Island Open? I can't just, just leave now, can I? I need to just . . ."

She trailed off, watching as a series of expressions crossed Levi's face. He seemed, uncharacteristically, to be in conflict.

He moved away and sat back down on the end of the bed. Then he said gently, "I think you need to take care of your heart a little, after all this, think what another Island Close means, and what you're wanting from it. Garrick ain't likely to have much to give, is all I'm thinking."

"Last night he called me a 'lapse.'"

"See, that's a word that's all about him, no thought for you. And if that's where he's at, it might not feel so good to be stuck here all that time, near him, away from your people." He dropped his head, clasping his hands at the back of his neck, stretching first one way then the other, deliberately not looking at her. "I don't know, Dolittle. Speaking on my own part, I'd enjoy you hanging around. But I ain't what matters in this equation right now."

"Would you? I didn't see you knocking on my door last night."

"You were drunk as a skunk, girl. In any case, I said I'd leave you in peace and I keep my word. You wanted me banging your door down trying to take advantage when you were wasted, like Zekri?"

"Yes."

"My daddy taught me better."

"Mine is a philandering humanist minister."

"*Guay de mi,*" said Levi softly. He shook his head. "You got what to think about, *kerida.*"

The sun moved, and the room was flooded with a new warmth of light. Charlotte turned to lean on the high windowsill, and crossed her arms, resting her chin on her wrists, and shutting her eyes, feeling the heat on her skin. A morning breeze sifted the cashew leaves and she heard the suggestive whistle of a calling cardinal. Out of sight, a coconut crashed from a palm into some dry shrubs below, and in response an invisible donkey stamped, and snorted. The jungle's green sap was on the air and something else, the brine of the ocean, and a reminder of last night's woodsmoke.

Charlotte heard the creak of the bedsprings as Levi stood, and her breath caught in anticipation. But he did not touch her. Instead he stopped a few paces away, the small distance between them hers to close. She longed to turn around, to open her arms and draw him near again. Instead she reached back and brushed her bare foot to his.

"My head is all over the place. I can't, you know I'm not really in a position to be starting . . . I am sending out mixed messages."

Levi hesitated. Then he moved behind her and slipped his arms around her waist, his chin resting lightly on the top of her head. She leaned back against the solid warmth of him. Each looked out in the same direction, over the water.

"Either way," Levi said softly, "whatever messages you sending, I'm listening."

Light fell on the ocean, rippling and shimmering before them, the horizon cobalt; exposed and unbroken, the beauty of the planet's curve. *Take care of your heart a little.* She had been wrong to see emptiness, Charlotte realized. Before her lay everything.

Epilogue

Marianne had taken out the pruning shears and was snipping bunches of lychees into a basket, listening to Taxi on Ruth's old portable radio.

"Some final announcements before I take up my post at the barbecue," he was saying, and Marianne paused. "Cargo is processed and on board for tomorrow's ship, the missing suitcase from arrival has been located and off-loaded, sorry about that, and that blue Kelpie pup is ashore, all checked and ready to collect first thing, if it's yours. Spencers, I'm looking at you, and let's hope this one don't chew my custom upholstery like the last one did. Tonight's tombola is at nine p.m., not eight p.m. like the posters says, that was an unfortunate error. It's just before fireworks and you ain't going to want to miss it, I'm telling you, when you've a chance of winning a snorkel, a nice smart yellow it is too, I've tried it on, or a two-kilo sack of wheat flour fresh off this boat is another, and the grand prize is a conch pearl. All right, all right, not a conch pearl, but it's something almost as good, if you can believe it, a fine pair of lambs, and you can go see the prizes in the Old Kal from now, I believe. All that remains is for me to say a happy twelfth birthday to Annie Goss and Alex dos Santos, you two behave yourselves, and be sure to save old Taxi a slice of cake. Come see me in Harbour Street if you're passing, everyone. *Paz*, and have a happy Island Day!" And Taxi signed off, leaving them with the twanging instrumental "Happy Birthday to You" recorded in 1961 by Cliff Richard and the Shadows, the

314

traditional track for every island birthday since the year of its release. For the rest of the evening the radio would loop a single compilation album, until the other DJ came back on air at midnight.

The children had been making Island Day decorations the night before, huge long strings of coconut shells to represent blue conch pearls, and there was sapphire paint spattered all over the red dust of the yard. The folding table was still out and covered with Ruth's best cloth, where earlier Marianne had held a small birthday tea. Now evening had fallen, and Alex and Annie had gone ahead into Town for the start of the Island Day celebrations, while Marianne stayed behind to tidy up. She had already changed from work clothes into a rare good dress and had been about to follow them when she found herself delaying for this last, trivial task. Ruth was unlikely to stir, but still. It felt wrong to leave her by herself on her final night at home.

This time tomorrow, Ruth would be on the ship. The trunk had gone, and Elsie had come that morning for her passport. All that remained was delivery of the traveler herself. It had already been agreed by the committee engineering this partial kidnapping—Katie, Dan, Marianne—that no reduction should be made to her medication until she was in England, probably not till after the surgery. To get her there was challenge enough. Charlotte Walker had agreed to share her cabin on her way home, and to titrate Ruth's drugs on the journey. Good luck to her, thought Marianne. The surgeon seemed sensible and sensitive. *We certainly won't be rushing her out, after the procedure*, she had written to Dan, implying that her supervision of Ruth as an inpatient could be extended a little, on a quietly compassionate basis.

Marianne switched off the radio and returned to her harvesting when Katie Salmon cycled into the yard, wearing what might be the only cycle helmet on the island, white and spangled, and with a plush unicorn horn Velcroed to its dome.

"All packed?" Katie asked, dismounting. "How is she?"

"Terrified. But we've read through the letter a few times and she knows she must go. She won't wake now before tomorrow." Marianne nodded at the black holdall slung on Katie's shoulder. "Is that—what you told me about?"

"Disposable incontinence pads, yes. It's enough for four weeks, so she won't need to worry about laundry even if there's a delay, but someone will need to go to Boots for her when she disembarks."

"Boots?"

"Sorry, I mean, just go to a pharmacy. And keep the receipts." Katie stepped closer and held up the basket for Marianne while she snipped. "Listen, I need to talk to you about something. You're not to worry, it will be fine, but Charlotte Walker wants to stay till Island Open, now."

"But Ruth can't go without—"

"That berth is for Ruth's chaperone, Dan won't let anyone release it, don't worry. We just need to send someone else. I wondered if you wanted to go."

"But I can't, I can't just leave the children for six months, it's Island Close coming, I . . ." Hot tears had come instantly to Marianne's throat, a rising tide of sorrow in her chest. "I need to . . . I can't think." (But already she had thought. Already then, she knew.)

"We've not got to this point to miss our chance, don't worry, she's going on that ship. Charlotte feels terrible that staying makes things complicated, she said a few times that if you don't find a replacement she'll still go, but we can't really expect her to do that when it was a pretty big favor in the first place. The community here is remarkable, though, and I know someone will do it. So before I put it out more widely I thought, perhaps you can think of someone you trust who wants to go to England for another reason? If you tell me tonight, I can sort out all the paperwork for you, they don't need to be aboard until mid-afternoon tomorrow."

Marianne took the basket briskly from Katie's hands and dropped in the pruning shears, preparing to go back into the house. She had a lot to do, now, and would have to ask around for another trunk.

Before she went she handed Katie a branch of lychees and then turned, and began to walk away. "Alex will take his mother to England. I pick late. Eat those today or tomorrow, they'll not keep longer."

There was woodsmoke in the air as Marianne walked into Town, and the scent of chilli and garlic. To honor the occasion, Taxi had used a black felt tip to touch up the peeling photograph of Kate Bush on his favorite T-shirt, and now stood over a painted oil drum grilling marinated octopus, together with something smaller and slighter to the back of the barbecue, bearing a suspicious resemblance to jump chicken. Three of the younger moshav children came past to look, and were nosed away from the heat of the grill by a huge collie with a bandaged forepaw, whose limp did not prevent his corralling his charges down Harbour Street like a herd of brightly colored sheep. On the next stall, Sylvester had run out of halved coconut shells and was passing out toddies in far less romantic polystyrene cups, all of which had been used many times before, and seen better days.

Across the street, Elsie was supervising the rhubarb-and-custard striped tent of the coconut shy, in which six blue coconuts balanced on six tall ironwood stakes. She wore a flat cap for the occasion, her bumbag requisitioned as a ticket and coin belt. Beside her stood Betsey, who had come merely to deliver a toddy from Sylvester, but was now hearing about the merits of underarm versus overarm techniques.

"It's like basketball, see. If your free throw is underhand, it's softer, a softer touch. Smoother," Elsie was saying, while Betsey smiled in incomprehension and wished she had a drink of her own. "They say it's for girls, see, but if you look at the best free-shooters in history that's just what works. Same with coconuts."

Betsey was spared further disquisitions by the approach of Walter and Rebecca Lindo-Smith, who handed in their tokens and each took a pyramid of colored balls. The little girl wore a huge party dress of spangled tulle and rainbow sequins, new not only to her but actually new-new, clearly expensive, and just arrived on the boat. But she did not look in the mood for a party. As Marianne stood watching, seven-year-old Rebecca picked up a fuchsia ball and threw it with such force that Betsey and Elsie leaped from the shy in surprise.

A strong arm was slipped through Marianne's, and Marianne started. Miss Moz patted her in reassurance, and together they observed Rebecca, whose frustration was mounting with each missed attempt, and was yet refusing to allow her father to help.

"Maia didn't come home this ship; in the end, she swapped for Island Open." Moz clicked her tongue. "We'll have to keep that scrap busy the next six months, she got some big feelings. Well, she would, wouldn't she. She had a calendar on the wall all this year, crossing off the days, and now she need a whole new one."

"Maia's doing it for her family."

"Oh, *kerida*, don't I know it. But since when did mothers get due thanks for any of our sacrifices? Since never is when, but that's not the point, is it. You had some dinner, *mi vida*?"

Marianne gave Moz a tight nod. She was looking around for Annie, and wished to change the subject. Close behind Moz, Saul caught her eye, unexpectedly casual in shorts and a pair of flip-flops, and holding a paper cone of grilled octopus. He was also drinking a beer, Marianne noted in surprise, and realized it must be the first Island Day for decades on which he did not have to remain sober for late-night splints and stitches, the inevitable results of the night's exuberance.

Marianne searched the Island Day crowds for the children. When she could not see them, she instinctively scanned upwards and there they were, on the unfenced flat roof of the Botika Moshav, long bare legs dangling, precisely where they were not supposed to be. Annie immediately caught her mother's eye and grinned, winsome, her expression betraying both the awareness that she had been caught in a transgression, and the belief she would be instantly forgiven. Annie nudged Alex, whispering close into his ear, and Alex offered Marianne a look of apology as the two of them began to gesture that they would come down, that they would watch the fireworks by her side.

They wanted so to please her. They surged forth into the world together each morning alive with experiments and schemes, drawn like magnets to mud and mess and scrapes, driven to explore, urgent to be free, but just as strong was their impulse to bring happiness to Marianne. Though their judgment was still forming and their risk assessment rarely aligned with her own, they never took pleasure in deliberate disobedience. The triumph of her rare permission would enhance their pleasure, not diminish it.

Marianne shook her head. She gestured for them to sit, to stay, to be very careful, that they could remain where they were until after the fireworks, and she watched as comprehension dawned, soaking in the pure sweetness of their delight. Alex gave her two thumbs-up, and Annie blew her mother kiss after kiss, theatrical with joy. Then they turned to one another, as they always did, an instinctive drawing-together whenever there was a pleasure to be shared. Marianne could stand it no longer, and looked away.

It was right for Alex to chaperone his mother. And it was right, too, that Alex be set free from the ache of his perpetual worry for her, together with the guilt he felt (lifelong, unspoken, palpable) that in giving him life, Ruth had all but lost her own.

By sending him on the ship, Marianne could grant him an opportunity to feel that he had truly helped. By sending him on to boarding school at the Fabian Academy, she could grant him something greater: the opportunity to set down his burden and make a bigger life, apart.

Marianne looked up to see that Annie was watching her again, checking perhaps, to reassure herself that her mother was OK, that she was also having a nice time. They carried so much, her children, when they deserved nothing less than everything.

She thought of Maia, alone in London, suffering her knowledge of Rebecca's sorrow. What was motherhood but the giving of one's whole self? To love without self-interest meant standing firm, keeping hold of one's own wisdom in the face of children's consequent pain, finding courage to deny the fierce wishes of an innocent, who could not yet know what choices cost. Annie was the bravest soul she knew. Now Marianne must be just as brave.

Tomorrow she would help Annie to understand that the journey was a gift to Ruth that they must grant with open hearts; that the destination was a lifetime's chance for Ruth's beloved boy, when Ruth had nothing of her own to give. They who most loved Alex must be brave, must palliate their grief with generosity of spirit. She could not pretend that Alex, once he had gone to England, would ever come back. They might suffer. But Alex now would fly. Marianne would teach her daughter that true love lets go.

High and free as fairy terns, twelve-year-old Annie Goss and Alex dos Santos sat together with fingers interlaced, and open faces lifted to the heavens. At that moment the sky above them exploded with ruby and emerald.

Acknowledgments

Not simply this book but the evolution of the island itself would have been impossible without the patience and professional expertise of Dr. Aniket Sardana, Joshua Powell, Dr. Justin Gerlach, Dr. Ben Tapley, Dr. Sean McCormack, and in particular Dr. Thomas Day, each of whom took such care to explain, to teach, to correct. Research is one of fiction's greatest joys, providing an excuse to bother and befriend world experts who have, without question, many and far better things to do. All the aforementioned experts were extraordinarily generous with their time and knowledge, catching errors and inspiring new avenues of thought. Any remaining errors or inconsistencies are thus entirely my own.

Thank you to Fred Kroner at Whiskey & Ink, whose beautiful map first brought Tuga de Oro to life.

Huge thanks and love to Adam, Adam, Allison, Cathy, Charlie, Davinia, Eloise, Elizabeth, Jo, Kaitlyn, Naomi, Nick, Olivia, Rupert, Susannah and Vikki for your reading and friendship, not in that order. I feel blessed beyond measure by the hours you've spent with me on Tuga (and additionally, in the case of Vikki and Naomi, days in the more temperate paradise of the British Library).

My mother, Karen Segal, whose wisdom, insight, and encouragement are essential from first draft to last. Thank you, endlessly, for your faith and high standards. Miranda Segal, thank you for your love, inspiration, and support. There is no one else with whom I'd rather run errands.

Gabe—always, for everything. You are the refuge and the adventure, both.

To everyone at Chatto & Windus, and Vintage—I have always been so proud to be on your list. Clara Farmer, Hannah Telfer, Bethan Jones, Jessie Spivey, Rosanna Hildyard, Nat Breakwell,

Carmella Lowkis, Graeme Hall, Sarah-Jane Forder—thank you all for taking such care of my books. Yeti Lambregts and Kris Potter, thank you for your beautiful and thoughtful design. Peter Haag and Sara Schindler at Kein & Aber likewise; I feel lucky to have had such loyal publishers from the beginning. Thank you to Helen Atsma and the brilliant team at Ecco, it's been a pleasure joining the gang. I am grateful to the Marie Fellowship for inspiring the earliest incarnation of this island. Zoë Waldie at RCW, I truly cannot imagine a better agent, thank you. Your steadfast loyalty and unwavering good judgment make art possible.